The Quarry

THE QUARRY

Iain Banks

REDHOOK

www.redhookbooks.com

Redhook Books/Orbit
Hachette Book Group
237 Park Avenue, New York, NY 10017
www.hachettebookgroup.com

First US Edition: June 2013

Published in Great Britain in 2013 by Little, Brown

Redhook Books is an imprint of Orbit, a division of Hachette Book Group, Inc. The Redhook Books name and logo are trademarks of Hachette Book Group, Inc. The publisher is not responsible for websites (or their content) that are not owned by the publisher.

The Hachette Speakers Bureau provides a wide range of authors for speaking events. To find out more, go to www.hachettespeakersbureau.com or call (866) 376-6591.

10 9 8 7 6 5 4 3 2 1

RRD-C

Printed in the United States of America

FOR ALL MY FRIENDS, FAMILY AND FANS, WITH LOVE.

WITH THANKS TO ADÈLE, RICHARD, LES,
VICTORIA, CELIA AND GARY.

1

M ost people are insecure, and with good reason. Not me.
This is probably because I've had to think about who I am and who I'm not, which is something your average person generally doesn't have to do. Your average person has a pair of parents, or at least a mother, or at least knows roughly where they fit into all that family business in a way that I, for better or worse, don't. Usually I think it's for the better, though sometimes not.

Also, it helps that I am very clever, if challenged in other ways. Challenged in this context means that I am weird, strange, odd, socially disabled, forever looking at things from an unusual angle, or however you want to put it.

Most things, I've come to understand, fit into some sort of spectrum. The descriptions of myself fit into a spectrum that stretches from 'highly gifted' at one end to 'nutter' at the other, both of which I am comfortable with. One comes from understanding and respect, while the other comes from ignorance and fear. Mrs Willoughby explained the thinking behind both terms. Well, she explained the thinking behind the latter term, the offensive, deliberately hurtful term; the thinking behind the former, respectful judgement seemed perfectly clear and valid to me. (She got that wincing expression on her face when I mentioned this, but didn't say anything. Hol was more direct.)

'But I am clever.'

'I know. It's not the being clever that's the problem, Kit. It's the telling people.'

'So I ought to lie?'

'You ought to be less . . . determined to tell people how clever you are. How much more clever you are than they are.'

'Even if it's true?'

'Especially then.'

'But—'

'Plus, you're missing something.'

I felt myself rock back in my seat. 'Really?'

'Yes. There are different types of cleverness.'

'Hmm,' I said, which is what I've learned to say rather than the things I used to say, like, *No there aren't*, or, *Are you sure?* – in what was, apparently, a sarcastic tone.

'If nothing else,' Hol said, 'other people *think* that there are different types of cleverness, and that's what matters, in this context.'

One of the ways I am clever is that I can pay very close attention to exactly what people say and how they phrase things. With Hol this works especially well because she is quite clever too, and expresses herself well, and mostly in proper sentences (Holly is a journalist, so perhaps the habits of her trade have had an effect). Also, we have known each other a long time. With other people it can be harder. Even

2

Guy – whom I've known even longer, because he's my dad, after all – can be a bit opaque sometimes. Especially now, of course, as he's dying. They don't think there is a tumour in his head affecting his mind, but he is on a lot of mind-muddling medication.

So, to return to Hol's last phrase, 'in this context': there was an almost audible clunk as she added these words to the end of the sentence. She put those words in there because she knows that I like them, that they make a difference to me. Both Hol and Mrs Willoughby have explained to me – sometimes at great length – that context matters a lot in various situations, and especially in social interactions, which is the stuff I tend to have difficulties with. Adding 'in this context' means she – Hol – wanted me to think about what she'd just said rather than just dismiss it out of hand because it seemed to me at the time that there was, plainly, only one sort of cleverness.

Anyway, other people '*thinking*' that there are different types of cleverness was, apparently, what I was supposed to focus on.

'Are you sure, Hol?' I asked, patiently.

'There you go.'

'There I go what?'

'There you go, sounding sarcastic and patronising.'

'But I wasn't being either. I was trying to sound patient.'

'Again, what you *meant* isn't what matters, Kit. What matters is how you appear, what other people think you meant.'

'It's not my problem if . . .' I began, then fell silent under a look from Hol. The look concerned involves her dipping her head a little to the right and her eyebrows rising while her lips purse a fraction. It was her look that says, as near as I can gauge it, 'Now, Kit, we've been over this before.'

'It *is* your problem,' she told me. 'If you've given people the wrong impression when you could have given them the right one, you've—'

'Yes yes yes, I need to make allowances for people,' I said, wanting to get back to the proper point. I may have waved my hands, too. 'So, what other sorts of cleverness are there?'

Hol sighed. 'Emotional cleverness, Kit. Empathising with others, getting on with people, intuiting what and how they think.'

'But if people would just say what they—'

I got the look again.

Now it was my turn to sigh. 'That's another area where I have to make allowances, isn't it?'

'Yes, it is. Plus, people don't always know what they think themselves, Kit,' Hol told me (and, in another turnaround, now *she* was sounding what you might call conspicuously patient). 'Not precisely, not so they can tell you clearly and unambiguously and without contradictions.' She paused, probably waiting for me to protest that, well, people just *should* know what they think, and express it properly (it was certainly what I was thinking). But I didn't say it. 'And a lot of the time,' she continued – when I just sat there and smiled the way she'd taught me – 'even when people *do* know what they think and why, they don't always want to tell you.' Another pause. 'Sometimes because they don't want to hurt your feelings, or give you something you might use against them later, either directly against them, to their face, or use against them by mentioning what's just been said to some-body else.'

'Gossip.'

'Often, yes,' Hol agreed, and smiled. Hol has a plain face but the consensus seems to be that it lights up when she smiles. I like to see her smile, and especially I like to see her smile at me, so I suppose this must be true. Hol has always been my favourite of Dad's old friends (not that he really has any new ones). Even before we came to our financial arrangement, I knew that I trusted her and I would listen to her and take her seriously. 'Sometimes,' she went on, 'they're ashamed of what they're thinking, or just need more time to decide what they really, truly feel, because emotions can get very . . . well, tangled.'

'So,' I said, 'what you're saying is, it's complicated.' (This is almost a joke between us. A lot of apparently simple things seem to end up being 'complicated'.)

Hol nodded. 'People are. Who'd 'a thunk?'

I thought about this. 'Well, everybody, obviously.'

Holly nodded. 'Well, everybody else, Kit.'

'So I ought to hide my light under a bushel?'

'Oh, Jeez, Kit, you haven't been reading the Bible again, have you?'

'Is that where that's from?'

'Yes. I mean, I think so.'

'No. But should I? Hide my light under a bushel, I mean?'

'Well, just don't insist on putting it under a magnifying glass.'

We were in the sitting room of the house, sitting on over-stuffed but threadbare couches on either side of the large, interestingly warped coffee table. A large vase of black glass containing real flowers sat between us. Usually we keep artificial flowers in this vase because real ones are such a bother and the only reason the vase is there anyway is to catch drips falling from the water-stained ceiling directly above. Holly had put the real flowers there. They were yellow; daffodils. This was spring, as in last spring, four Holly visits ago, when Guy seemed to be on the mend, or at least when the cancer was in remission.

I sat back in the seat and nodded in what I hoped was a decisive manner. 'I understand.'

Hol frowned. 'Hmm,' she said. 'Hu-fucking-rah.' (She is, unfortunately, somewhat prone to swearing, so arguably not that clever after all.)

Holly is wrong. I do understand emotions. When I see her shape in the frosted glass of the inner door of the porch, framed against the grey light by the storm doors bracketing her, I recognise her and feel a surge of good emotion. I run down the stairs to the door before Mrs Gunn can get there from the kitchen at the back of the house. I want to be the first person to greet Hol.

Mrs Gunn says that I 'thunder' when I run down the stairs. I don't care. I jump down the last two steps, landing as lightly as I can – which is surprisingly lightly, I think – then take the last two and a half paces to the front door at a calm walk because I don't want to appear too overenthusiastic. I can be a bit full-on, I've been told. (I've always thought this is really a good thing and people are just embarrassed and jealous that they're not as forthright as I am, but both Mrs Willoughby and Hol have explained . . . Well, I'm not sure I could be bothered to listen on either occasion, but it was definitely one of those complicated areas where I have to pull back a bit and restrain myself.)

I open the door. 'Holly!'

'Hi, Kit,' she says, and comes forward and hugs me, kissing me on both sides of the face. She rises on tiptoes to do this, and properly applies lip pressure to my cheeks, a couple of centimetres forward from each of my ears. There is no moisture transferred (thankfully, even if it is Hol), but it is more than the usual mwah-mwah that I know, through Hol, media people exchange, when there may be no physical contact between heads at all, just cheeks put briefly in proximity.

Hol's hair looks the same so I don't have to remember to compliment her on this, and she appears similar otherwise, which is good. She is dressed in blue jeans, a black T-shirt and a green fleece. It is mostly thanks to Hol – and a little due to Mrs Willoughby – that I know to look for these things and consider commenting on them, to keep people happy.

'How are you, love?' she asks me.

I like the way Hol says 'love'. She was brought up near Bolton but her accent is sort of placeless; if you were forced to, you might say she sounded vaguely like a Londoner – or at least somebody from the Home Counties – with a hint of American. Dad says she completely lost what he calls her 'Ay-oop' accent within the first year of uni, remaking herself to sound less provincial, less identifiable, more neutral and bland. But she still says 'love' like a northerner, with the vowel sound like the one in 'low', not the one in 'above'. I realise I am thinking about this rather than actually replying to her question when I notice that there's an ongoing silence and Hol is looking at me with both eyebrows raised.

'Oh,' I say. 'Generally pretty well, thanks.'

'Huh,' Mrs Gunn says, appearing silently, suddenly at my side. Mrs Gunn is small, wiry, seemingly always bent over – forwards – and wears what we're all pretty sure is a tightly curled auburn wig. 'It's you,' she says to Hol. She turns away again, heading back down the dark hall, drying her hands violently on a dishcloth. 'I suppose you'd better come in,' she says as she goes.

Apparently Mrs Gunn is not the world's most welcoming person.

'Nice to see you too, Mrs G,' Hol says quietly to our housekeeper's retreating back. She pushes a small rucksack into my arms.

'Oh,' I say, startled, looking at it. 'I haven't got you anything.'

Hol sighs, takes the rucksack back. 'Never mind. I'll take this; you can get my case from the car. Heavier anyway.'

She stands aside and I go out to the car – the same old Polo – and take her case from the hatch. The car is red – the paint is faded on the short bonnet, which I've noticed tends to happen with red cars – and its rear is grey with motorway grime, making the hatch release feel gritty. I wipe my hand on my trousers but I'll need to wash it again as soon as I can. Or I could just stand here with my arm outstretched and my hand flat like I was looking for a tip from God; it is, as usual, raining.

'How's Guy?' Hol asks as we go up the stairs to her old room.

'Oh, still dying,' I tell her.

'Jeez, Kit,' she mutters, and I see her looking along the dark corridor towards his room.

I open the door for her and bring her case in as she stands there, looking across the rucked carpet and the sagging bed to the window with the faded curtains and the view over the densely treed back garden. The trees are only now coming into bud, so you can see the quarry between the network of restlessly moving twigs and branches; a grey depth opening into the rainy distance.

'Was I being insensitive?' I ask her.

'He might have heard you,' she tells me, not looking at me, still staring out of the window.

'He's probably asleep.' I leave a space. 'And anyway, he

8

knows he's dying.' Holly is still looking away from me, but I see her head shake slightly. 'Anything else I've missed?' I ask her. 'So far?'

She turns to me. She wears a faint smile. 'You might have asked me how I am, how my journey was, Kit.'

'Sorry. How—?'

'I'm fine. The drive was mostly shit; it usually is, especially on a bank holiday. But never mind. I'm here now.' She puts the rucksack down. Her glance flicks to the half-open door behind me. 'How are you doing, Kit, really?' she asks. She has lowered the volume of her voice.

I am about to repeat that I am generally pretty well, thanks, when I realise that the glance to the door and the lowered voice mean that she is thinking of Guy, and – I'm guessing – how I might be feeling about the fact that my father is going to die soon. I've got quite good at thinking about this sort of stuff, and quick at it, so I leave a little extra time before – with a serious expression on my face and also at a lower voice-volume – saying, 'I'm okay, Hol.'

'This must be hard for you, though,' she says, coming up to me and putting her arms round me, hugging me and putting the side of her head on my upper chest. Hol is smaller than me. Most people are. I put my arms round her and hug her in return. I think about patting her on the back, but she is the one trying to comfort me, so I don't.

'Little whiffy, to be blunt, Kit,' Hol murmurs, though she doesn't lift her head away from where it is, her nose near my left armpit. She briefly squeezes me a little tighter, as though to compensate for the personal criticism. 'You showering every day?'

'Normally every second day,' I tell her. This is my winter regime. In the summer I shower every day.

9

'Hmm. Maybe you should change your T-shirt more often, hon.'

This is a regular theme with us. Usually I wear camouflage T-shirts and trousers – mostly green NATO fatigues, though sometimes I wear the basically beige British or US desert gear that has become more and more prevalent in the sort of shop or on-line store that sells such apparel. Sand-coloured fatigues don't make much sense here amongst the browns and greens of the frequently damp north-east of England, but I don't wear this stuff because I want to crawl around the countryside unnoticed (I don't go out much beyond the garden at all, and I hate mud); I favour camo gear because you can wear it longer before you have to bother washing it. Stains just disappear. Dad says I'm a messy eater and shouldn't wipe my hands on my T-shirt so much.

Today I'm also wearing an old yellow checked shirt of Dad's and a padded olive gilet, because it's cold.

'Do you want me to go and change now?' I ask.

'No, love,' Hol says, sighing. She pushes herself away and looks up at me, her gaze criss-crossing my face. 'You getting proper help from the local health people?' She still holds me, her hands on my forearms. She blows once, quickly, out of the right side of her mouth, attempting to shift some black hair from near one eye. Holly has collar-length straight brown hair, which she dyes black.

'We're getting some help,' I tell her. 'Though there seems to have been some sort of mistake with his last Work Capability Assessment. He was too ill to get there and we got a letter a week later saying he's been put back on the able-to-work register. I think. Guy wouldn't let me see the letter.'

Holly lets go of me and turns away, shaking her head. 'Jesus fuck.'

'I wish you didn't swear so much.'

'I wish there wasn't so much to fucking swear about.'

The door is half open behind me. Across the hall the stairwell window facing the front of the house is as tightly shut as it can be but its frame is wonky and it admits both draughts and sound – and leaking water, too, if the weather is from the south. I can hear a noise of crunching stones from the driveway beyond.

I nod backwards. 'Somebody else,' I tell Hol.

We go out onto the landing, to look. Out beyond the slope of the front garden lawn, the straggle of assorted, unkempt bushes and the stone gateposts guarding the drive – the left one tipped precariously, as though trying to block the entrance, replacing the long-sold-off gates – a swell of ridged brown field hides most of the city; only the triplet towers of the Minster and the spire of St Thomas's church show dark grey above the brown corduroy of the land.

A large white Audi swings round the loop of driveway in front of the house, narrowly avoids hitting Hol's little red Polo and scrunches to a stop out of sight below, right by the front door.

'Buzz Darkside's arrived, then,' Hol says.

She means Uncle Paul. As we start down the stairs the Audi's horn blares quickly, twice. It is quite loud. Moments later a bell jangles distantly in the kitchen, as though the house is answering back.

I can tell the difference between the sounds of the bells for different rooms. 'Dad's awake,' I tell Hol as we get to the bottom of the stairs. A car door slams.

'Thoughtful as ever, Paul,' Hol mutters, though her pace quickens as she approaches the door, where a shadow is looming. Her hand is out towards the handle but Uncle Paul

11

opens the door himself, breezing in, kicking it shut behind him. Paul is below average height for a man but carries himself bigger. He looks tanned and has naturally black curly hair he keeps tidily short. He works out a lot, he says, though his face looks a little puffy. Hol thinks he's had work done, certainly on his teeth and probably on the bags he used to have under his eyes. He's about thirty-nine. They all are, because they were in the same year when they went to uni and this was their home in term time. Only Guy breaks this pattern; he's a couple of years older.

'Hey, Hol. Kit! Wow. You look even bigger! Here, take this.' He shoves an old battered-looking leather briefcase into my arms. 'We can get the rest later. Hol.' He leans in, kissing her, cheek against cheek, while Holly cooperates resignedly. 'How's my least favourite movie critic?'

'Fuck off, Paul.'

Uncle Paul looks at me as he lets Hol go. 'Aww, her first words.' He pulls in a breath as he steps back to take in Hol's appearance. 'Great to see you too, petal.'

'If this is about *Kinetica*, it was still shit.'

Paul shakes his head. 'Grossed one-fifty worldwide, for a budget of thirty. Slightly south of thirty, actually. If that's shit let's hope they all are.'

'So it's shit that grossed one-fifty worldwide. Still shit.'

Paul smiles broadly at her. 'You are welcome to your biased, bitter and basically totally bizarre opinion.'

Paul is a corporate lawyer for Maven Creative Industries. Maven Creative Industries make high-concept cinema (movies, according to Uncle Paul; films, if you listen to Hol), have multiple interests in theme parks and are increasingly moving into electronic games and other virtual arts and entertainment spaces where they are poised to exploit the synergies offered

12

by multiple-platform cross-conceptualisations. So says their website. (HeroSpace, the game that I play, is not one of theirs.)

When they all lived here back in the early-to-mid nineties, before I was around but when I was conceived, everybody coming here this weekend was a student in the Film and Media Studies department of the university. Except Dad, who was, nominally, originally with the English faculty before he changed departments. He changed courses a lot. His status was such he was sometimes described as the Student Without Portfolio (a Hol coining, apparently. It sounds like one of hers).

'How are you, anyway?' Paul asks Hol.

'Just about keeping my head above water. You?'

'Water-skiing.' Paul grins. 'Things are good. You heard I might be coming up here to, ah . . .'

'Get parachuted into the local safe seat over the heads of the loudly protesting local party?' Hol says, folding her arms in front of her. 'Yeah, heard. Well done; you finally made it into *Private Eye*.'

'Yeah, I know; having that issue framed.'

'I thought that was the police's—'

Uncle Paul – he's not a blood relation, he's just always liked me calling him Uncle Paul – turns from Hol and smiles at me. 'Hey, Kit, I could end up being your MP!' He laughs. 'I should court you!' He frowns. 'You are allowed to vote, aren't you?'

'Jeez, Paul,' Hol begins.

'Can I count on your vote, Kit, yeah?' Paul says, smiling broadly at me.

'No,' I tell him. 'We're in Bewford South here. Not Bewford City.'

'Really?' Paul looks taken aback. He's frowning. He reaches

13

out and takes me by the right elbow. 'Well, never mind,' he says, sounding sympathetic. His attention leaves me. 'Hey, Mrs Gunn! How you doing?'

I think I hear a distant 'Huh', then the sound of the kitchen door closing.

Paul frowns briefly, shrugs. 'Same old Mrs G.' He looks around the front hall, inspecting. 'Same old everything, I guess,' he says, more quietly. 'Place looks a bit shabbier, that's about it.'

I suppose the place does look shabbier. It is deteriorating all the time because although we have a big house we don't have much money and Guy sees no point in keeping the place in good repair anyway. There are various leaks in the roof and many slates are missing or flap loose in gales and storms. (When the wind blows, it is, I've heard Guy say, 'like living in a castanet factory in an earthquake'.)

Most of the gutters and downpipes are blocked – a small tree at least as old as I am is growing in the down-pipe on the north-west corner of the house. There's a crack big enough to fit a finger into running down two storeys of the back wall facing the quarry; two internal doors fit so poorly they have to be shoulder-charged to gain entry to the bedrooms concerned – or hauled open with both hands if you're inside and want to get out – while another fits in its frame so loosely that just walking past it on the landing outside is enough to make it click and creak open (easily confused people find this 'spooky').

Several windows are cracked across their corners and the one in the boxroom fell out entirely ten years ago and was replaced with hardboard, itself now warped with damp. The electrical system needed refurbishment twenty years ago (I estimate we go through about a metre of fuse wire per

14

annum); the fire in the parlour produces a strong smell of smoke in the bedroom immediately above it, the two above that and the attic above those; the plumbing clangs and bangs; the boiler or something close to it groans and wheezes when called upon for hot water; and the central heating makes a noise like a slow drill and never really heats the two furthest bedrooms much beyond taking the chill off. The upper floor, which housed the servants in the old days, isn't heated at all, though a little warmth finds its way up there anyway because nothing in this house fits or insulates properly.

Guy still talks with surprising bitterness about the folly of removing the Aga that used to take up half of one kitchen wall and replacing it with an electric cooker. That happened nearly a quarter of a century ago, when his parents were modernising the place. He used to talk of buying a new Aga, or at least one new to us, but he never did, and now, of course, never will.

I've grown used to the house slowly crumbling away around me – I've grown up with it – and of course I see it happen very slowly and incrementally, every day, while Paul visits only about once a year, so any changes will look more dramatic. He glances back to the front door. 'Think the rain's going off. I'll get my gear.'

'I'll help,' I say, remembering to be helpful. Holly comes out to the car, too. Paul points the key fob at the giant Audi and the rear hatch hisses up. 'Cool,' I say. We have a dark blue Volvo estate, which is older than I am. Guy bought it from an antique dealer in Buxton twenty years ago and now it's practically an antique itself, he says. It lives in the wooden garage, which sort of leans against the south side of the house. I can drive it, after passing my test last year, though I've never driven it very far and I'm frightened of the motorway.

I keep it maintained, too, though it's a messy business, requiring several sets of overalls, and surgical gloves. Sometimes two layers.

'Grab that antique Halliburton, will you, Kit?' Paul says, nodding at an aluminium case. I lift it. Paul pulls out a posh-looking suitcase. I think it's made from carbon fibre. Hol steps forward, hand out. 'Hol?' Paul says, sounding concerned. 'You sure you should be carrying anything, in your condition?' Hol glares at him. 'You know, with that enlarged spleen and overactive bile duct of yours? Sure we're not going against medical—'

'I thought you might need help getting your ego into the house,' Hol tells him.

Paul just laughs, then says, 'Still working for *Sight Unseen?*'

'*Sight and Sound*, and fuck you again. And don't pretend you don't read it, even if it's just because you have to.'

He laughs again.

'I'm not any bigger,' I tell Paul as we head back into the hall.

'What?'

'I'm the same size as I was last summer, last time you were here.'

'Oh. Are you?'

'Yes. I'm one hundred kilos.'

'Are you now?'

'I'm always one hundred kilos. I have been since before I was sixteen.'

'Really.'

'I just like being one hundred kilos.'

'I see,' Paul says, as we troop up the stairs. 'Well, that's, ah, that's a nice round number.'

'Yes,' I say. 'Exactly.' I'm leading the way up the stairs at this point so I can't see his expression.

16

Guy's bedroom bell jangles again and a moment later I hear Mrs Gunn bustling out of the kitchen, muttering, 'Yes, yes, I hear you. Can't be in three places at once.' She comes stamping up the stairs behind us.

'Hello again, Mrs G!' Paul says cheerily as she passes us.

'Mm-hmm,' she says, not looking at any of us as she passes. She has her outside wellies on and is taking off her gardening gloves as she goes, disappearing round the corner at the top of the stairs.

'How is Guy?' I hear Paul say quietly.

'Haven't seen him yet,' Hol tells him. 'No better, from what—'

I turn round, lower my head and my voice and whisper, 'He's still dying,' to Paul.

Paul looks instantly serious. 'Sorry to hear that,' he says.

Behind him, Hol seems to be keeping a neutral expression.

We're in the kitchen ten minutes later, drinking tea that I've made and eating shortbread that Mrs Gunn has made – she is still upstairs, probably helping Dad get up – when the doorbell rings.

The doorbell also links to one of the kitchen bells. These are over one hundred and thirty years old, as old as the house itself. The bells exist in a long box up on the wall of the kitchen. They look like little handbells hanging on the ends of metal springs shaped like question marks. A white-or-red disc under each bell used to show which one had rung most recently even after the bell had stopped ringing and the spring had stopped quivering, but the discs haven't worked for at least the one point eight decades I've been around.

When the quarry on the far side of the back garden wall was still being worked, up to four years ago, the twice-weekly

17

blasts used to shake the whole house and make all the bells ring faintly. It was as if the house was trembling and crying out in alarm.

Now they're going to extend the quarry and the house is going to have to go; Guy is selling the place to Holtarth Moor Quarries and it'll be demolished. I don't entirely know where I'll end up but if there is one thing I'd like to keep from the house itself – I mean, apart from all my own stuff, in my room – it might be this box of bells here in the kitchen. I'm not sure why.

'Anybody home?' a distant female voice yells from the front hall.

'Hey, it's the fatuous Baker girl,' Hol says as we all stand, chairs scraping on the flagstones.

'We just came in,' says a male voice from the same direction. 'Hope that's all right . . .'

'Oh,' Hol says brightly, 'and Mr Bobby.'

'What does she call me?' Paul asks me as we file out of the kitchen to the hall again.

'Buzz Darkside,' Hol says, before I can answer.

Paul looks unimpressed. 'Still with that? Needs reimagining. Hey!' he says, raising his voice as we see the others. 'Hey!' he shouts, even louder. 'It's the whole gang!'

I'd expected two more people – Alison and Rob – which I think I could have coped with, but instead there are four and I feel overwhelmed. The other two are Pris and Haze, who used to be a couple but now aren't and yet they've turned up together. Everybody crowds into the hall except Mrs Gunn and Guy, who are still upstairs, and I back into a corner near the cupboard under the stairs, feeling suddenly hot and a bit dizzy, while people, us from the kitchen and the rest from the still-open front door, mill about and talk and shout and put luggage down and embrace one another and slowly start to sort themselves out, though in the meantime they all talk at once and talk over one another, so it's difficult for me to tell who's saying what.

'Yeah, bit mob-handed, as my old da would have said. We did ring, but—'

'Still not where the sat-nav says it's supposed to be.'

'Come in! Come in come in come in come in.'

'It doesn't *matter*.'

'Paul. Ah, thanks. Yeah, thought that must be your great white behemoth blocking the front door.'

'Yeah, look, I missed out on getting to the supermarket so I haven't got any booze. But I've brought all me special spices and secret ingredients with me. Thought I might make a curry. I mean, I can go out specially later for drink, yeah? Oh, hi, Hol. Hey, Paul, what's up?'

'Yes, but it should get it *right*. The place has *been* here long enough.'

'Passed Pris and her new chap on the motorway so I texted them. Met up for a coffee in Ormers and bumped into Haze.'

'Well, not for much longer. Evening, all. Oh, look; decent mobile reception. That's an innovation.'

'Yeah, that was just a misunderstanding, that disabled space.'

'Where's, ah . . . ?'

'And can I just say now, I've brought some lacto-free milk, and I'm not saying nobody else can't have any at all, but I will need some each day, so . . .'

'What did you buy?'

'Might ask you to move the Audi at some point, Paul; going to need access to a plug to recharge the Prius.'

'Rick, Paul. He's called Rick. He's staying in Ormiscrake. The King's Head.'

'Hey, Paul, Hol; good to see you, Kit.'

'What, is he just shy or something?'

'Oh, like, no, I wasn't . . . I was, um, donating, you know?'

'You've got a plug-in Pious?'

'He doesn't want to intrude, Paul. I know that's a hard concept for you to cope with.'

'Oh. It's just that you came out with a bag.'

'Hol the *doll*! You good? Look at you!'

'He looking after Mhyra?'

'Yew, harsh!'

'Well, you're kind or blind and I'm a mess, but thanks.'

'Nah, we left Brattus Norvegicus with my sister in Hemel.'

'What? Oh, ah. No, yeah, that was, like, stuff they couldn't . . . Hey, there's our Kit! Hey, Kit. Yeah, yeah. How are you, my friend?'

By early evening, when it is already dark but the rain has eased off again and a little watery moonlight is painted over the limbs of the trees crowding the back garden, they are all fed and watered and Guy is up and we are all in the sitting room, sitting.

Mrs Gunn has gone home. She lives in a neat little timber-frame, brick-skin bungalow in a cul-de-sac in the leafy suburb of Quonsley, which is a couple of kilometres away, just over the big bulge of field on the hill that hides most of the city from the house. I have been to her house once, when I missed the bus from school and was told to go to hers to wait for Dad, who was coming with the car. She keeps clear plastic covers on her couch and chairs in the living room. Her house was warm and draught free, and smelled of clean. It could not be much less like this place.

Willoughtree House. That's the name of this place, the name of the house we are talking about and which I live in with Guy, my dad.

'I *still* can't fucking believe it. I certainly couldn't believe it the first time . . . *especially* the first fucking time. I remember thinking, Boris fucking Johnson as mayor of London? What next? The Chuckle brothers as secretaries general of the United Nations?'

'Boris isn't so bad.'

'*What?*'

'Yeah, come on, Hol; at least he's, like, real.'

'Fuck off. He's a fucking right-wing Tory, friend of Rupert fucking Murdoch and defender of the fucking kleptocrat bankers. Another Bullingdon Club bully. How does coming across as being an incompetent bumbler at whatever he does make him *better?*'

'I've met him. He's not so—'

'Oh, I bet you have. I bet he's fucking charming. So was Blair. So what?'

'Look, I didn't feckin vote for him, all right?'

'But Haze is right,' Rob says. 'Boris seems more like a normal person.'

'Yeah!' Haze says. 'Not one of these robot guys, never giving a straight answer or anything. Just, just . . .' Haze flaps both hands. 'Yeah, like . . .' His voice trails away.

'You would have fucking voted for him, wouldn't you?' Hol says, looking straight at Paul.

'I just told you I didn't.'

'Yeah, you're contractually bound not to because after giving it a lot of thought you've plumped for Labour for your political career. I bet you would have if you could, though. And for all we know—'

21

'Like I say—'

'Look me in the eye, you twat, and tell me you weren't tempted to vote for him. Especially against Ken; you're more of a Blairite than that lying, war-mongering scumbag is himself. I bet you had to grit your teeth, if you did vote for Ken. Tell me you didn't want to vote for Boris.'

'Never even occurred to me.'

'You lying bastard.'

Paul spreads both arms, looks round at everybody else, as though appealing to them. He even looks at me. 'Holly,' he says, when his gaze returns to her, 'I don't know what to say to you when you're in this sort of mood. I don't know how to handle you. Politics is politics and there are some decent people on the other side just like there are some twats on our side, and until you accept that you're always going to sound like some Spartist caricature. Get a fucking grip, why don't you.'

'Can we talk about something else?' Alison asks.

'I'm not arguing there are no decent people in the Tory Party,' Hol says to Paul. I think she's trying to keep calm now. 'But they're like bits of sweetcorn in a turd; technically they've kept their integrity, but they're still embedded in shit.'

'There you go,' Paul says, laughing lightly.

'Yeah, come off the fence, Hol,' Haze says. 'Tell us what you really think!'

'Things have changed, Hol,' Rob tells her. 'Phase-changed, even. We're just not where we were.'

'I'm being serious here,' Alison says. '*Can* we talk about something else? I mean, does any of this really *matter*?'

Hol shakes her head. 'What a choice: Neo-Labour, the toxic Agent-Orange-Book Lib-Dems or the shithead

22

rich-boy bastardhood that is the Tories. We really are all fucked, aren't we?'

'Finally a note of realism,' Paul says, shaking his head.

'There's always UKIP, Hol,' Haze says.

Hol looks at Haze as though she's about to say something, but then her face sort of screws up and she just makes a sound like 'Tschah!'

A bell rings in the hall, not the kitchen. It's the special one we put in last year. Guy isn't in the room with the rest of us right now; he left about five minutes ago, pushing on his Zimmer frame and refusing help.

While he's been absent, I have been asked again about exactly how Guy is. I've done my little speech about how he has good days and bad days and good weeks and bad weeks, though month-on-month he's very obviously heading downwards, and the good days and good weeks now are like the bad days and bad weeks of just a few months ago. Everybody seems satisfied with this.

The thing is, with Mrs Gunn gone, I'll have to answer the bell if it goes again (we have a code), though I'd rather not. I'd rather stay here with the others, even though I'm just sitting on the edge of the group and only listening, not taking part. This is where I'm comfortable, being with a few other people rather than just with Dad, but not actually having to do much except listen.

The numbers have to be right. Too many people – more than ten or twelve, say – and I clam up anyway, confused by all the different voices and the interrupting and the trying to work out what people mean behind what they say and what their facial expressions and body language are telling me, but, on the other hand, if there are too few people, then they seem to feel they have to try to involve me in the conversation, because they don't want me to feel left out, or because they don't see why I should get to listen in without contributing something.

I'm still waiting for the other bell, dreading it. I am Pavlov's dog, though instead of salivating I have a little jolt of fear in my guts each time it rings.

'And don't think I didn't hear that bit about "For all we know",' Paul is saying to Hol, pointing at her. 'You didn't actually get to the point where you might have impugned my word, but you sailed pretty close to that . . . to that particular waterfall.'

'What the hell are you—'

'Seriously,' Alison says, '*can* we talk about something else?'

'And who the fuck uses words like "impugned" amongst their pals, for Christ's sake?' Hol asks, sounding angry. 'Is that, like, lawyer talk or something?'

'All I'm saying—'

'Or is it politico lingo?' Hol is asking Paul. I think she's still angry but she makes a sort of small laughing sound as well. 'Have they put you through some sort of Talking Like a Politician induction course? Is that Spad-speak? Now you're probably going to be an MP, are you going to start talking about straw men, and things getting knocked into cocked hats? Is that how it works?'

'Politilingo? Polingo?' Haze is saying.

I have seen Hol and Paul argue and talk and shout like this before. According to Guy they were always the same.

'Anyway. Think I'll get another drink,' Haze says, standing. 'Anybody else need another drink?'

'Yeah, that's what this conversation needs,' Pris says. 'More alcohol.'

The sitting room is probably the most civilised space in

24

the house, and the warmest. It has that long rectangular coffee table made of wood in the middle; the one with the flower vase at its centre. A three-seater couch faces each of its long sides and an easy chair faces each of its short sides. One of the couches and a chair are matching blue velvet; the other couch is brown, pretend leather. The other seat is a swivel chair made of stretchy red fabric pulled tight over an expanded polystyrene moulding. Pris has told me this is a piece of authentic seventies batwing kitsch and so old it's been back in fashion at least twice. Or would have been but for the tears in the fabric and the stains on it. (Last time we talked, she wasn't sure of the current position of such furniture – she said she'd have to consult a magazine called *Wallpaper*. Which I found confusing, because we're talking about a chair.) Anyway, the red chair and brown sofa don't match anything else in the room.

Guy was sitting in the red chair until he left. He used to always sit in the blue velvet armchair when we had guests, until his back got so bad and getting out of the chair became so difficult. Paul is sitting there instead. Hol and Pris are sitting on the blue velvet sofa. Alison, Haze and Rob are on the brown one.

I've pulled out the blue velvet pouffe that usually squats under the table in the bay window. I'm sitting on it, hunched, with my hands clasped between my pressed-together knees. The pouffe has lost a lot of its stuffing, or it's compressed over the years, so you sit quite near the floor on it, plus it makes a sort of crackling noise when you sit on it and you have to kind of waggle your bottom to get comfortable, but I don't mind.

I'm sat by the side of the blue velvet sofa, near Hol. Hol has said a couple of times I should sit up on the couch with her and Pris but I don't want to; I'd feel too big and obvious and people might expect me to join in. From here, low down, I can watch and listen without disturbing anybody.

Hol has put on a faded orange cardigan instead of the green fleece, and big thick blue socks. Paul is wearing neat-looking blue jeans and an open-necked pink shirt. Pris wears tight glittery trousers and a baggy black jumper, Rob wears black chinos and a grey polo neck, Alison is in a black knee-length dress with thick black woollen tights, and Haze has olive trousers and the same dark green Therapy? T-shirt and loose padded tartan shirt he arrived in.

Pris is pretty and curvy and the colour of coffee with milk, with dark eyes and shiny black, scraped-back hair with lots of ringlets. Rob is about average height but quite wide; gym-fit, Hol has said. He keeps his head shaved but he has brown hair, I think. Alison is small and blonde and always wears make-up. Hol says Alison used to be fat and now exists in a state of perpetual semi-starvation. Haze is nearly as tall as me, though he doesn't carry himself that way. He's been slowly putting on weight ever since I've known him and his thin brown hair is receding in an orderly fashion straight back from his eyebrows, which are usually slightly raised.

Hol's face looks a little flushed, as does Paul's. This might be because they have been arguing, or because they have been drinking wine. Paul arrived with a crate of red wine from the French region of Médoc, and so far four bottles have been opened and three finished. I tried some, though I prefer sweet white wine if I feel I have to drink. Drinking isn't really for me. I suffer from acid reflux but more importantly I don't like the feeling of losing control. (I think most people drink because they're not happy with their sober self and wish to alter matters, whereas I am quite happy with who I am.)

26

Though Hol looks flushed, she seems more alive than she did before, her facial expressions both more animated and drawing from a longer menu. Paul appears deliberately relaxed, as though his instinct is to shout and gesticulate but he's decided not to.

Guy put on what he calls his Sunday Best to be with the others: the trousers and waistcoat of an old three-piece, lavender-coloured suit and a dove-grey leather bomber jacket. These clothes date from twenty years ago when he was a size thirty waist the first time, but they hang off him now, he's grown so gaunt. Most people who knew him from the old days and who haven't seen him for the last few years tend to go quiet and look shocked when they see him because he's lost so much weight and his face, which was always thin, now looks cadaverous. There are dark circles under his large, blue, hooded eyes and his skin is dry and flaky. His lips look bruised all the time.

The people who don't go quiet and look shocked when they first see him usually haven't recognised him at all, and think he's somebody much older.

He wears a hat knitted from brown wool, to hide his bald-ness after the chemo treatment. He used to have long blond wavy hair he was very proud of. Originally the hat had a sort of woolly bobble on top like a little fronded pompom, but Guy thought that looked silly so he cut it off with a kitchen knife. As a result the hat has started to fray and unravel at the top, so you can see a little of his baldness through the two-pence-sized hole. Mrs Gunn and I have both offered to repair this – she was going to darn it (I'm not sure what that involves) and I could at least have sewn it back together – but Guy has refused so far. He can be stubborn. Hol says this is where I get it from.

There's no second bell, so I start to relax.

'Did I hear a bell there?' Hol asks nobody in particular.

'Just Guy letting us know he's on his way back,' I tell her. 'Ah.'

'Well, there is stuff we could talk about,' Paul says, glancing at me. 'But maybe not with Kit here.'

'Ah,' Haze says, 'yeah. The, ah . . .' He sticks a finger in his ear and waggles it this way and that. 'The video. The tape, the . . . yeah.' He looks round at the rest of them. 'Yeah, that.'

'Don't see why we have to excuse Kit,' Hol says, though she doesn't sound very sure.

'Oh,' Paul says, smiling, 'I think we do.' He smiles at me. The rest look or glance at me.

I'm feeling hot.

Silence. Suddenly Alison leans over and glares at the bottom of the couch she and Rob are sat on, concentrating on the little fringe of grubby green tassels that hang down almost to the threadbare rug. 'I thought I could feel a draught,' she says. She nods at the fringe. 'Those . . . That fringe is *moving*.' She stands, then uses her knees and hands to push the sofa back, making it scrape on the floorboards.

'*Now* what are you doing?' Rob asks her, tutting as he's moved back along with the couch. He is holding a glass of gin and orange juice.

'Yeah, don't offer to help or anything, lover,' Alison says, pulling the rug back. 'Look!' She nods down at the floor. 'There's a damn great hole.'

We all sit forward, crane our necks; whatever. There is a fist-sized hole in the floorboards there.

'That's where a large knot fell out,' I tell them. 'Out of the floorboard,' I add, which is probably unnecessary, though

28

on the other hand they are all quite drunk. 'Though if you ask Guy he'll tell you a rat gnawed it.'

'What?' Alison asks, looking horrified.

'Definitely a knot, though,' I tell her. 'No teethmarks.'

'Jesus,' Alison says, and starts trying to pull the sofa back to where it was, grunting.

'Fucking place is falling apart,' Paul says, looking around.

'Yeah, well,' Haze says.

'Guy says he doesn't think they'll need to actually pull the house down,' I tell them (they all look at me). 'Says it's only held up by us being in it; him and me. Once we're gone, once we stop believing in it, it'll fall down all by itself.'

'Plausible,' Alison says, tugging at the sofa. It's harder to move it that way; I think it's the grain of the wood or something. She gets the couch to jerk forward a centimetre.

Rob tuts again, licks at his hand. 'Do you mind?' he says. 'You're spilling my fucking drink.'

'Oh, help her, Rob, for goodness' sake,' Hol says.

Rob shrugs. 'Wasn't my idea to start moving the fucking furniture around.' He drinks his drink. 'This happens at work, too, you know,' he tells Hol. 'She starts out on some irrelevant, seat-of-the-pants new project, causes chaos everywhere and then I have to come along and clean everything up. I'd probably have advanced a lot further in the company if I didn't spend so much time sorting out Ali's messes.'

Alison smiles widely at Hol. 'That's Rob-speak for I initiate some bold new venture taking the company in an exciting, fresh but entirely course-complementary direction and then he breezes in when all the hard work's done and takes the man's share of the credit. *I'd* be a couple of rungs further up by now if I didn't have him constantly in tow.' She tugs hard at the couch, grunting.

'Jesus!' Hol says, getting up and going round the back of the couch to push it. It slides back to where it was. Hol looks at me as she sits back down again. She's frowning. I wonder what I've done wrong now.

Then there's a double ring on the hall bell.

Shit. I don't want to have to go. On the other hand, I sort of do want to go now.

I stand up. 'Excuse me.'

'Kit,' Hol says, extending one hand towards me, 'you don't have to—'

'Yeah, Kit . . .' Haze says.

'No,' I say, pointing to the door, 'I have to . . . Excuse me.'

'Is there blood?'

'There is a little blood.'

'Well, what does that mean? What does "a little" mean?'

'It means there is a little blood.'

'Don't be fucking smart, Kit; just tell me how much blood there is. And what colour? Red? Brown? Black?'

'Are you sure you can't turn round and take a look?'

'Not without going out into the fucking hall, waddling, with my trousers round my ankles and my cock hanging out, so, no.'

'If I had a smartphone I could take a photo and show you.'

'I'm not buying you a fucking smartphone. Will you shut up about the fucking smartphone? You don't need one. And you'll just post the photos on Facebook. Or find a way to sell them in your stupid game.'

'Course I wouldn't,' I tell him. 'Though you could have Faecesbook, I suppose,' I add. Well, you have to try to lighten the mood.

'Oh, Christ.'

'There's only a smear,' I tell him. 'And it's red.'

'Good, fine. Look, just, just, you know, wipe me off and . . . Christ, this is . . . Just, would you? Okay?'

This doesn't happen all the time but, sometimes, I have to wipe my dad clean after he's moved his bowels. He can't stretch round or underneath any more to do it himself; even on the opiates the pain is too much now that the cancer has moved into his spine. Often Mrs Gunn will do this. She is paid to be a carer now, though I'm not sure this whole arse-cleaning thing is really within her remit. Guy cried following the first time she performed this service for him. He doesn't know that I know this; I heard him through his bedroom door, afterwards.

The first time I had to help Guy wipe himself I tried to do it with my eyes closed. This was unsuccessful, and messy. My compromise these days is to breathe through my mouth so I don't smell whatever might be in the toilet bowl (I resent being made to look in there but Guy feels a need to know whether there is blood in his stool). Obviously I am wearing a pair of blue surgical gloves; we keep a box by the door. I can let myself into the downstairs loo because it has a relatively modern mechanism that can be unlocked from outside via a slot in a small metal stub projecting beneath the handle. You use a screwdriver, or a penny.

The bell that Guy rings when he needs help in here is attached to a length of string that rises from beside the toilet bowl, goes through a couple of U-nails hammered into the ceiling and out to the hall through a hole I bored using our electric drill. The bell in the hall hangs from another grey galvanised U-nail. It is spherical and from a budgie's cage, so it's quite quiet.

You have to listen for it, and once or twice I've tried to

pretend to myself that I haven't heard it, but then it'll ring again, and again, and even if I leave it for half an hour Guy still keeps ringing it and still can't wipe himself and so I have to go in the end. When I do eventually go to help him he is sometimes crying, and always grateful, not angry, and that is how I know, I think, that he really can't do this simple thing by himself and really does need help and isn't just doing it to be cruel to me.

In theory we could just keep our mobiles about us and he could phone or text when he needs me, but Guy is not very good with mobile phones and frequently forgets to carry his, or keep it charged. I've tried reminding him about this sort of thing and have offered to make sure he always has his phone and it's properly charged, as well as taking over responsibility for his meds (he forgets to take his medication, a lot, then sometimes takes too much), but he just accuses me of trying to run his life and tells me to back off.

Guy stands, bending forward to rest on the Zimmer frame. I flush the toilet, to be rid of the sight, then, while his always skinny, now scrawny, legs quiver, I carefully wipe him down. Once you get over the simple unpleasantness of it – I suspect most people would gag, the first time – it is easier to wipe somebody else's bum than it is your own, because you can see what you're doing and use both hands at once if necessary. The whole process is much more efficient and uses no more toilet paper than is strictly required, so it's better for the environment, too. If we were being really green we'd all have somebody else wipe our bums, though I can't see it catching on.

'Fucking portable prison,' Guy mutters, and slaps at the Zimmer. Dad hates his walking aid, even though it helps him a lot. He can still move around fairly easily on the flat, even out in the garden, using his Zimmer frame and, on good days, just a single forearm crutch. On really good days he can get by with just a walking stick.

Guy starts coughing. He sits back down to do this. Probably wise; sometimes when he coughs really hard a little poo can come out. His cough makes it sound like his chest is full of Lego bricks. He stopped smoking five years ago, about twenty years too late. He's taken it up again recently, reckoning there's nothing left to lose, and also, I think, as an act of defiance. He's shared a roll-up with Haze already this evening and I can smell the tobacco on his clothes.

After half a minute or so he stops coughing and goes back to just wheezing.

'That you okay?' I ask him.

'Fucking never been better,' he says. He hauls some phlegm up into his mouth, shuffles back a little further on the loo, and carefully spits between his spread legs. I choose not to follow the whole process. 'Christ,' he says, sitting back against the cistern and breathing hard, a noise of gurgling coming from his lungs, 'knackers me just having a cough these days.' He sighs, wipes his lips, looks at me. 'I hope the shareholders of British American Tobacco are fucking grateful.'

'Think we're done?' I ask him.

'Done and dusted, kid,' he tells me. 'Done and dust-to-dusted.'

I flush a second time, strip off the gloves and dump them in the bin, help Guy on with his pants and trousers and run the taps, holding the towel ready while he rests his forearms on the Zimmer and washes his hands.

'Okay, okay,' he says. 'I'm all right. Stop fussing.'

I don't think I was fussing but I've learned there's no point arguing.

I head back to the sitting room and hear him lock the loo

33

door. He doesn't like me to accompany him back into the room when we have guests, so making it obvious he needs help in the toilet. There are still proprieties – or at least little face-saving deceptions – you can observe even when you're reduced to this level of helplessness.

And, of course, it's only going to get worse, as we both know.

The whole thing about the smartphone is a bluff, by the way; I have one, though Guy doesn't know about it. I bought it via Holly with money I made on HeroSpace.

I go back to the sitting room, hearing their voices from the hall. When I enter they fall silent. I suppose I wasn't away long enough for them to talk through whatever it is they needed to talk about.

I know there's something about a tape – an old audio-cassette tape or digital videotape, I think, from what I've gleaned over the years from a few partially overheard mentions, muttered between them during previous visits – but I also know there's been talk about what will happen to me after the house is demolished and Guy is dead (or Guy dies and the house is demolished, though I'm not sure the order makes much difference).

Possibly, also, they might be talking about exactly who – and possibly even which one of them – is my mother.

That would be nice to know.

2

In a sense I don't really live here. The place where I really live is HeroSpace.

Obviously I do live here; this is where my body and my brain are, where sleep happens and real food has to be consumed and bodily functions experienced and coped with, where other people and officialdom have to be encountered and managed and so on . . . But over the years that has all increasingly started to feel like the part of my existence that just has to be got through with the minimum of fuss so that I can get back to the really important part, which is my life on-line, and especially my life in HeroSpace.

It's as though what we call reality is the boring motorway journey to the exciting place where you actually want to be – something to be borne, even suffered, so that you can get to the place where you can do the things you really want to do. Like going on holiday, in other words. Not that I've done that very much; I prefer staying at home.

I even stay home in HeroSpace sometimes, wandering my castle in the Moonwrack mountains. But that quickly becomes boring and I head out to seek quests, battles, honour and treasure.

I have played both Warhammer and World of Warcraft in my time, but HeroSpace is the game I've settled on, the one I find most satisfying and pleasurable. It's a massively multi-player, on-line, role-playing game, rated number one by several forums and the more discerning on-line magazines, and, in its various incarnations and iterations, it has received every significant games industry award there is.

I've been playing it for four and a half years and have watched it grow from small beginnings and only a few thousand players to its current mind-boggling size, and many millions of players. I like to think I've grown too, in that time. I have certainly accrued status, power, combat experience, loot, respect and even comrades and friends over the years.

I love HeroSpace partly because it allows me to be myself, my true self, and because the rules, though many and complicated and gradually evolving, are definite and clear. Mostly, though, I love it because it's just more vivid than real life, and much more exciting without being truly terrifying. You can have proper adventures, battle the forces of evil, and triumph – definitely, unambiguously – in ways that in reality are either life-threateningly dangerous, or almost unavailable.

HeroSpace is set in a future world where computers have developed to become Artificial Intelligences, but then departed for the stars. Humanity has been left behind to fend for itself, using the powers and gifts the machines have out-grown. On this future Earth, most people exist in giant hive cities, lying, dreaming comfortably, blandly, in pods, but those who wake up can wander the landscape beyond, where the degenerated descendants of the last generation of machines, those abandoned after the AI diaspora, are forever trying to destroy the hive cities and their brave defenders (that'll be us game players), and find whatever assets and weaponry the long-departed AIs have either bequeathed, forgotten or just not been sufficiently bothered about to take with them.

(That's my précis of the introduction to the generally accurate and fair Wikipedia entry, though personally I've never understood how a brilliantly clever AI ultra-computer can just 'forget' something . . . Or anything really. But then I didn't invent the game. And that's almost the only point I find particularly troubling, which puts it well ahead of anything else out there, believe me.)

I think part of HeroSpace's appeal for gamers is the implication that it might just, somehow, at a stretch, be true; that the dreamed life the people in the hive cities are experiencing is basically our own life, this real life, right now, only they have to want to wake up from it and follow certain clues distributed throughout what appears to be reality so that they can truly awaken and thus enter the genuine real life of HeroSpace. (If this sounds a bit like the *Matrix* films, it may not be a coincidence; there was a legal dispute, a court case and a financial settlement – details undisclosed for reasons of commercial confidentiality – between the film and the game people.)

Not that I believe any of that at all, not even for a moment; what looks like reality is reality and HeroSpace, much though I love it and sometimes wish it was real, is just a game.

I do, though, make money from it, so it's not all *just* about playing and having fun. Within the first year I was doing so well in single-combat confrontations, tactical skirmishes and even battle-sim choice spreads I'd accumulated more points than I knew what to do with. So I sold them. Because you can. There are internal markets in the game itself, using *gelt*, the game's own currency, but there's nothing to stop anyone building up points on any level and trading them with other people for real money, in the real world, using PayPal or direct bank transfers.

I was stupid at first and ran into problems with cheques bouncing but then Hol offered to help out. She's always taken an interest in my game-playing (Guy treats it with contempt) and for the last four years she's taken care of the money. I was too young to have a proper bank account when all this started and I didn't want Dad to know about it so I needed some other adult to look after things. Now I'm eighteen I can handle my own financial affairs. One of the reasons Holly is here this weekend is to hand over control of the money I've made.

It's not a serious fortune – about eleven or twelve thousand pounds, I estimate – but it's mine, and I could easily make more. For the last two years, though, Hol has told me to have more fun in the game and be less single-minded about accumulating loot-points, or I'd go over some sort of threshold and have to start paying income tax back in reality, which might cause problems with Guy.

Anyway, I know from bitter past experience that most people find the whole subject of HeroSpace astoundingly boring, so I won't go on about it. Suffice to say it's where I'm happiest, even if some people think that is, in itself, sad.

I don't care; happiness is happiness.

Hol and I are in the kitchen doing the washing up. Alison and Rob have gone to their room; the rest are still talking. It's well past Guy's usual bedtime but he's excited and energised because there are other people here so he's staying up late. He's even swapped his Zimmer frame for his stick, which is both worrying and positive at the same time. I came through to stack the dishwasher and wash up and Holly came through to help.

I had to partially unstack the dishwasher first; Mrs Gunn has her own way of stacking it but it's wrong. My method is more efficient and cleans both cutlery and crockery better.

For the hand-washing part, Hol is washing and I'm drying and putting away, because I know where everything goes, having recently rearranged things to be more logical.

'What is this tape you're looking for?' I ask her. 'I might be able to help. I know the house better than Guy does now. I know where most stuff is stored.'

Holly stares at the suds in the sink, then lifts out one yellow-gloved hand and takes up her wineglass, drinking. 'Just an old videotape,' she tells me. Her voice sounds sleepy, the words slightly slurred. 'Something kind of embarrassing on it.' She shrugs. 'If it's even still around.' She looks at me. 'An S-VHS-C; old format. Thick as a VHS cassette but about, I don't know, a quarter of the size. Small enough to fit into a hand-held camera of the day but you could play it . . . Well, you could play them straight from the camera, but if you've got this' – Holly is waving one gloved hand around, distributing foam – 'mechanical sort of gizmo the size and shape of a VHS tape, then . . . you inserted it into that and then put the whole shebang into your standard VHS video player under your telly and played it from that.' She blows out her cheeks and shakes her head, then uses the heel of her hand to push some hair back from her face. 'All very complicated. Lot easier these days, just use your phone. Anyway.'

'Would it be identifiable? The particular one?' I ask. 'I mean, if I find a whole box of them. Will it say anything on it to identify it?'

'Can't remember,' Hol says, though after a very slight hesitation. Then she burps. Ah, that might have been the cause of the hesitation, not a pause to choose whether to tell the truth or not.

'Okay,' I say. 'I can't remember ever seeing any of those, though there are boxes in some of the top bedrooms I've never investigated properly. And some in the outhouses. Though . . . No, the ones in the attic are empty, or just have packing material in them. We moved all the heavy ones.'

'Hmm,' Hol says, twisting her empty wineglass in her hand and looking at it thoughtfully, then lowering it into the water and carefully washing it.

'And then there's the shed, and the garage,' I add, after thinking about it. 'And the old outhouses.'

'There you are,' Hol says, sounding tired. She hands me the glass.

I dry it, looking out the window to the darkness. The rain is back on, sprinkling the window with drops and streaks, making a sound oddly like a fire crackling in a grate. 'We have a lot of junk,' I say, realising. 'I don't know where it's all going to go when we have to move out.'

'Drop it over the back garden wall, into the quarry,' Hol suggests. 'Stuff you don't need.' Her glass was the last thing needing to be washed. She starts stripping off the yellow gloves. 'Actually, why bother?' She drapes the gloves over the taps. This is not where they go but I can wait before putting them where they are supposed to go (Mrs Gunn and I disagree about that, too). 'Just leave it all in the house; end up in the bottom of the quarry anyway.'

'What's on it?' I ask. 'What's on the tape?'

She shakes her head. 'Embarrassing shit.' She holds up one hand. 'We made a lot of embarrassing shit. Embarrassing shit

40

little mini-movies. They were shorts, nothing longer than half an hour, most less than that, but we dressed them up like they were features.'

'I've seen them,' I tell her.

'Hmm? Yeah, yeah, course you have. Forgot. Yeah, like I said; embarrassing.'

They used to make short films, nearly twenty years ago, when they were all in the Film and Media Studies department at Bewford. The films were pastiches of proper films by famous directors; their Bergman was called *Summer with Harmonica*, their Kubrick was *Full Dinner Jacket*, their Chabrol *Madame Ovary* and their Landis *An American Werewolf on Lithium*. There were others.

They made these to amuse themselves and impress their fellow students rather than as part of their coursework. The films were made quickly, usually over a single weekend, and edited only in the sense that they would do multiple takes if they felt they really had to; the idea was to use just one tape and record everything sequentially on that, with no further transfer or re-editing allowed. ('Fuck Dogme 95,' Guy said once. 'We were years ahead of those fuckers.') Second takes were common because they were usually laughing so much during the first one, but third takes were relatively rare. They all took turns behind and in front of the camera; Guy was probably the most natural actor and least talented director.

'I thought I'd seen all the films,' I tell Hol.

She shrugs. 'Well, I guess you missed seeing that one.' Then she folds her arms, frowns at me. 'Really? He showed them to you?'

'He used to like showing them to people who came to visit, though not so much any more.'

41

'Did he?' Hol frowns. 'Never showed them to us. Well, never showed them to me, not after we'd finished them. He show them to any of the others?' she asks, glancing towards the door.

'I don't think so. But then you'd all already seen them.'

'Huh. Maybe he was more proud of them than he pretended to be. He ever finish transferring them to digital? I'd have liked a copy, but . . . we kind of gave up asking.'

'No,' I tell her. 'What's it called?' I ask. 'The missing film?'

She shakes her head. 'Not sure we gave it a title.'

'Anyway, Dad stopped showing them to people.'

Hol nods, staring at the floor. 'Age thing, maybe,' she says, sighing. 'Beginning to feel dismayed by the difference between how he looked then and how he looks now. Worse for him, I suppose, given how he's . . . deteriorated over the last . . . whatever years.' She smiles, slightly. 'He used to claim he was ashamed by the amateurishness of the films. But they're not that amateurish, and I think what's really happening is he looks at the young self captured on those chunky little tapes and sees somebody full of hope and fun and the joys of life, and can't stand the contrast with what and who he's become.'

'Also,' I say, 'perhaps because the video player that could show them stopped working.'

Hol nods. 'Yeah, that. That too. Like I said; he never did get them all transferred to digital.' She makes a sort of small grunting noise. 'Never exactly your go-to person when you were looking for a sense of urgency, our Guy.'

It was always strange seeing Guy looking so young in the films. They were made between 1992 and 1995 when he was only five years older than I am now – the others were only a couple of years older than I am now – so the fashions of the time, and the hairstyles and so on, are not too ridiculous (or, at least, not yet), but that still feels like a long time ago. Perhaps this is because I hadn't been born, hadn't even been conceived when they were made.

Back then they all looked young and fresh. You can see how they've changed from the people they were then to the people they are now, though I don't know that you'd have been able to guess exactly how they would age; it's more than just people getting more wrinkled. It's like their bones change and their whole face alters. Maybe it's not a bone thing. Maybe it's muscles, and facial expressions that change. I've watched Guy when he's asleep and his face is quite different when he's in that closed-down, unconscious state. I suppose everything just relaxes, but it looks like more than that. It looks like the person is somebody else, or suddenly very old, or at least that you are getting to see how they will look when they become very old. Sometimes it looks like they're dead.

I've watched a few people when they're asleep, and they're all the same: old-looking, or dead. I probably ought to have felt depressed at this, though at the time I felt oddly comforted, and in a strangely satisfying position of power. Also, I was usually more worried that they were about to wake up and start screaming. (I'm not a murderer or a rapist or anything; I just wanted to look, but I can reveal that people most definitely don't like waking up in the middle of the night to find somebody staring at them from a half-metre or so away. Or even a whole metre.)

Hol is right, though: Guy has aged the most since they made those films, because of his illness. Back then he was probably the best-looking of all of them; I mean that if there was some absolute, objective standard of human beauty or handsomeness that applied across both genders, then he would have scored higher than the others. He was a golden boy then, all flowing blond locks and sparkling blue eyes, lithe and graceful and with the best voice too. The others looked like kids in comparison.

'You sure you're going to be okay?' Hol asks. 'When Guy goes. Will you be able to look after yourself?'

'Oh yes.' I nod. 'I'm sure I'll miss him, but I'll be fine.' It's odd, though, because when I say this sort of thing I always get an image of myself living here alone, in this house, just me, all by myself, and that's not what's going to happen, because the house is going to be demolished to make way for more quarry, and I know this, but still; that's the image I have of my life after Guy dies.

Also, I think I still find it hard to believe he's actually going to die. I've watched him get worse and worse over the last few years and I've usually been present when the medics have delivered their sombre assessments, but even though everything points to him being dead in the next few months, it seems some part of me can't accept it's actually going to happen. I think it must be quite an important, if deeply buried, part of me, because otherwise I'd feel more. I mean, about him dying soon. As we stand, I mostly feel numb, and I've yet to break down, yet to cry properly, yet to feel any terror or impending sense of doom. Maybe that'll change once he's bed-bound and immobile, or in a coma, or at the moment he dies. Or later. Maybe this strange numbness is just a survival mechanism, to let me cope.

It has all made me question what I really feel for my dad. I love him, I suppose, the way you have to love your mum or your dad, the way people expect you to, and I'm grateful to him for looking after me by himself all these years, but I don't love him twice as much; I don't love him with all the love he might expect to be his, plus all the love that a mum might have got as well. Maybe it never works like that anyway.

Sometimes I think I love him only because he's there, because there was never anybody else around. I once watched a TV programme about a bunch of ducklings who'd become imprinted, immediately after hatching, on a pair of red wellington boots; they treated the red wellies as if they were their parents, following them everywhere, and always expected to be fed by the person wearing them. Maybe that's the way I love Guy.

Dad's hinted more than once that when it seems like he's being horrible to me, it's just to toughen me up and get me ready for living by myself, or at least without him, and even to make me look forward to him dying, rather than getting all tearful about it.

Though, frankly, Guy being who he is, that could just be an excuse.

'I mean, you'll get money, won't you?' Hol asks, wiping hair back from her brow again. 'For the house. There's money coming to you, isn't there? There isn't anybody else.'

'Not that I know of,' I tell her.

'I mean, there's the money I've got for you, obviously, but there'll be more from the house. A lot more. Should be fairly serious money, I'm imagining.'

'There will be some,' I confirm. 'If he leaves it to me.'

'Good.' She nods slowly a few times, staring at me. I feel that perhaps she didn't really hear the second sentence. 'Good,' she says again, and sighs. 'You look tired,' she tells me. 'You should go to bed.'

'I can't, until Guy's gone. He needs me to help him get undressed and into bed and that sort of stuff.'

45

'Oh.' She seems to think about this. 'None of us could help him, no?'

'Hmm.' I try to make it look as though I'm thinking about this, even though I know the answer perfectly well already. 'Probably best not. Unless it's me or Mrs Gunn he kind of gets upset.'

'Huh. That's tough.'

I shrug. 'Thank you for the offer. This tape.'

'Hmm?' she says.

'It's not a sex tape, is it?' I'm really hoping it isn't.

Hol laughs. She shakes her head once, or at least moves it. 'No,' she says. Though it could be 'Oh' that she says rather than 'No'; it's hard to tell. She's still slurring her words. 'It's . . . embarrassing for other reasons . . . Nothing to do with sex.' She smiles at me.

'Fucking parliament of crows, vultures,' Guy says as I tuck him into bed. 'Fucking circling vultures, so-called friends.'

Guy is quite drunk. His eyes, looking large in his thinned head, appear glazed and don't seem to be focusing well, pointing in subtly different directions as if he's become part chameleon, though without the interesting ability to blend into the background through changing skin colour.

'You did invite them, Dad.' I check his meds. They're held on the upturned lid of an old biscuit tin sitting on the bedside table. Only just held; they almost overflow. He has to take quite a lot.

'Yeah, well, nice to have some normal people in the house for a change,' he tells me. 'Some decent company, adults I can talk to. The bastards are only here to gloat, though, watch me suffer.'

'Why would they do that? They must have better things

46

to do.' I can see the opiate capsules have gone early; they usually do.

'Because people are vicious bastards, that's why. They don't all run flow charts in their heads before they decide what to say next. They're not all fucking Dr Spocks like you.'

I think about this. 'I think you mean Mr Spock. After the character from the original *Star Trek*.'

'Fuck off. You know what I mean.'

It has taken us even longer than usual to get up the stairs this evening. Usually it takes less than two minutes, with me helping Guy and him resting on each step, but tonight it took nearly three minutes. The others offered to help – especially Pris, because she used to be a nurse and still deals with a lot of old and mobility-impaired people – but it's not really about numbers. We have applied for a stairlift device but there's no word of it yet. Guy reckons if it ever does get installed it'll turn up just in time to bring his coffin down the stairs, assuming he has the good grace to die peacefully in his own bed.

'Anyway, they're here because they're your friends. They're all busy people. They didn't have to come.'

'All right! I heard you! Take their side, yeah, why not; just you do that. Why support me, eh? I'm just your dad.' He looks up at me from the bed. He lies half propped up against a slope of pillows and cushions because that's the most comfortable position for him to sleep in. He stares at me. 'You're all just waiting for me to die,' he says. 'You are, aren't you?'

'Now, Dad,' I begin, checking his water bottle on the bedside table is full.

'I'm not an idiot. I'm not losing my mind. Fucking shitty horrible fucking cancer hasn't got there yet!' His voice has grown louder and a little higher in pitch. 'I know you're just waiting. I know you hate me. I know you can't wait for me to go. I'm not fucking stupid.' He makes a noise like a sob. 'Don't think I'm not fucking stupid.'

He means 'Don't think I'm fucking stupid', not what he actually said, with the almost certainly unmeant 'not' in the phrase, which entirely turns the meaning on its head.

Up until as little as a few months ago I'd have pointed this out, because, well, it's just wrong. However, I am learning not to do this all the time. He's very ill, and constantly either in a lot of pain or so loaded with opiates he struggles to think straight, so he deserves to be indulged. I recognise this. Also, picking him up on this kind of minor mistake only leads to further argument and vexation, and it's pointless. I'm not dealing with a child still learning the ways of the world and how language works; he's a dying man. There's nothing to be gained trying to teach him new things or reinforce stuff he ought to know because he'll need this information for his life ahead; he hasn't got one.

And, of course, he's right, in a way. I am waiting for him to die. I don't necessarily *want* him to die (my deepest wish is that things could go on the way they were, just the two of us living here, minding our own business, like we did before the cancer got so bad and spread so far and he became so dependent on me), but knowing that his death is as close to inevitable as these things get, and not far off, makes me wish it was all over with sometimes. Apart from anything else, my knowing he doesn't have very much longer to live helps make it easier to ignore the insults and curses and the general unpleasantness that him being in this state leads to.

If I faced a lifetime of this, or let's say ten more years – or maybe just five, or even two – I think I'd kill him, or myself, or run away.

I point at the biscuit-tin lid of drugs. 'Have you taken the purple ones?'

'What?' He glances, then winces with the pain that must have come with the movement. 'No. Maybe. I don't know.'

'You should wait until I'm here before—'

'Oh, shut up. I don't know. What are they?'

I pick up the pack. 'Larpeptiphyl,' I read off the label.

'Stupid fucking name. Stupid as the names in that idiot game you play all the fucking time. I think you make half of these up. Is that really what it says? Let me see it.'

'Here.'

'Well, where are my *glasses*? What am I supposed to do with . . . What have you done with my glasses?' For the last couple of years Guy has needed glasses to see things close up. He is vain about this; he would have had laser surgery on his eyes to correct them instead if he'd been well enough.

'I haven't done anything with them,' I tell him. 'Last time I saw them they were round your neck.' I wish they were on his head; that's where they would be in a sit-com. 'They'll be in a drawer probably . . .' I go to open one of the bedside cabinet drawers but he flaps a hand at me.

'Never mind. You've worn me out with all this bollocks. Just let me sleep.'

I look at the pack of Larpeptiphyl, counting the empty, punctured blisters. 'You need to take two of these.'

'Trying to make me overdose now, are you?'

'No. You haven't taken the ones for tonight. See?'

'How do you know?'

'I counted.'

'You counted,' he says, as though spitting the words. I pop

the purple pills from their little clear plastic bubbles. 'Yeah, that's all you can do, isn't it? Count. That's what you're good at. That's all you can do: just count. You don't even have the people skills to be a fucking accountant, do you? I wasted my fucking life on you. I don't know why I bothered.'

'Here.' I offer him the pills one at a time and hold the water glass to his lips as he leans forward and up and gulps everything down.

He seems to choke, and splutters. 'All right! Don't fucking drown me!' He collapses back amongst the pillows. His lips look livid against the pale skin of his face. They're a sort of strange purple-brown, like the lips of giant clams on the Great Barrier Reef. I wipe the glass, top it up from the bottle.

'I think that's everything. Are you all right now?'

'Of course I'm not fucking all right! Do I look fucking all right? Look at me!'

'I meant—'

'You meant can you fuck off with a half-clear conscience and play your stupid fucking game and leave me to die, that's what you meant.'

'I think it's time we both went to sleep.'

'Put to sleep,' he mutters, though his eyelids are fluttering with tiredness. 'Put to fucking . . . yeah, you go. Just leave me,' he says, voice fading. 'Fuck off.' His eyes are closed now. 'Oh, fuck . . . I'm sorry, son,' he says, sighing, eyes still closed, lids fluttering. 'Shouldn't talk to you like that. Know you're just trying to help. You shouldn't listen . . . You'll be better off without me.' He sighs again, as if it's his last breath easing out of him. 'You go. Have a nice wank. Wish to fuck I could.' But he can't even manage the hard '-ck' sound; the word comes out more like 'fuh', and while I'm still tidying up the lid of drugs he relaxes at last and with a long sigh his breathing slows and his face goes that slack way, mouth opening a little, giving him that look that people get, so that he seems even older, or already dead.

I stand over him for a short while, looking down at him as he sleeps. Then I put the light out, turn the night light on, and leave.

I don't go out much. I never liked having to go to school every weekday and it's a relief that that's over. I didn't hate school; I learned things and even met one or two people I still keep in touch with, plus I was too big to bully efficiently – and I have been known to lose it and lash out – but I always hated leaving the house.

My main exercise is walking round the garden. From my bedroom window I can see a large part of my regular walk. My bedroom is on the opposite side of the house from Guy's and looks out to the north-east, over the back garden and the trees towards the wall and the quarry. My regular walking route takes me from the kitchen door, curves away to skirt the rear of the garage and the sides of the outhouses, passes between the vegetable patches, disappears into the rhodo-dendron clump, crosses the lawn at a diagonal, veers past the weed-choked bowl of the long-drained pond, weaves between the trunks of the trees – mostly alder, ash, rowan and syca-more – before arriving at the remains of the old greenhouses and the tall stone wall defining the rear limit of the property.

The wall is about two metres high but there is one place where a pile of stones at its base and a projecting piece of ironwork a metre up allow you to climb it and see over the top and into the quarry. On the other side, there is only a metre to two metres of level, sparsely grassed ground before the earth falls away. The quarry is at least forty metres deep, stretches back for over a kilometre and widens out in a giant, irregular bowl shape nearly half a kilometre wide. It is tiered, with stone ramps for trucks cut into the different levels; big rocks line the edges of the clifftop roadways to stop trucks falling in. The bottom is a series of flat arenas on different levels, the lowest filled with green-brown water. The rock is the grey of old warships.

At the far end, where the remains of the hill curve round like cliffs, with just a small gap giving a glimpse of the agricultural land beyond, there are some tall, gawky structures made of rusting iron. A few stand like upside-down pyramids on skinny metal legs, while others sprout wonky-looking conveyor belts that straggle across the ground like fractured centipedes, disappearing behind piles of stones sorted into different sizes. It's been years since I saw anything much move here. I can remember when piles of rocks undulated along the conveyor belts and dust rose from the stone piles as the big yellow vehicles swung across the ground, scooping up stones and dropping them again. When the wind was in the right direction you could hear distant clanking and thudding noises.

Back then, twice a week, most weeks – after the sirens had sounded for a couple of minutes, usually at about two in the afternoon, so that I experienced it only when there was a school holiday that wasn't an everybody-else holiday – there would be that sudden quiver that shook the whole house and made the old servant-summoning bells in the kitchen ting faintly. It rattled the windows in their frames and once or twice made dust drift down from cracks in the ceiling. The noise of the blasting charges came a second or so later, because the shock waves propagate faster through rock than air.

The local crows and the rooks from the nearby rookery would already be in the air; other birds reacted to the detonation rather than taking the warning of the sirens, and went flapping and panicking into the skies, chirping and calling. The corvids made sounds it was hard not to think of as contemptuous, or just as laughter.

Then there would be another, longer, rumbling sort of shaking; this was the curtain wall of stone that had been shattered free from the bedrock, falling and slumping to the ground beneath. More tinkling and rattling. A noise like a heavy, distant crump came and went. The sirens shut off half a minute later.

I used to watch from my room, when I could, when I heard the sirens, and a couple of times I was able to be at the back wall, standing on the footrest of the loop of iron projecting from it – even though I was banned from being there for safety reasons – but I only once ever saw the explosions and the falling face of rock, from my room, when it was raining and the view was slightly misty. The blast was far away, near the end of the quarry where the rusty structures were, and disappointingly undramatic: just some small vertical bursts of dust appearing suddenly from one or two of the half-dozen blast holes on the ledge above, then the cliff collapsing along a thirty-metre front and briefly flowing like a mush of dirty ice, spreading out across the ledge beneath and quickly coming to a stop, with more grey dust that quickly joined with or was defeated by the mist and rain. I was watching through binoculars, but still saw hardly anything. Even the shake the house got from that blast was substandard; the kitchen bells stayed silent.

The machine that drilled the holes for the blasting charges looked excitingly like a complicated anti-aircraft gun, tipped up near the edge of a cliff, producing dust in dry weather. Sometimes you could hear it, working away.

My return walk takes me from the back wall via the other clump of rhododendrons, skirts the lawn on its western edge, loops round the remains of the summer house with its fallen-in roof and broken windows, and reaches the house along the side of the old flower beds and the terrace, with its kinked, uneven stone balustrade and its weed-outlined flagstones, roughly a third of which have suffered significant cracking.

If I stand by the window of my room I can see approximately ninety per cent of my garden walk. In some places I can see where individual footprints occur as I pace out the same walk day after day, so you can see where I've left my mark on the garden. This makes me smile.

The whole walk, disregarding the bit about shinning up the rear wall to look into the quarry, consists of 457 steps. The number 457 is, satisfyingly, a prime. The original walk was – completely naturally, as it were – 456 steps, but I adjusted it.

In the morning I am in the kitchen when Pris comes in, wrapped in a big white towelling robe. 'Hey, honey. You're up early.' Her face looks a little crumpled, eyes puffy. Her glossy black hair needs brushing but it looks attractively tousled on her. When my hair needs combing I look like an axe murderer.

'I'm making Guy's breakfast.' I look at the clock on the wall. 'And it's not really early.' I am boiling a couple of eggs in a pan.

'Early for the weekend, sweetheart. It's weekend early.' She scratches her head and goes over to the kettle. 'New kettle. There you go. Something has changed.' She looks out of the window at grey clouds and dripping black trees. 'Though sadly not the weather.'

She makes a mug of tea, sits at the table. She glances at the clock. 'Just having a cup of tea,' she tells me, unnecessarily. 'Meeting the other half in Ormers for breakfast.'

'That's nice,' I say.

'That's nice' is one of those pointless phrases I would never have used but for Hol. My natural response to something like what Pris has just said would be to say nothing. So, she is going to Ormiscrake to meet her relationship partner for breakfast. Does that really require any reply from me? No.

Yet Guy would sneer and be sarcastic towards me on such occasions. 'Still perfecting the blank look, are we?' he'd say (or something similar). 'Good for you, kid. Treat these phatic fuckers with the contempt they deserve.'

Hol eventually took exception to this behaviour, too. 'You just say *something*, Kit,' she told me, when I protested that usually these misunderstandings occurred when I had nothing useful to say in return to something I'd just been told. 'A nod, or a grunt, would be an absolute minimum, or an "Uh-huh". Just a "Really?" or "That's nice", or "I see", or partially repeating what you've just been told, or thinking it through a little so that if they say they're going out you ask, "Anywhere exciting?" or suggest they take a brolly cos it's pissing down. You don't just stare blankly at them. Apart from anything else these meaningless replies are like saying "Roger", or "Copy that"; you're letting people know that you received their message. If you don't use them you're getting the whole communication thing wrong. You're making them think they need to repeat themselves or rephrase what they've already said because you didn't get it the first time. That's unneeded redundancy and inefficient and, frankly, I'd expect better of you. Get the procedure right, Kit; your comms protocols need refreshing.'

I think this little diatribe shows Hol knows exactly which of my buttons to push. I took note of some of the phrases she'd mentioned, and started using them. I still find it bizarre that we get away with spouting such inanities, but they seem to work. I get fewer funny looks.

That said, I'm still thinking of replacing 'That's nice'. I think 'Aha' serves just as well and sounds less potentially sarcastic. '*What's* fucking "nice"?' is Guy's usual, half-sneering, half-incredulous reply to that particular phrase.

'Have you met Rick?' Pris asks, frowning. 'My chap?'

'No,' I tell her. The sweep hand on the kitchen clock reaches twelve; I switch off the ring beneath the pan with the eggs. I think about Hol's advice regarding thinking things through. 'What's he like?'

Pris snorts a little laugh. 'Mostly he's not like Haze,' she says. She and Haze used to be a couple. 'Got some gumption. Some get-up-and-go.' She plays with the fluffy white belt of her gown. 'Not sit-down-and-whine.'

'Aha.'

(That was definitely not a gap during which to employ 'That's nice'. I feel quite pleased with myself and I am liking the neutrality of 'Aha' more and more.)

'He's sweet,' she tells me. 'I mean, he's not like, you know, one of . . . He's not been to uni or anything, he doesn't . . . Anyway, hopefully you'll see him later. Hope you like him. Be nice if people liked him.'

'Of course,' I say.

'Anyway,' Pris says, in that slightly drawn-out way that I've come to recognise means we're finished with that particular topic (and it's cross-platform; by which I mean that this signal is used by other people, not just Pris). 'How are you, Kit? Really, I mean.'

'Really?' I say (look for a part of the question you can repeat). I nod. 'I'm well.'

'Yeah, but *really* really?'

'No, really, I'm—'

'I mean about Guy; about the house,' she says, interrupting.

The kitchen clock's second hand reaches the top of its arc again. I remove the pan from the hob, take it to the sink and run cold water into it. The eggs shake and bounce around in the water, clonking against the pan's sides. 'You know when—' I begin, at the same time as she starts saying something.

'Sorry,' she says, 'what were you—'

'No; you, please,' I tell her, taking the eggs out and placing them on the breadboard.

'I was just going to say,' Pris says, 'that we all . . . We all feel for you, Kit. We all love you. We're maybe not all very good at showing it, but . . . That's always been . . . None of us . . .' She makes a noise like she's exasperated with herself. 'Well, we do. We just do, okay?' She gives a laugh that isn't really a laugh. 'Listen to me, eh? Anyway, I interrupted . . . What were you saying?'

I'm shelling the eggs. The eggs were past their use-by date but they smell okay.

'I'm just taking it one day at a time, Pris,' I tell her, and feel suddenly very mature. It's one of those phrases you hear a lot on television that seem to work well in reality. 'It's all you can do.' I feel even more mature now; that's sort of my own embellishment and seems to reinforce the first statement, so it's not left hanging out there alone like the cliché

57

it is. I smile quickly at her, look back to the eggs. I chop them up. The yolks are just off completely hard, which is how Guy prefers them. I put the warm pieces in a mug pre-warmed with water from the kettle.

'Well,' Pris says, 'that's all you ever can do. But if you want to talk, about anything – anything at all – you know you can talk to me. You do know that, don't you?'

'Yes, thank you,' I tell her.

'I'm serious, Kit. I deal with people facing bereavement in my job all the time. In some ways it can be harder for the people being bereaved than it is for the person who's going to die. There can be all sorts of emotions involved, often conflicting, often – usually, even – ones people feel anxious, even ashamed, about having. If you need to talk about any of that you can talk to me . . . you know; completely confidentially. I mean, as a friend, I hope, but also as somebody who knows about this kind of thing, who's dealt with it professionally.' She has an expression on her face that looks like she's in some pain. 'I always wanted to be more of a friend to you, Kit. More like Hol's been, you know?'

I nod.

'I'm so sorry I just never had the kind of job where I could take that sort of time off, not when I always had other people to think of as well. I just want you to know that.'

I nod again.

'So, please, let me do this for you, if I can. Talk to me, any time, about anything. Okay? Yeah?' She smiles.

I set my mouth in a tight line. I wait a moment or two, then nod. 'Thanks, Pris,' I tell her. 'I'm okay for now, seriously, but thanks.' I go back to the breadboard.

'Okay,' she says, letting a breath out. 'So . . . how long

do they think he's got, now?' she asks, watching me dice up a piece of soft white bread.

'Maybe a month,' I tell her. 'Maybe two.'

'Jesus. Well . . . that's what I'd heard, but . . . really? Is that all?'

'Yes. That's the oncologist's best estimate. But she did say you should never give up hope.' I scoop the little squares of bread into the mug and stir with a teaspoon. Pris looks at the eggy mug like she wants to say something, but she doesn't.

'Is there nothing more they can do?' she asks.

'There is more they can do,' I tell her. 'But Guy doesn't want it done. They could continue the radio and the chemo and maybe get him another month, but maybe not, and none of it's very pleasant. The side effects are . . . distressing.' I'm doing, I reckon, really well here, using euphemisms and semi-technical terms and everything. Guy would be a lot more blunt. 'They seem to have his pain relief sorted now,' I tell her. 'That's been a good change.' There is a plastic tomato sauce bottle half afloat in a basin of warm water in the sink. I add a generous squirt of the sauce to the mug of egg and bread, wipe off the sauce bottle and return it to the cupboard.

Warming the sauce – as well as the mug – is my innovation, to ensure the mixture is at the right temperature when it gets to Guy. There used to be complaints.

Pris is silent, staring at her mug of tea, so I add, 'When Guy asked the oncologist whether she'd continue with the treatment if it was her, she said she was supposed to dodge the question and say, well, it had to be his decision, but the honest answer was just no, she wouldn't.'

'Yeah,' Pris says quietly. 'Medics. Most medics are okay . . . Do you think we'll find this tape?' She looks up at me.

I have to think about this. 'Probably?' I suggest.

Pris looks down at the table again. 'Wouldn't be good if that came out. The others would . . . Well, they're not in the sort of job I am. You know, caring. For vulnerable people.' She makes a noise like a laugh. 'Leaves me vulnerable, too.'

'I'm sure we'll find it,' I tell her.

There is a pack of playing cards on the table. Guy likes to play a game called Patience sometimes. Pris lifts the pack up, turning it over in one hand. 'Funny,' she says. 'It's mornings when I miss smoking. First one of the day, with a cuppa.' She looks up at me with a small smile. 'Most people, it's the evening, after a drink or two.'

I do a last stir of the egg mug with the teaspoon, take a glass of chilled milk from the fridge and a fresh teaspoon from the drying rack, put everything on a small tray and head for the doorway. I stop there and look back; first at the window, then at Pris. She looks quite small, all of a sudden.

'Don't forget a brolly,' I tell her.

'You still on the radio?' Paul asks Holly as I put his toast in front of him. 'Haven't heard you for a while. Oh, ta. You got any napkins, Kit?'

I nod to show I've heard and tear him off a square of kitchen towel. He looks at it, sighs, and places it delicately on the lap of his dressing gown, which is deep blue and slightly shiny and might be silk.

'Yup,' Hol says, not looking up from the open magazine on the kitchen table in front of her. She is wearing green PJs I've seen her in before. They remind me of hospital scrubs. 'Still on the radio.'

'A face for radio, eh?' Haze says, looking round at the others, then adds, 'Just kidding, like, Hol,' though she is already speaking.

60

'Uh-huh,' she says. 'And a voice for mime.' She looks up. 'Anybody else?'

'What are you on?' Alison asks her.

Hol looks at her.

'What radio station?' Alison says, smiling.

'Greater London Local,' she says. 'Horizons strictly fixed within the M25.'

'I really should listen,' Alison says. She and Rob are dressed in matching white PJs and cotton gowns. Alison's blonde hair looks perfect; Rob's shaven head gleams even more than usual.

'I still listen to you, Hol,' Rob says, putting his fork down. He had the last of the out-of-date eggs, scrambled.

'*Do* you?' Alison says, turning to him and sounding terribly surprised. He doesn't look at her, but smiles and winks at Hol. Hol frowns and goes back to her magazine.

'It's on podcast,' I say. They all look at me. 'I listen on the podcast,' I explain. They go back to their breakfasts. Except Hol, who is still looking at me. 'I saw *The Hobbit*,' I tell her. 'I didn't think it was that bad. You said it was Peter Jackson's *Phantom Menace*.'

Paul chokes on his toast, or pretends to.

'Phwoar,' Haze says, sort of half laughing. 'Harsh!' Haze is wearing a brown dressing gown with a green cord. The gown has some interesting stains. The pale ones are probably toothpaste.

Hol shrugs. 'Yeah, I didn't think it was quite that bad, either, Kit, but it's still a piece of disproportionate, self-indulgent wank with values driven entirely by the needs of the studio and the distributors, not the original story, and it needed saying.'

Alison sighs. 'I loved it.' She shrugs. 'I can't wait for the

61

next two films. Sorry,' she says to Hol, who has gone back to reading. 'Guess I'm just such a low-brow these days.'

'Always were,' Rob says.

She play-punches him. 'Why I married you. Darling.'

'Knew there had to be a reason!' Haze says, but then – when they both look at him – he clears his throat and starts humming while he pushes the last of his sausages round his plate with one finger.

'Really?' Rob is saying to Alison. 'I thought you'd been sent by Fun-Be-Gone Industries to stop me enjoying myself too much. Or at all.'

'What,' Alison says, 'shagging everything with an infrared signature and a cleft was your idea of fun?' As Rob looks thoughtfully up at the ceiling and gives a small shrug, Alison turns to look round at the rest of us. 'You'll have to excuse my husband; he's still having trouble with the whole quantity/quality dichotomy.'

'You weren't exactly parsimonious with your favours yourself, my love, were you?' Rob says, smiling at her.

'We ran the figures, remember?' she says to him. 'The ratio was – what? – one of mine to four or five of yours?'

'Four point six,' Rob says, grinning.

Alison spreads her hands. 'Rest my case.'

'Oh, get a room, you two,' Haze says. Rob and Alison both look at him again, frowning. Haze goes back to humming.

'Guy awake?' Paul asks me.

I shake my head. 'No, he's sound.'

Hol, still focused on her magazine, mutters, 'That's a first.'

Haze stops humming just long enough to look at me and say, 'Pris gone off to see what's-his-name?'

'Rick,' I say. 'Yes.'

Haze sighs.

Haze – his real name is Dave Hazelton but he's been known as Haze since Fresher's Week '92, allegedly – is in local government; planning. Career-wise, according to Pris, he's currently in a sort of 'slumped, drooling-with-the-autopilot-on' state and has been for the last ten years; they split up six years ago. His interests and hobbies have varied over the years as he's looked for something he can invest his declining supply of enthusiasm in (this is all from Pris). Apparently he's been through surfing, hang-gliding, green politics, landscape sculpture and Lib-Dem politics. He is currently managing an amateur women's football team. They are bottom of their league.

Pris is back in the single-bed room she had when she first lived here; the original plan was for her and Rick both to stay here and have Guy's room this weekend, before he got so poorly that this became impossible. Instead, Haze was asked to give up his double-bed room for them, but he didn't want to.

Pris is an ex-social worker now running the local franchise of a care services outsourcing agency on the south coast.

Alison and Rob work for Grayzr. They're back in the London office for the year but they've been all over the world, fast-tracked for the executive heights, apparently. I switched from Google to Grayzr last month but I feel shy about telling them for some reason. Hol calls them corporate bunnies.

Last year, when Alison and Rob dropped in while driving back from Scotland, Hol happened to be here for the week and I remember this exchange, over tea and cake:

'. . . No, we're thinking about buying a place out there.'

'Oh, good grief,' I heard Hol mutter.

'Yeah,' Rob said, 'but not on one of the islands. Those are a bit . . . you know.'

Alison nodded. 'Yeah. No. But there are lots of beautiful apartments near the Burj, though. Really tasteful. Cheap now but a really good investment in the medium-to-long. Honestly, Grayzr Arab Street is growing scary-fast, even faster than vanilla Grayzr. Ground-flooring there would be a sound move, strategically.'

Hol looked at both of them. 'Seriously?' she said. 'Fucking *seriously?*'

'And there's more autonomy out there,' Rob added. 'You're not exposed to the beady gaze of Head Office the way you are in Londinium.'

Hol looked at them for a bit, then nodded. 'You should move to Saudi,' she told them. 'They take an even more hands-off approach there.'

. . . I believe the remark might have caused a certain frostiness.

But back to now, and breakfast:

'Hon,' Hol says to me, 'you've been running after us for over half an hour. Sit down; have something yourself.'

'I'm fine,' I tell her.

I've been up for a while. I woke really early, played an hour of HeroSpace and then spent forty minutes in two of the top-floor bedrooms – where all the spiders live and there's a near-constant sound of dripping water even on dry days – peering into old packing cases and soggy cardboard boxes, looking for S-VHS-C tapes (nothing, though if we ever discover an urgent need for damp back copies of the *Bew Valley and Ormisdale Chronicle and Post* dating from the nineties, I know just where to lay my hands on them). Then I had a shower, because Hol said I was a bit whiffy yesterday. I'm wearing a fresh set of clothes, three days early. I even stripped my bed; I'll put new sheets on it tonight.

'Paul,' Alison says. 'You still see Marty F?'

(I have no idea who Marty F is.)

'Not for a while,' Paul says. 'He's in LA these days. Married with two.'

'What?' Haze says. 'Two *wives*?'

'Yeah . . .' Paul says, smiling faintly at him as he munches his toast.

'Weren't you thinking about going out to the States, Hol?' Ali asks. 'Thought you seemed all set at one point. What happened with that?'

'It was being talked about,' Hol says.

'*New Yorker*, wasn't it?' Rob says.

'Mm-hmm.'

Haze whistles appreciatively.

'Hmm,' Ali says. 'That's quite . . .'

'Prestigious?' Rob finishes for her. 'About as cool as reviewing gigs gets, I guess.' He smiles at Hol.

Hol just shrugs.

'Way to go, Hol,' Haze says. 'The *New Yorker*; yeah.'

'And?' Ali says, gesturing. 'Just . . . deal fell apart? Visa knocked back? You owned up to being in the SWP? What?'

'I thought I could do it from here but it turned out it would have meant moving to the States,' Hol tells her.

Ali glances at Rob. 'Preferring London to New York, Hol? Really?'

Hol shrugs again. 'Preferring home to away.'

'No idea you were such a home-loving gal,' Rob says.

'But I thought you hated it here,' Ali says.

'No, just what and who's happened to the place.'

'Arooga,' Haze says. 'Politics alert!'

'Amber warning of rants ahead,' Rob says, and winks at Hol, who smiles thinly back.

'But I thought that was your ambition, wasn't it?' Ali says. 'Moving to NYC or LA? Get stuck into Hollywood at closer range? No? Once?'

'Once,' Hol says. 'That was a while ago. There's still the occasional decent film made here in dear old Albion, and our Continental cousins haven't given up the medium entirely either.'

'Yeah,' Haze says, 'but compared to Hollywood . . .'

'They make more movies in Bollywood,' Rob tells him.

Haze's nose runkles. 'Yeah, but they're all musicals and that, aren't they?'

'The death of the British film industry, like its revival, is constantly being exaggerated,' Hol tells them. 'Anyway,' she says. 'Enough about me. What about the aforementioned Marty F?'

'Hmm,' Alison says. 'It's just . . . Wasn't he on *Jim'll Fix It?* When he was a kid. Wasn't he?'

Paul chews on his toast, frowning. 'Oh, yeah.' Looks are exchanged. 'Now you mention it.' Paul nods slowly, then shrugs. 'That'll be something to tell his analyst.'

Haze seems to hesitate, then leans forward and says, 'Yeah; in LA, if you're not in therapy there's something wrong with you!' He sits back. There are more faint smiles. 'Aww,' he says, 'come on . . .'

I have another walk, much longer than my round-the-garden walk. This walk means going down the driveway at the front of the house to the minor road there and turning left, heading slightly uphill, then after about eighty metres climbing a gate into a field and skirting two of its sides to the far corner, where there is a part of the drystone wall with projecting stones designed to be used as a sort of rough stairway. On the other side of the wall the agricultural land gives way to moorland. This is Holtarth Moor. Technically our house, Willoughtree House, stands on Holtarth Moor. That is also why the quarry is called Holtarth Moor Quarry.

Beyond the wall the land rises gently towards the sky and there is a sort of faded path across the grass and heather for a little more than a kilometre, then it peters out completely. You have to navigate by compass, GPS or dead reckoning, the last of which is made easier by there being a single, stunted, wind-blasted tree away to the north-east, which should start off at one's eleven o'clock and which should be passed to one's left at about a hundred and fifty metres.

As the swell of the ground summits, you start to see the distant hills forming the rest of the Pennines, while off to the east, on a clear day, you can see the North Sea, though it's just a line. I suspect that on a mostly clear night, with the right amount of cloud directly above the city, you might see the glow of the lights of Newcastle, but I'm not sure – it's a biggish city but it's a long way away. Anyway, I'd never do this walk at night.

A small declivity starts to fold itself into the land once the lone, leaning-away-from-the-west-wind tree has been passed. The route then keeps to the right of this as the fold becomes a stream and then a shallow valley. Finally – and if the wind is from the west as usual, by now it's normally possible to hear the motorway – a curving walk round the limit of a sort of scattered tor of rocks to the right brings you up over a last small rise to the cutting through the hill where the motorway lies.

The M1(M) slants south-west to north-east here; a B-road, following an old pack route through the hills and coming up from the south-east, crosses the motorway on a long arched bridge. You used to have to climb the wire fence meant to separate the moor from the road but it's fallen into disrepair over the last few years and so you can just step over it now. The walk from there to the centre of the bridge takes a minute. I've looked on the relevant maps for a name for the bridge, but it doesn't seem to have one.

There, at the middle of the span, is where I like to stand, leaning on the chest-high safety barrier, watching the traffic beneath.

There is rarely any traffic on the B-road: the odd car, a van or light truck or two (sometimes lost; twice in the last couple of years delivery trucks have stopped to ask me directions, confused by some sat-nav glitch; I'm not much help). I'm always convinced, when the people stop their car or van behind me, that they're doing so only so that they can get out and beat me up or kidnap me or do something else terrible to me. Though so far this hasn't actually happened.

Three times, a small herd of sheep have crossed the bridge, followed by a farmer on a quad bike. The sheep hesitate when they see me, then are forced onwards by the farmer. They flow, bleating, round me, trying to keep at least a metre or so away from me, scurrying at the last moment and sometimes jumping into the air, kicking their skinny rear legs. I have been nodded to by the same farmer man twice now, and nodded back. Frankly I'd always prefer to have the bridge entirely to myself but I get an odd thrill when I perform this minimum exchange of pleasantries.

I have fantasised about an attractive young farmer girl coming along on her quad bike, and the bike breaking down and needing a push to get it going or something, or her requiring some other sort of help that I am able to provide, and her giving me a lift, or the two of us just starting to talk and this leading to – well, in the wilder versions, going back to a rather implausibly clean and deserted farm where we literally roll in the hay or have a shag in a hot tub or whatever. However, these are just fantasies; a single, terse-seeming nod from a dour, taciturn male farmer is as warm as things get up here.

The traffic is what attracts me. I love to watch the steady rolling streams of it heading north and south. To the south the land drops away and curves slightly further eastward so that you can see less than a kilometre of the motorway, but to the north there is a straight nearly four kilometres long, heading very slightly downward to the floodplain of the river Bew and the flyover complex affording access to and from Bewford.

I find the sound of the traffic soothing. This is a busy stretch of motorway with only two lanes in each direction and at most times of the day the noise is almost continuous, with cars and light vehicles tearing past on the steel-grey tarmac below, the laden trucks labouring slowly and the unladen ones thundering quickly past underneath. Their engines create one wash of sound, their slipstreams a second and their tyres on the road surface another. It all makes a sort of throaty choir of white noise, roaring a long shout of nothing into the sky from the cutting through the land. Rain on the tarmac makes the tyres sound louder but softer at the same time.

Towards dusk the lights form twin bands of colour, white and red, glittering and beautiful. I used to be unable to stay late enough to see this for long because it never seemed wise to make the walk back across the moor in the dark. Now that I can drive I've brought the Volvo out here a couple of times at night, parking it and walking out into the middle of the bridge to watch the lights. It's not quite the same, though; the walk is part of the experience, even though I find it stressful and don't like having to walk through dirt or mud.

Being here at night is even more nerve-racking, though; the threat of people turning up to attack or kidnap me seems all the greater. I know the crime statistics indicate this is highly unlikely to happen, but I just can't ever stop thinking about it. So mostly I come here in daylight.

Mist, fog and low cloud ought to make it barely worth coming, but it doesn't always work that way. If it gets too dense you can see almost nothing – the vehicles appear directly below only briefly and disappear again – but, if there's just enough, it can make the whole scene look serene and other-worldly. The traffic looks like it's made up of ghost vehicles forever solidifying out of the atmosphere and rolling along an enchanted highway to somewhere exalted, exotic and fair.

The very best thing to see, though, is a random jam. A random jam is when the traffic backs up for what looks like no particular reason. Roadworks and crashes produce non-random, perfectly explicable jam-ups, but random jams seem to come out of nowhere. One moment the traffic is flowing normally, then the next it's as though the liquid of the traffic suddenly sets, with the wave-front of halting vehicles propagating rapidly upstream. Later, after a few seconds or many minutes, as the traffic at the front of the queue breaks up like ice on some Alaskan river in spring, the flow resumes, and everything gets back to normal.

It's fascinating, and oddly beautiful. Sometimes it leads to skids and shunts and road traffic accidents, when people don't pay attention and fail to brake in time, and that isn't so good, but generally this doesn't happen and the random jam is like some strange, harmless, ephemeral work of art.

I rarely drive on the motorway and I've never been in a random jam. It must feel like any other except you never see what caused it, so a random jam can only really be appreciated by an external observer, like me on the bridge.

The best one I ever saw was the first, when I was only ten and had just started venturing as far over the moor as the motorway and the bridge. It started to the north, at the far end of the straight before the Bewford turn-off, and I watched the traffic congeal all the way up to where I stood until it passed beneath me and went on out the other side of the bridge. When I looked back to where it had begun it was already clearing, and the wave of spreading-out, accelerating vehicles came rolling up the hill as quickly as the original jam.

I remember laughing.

Random jams only ever occur when traffic is heavy and bunched up. I think they're triggered when something seemingly trivial takes place, like somebody changing lanes suddenly, and the person behind brakes, then the person behind them brakes a little harder, and so on, until people further back are having to slow to a crawl and then a stop, while people changing lanes to avoid it just spread the blockage further.

Ideally, to study the phenomenon under controlled conditions, you'd want to start one of your own. I have toyed with the idea of dropping something from the bridge – a plastic bag full of leaves, maybe, so it wouldn't cause any damage if it hit a vehicle – but that would still be dangerous and irresponsible, plus I'd be frightened I'd be caught and imprisoned.

71

Lastly, it has occurred to me that the person who initiates a random jam probably never knows what chaos they've caused behind them. I've seen six random jams over the last eight years – three in the last eighteen months as I've adjusted the times of my walks to make witnessing them more likely – and it took me a while before I realised that they might stand as a symbol for life in general; trivial actions leading to proliferating consequences that affect hundreds of others, but which we never know about.

I can be slow that way.

'Yeah, Kit, mate, hi. How you doin'? Just having a cup of tea, yeah?'

I am standing stirring a mug of tea with the tea bag lying steaming on the draining board right beside the mug, so I'm not sure Haze's statement needs even the most cursory acknowledgement. I think I'll risk it and say nothing.

Everybody has finished their breakfast, including Guy, though he had only about half the eggy mug and complained there was too much tomato sauce (that's a first). I've eaten the sausage Haze left, the bits of bacon Alison removed from her bacon roll – mostly fat, but well crisped; the best bit if you ask me – three half-slices of toast off various plates and assorted other bits and pieces. I was able to do this quickly while clearing up after everybody had left the kitchen, and obviously I watch people carefully to make sure they haven't sneezed over their food, or are inclined to spray saliva when they talk, or insert something into their mouth and then put it back on their plate, uneaten but contaminated.

I'm not really comfortable eating in front of people at the best of times, but this sort of scavenging-eating – even though it's really just about not wasting food – can look a bit sad;

72

people think you're destitute, or – God help us – have Eating Issues. And I draw the line at finishing the contents of Guy's eggy mug.

Anyway, thanks to Haze, now I've lost count of how many rotations and contra-rotations I've performed with the spoon to stir the milk and sugar in. Oh well; I was probably about there anyway. 'Hi, Haze,' I say. He's dressed in his jeans and the same Therapy? T-shirt.

'Yeah,' he says. 'Just thinking; what time did Pris head off to see this, um, what's-his-name?'

'Rick.'

'Yeah, him.'

I think back. 'About eight-fifteen, eight-thirty?'

'Right, right, yeah. She say what time she'd be back?'

'No. I think we're all meeting up for lunch.'

'Right. Yeah, I see.' His face scrunches up. 'Don't see that lasting, really, do you?'

I stare at him. Eventually I shrug. Then I drink my tea; sometimes it's good to have a prop.

'Always a bad sign, when you sleep apart, isn't it? Well,' he says, scratching his head through his thin brown hair, 'you wouldn't . . . But it is, know what I mean?'

'Aha.'

'Yeah,' he says, grinning now. 'Yeah,' he repeats. He takes a deep breath. 'So, this tape, eh?'

'Aha. Yes. The tape.'

'Yeah; the tape.'

'Is it a sex tape?' I ask him.

Haze's eyes widen and his mouth opens. 'Oh, yeah, totally.' Then he laughs loudly and shakes his head. 'Nah, not really. But there is, ah . . . embarrassing stuff on there. Would hurt me a lot if it, you know, came out.' His nose wrinkles. 'Others

73

are all right; they're, you know, secure. Career. Money. That sort of boring, conformist shit.' He shrugs. 'I'm . . . I'm sort of, a bit more . . . out there, you know? Bit exposed, yeah? Result of living on the edge a bit. Certain . . .' He waggles one hand. 'Certain sensitivities with . . . certain people around me about, you know, activities . . . exposed positions, that sort of thing.' He nods.

'I see.' (I don't.)

'Yeah,' he says, frowning. 'Anyway, so . . .' He has started gently, rhythmically, bouncing one fist off the shoulder of one of the kitchen seats as he talks. He's not looking at me now; he's looking at the table. 'It's just, I've, like – oh, man, it's really annoying,' he says through a laugh, ' – but I've only gone and come out and left home without me wallet, haven't I?' He reaches round and pats a hip pocket. His gaze flicks to me and then away again. 'Well, I mean, I've got the actual *wallet*, but I forgot to bring, like, dosh, and my card, you know what I mean?'

I feel like the Terminator sometimes. I can almost see the lines of potential dialogue scrolling down in front of me.

'Fuck off, asshole' and 'Uzi nine millimetre' both being inappropriate, I decide to go with:

'Oh dear.'

'Yeah, I know!' Haze says, nodding vigorously. 'So I just, like, wondered if you could, you know, like, spot me for a shekel or two, know what I mean, mate?'

'Lend you some money?'

'I'll give you a cheque and everything. I always carry a spare cheque in my wallet, so that's not a problem, I mean, it really isn't. Yeah, so, that'd be great. Hundred would . . . Hundred would do. Shit, man, really hate having to ask you. This is so embarrassing, but . . .' He looks back at the kitchen door and drops his voice a little. 'You're sort of the man of the house now, aren't you?' He looks at me, smiles and shrugs.

I shake my head. 'I don't think I have much cash, Haze, sorry.'

His face falls. 'Oh.'

'Maybe a fiver in change, if that.'

'Well, that would—'

'But' – I look up at the ceiling, to give the appearance of thinking; there's a new stain there, I'm fairly sure – 'I'll need a pound coin for the shopping trolley,' I tell him. 'And then, later in the week, if I have to take Guy to the hospital, there's the parking. You have to pay, now.'

'Oh. Oh, right. Yeah, I see. Well, okay. Yeah, right, yeah; bummer, eh? Never mind. Thanks.' He pats the seat-back as though congratulating or commiserating with it, then starts to retreat to the door. 'Yeah, well, so; if you could get any money when you're out, or anything, then, you'll, you know . . .' He looks at me with an expectant expression on his face. I smile at him. 'Right,' he says. 'Yeah; right. Okay then. Like, later, crocodile.' He leaves.

I have a biscuit with the tea. There's a syrupy residue of partially dissolved sugar left in the bottom of the mug.

I knew I hadn't stirred it enough.

'Where now?'

'Aldi.'

'I thought we'd been there.'

'No, we haven't.'

'You sure? Where did we go first?'

'That was Lidl.'

'Ah.'

'They share seventy-five per cent of the letters in their names.'

75

'Yeah, that'll be it. Why are we going to Aldi?'

'For bread.'

'We got bread in Sainsbury's.'

'That was brown wholemeal, for me. We still need plain white, for Guy.'

Hol nods behind me. 'There's some right there.'

I don't even need to look. 'Yes, but it's not on special offer.'

Hol squints. 'Doesn't exactly look expensive.' She has a pained expression on her face. I have come to recognise this look, over the years. Not just on Holly, either.

'Yes,' I tell her, 'but it's still not on special offer. It's twenty pence cheaper in Aldi this week.'

'Twenty pee? Is it even worth it? How far is it to Aldi?'

'It's one point four kilometres. Given that the car's engine is already warmed up, our additional fuel consumption, even allowing for the extra eight hundred metres added to our journey from Aldi to home, compared to from here to home—'

'No need to show your working, Kit,' Holly says, holding one palm up to me.

'It's worth it,' I confirm, cutting to the chase.

'Okay.' Hol sighs. She looks down the aisle. 'Any particular checkout? Do you have a strategy for that too?'

'One of the self-checkouts.' I nod. 'There's a single queue; more efficient. Why we have a basket.'

The other reason I like to exit via the self-checkout lanes is that I don't have my own proper bank card yet and so I have to use Guy's debit card to pay for the groceries – I usually get some cashback from the first supermarket I visit, to pay for any subsequent smaller orders – and it's less stressful using a machine to enter the PIN than looking into the eyes of a checkout staff member when technically it's not actually your name on the card you're using. That makes me sweat and sometimes fumble or even temporarily forget the PIN.

Sometimes machines can be more forgiving than people.

Today there's even a queue for the different queues. That's new. We join it.

'Does it even make sense to shop on a Saturday?' Hol asks, as we pull up behind a large family with a full trolley. I put our heavy, piled-up basket on the floor so I can nudge it along with my foot as we all shuffle forward. 'I mean, you can shop any day of the week, can't you?' she says. 'Isn't Saturday the busiest day?'

'Yes, but you get the best special offers at the weekend, and by Sunday usually some have sold out. I have no time constraints, so I can afford the extra minutes spent in queues.'

'You do this every week?'

'Yes. At least. Sometimes we need to top up, though I try to avoid that.'

'That's a lot of extra time in queues.'

'It gets me out of the house.'

Hol looks at me. 'God, you're being serious.'

'We could have groceries delivered, but I don't like leaving the choice of fresh stuff to somebody else, their substitution choices aren't to be relied on and, in theory, to maximise the savings we'd have to have up to six separate deliveries, most of which would be too small to qualify for free delivery anyway, so—'

'You really have worked this all out, haven't you?'

'Of course. It's fun.'

Holly smiles. 'I bet it is.'

'I started with a flow-chart and considered writing a small program but I just do it all in my head now. The main

77

problem used to be convincing Mrs Gunn it was worthwhile, and obviously she did have other calls upon her time so the extra waiting wasn't irrelevant to her. Sometimes she would cut out a store altogether if there was only one or two items to be bought there. Also, I don't think she likes being seen shopping in Aldi or Lidl.' I have a think, remembering. 'Or Poundshop,' I add.

'Aha,' Holly says. She is making faces at the young girl sitting crying loudly in the fold-out seat of the trolley in front. The child's mother is ignoring her while she scolds another child.

'She had particular problems with the results of me calculating the best order in which to visit the local supermarkets so as to balance the priority of securing those items most prone to selling-out quickly while minimising the time that fridge and especially freezer stuff might spend warming in the car.'

'No kidding?' The child in the fold-out seat of the trolley in front has stopped crying. Instead she is staring at Hol, who is making her ears waggle and crossing her eyes.

'It's a seasonal thing. I think that's what really used to mess with Mrs G's head. She seemed annoyed at the time, but I think she was secretly pleased when I told her that now I could drive I'd be able to do it all myself.'

'We used to employ sacrificial peas,' Hol says, turning away from the little girl as her mother picks her out of the trolley and puts her to her shoulder, cuddling her.

'Did you say, sacrificial peas?'

'Yes I did.'

I shake my head. 'Not familiar with that term.' Even as I say this, I realise I've left the personal pronoun off the beginning of that sentence. This is probably because I'm excited;

I find all shopping expeditions a little stressful, but a successful one is positively invigorating.

'If you were going out on a picnic,' Hol says, frowning at the queue ahead of us, 'or taking some bubbly to somebody's room in the summer or something, you'd buy a packet of frozen peas to pack round the bottle to keep it cool. Then you threw the peas away.'

'Without even opening them to see if they were still viable?'

'They were only there as a cooling device, Kit. The priority was the drink.'

'Still; very wasteful.'

'It was drink, Kit. Often drink linked to the possibility of copping off with somebody who'd helped consume said alcohol. Dumping a cheap packet of peas invariably seemed like a small price to pay.'

'Hmm.'

'Anyway. How is Mrs G? I tried to talk to her yesterday but she was in full-on Ted mode.'

'Ted mode?'

'Ted and Ralph? *The Fast Show?* Paul Whitehouse? "I don't know about that, sor."' Hol lowers and deepens her voice and assumes what I think might be an Irish accent for the bit that sounds like she's quoting.

'I thought you meant *Ted*, the film with the teddy bear that comes to life.'

'Ah, yes, our Seth, the nipple man.' Hol sighs. 'No. Anyway, sorry; dated reference for an eighteen-year-old, I guess.' Hol shakes her head. 'Point is, Mrs G was being taciturn last night. I just wondered how things are with her.'

'She is well,' I tell her. I think. 'I think.'

'What other help are you getting?'

'I still see Mrs Willoughby. Only once a month now.'

'I meant with Guy,' Hol says. 'His illness.' She touches me lightly on the forearm. I find this less intrusive than the same gesture performed by anybody else.

'Things have gone quiet now he's back home and off the treatments,' I tell her.

The queue edges forward and I push the basket along the floor. Another reason for using a heavily loaded basket rather than a lightly loaded trolley is that whenever I choose a trolley it always seems to develop a squeaky wheel, which is annoying. I've been known to bring a small oil can with me on these expeditions, to obviate this very problem.

'It's been a relief,' I tell Hol. 'So Guy says, although I thought it was quite nice having so many people to the house, and driving him to the hospitals and the units when there was no ambulance available. Doctor Chakrabarti comes out to see Guy once a week. A Tuesday or a Wednesday, usually.'

'Hey, Kitface,' one of the shelf-fillers says to me, pushing through the queue one trolley behind us with a shrink-wrapped pallet. 'You all right?'

'I'm fine, thanks,' I say. 'You?'

'Cool, yeah,' he nods.

I nod at the queue. 'This a new queuing system or something?'

He rolls his eyes, then shakes his head. 'Yeah.' He pushes the pallet on through.

'Say hi to—' I begin, but Clodge – his real name is Colin – is already out of earshot. He is taller but much thinner than me, with ginger hair and poor skin.

'Friend?' Hol asks.

'I suppose. Ex-colleague.'

'You worked here?'

'On a placement. Sort of work experience.'

'That where you work for nothing and get your dole docked if you don't? And this place gets a free worker?'

'I was told it would be valuable experience.'

'Uh-huh?'

'It taught me not to suggest and then unilaterally enact too many innovations within the retail environment, as this would inevitably impact adversely on my employment prospects.'

'You got sacked?'

'Yes. I had my Unemployment Benefit stopped for six weeks, too.'

'Jesus.'

'Did you know supermarkets deliberately change their layouts so people who've become familiar with the previous layout will subsequently be forced to wander around more, looking for the things they want, and so seeing and potentially purchasing products they stumble upon?'

'Yes.'

'Well, that's so inefficient!'

'No, it's very efficient at increasing profits. You're just looking at it wrong.'

'I sort of know that, but I still find it offensive.'

'We'll make a socialist of you yet.'

'I doubt it; I'm not sure that's that efficient either.'

The queue processes forward again. We're almost at the split point where an elderly employee I don't recognise is directing those queuing to the first available aisle or the self-checkout area.

We are close enough to the latter to hear the soft chorus of phrases, delivered by a female voice stored on a chip: 'Next item, please', 'Unidentified item in bagging area', 'Please insert card or cash now', 'Please wait for help, an

81

attendant is on the way', 'Would you like cashback?', 'Please enter your PIN number' (though of course that one really ought to be, 'Please enter your PI Number' – not that anyone takes any notice when you point this out – not even management), 'Please enter your voucher number', 'Please take your change', 'Notes are dispensed from beneath the scanner', 'Have a nice day'.

As well as this subtle, lilting choir, there are many mellifluous little chiming noises issuing from the till units, pinging out over the controlled chaos of the queues with each programmed action.

It is, I contend, music, and beautiful. I used to like hanging around here during busy periods just to listen to it. I think that might have impacted adversely on my employment prospects too.

'Do you know what you're going to do, once Guy's gone?' Hol asks. I think she's keeping her voice low. 'And once you have to leave the house?'

'I think it depends on too many things for me to be sure,' I tell her. 'Guy might stage a recovery if the cancer goes into remission again. And there's a final appeal by a local action group against the quarry extension with the result still pending, so that might not happen either. Even if both do happen, I don't know how much I stand to inherit. Guy won't say. He says it's complicated, and there are debts to be settled first. Plus there's the whole Power of Attorney thing, of course.'

Guy started a Power of Attorney action in the courts years ago, to protect my interests once I was no longer a child. I was suspected of being unlikely ever to be able to look after myself properly, and to be psychologically unfit for the full range of adult responsibilities. Both Mrs Willoughby and

Holly swore statements testifying to the contrary. Given her professional status, I think Mrs Willoughby's carried the greatest weight, but I thought it was good of Hol to support me as well.

'*What?*' Hol says. 'I thought that had been dropped!'

'It was adjourned, but technically the issue is still open. It's up to the local authority now. Mrs Willoughby says not to worry and they're probably too snowed under with other stuff to think it worth proceeding with, and it'd probably go in my favour anyway, but you never know.'

'Good old Mrs Willoughby.'

'She said to say hello.'

'Say hello back. Wish her well from me.'

'She's retiring in June but she says she'll continue to take an interest and she'd willingly swear another statement and appear in court if required.'

'This is bollocks, Kit. What was Guy thinking?'

'He was thinking of my best interests. Everybody is, apparently.'

'Yeah, so they all say.'

'Also? I think the whole issue with my mother complicates matters.'

'Shit. I bet it does,' Hol says. We move forward again.

I feel slightly incompetent, not knowing who my mother is.

Not knowing who your father is is not so unusual; not knowing who your mother is is just plain weird. Guy always maintained he was my father and I've always looked like him about the face, especially when I was younger, plus we finally did a DNA test two years ago and he definitely is – but he has variously claimed that my mother is an emigrated-to-Australia ex-barmaid from a long-closed pub in Bewford; a married, middle-aged member of the aristocracy somewhere between one-hundred-and-fiftieth and two-hundredth in line to the throne; a disgraced Traveller girl now settled quietly in County Carlow (which is in Ireland); an American exchange student from the Midwest with hyper-strict parents, belonging to some bizarre religious cult; or possibly just some random girl/conquest he promptly forgot about even at the time, who literally abandoned me on his doorstep one evening. (He tells people he came back drunk from the pub that night and assumed the warm bundle inside the front porch was a takeaway meal delivery he'd forgotten ordering. He claims to have been quite peeved when he discovered it was actually a newborn baby.)

Also, this is why my first name is Kit; it's short for Kitchener, as the kitchen was where Guy first clapped eyes on me.

He has also hinted that it's possible Hol or Pris or Alison might be my mother. I know they each spent the year or so abroad immediately following graduation, which would sort of fit. He's since claimed he was just kidding about this and sworn me to secrecy regarding ever even mentioning this to any of them, but the idea has been planted.

However, it's not a topic I like to dwell on. I'm going to change the subject.

'Haze asked to borrow money from me,' I tell Hol, 'just before we came out.'

'Oh, good grief. Did you give him any?'

'No. I lied. I told him I didn't have any. Actually I didn't quite lie outright, but it was as good as.'

'He done this before?'

'Once before. Last time he was here, a couple of years ago. Just a tenner, but it was all my pocket money.'

'Twat. Did he pay you back?'

'No.'

'Yeah, well, you did the right thing. He'll probably ask me next.' She smiles at me. 'Don't give him any money.'

'I wasn't intending to.'

'Also . . . I wouldn't mention that you have opiates in the house, either. Just to be on the safe side.'

'Okay.' Guy has already said as much.

'Haze has always been like this, Kit,' Hol says. 'He's surely had his problems, especially after Pris left him, but they're pretty much all of his own making.'

'Till number five, good people, please!' The elderly-looking gent directing customers calls out to the family in front of us with the trolley. 'Basket; this way, this way!' he says to us, gesturing extravagantly.

'Haze was a big part of my life, and he'll always be a friend,' Hol says as we start passing the groceries across the laser scanner, to the accompaniment of beeps and 'Next item, please'. 'But he taught me an important life lesson a long time ago.'

'A life lesson?' I say, because this is an unusual turn of phrase for Hol.

She nods. 'Just because you'd trust somebody with your life doesn't mean you can trust them with your money.' She looks at me and arches her eyebrows.

'I'll remember that,' I tell her.

Beep.

3

We're all supposed to meet up for an early lunch in The Miller's Boy pub. Hol and I are going to have to be late because I've seen the temperature display on the side of the Corn Exchange shopping centre and it's a degree too high to leave the shopping in the car so we have to go home and drop it off and put the things in the fridge and freezer that need to go in those. I've offered to do this myself and let Hol go to the pub to meet the others but she insists on helping. She phones Paul to let people know.

Guy, who had said last night he reckoned he'd be able to go along to the pub, is still in the house, sitting in the kitchen feeling sorry for himself. He looks even more gaunt and haggard than usual and hasn't put his woollen hat on, so his head looks still more like a skull.

'Come on,' Hol tells him. 'Come to the pub, if you're up to it; won't be the same without you.'

'I'm up to it, Rupert isn't,' he says, though he is now pulling on his knitted hat, which might be a positive sign.

Guy calls his cancer 'Rupert', an idea he says he got from the dead playwright Harold Pinter.

I smooth and tidy what's left of his hair and he flaps a hand at my fussing, though there is a quality to his tutting and sighing that I think indicates he's persuadable. 'Yeah, please come, Dad. You'll perk up once you're somewhere different, with lots of people; you know you will.' (This is true.)

'Yeah, you only call me "Dad" when you're trying to get me to do something, don't you?' he says to me. (This is not true.)

'Or stay here and I'll stay with you,' Hol says. 'Won't see you sitting here alone.'

'I'll sit here alone if I want to,' Guy tells her. It is probably meant to sound rebellious or determined but actually it just sounds pathetic.

'Fine,' Hol says, 'I'll sit through in the parlour, have a sandwich, read the paper.' She looks at me. 'Kit, you can go to the pub. We'll be fine here.'

I feel torn; I should probably offer to stay too but I'm quite excited at the idea of going to the pub to be with the others, even though it's a public space and will doubtless be full of people.

Guy sighs dramatically. 'Oh, all right, all right,' he says, and starts trying to get up, so we go through a bit of nego-tiation – I would prefer him to take his Zimmer frame but he says he won't be seen looking like some effing geriatric, so we compromise on one of his aluminium and grey plastic forearm crutches – then I drive the three of us back through a sudden, briefly sunlit shower and park in the multi-storey next to Thaxton's.

Thaxton's is the big department store in the centre of town and the place where I thought I'd invented escalator shoe-shining, which is when you clean and shine your shoes by using the black plastic fibres at the stair edges. I was quite proud of this and demonstrated the technique to Hol on one of her visits about three years ago. She told me she'd heard the idea before and other people had obviously had it too.

I got quite upset and had to be mollified with tea and an éclair in the top-floor café. That was where Hol brought up the idea of the Many Worlds theory – possibly in desperation, as I was crying a bit – and said that on the other hand there must be a universe – perhaps even an infinite number of universes – where I really was the first person to think of escalator shoe-shining, and this made me feel better. It helps you to feel normal if you think there's an infinite number of other yous, somewhere.

We find the others gathered around a pair of tables in the River Room Brasserie.

'Hey! He made it! Yeah; cool!'

'Wow, Hol's charms worked.'

'Guyster! Come on down! Here; have this seat. I'll fetch another.'

'Guy, this is Rick,' Pris says, a little redundantly, as she's sitting beside him holding his hand. Rick is a bulky, muscled man with a shaven head and an earring in his left ear. I'm not very good at telling how old people are but I think he's a bit younger than Pris. He's a telephone engineer. He is wearing jeans and a black leather bomber jacket over a yellow farmer's shirt. He says hi and shakes Guy's hand like he's afraid he's going to break it. He sounds like he's from Essex but in fact he's from Kent.

'So, I was just getting a round in and I saw this guy I sort of half knew sitting there with an empty glass – this was in the old union, so it was probably a plastic, but you know what I mean – but anyway there was this *hippyish*-looking first year who looked like he needed a pint so I said, you know, hello, hi again, and he said hi and I said, "What are you for?" and Haze – as I now know the fucker to be – just looks up with this expression of *real concentration* on his face and stares off into the middle distance and nods like, really, really slowly and says, "Yeah . . . yeah . . . Like, what *are* we for? What is it all about? Where do we fit in?" and I'm sort of staring at him, thinking, What the fuck? But I got him a pint anyway; I'm generous that way. Still waiting for one back, mind.'

The others laugh, though we've all heard this story before, apart from Rick, I suppose. This is Guy telling this story. He's as animated as I've seen him in a year; his eyes look glittery and bright and although he's barely touched his shepherd's pie (I told him he wouldn't need a full-size main course if he was going to insist on a starter, but he wouldn't listen) it doesn't really matter because we're not paying and it's just good to see him so alive and holding court, as they say, and telling stories of the old days and being so obviously pleased to have people gathered round listening to him and laughing at what he says, even though they're probably laughing a bit more than they would if he wasn't so ill.

Haze laughs with the others and nods. 'Yeah,' he says. 'Fair enough. I was kind of stoned that day and—'

'You were stoned that *year*, Haze,' Pris tells him.

'Yeah, all right, all right. I was thinking of doing Philosophy as a subsidiary to make up my credits, wasn't I? And anyway it was, like, research, know what I mean? I had to road-test all those drugs I was providing for you sods, yeah? Didn't want you lightweights OD-ing on me, did I?'

'"Providing"? Ripping us off—' Paul says.

'I think you'll find most of the nefaria consumed came via Guy,' Rob says.

'I was fucking growing most of the green stuff,' Guy agrees.

'So,' Rick says, 'was that, like, when you first started to meet up, you lot?' He looks at Guy. 'Cos you're that bit older, right, Guy?'

'Just a couple of years,' Guy says, lifting his half of Beamish. 'Lot more fucking mature.'

'Whoo!' Alison says.

Paul puts on what I think of as his newsreader voice and tells Rick, 'Guy had had an . . . interesting, diverse and involved university career up until that point, I think it would be fair to say.'

'What can I tell you?' Guy says. 'I'm a fucking Renaissance man, me. I had eclectic tastes.' He nods at Hol. 'Actually, first one of this lot I met was prickly little Holly here.'

'You may have mistaken me for mistletoe,' she tells him. 'First thing you did was try to stick your tongue down my throat at the Freshers' Disco.'

'I were probably trying to shut you up, lass,' Guy says. He seems to be sounding more deliberately northern right now, as though Rick being so conspicuously from the south has brought out some sort of regional competitiveness. He grins round at the others. 'Anyway, you were unable to resist my bluff rustic charms for long, isn't that right, love?'

Hol is nodding slowly, and smiling. 'Next day I happened upon Guy, nursing a pint of Guinness and a cheap cigar and looking studiedly louche in his best Young Fogey gear, in the snug of The Northumberland Arms—'

'God, that place was a dive!'

'Supposedly this was the pub where all the lecturers used to go,' Pris tells Rick, 'to get away from the likes of us.'

'Looking very world-weary and disillusioned, he was,' Hol continues, still smiling softly at Guy.

'I were practising me fin-de-siècle look for the fin-de-fucking-siècle,' Guy says, sipping at his beer. He's not supposed to drink anything at all because it interferes with some of his medication, but it's hard to deny him the pleasure.

'About eight years early!' Haze says.

'Soulful-looking, I thought at the time,' Hol tells everybody else, though mostly keeping her gaze on Guy, who is sort of smiling into his half-pint glass.

'Naive like that, you were,' he says, not looking up.

'Not the first to fall for that look,' Pris says, laughing.

Alison nods. 'And certainly not the last.'

'I asked him what he was drinking,' Hol continues, 'and he said, What did it look like? and I said, "Well, Guinness, the old man's drink", and he just sort of took a deep breath and sat back on his bar stool and held the glass up and looked at it like he was studying it for the first time and said, "That's the thing about a good porter" – and he shrugged, or shook his head and sounded so rueful and sort of growly as he said, "Deals with all your baggage."'

'Oh, God . . .' Rob says.

Alison shakes her head. 'I don't know if that's cheesy or profound.'

'Preesy?' Haze suggests. 'Chofound?'

'I don't get it,' Rick says, looking round. 'What's—'

'Porter,' Pris says, squeezing his hand. 'It's the old-fashioned name for the sort of beer Guinness is.'

'Aww, right,' Rick says, though he still looks confused. 'I thought it was stout . . .'

Hol is laughing. 'And I was just *smitten*, I thought—' She puts her right hand flat on her chest, just below her neck. 'Oh, my . . . This guy is so *deep*.' Her eyes go wide.

'Not me, love,' Guy says, though he's smiling. Also his face looks a little flushed. 'Deep as a reflection. Known for it.'

'Thought you were in love, did you?' Alison asks Hol. After a moment, Ali makes a slight smile.

Hol nods slowly. 'At the very least, I thought he ought to be in love with me.'

There are a couple of low *Whoos* from round the table. Hol looks at Guy with a sort of smirk and he looks back at her.

'Swept off your feet, weren't you?' Haze says.

'Yes,' Hol says, drawing the word out. 'Though of course the usually unspoken consequence of a girl being swept off her feet is that she almost immediately ends up on her back.'

'Had his wicked way, did he? Eh?' Rick says, winking at Guy.

'Oh, my ways are pretty wicked too,' Hol says. She drains her G&T and raises one eyebrow. 'Arguably wickeder.'

'As we all know!' Haze says, laughing, then looking quickly round at everybody else. He even glances at me.

'Excuse me,' Paul says as his phone trills. He gets up and walks off to take the call.

'Anyway,' Hol says, 'that, unless I'm much mistaken, was the start of us all meeting up and spending years two and three of our distinguished academic careers as one big happy disfunctionality up at Willoughtree House.' She stands, holding her empty glass, looking down at Guy. 'And now, it's my round, I do believe.'

'Fuck me: Creation Myths of Bewford Uni Film and Media Studies Faculty Ninety-Two Intake,' Guy says, holding his glass out to Hol. 'Make mine a pint of Guinness, love; I think I fancy me chances.'

She just smiles at him.

*   *   *

'Hey, Kit.'

I am in the Gents' toilet of the The Miller's Boy. They have Dyson Airblade driers and I can hardly hear Paul over the sound of the appliance. The line of super-fast hot air on the skin of my hands feels pleasing. I confess I had been wondering what it would feel like if you could sort of swing one of these off the wall like a drawbridge or something and fit your cock into it, letting the blade of hot air pummel it as you moved it in and out . . . so I react in a slightly startled way when Paul says hey.

I clear my throat. 'Uncle Paul.'

'Yeah, we can probably drop the "uncle" bit now, I think. You finished with that?' he asks, nodding at the hand-drier and standing with his hands raised from the elbows like a surgeon before an operation.

'All yours,' I say, realising my hands have been dry for a moment or two and I've just been sort of mindlessly moving them up and down and in and out.

He inserts his hands into the drier, watches the only other guy in the place leave, then says, 'Hol tells me you're on the case of the missing videotape, yeah?'

I nod. 'I've been looking.'

'Think it's going to turn up?'

Shrug. 'I don't know.'

He looks at me, his eyes narrowing a little. Those are probably laughter lines, though he doesn't look like he's laughing. 'How, ah, assiduously are you searching?'

I have to think about this. Obviously I know what 'assiduously' means, but I'm not sure how you measure or express assiduousness or calibrate for somebody else's working definition. What would be the SI unit? The assid? The ass? Assaying assiduousness. Tricky.

'Look,' he says, taking his wallet out. I look. There are a lot of notes in there. He takes one out. It's big and red. He refolds it and presses the fifty-pound note into my hand. 'Bit of an incentive,' he says. 'Advance on a finder's fee, yeah? Let's say, another two of those if you find it and you're able to let me know first, let me have sight of it? Deal?'

I stare at the note. I've never held one of these before, and only ever seen them on TV or in films. Maybe the ATMs of London dispense these. They certainly don't up here. I can't think of anywhere local that would accept one; it might as well be foreign currency. A bank would convert it into the more practical shape of two twenties and a tenner, I suppose. Also, I'm fairly sure the one time I ever heard mention of a 'finder's fee' was in the Coen brothers' film *Fargo*, and I seem to recall things didn't turn out too well for the person who expected to be on the receiving end of one.

'I think technically the tape would still be Dad's property,' I tell Paul.

'Understood,' he says, folding my fingers over the note so it's hidden in my palm. Again, I've only ever seen this done in the movies, but Paul performs the act like he does this every day. 'Just want to be told first, see it first. Can you do that for me, Kit? I'd be . . . very grateful. Like I say, another couple of those to come. This is strictly between us, of course. Man to man. Yeah? That has to be a condition.'

There's no question I'm going to take the money – of course I am. This is free money for something I was going to do anyway so I'd be mad not to and I – we; Dad and I – need the dosh. I'm already thinking of loopholes in this verbal agreement Paul and I seem to be setting up here where I could make sure I see him first after I find it – if I find it – and show him the tape and let him have it and then almost immediately tell Dad or Hol or one of the others, telling them Paul asked to see it like we'd just bumped into each other rather than set it up in advance. Or I could just lie and take the fifty and not say I've found the tape – again, if I find it – until they've left on Monday and there's just me and Guy in the house.

Too much to think about. I'm probably looking hesitant.

'In fact, let's . . . Let's make it another four of those; two-fifty altogether. Yeah?' Paul says. He's standing close enough for me to smell his aftershave. 'Best offer.' He winks at me.

Two hundred and fifty. Blimey; that's as much as you get for a clip used on *You've Been Framed*.

'What's on this tape?' I ask him.

'Embarrassing shit,' he says ruefully, nodding.

'Not porn?' I ask, jokily (I think).

'Definitely not,' he says immediately, like he was just waiting for the question. I'm starting to think it is porn. 'So,' he says, standing back and looking at the inner door of the Gents' as it trembles and the outer door makes a flapping-open noise. 'Deal?'

'Deal,' I tell him, and slip my hand and the note into a gilet pocket.

'Really?' Hol is saying to Rick, as Paul and I come back to our shunted-together tables. Rick is folding a newspaper and sticking it into an inside pocket in his leather jacket. 'The *Daily Mail*?' Hol says, gaze flicking from Rick to Pris. 'Hate-filled, right-wing rant-rag the *Daily Mail*, to give its full title; the newspaper with its knickers permanently in a twist?'

'Yeah,' Rick says, shrugging inside his jacket. 'They were out of *Morning Stars*, weren't they?' He glances at Pris, who is looking round at the others and rolling her eyes.

'Oh, Christ, here we go,' Paul says. 'Leave it, Hol.'

95

'Hol finds the *Guardian* a tad right-wing,' Pris tells Rick.

'I was getting the *Sun* till about six months ago,' Rick says reasonably. He nods sideways towards Pris. 'Herself took offence. Think she was jealous of page three.' (Pris rolls her eyes again, though she is smiling as well.) 'Bloody hell, eh? Thought I was moving up in the world.' Rick grins, looks at Paul, Rob, Guy and Haze. 'Still miss the football in the *Currant*. Bit shit in this.' He taps his jacket where it bulges over the newspaper.

'You'll have to excuse Hol, Rick,' Guy tells him. 'She blames herself for the past twenty-odd years of neocon excess, bless. Feels if only she'd been a more engaged, political journalist and properly inspiring – you know, rather than a hack sitting in the dark regurgitating bile onto undeserving Hollywood product – it might all have been so different. Eh, Hol?' He gets to the end of this little speech and sits shaking with what might be a suppressed cough, swallowed laughter, just hiccups or a malfunctioning gag reflex – it's impossible to say.

'Yeah, I take full personal responsibility for everything,' Hol says, glaring at Guy, her mouth a tight line.

'You read what the fuck you want, mate,' Rob tells Rick, and sits back.

'Don't you worry, chief,' Rick says. He drains his pint glass. 'My round. That be a red wine, Holly?'

'No thanks. I'm fine.'

'Come on; just kiddin you. Have a G&T. It's only a paper.'

'Fine,' Hol says, handing him her glass. 'Make it a double. You persuaded me.'

'Never taken much, has it, Hol?' Alison says.

'Never,' Hol agrees promptly. She smiles a broad smile but her voice sounds like she doesn't care.

*   *   *

96

'So, Rob,' Rick asks, 'what is it you do?'

'I solutionise outcomes,' Rob says.

Hol, who had been talking to Pris, looks over and says, *'What?'* but Rob doesn't notice, or pretends not to.

'We're both in Grayzr Corps,' Alison tells Rick, glancing at Rob.

Rob nods sideways at Alison without looking at her. 'We work in Moral Compliance.'

'Bloody hell,' Rick says. 'What's that then?'

'Pre-identing up-torrent crisis nodes and realitising positive issue-relevant impending-threat-modulated countermeasure envision-sets within the applicable statutory and regulatory challenge/riposte-space,' Rob says, without taking a breath. He looks round at the others.

Guy and Haze, who had been arguing about drugs, are looking at him.

Hol is staring at him, then she looks at Alison. 'That was a joke,' she says. 'That *was* a joke, wasn't it?'

Alison smiles at her.

'What's the big problem?' Rob asks. 'It's just what I *do*.'

'Sorry, mate,' Rick says. 'I'm none the wiser.'

'Think we knew that from the—' Guy starts to say, but Hol, who is sitting beside him, flicks a fist into his thigh. 'Fuck's *sake*,' he says, rubbing his leg.

'Sorry,' Hol says quickly. 'That was harder than I meant.'

'I've nothing left there, Hol,' Guy grumbles, wheezing. 'Fucking fuck-all muscle-mass. I have to sit down to pee; can't stand up long enough to take a piss. Jesus.'

'I'm *sorry*!'

'Modern multinationals in a high-choice environment are largely about image, customer perception and the moral integrity of the brand,' Alison is telling Rick. 'While everybody else is, rightly, focused on prompt product deliverance, positive quarterly results and increased shareholder value, Grayzr has an entire, vertically threaded division thinking about how we appear to the public and the various national and supranational regulatory and licensing bodies, not just right now but in the foreseeable future. It's the sort of function that CEOs and the board are involved in as a matter of course across all industries but Grayzr intrinsically recognises that the positional privilege and remuneration-inspired lifestyle gap implicit between those in such positions and their concerns' fundamental client-base make that task challenging without a dedicated in-house heuristic support structure, providing concept provenance, positional analysis and ethical guidance.' She pauses, then puts her head to one side a little to look at Rick, who is staring at her, mouth hanging open. She shakes her head. 'No?' She shrugs, frowning. 'I'm sorry. I don't know that I can put it any more simply than that without trivialising it.'

'Yeah,' Haze mutters, after a moment. 'What she said.'

'I think Alison means they try to look ahead, for the company they work for,' Pris says, squeezing Rick's hand. 'To make sure it doesn't appear evil.'

'They watch their bosses' arses,' Hol says to Rick.

Guy looks at him and says, 'They're cunts.'

Alison whirls to face Guy. '*Do* you fucking mind? There's no need for that sort of language!'

Guy continues to look at Rick, takes a sip of his Guinness and says, 'They're touchy cunts.'

'Sure you won't come back to the ranch, Rick?' Guy says. 'Hot and cold running sarcasm in every fucking room.'

We're outside The Miller's Boy, on the wide curved sweep

of pavement guarding the entrance to Uppergate Pedestrianised Precinct; I've been to get the Volvo, which is now sitting idling in one of the Disabled spaces (legally; we got a Disabled badge for Guy over a year ago). Guy is resting against a black-painted, Heritage-themed litter bin, his forearm crutch splayed out to one side as he leans over a roll-up, protecting the makings from the rain with his head. I got the brolly from the car and went to shelter him with it but he told me to stop fussing, so I'm standing nearby waiting for them to sort themselves out.

Rain patters on the stretched fabric above me. If you turn the umbrella right so the saggy bit's behind you, you can't see it's broken.

'Nah, my mate's picking me up in half an hour, thanks,' Rick says, pulling his collar up and holding his newspaper over his head. 'We're off to near his, by Preston. He's got me a spare rod and everything; I'm sorted.'

Paul looks up at the winter-grey sky from inside the fur-lined hood of his white parka. 'Bit late to be going fishing, by the time you get there, isn't it, Rick?'

'Yeah, we're losing the light here,' Hol says. She has the hiccups. Another *hic!* shakes her body and she looks away, stamping her foot in annoyance and tutting. (And actually it's only half past three.)

Rob and Alison are standing under a giant, colourful, Grayzr-branded umbrella. They brought their own car; Rob has stayed sober, though Alison hasn't drunk much anyway.

'Not for night fishing,' Rick says, grinning at Paul.

'Ah,' Paul says. He turns to Pris, who is holding onto Rick's left upper arm with both hands. 'That's not code, is it?'

Pris laughs. 'Sure you won't come back?' she says, looking up at Rick.

'Yeah, mate,' Haze says, approaching and holding up his right hand for a high five, which Rick responds to dutifully. 'I feel really bad, now, I really do. I feel I should have made more of an effort, know what I mean? With the offer of the bed and everything. It's just with this back of mine, you know . . . But you should come back. You should. And we could still switch rooms around or something, eh?' he says, looking at Pris.

'Nah, seriously,' Rick is saying. 'You lot have your weekend together; I'll be fine. I'd just be like a spare one at a wedding, I would, wouldn't I? You lot are like Monty bloody Python. Wouldn't be right.'

'No!' Pris says, almost hanging off his arms now, pivoting. 'You'd be great!'

'You'd fit in brilliant, you would,' Haze tells him.

'Don't listen to a fucking word, Rick,' Guy says, lighting up the rolly. 'You're well out of it. I was just being polite. These fuckers have decades of form. You stick with your gravel ponds, chum.'

'Yeah,' I hear Hol say quietly as she looks away, 'shallow and full of carp.'

I fold the five, bank-fresh, ten-pound notes and stick them into my number four safe, which is a hole in the concrete behind the tiles of the fireplace in my room. I nipped out and changed the fifty for five tens in the Lloyds branch next door to the pub while they were all putting on their coats and arguing about the bill (Paul and Rob/Alison both insisted on paying for everything but eventually split it; Hol left the tip).

I have five 'safes' – as I've called them since I was a kid – dotted around my bedroom, plus a few others elsewhere scattered throughout the house and in one or two of the outbuildings. To the best of my knowledge, none of them has ever been compromised. The one behind the loose tiles of the fireplace is a fairly quick one to get to and relatively commodious after I hollowed it out when I was ten or eleven. I used to hide food in there sometimes; it has a maximum capacity of two standard Mars bars.

Another good one is inside the hollow frame of my ancient iron bedstead; you unscrew the brass ball on the bottom left upright and reach in with your finger to feel for an inconspicuous black thread superglued to the inside; you pull it up carefully and there's a plastic container at the end that looks like a sort of giant med capsule. It can hold one Mars bar.

I need to get back down to the others, but I take a quick look round the room, just to reassure myself.

My room is my haven, my citadel. I fitted a bolt to the door years ago so when I'm in here I'm fully secure, though Guy was never one for just walking in anyway.

The bed is just a single but that's okay as there's just one of me. It used to be a real plus, it being small, as it meant it left more room on the floor for other stuff like the Scalextric set I used to have, and battle landscapes made of sheets draped over pillows and cushions and piles of books, where I'd play with my model soldiers. I don't bother with that stuff any more, of course; it was all kind of retro at the time anyway – basically I was getting birthday and Christmas presents that people Guy's age wanted when they were my age, not what I wanted – but now all that limited, physical gubbins has been replaced with the worlds that exist inside the computer and are distributed across the Cloud's server farms scattered across the world, where HeroSpace and the other game environments are.

The current machine – sitting on an old dressing table, so flanked with infolding side-mirrors – is a two-year-old Dell

101

with a sixty-centimetre flat screen. I used to really care about the hardware and built my own computer when I was fourteen, but it seems kind of irrelevant these days; just the gateway you pass through to get to the landscapes on the far side. Big screens and fast graphics chips are useful, but they don't compensate for lack of skill or experience.

The main expense I incurred over the last few years was getting in decent broadband. Guy doesn't even know about that. I feel a bit bad having this wired straight into the Dell and not home-hubbing wi-fi throughout the house, but I need it for intense HeroSpace moments, and letting Guy know about the broadband might raise awkward questions about where the money for it came from. The broadband is like my secret, high-speed tunnel out of the house into the rest of the real world, and those beyond.

I have a bookcase full of books and old toys, a few CDs, a third-generation iPod with a cracked screen and a travel dock, and a chest of drawers with clothes. The room has a single, very worn old carpet covering the floorboards. It's allegedly Persian but actually made in Belgium according to the label underneath. The room's other principal feature is translucent plastic Really Useful Boxes, some individual ones and some stacks, varying in capacity from one point four to sixty-four litres.

I like boxes that stack and that fit neatly inside other boxes. I keep a pair of cardboard tubes from whisky bottles for no other reason than the fact one fits so neatly inside the other that when you insert the smaller one inside the larger and let go, it takes a full fourteen seconds for it to move slowly all the way down, air sighing smoothly out around it. I suspect even the Volvo's pistons aren't that tight.

*   *   *

'You've learned the *words* to "Gangnam Style"?' Hol says, plonking herself down on the velvet sofa in the sitting room. She starts laughing.

'Yeah,' Haze is saying, 'I heard this girl on the radio doing it and I thought, *You know what? That sounds quite cool, that does. That's better than just doing all the actions, like.*'

'But you *can* do all the actions?' Paul asks, a deep frown on his face.

'Yeah,' Haze says. 'Of course.'

'Thank God,' Paul says. He pours himself some red wine and holds the bottle towards Hol. 'Sure I can't . . . ?'

'Positive you can,' Hol says, drinking from her pint glass of water, 'but later, not right now.'

'Pacing yourself, are you, Hol?' Alison asks. Like the rest, she's sitting where she sat last night.

'Yup.'

'*Pacing* yourself?' Guy says. 'Fuck me, Hol. When did this radical new regime surface?'

'No idea,' Hol admits. 'Must have crept up on me.'

'Think I'll pass on that.' Guy takes a last drag on the roll-up he started outside the pub, then folds it with deliberation into an old John Smith's Bitter can by the side of his seat.

'Yes,' Hol says, looking at him. 'Late-onset maturity remains a distant dream for you, doesn't it, Guy?'

'Yeah, Hol,' Guy says. 'Looks like I'm going to get to miss out on it altogether. Even the chance of it, ta.'

Hol looks at him for a while longer. Her eyelids droop and she shakes her head. 'Yeah, that might have been insensitive,' she says. 'My apologies.'

'Another first,' Rob mutters. He holds a glass out to Paul. 'I will, Paul, if you don't mind.'

'My pleasure,' Paul says, reaching.

103

'Fill it full as you like,' Rob says as Paul pours. 'I've got some catching up to do.'

'Certainly have.'

'Me too,' Alison says, also holding out her glass. Then, to Rob, as he looks at her, she says, 'Intending to maintain my lead, darling.'

'Wasn't aware it was actually a competition,' Rob tells her.

Alison looks at him for a moment. 'You're right,' she says, withdrawing the glass a second or so before Paul starts to pour. 'No need for both of us to get drunk and objectionable. I'll make myself a nice cup of tea like a good little girl, shall I?' She gets up and leaves, twirling the glass in her hands.

Rob looks at Paul and rolls his eyes.

'It's all right, love,' Guy is saying to Hol. 'We all know I'm dying, but we're all pretending otherwise. It's just that I'm the only one who has to live with it.'

He starts coughing, though you can see he's trying to stop, not putting it on to prove his point.

Hol is looking at me. 'Think you're forgetting your boy wonder here,' she tells Guy.

'Nah,' Guy says, glancing at me and clearing his throat. 'He's the batman, I'm the officer. Eh, kid?'

'Yeah,' Pris says, settling into the other sofa and curling her legs underneath herself. She's been up to her room to change after getting wet in the rain and now wears a fresh pair of jeans and a loose, too-big silvery jumper that keeps falling off one shoulder or the other. It looks like she's not wearing a bra. 'How you doing, Kit?'

'I'm fine, thanks,' I tell her. I'm sat on the pouffe again, near Hol. I raise my teacup. 'Got my tea.' I'm quite full; I ordered only a couple of starters in the pub, anticipating Guy wouldn't manage his main, which I got to finish. 'Might have some wine, later.'

'You found that fucking tape yet?' Guy asks me.

There's sudden silence in the room. Guy looks round at them all and says, 'What, I'm not supposed to know? I'm not fucking deaf.'

'Well,' Paul says, sitting back in his seat. 'This is a bit more like it.'

He doesn't look at me, which is good. I hope he doesn't want his fifty back.

'Where is it, Guy?' Rob asks.

'No fucking idea,' Guy says. 'Might have recorded over it anyway, years ago. Not fucking kidding, either. Think I did. Record over it, I mean. My first living will.' I fetched Guy another can of bitter before I sat down earlier; he opens it and drinks. 'Little bit of ferrous-oxide irony for you there.'

'Wouldn't be with your lawyers, would it?' Paul asks.

'Don't fucking trust lawyers, Paul,' Guy says to him.

Paul smiles slowly. 'Me neither.'

'Who does?' Haze says. He's building a joint.

'So it's *not* with your lawyers?' Paul asks.

'Like I said,' Guy says, 'I don't know where the fuck it is or what state it's in but I think I might have recorded over it and then it became redundant anyway.' He looks at me. 'You're very quiet, even for you, lad. Guilty conscience, or are we to take your silence in the negative? You haven't found it then?'

'I haven't found it,' I confirm. 'I've not looked much. This morning I looked in the two old servants' bedrooms above my room but it's not likely to be there.'

'So . . .' Rob says, '. . . *why* did you look there?'

'Because they're above my room and I knew I wouldn't

105

be disturbing anybody when I started moving boxes about,'
I explain. I'm feeling a little hot after Guy's remark about a
guilty conscience. Annoyingly, he can usually tell when I'm
trying to hide something. I think of the five tenners, folded
into a neat compression of papery linen in their new hole-
in-the-wall. 'The other rooms up there are above somebody
else's room. I thought I might disturb people below if I
searched in them.'

'Ah,' Pris says.

I used to disturb people. I bet I still could if I wanted to.
At one time, way back when I was thirteen or fourteen, I
had this thing about height. I'd just put on a growth spurt
and I was – suddenly, it felt – nearly as tall then as I am now
(one point nine-one metres then; one point nine-three now).
For some reason I felt a real and pressing need to know how
tall other people were. It's amazing how few people are sure
how tall they are, and how many add a few centimetres to
their real height because they feel they need to, and how
many, even now, measure themselves in imperial units, using
hopelessly outdated feet and inches rather than the far more
rational metric system. Even my own father wouldn't tell
me how tall he was, though I could see he was about eight
or nine centimetres shorter than I was (eventually I measured
him when he was lying drunk on the hall floor; one point
eight-three).

I decided I needed a technique to discover how tall people
were, objectively. Triangulation was never going to work;
people are loath to stay still long enough while you measure
the angle. You might as well ask them to take their shoes off
and stand in a doorway with their back straight, and I knew
from past experience how unsuccessful that was.

I tried attaching threads of different lengths weighted with

106

little plastic beads to the tops of doorways, both here at home and in school, so they'd just brush against the heads of individuals passing underneath, but I discovered that people tend to flinch, instinctively, as soon as they feel their head or even their hair touch something hanging above them, which made the observational side of things a bit hit-or-miss, plus it was usually hard to see exactly which of a bunch – or a little curtain – of threads they'd just made contact with or just missed. In theory you would need to hang up just one thread of a certain length at a time for each individual, gradually increasing the length of the thread/reducing the height being measured, until they just brushed the plastic bead and no more. With various people entering a room almost at random (as happens especially in school), this was almost impossible.

I gave up on that approach.

I decided to measure people while they slept, creeping into their rooms late at night to take a tape-measure to them in bed. This worked fine with Dad, who passed out fully clothed, on his back, on top of the covers, with the light on, at least once a week, and this may have given me a false sense of confidence in the technique. I knew I was reducing the sample size – it would mostly be restricted to Dad's drinking buddies from the pub; the occasional ex-colleague from the local radio station (he was a presenter and producer on *North 99* until his health got too bad); a sparse scattering of his few and mostly surly relatives; and his old uni pals: Hol, Paul, Rob, Alison, Haze and Pris, with or without other partners and subsidiary friends in tow.

As it turns out, though, most people lock their rooms at night, where possible, and/or sleep under the covers, making it hard to know which part of the bulge in the bedclothes is where their feet are to measure from, and/or they are amazingly light sleepers and tend to wake up and freak out when they see you padding stealthily up to them holding a tape-measure (or standing exasperated over them, trying gently to coax their legs straight). Plus, frankly, few people sleep lying flat out anyway; they tend to curl up a bit, making the measuring process highly problematic even without the whole waking-up-and-screaming thing.

I gave up on that method too, and just determined to get better at judging people's heights, especially as they passed through doorways. Most modern domestic doorways are close to two metres in height, for example, and although Willoughtree House, being Victorian with minor-gentry pretensions, has taller doorways, not all of a uniform height, it was a trivial matter to memorise all of them and recalibrate for each.

No sooner had I done this than I started to lose interest in the whole subject.

On the other hand, it was around this time I started to take an interest in how much people weighed. Though this quickly narrowed down to deciding to anchor my own weight as close as possible to one hundred kilos, a goal and limit I have stuck to ever since, even if it does sometimes mean that I have to eat a little more than I really want (a problem that seems to be easing, it has to be said).

'So you think you've recorded over it?' Paul asks.

'Might have,' Guy says.

'That's not exactly the impression you gave on the phone, when we were talking about arranging this weekend, earlier in the year.'

'Things change, mate,' Guy tells him. 'Circumstances, recollections, situations; all sorts of things. They all fucking change.'

Paul makes a sort of clucking noise. 'Oh well, you got us here, I suppose.' He shrugs. 'Really, Guy? Did you think we wouldn't have come otherwise?'

Guy looks at him. 'Seems to be a very embarrassing thing, even quite distressing and upsetting for people, being around somebody dying, coming to visit them. Specially when they can practically see an old mucker shrivelling away in front of them, like he's letting the side down by doing something none of us is supposed to do for another forty years or what-ever, and they hear what sounds like little individual tumours rattling around in their chest every time they cough, like nutty fucking slack.'

'Christ,' Pris says, looking up at the ceiling, blinking rapidly. 'Guy; please.'

'Sorry, Priscilla, love,' Guy says. 'Didn't mean to offend you, petal. Just trying to make the point that most of us don't like being around very sick or very dying people. We don't know how to react to them, how to treat them, how to maintain the usual isn't-everything-marvellous and aren't-we-all-on-the-up-up-up bullshit like we usually do. So people find excuses not to visit, or put a visit off until some time after you're safely dead – I've noticed the funeral seems to be a popular point when people can suddenly find the time they couldn't spare when you were actually alive and might have benefited from the attention—'

He breaks off to cough, once. It's just a single cough but it has a hard edge to it like the sound of splintering wood. I see Hol wince.

'Or people decide for you that you'd rather not see old pals,' Guy continues, 'because it might remind you too much of the old days and you might break down in tears and then they *really* won't know what to do or where to put their face.' He takes as deep a breath as he can, wheezing. 'Or they're worried the contrast between their so-fucking-wonderful lives and your own sad, pathetic, wasting-away terminal state will be too much to bear and only make it worse for you. So, anyway, yeah,' Guy says, breathing hard now and looking round at them, 'thank you all for coming.'

Pris gets up and goes over to Guy and kneels at the front of his chair and hugs him carefully, gently. 'Oh, Guy,' she says, and it sounds like she's crying. 'Oh, God, oh, Guy.'

Guy seems to shrink under her embrace. He looks awkward, angular, unsure what to do. Then he reaches round and puts one arm around her, patting her back.

'All contributions welcome,' he says, wheezing. He pats her back some more, then strokes the silvery fabric. 'Oh; no bra, that's thoughtful, love. You've made a prematurely old man very happy. Give us a jiggle.'

'You!' Pris says, pushing away from him then getting up and going back to sit on the couch, hitching her top back up to her shoulder from where it's slipped down her arm. She dries her eyes with the sides of her hands. Guy wheezes with laughter, or at least amusement.

'So, are we going to look for this tape or not?' Alison says.

'I think I need to sober up some more,' Paul tells her. 'Feeling a bit sleepy, to be honest.'

'Yeah, calm down,' Rob tells Alison, who glares at him. 'There's time. Wait till we're all a bit closer to the top of our game, not post big-boozy-lunch.'

Alison stares at Rob for a little longer, then takes out her iPad and snaps the screen open, stabbing at the touchscreen.

A little later, after more wine and much more tea – 'We are definitely getting older; we never used to be this sensible,'

Rob says – it's decided we can't stick around the house all afternoon drinking or playing games (a game of Trivial Pursuit or even Risk has been suggested, for old times' sake, or maybe poker or some other card game, only they can't agree on what they want to play).

The day has, remarkably, brightened a little and the rain eased almost to nothing, with suggestions of gauzy blue sky off to the west, where the weather's coming from, so an expedition to Yarlsthwaite Tower is suggested and agreed upon.

'We sure?' Paul asks. 'It's nearly five. There's only an hour of daylight left.'

'Half an hour there, same back,' Hol says. 'You'd struggle to spend thirty minutes at the place itself – it's just a bloody tower.'

'Might even be a nice sunset,' Pris says.

'I can take another two in the Prius,' Alison says. She has declared herself sober. 'Who's risking their lives in the Volvo with Kit?'

Volvos are very safe cars, I want to say, but don't.

'Kit could drive Paul's Audi,' Haze suggests. 'There's more room, eh, don't you fink?' I'm sure Haze says 'fink', not 'think'. It's like he's taken on something of Rick's accent, though, come to think of it, I'm not sure I heard Rick say 'fink' or anything like it at any point.

'Um,' Paul says, pressing his lips together and frowning.

'Actually, I'd best stay back with Dad,' I tell them as they start getting up from their seats.

Guy looks at me. 'You'll be staying home by yourself then, lad. I'm going too.'

'Oh,' I say, thrown. I was sure he'd need a snooze and I was looking forward to going tape-searching in some of the

111

other rooms. 'We'll need the wheelchair.' Guy has been very reluctant to use his wheelchair.

'Throw it in the back of the Vulva,' Guy says. This is what he calls the Volvo estate when he's being childish. 'I could use some fresh air.'

I bet you get there and smoke, I think of saying. Instead I say, 'Okay. I'll fetch the chair.' I get up, hesitate. 'You sure you won't be too tired?'

'I'm fine!'

'Well . . . Maybe loo first, yeah?'

'Will you just stop fucking fussing and fetch me my fucking cripple-chariot?'

'Yeah, she just sat there staring at the screen after the final fade-out and said, "Hmm. More *Citizen Smith* than *Citizen Kane*," cheeky bint,' Guy says.

'Sounds like me,' Hol agrees. She and Haze have joined us in the Volvo. 'May even have been my first proper bit of criticism.'

'Surely fucking not,' Guy says. He has the front passenger seat, as is usual since he stopped driving. We are heading through the country lanes, swishing along the wet tarmac, thrumming through puddles and larger stretches of standing water, and rattling over broad fans of gravel and small stones washed out of the surrounding fields.

'First bit of passing-for-properly-thought-out film criticism, then,' Hol says. 'I tried developing that theme, but "More Vegas than Degas" really only works on the page, and, frankly, barely even there. What was it even about, this film? Which one was it?'

'*Un Chien On Da Loo*, I think, wasn't it?' Haze says, then adds, 'Oh, yeah; terrible.'

112

'I vaguely remember,' Hol says. 'Some pretentious piece of black-and-white bollocks.'

'I was proud of that little film,' Guy says. 'It was a fucking heartfelt *homage*, you cow. Just because you—'

Hol starts laughing.

'What?' Haze says.

'It was cheesy,' she says. 'More like *fromage*. Ha ha ha.' Her laughter turns to hiccups and then she starts crying with laughter and sniffing as well.

'Buggering fuck,' Guy mutters, though it sounds like he's smiling. He looks at me. 'We nearly fucking there yet?'

'Bugger. I need a pee,' Guy announces when we're about five minutes from Yarlsthwaite.

'They installed any loos at the tower car park?' Hol asks.

'No,' I'm saying as Guy says,

'I need a pee *now*!'

I pull over into a field entrance, between high hedges. The road is narrow but I think there's about enough room for the others in the Audi to squeeze past the Volvo; they're somewhere behind us but Alison was taking it very easy in the big, wide Audi and I kind of lost patience.

'Sorry, obviously,' Guy is saying as Hol and I help him out of the car and fit the forearm crutch to his right hand.

'Leave you to it,' Hol says as we get Guy to the side of the hedgerow. He makes a sort of tripod of his legs and the crutch and begins undoing his zip with his free hand.

Guy's barely begun peeing when there's the noise of a big engine from behind us and I think at first it's the Audi, but it isn't; it's an enormous green tractor with an orange flashing light on top. It's towing an even bigger, high-sided trailer and it's signalling to come into the field.

113

'What's that?' Guy asks, trying to look behind him.

'Nothing,' I tell him, watching his thin dribble of wee falling into the tussocky grass. Guy's no better than most men at peeing when there's any pressure.

Hol appears on the other side of Guy. 'You shift the car,' she tells me.

'But—' I begin.

'Yeah,' Guy says, his wee-stream drying up completely. 'But.'

'I'm not touching the car,' she tells me. 'Still drunk. With my luck, tractor-driver Seth here will turn out to be a special constable or something with a thing about even the most cursory drink-driving and a chip on his shoulder about sexy, middle-aged, metropolitan film critics. You shift it. I'll get the gate. You okay for a moment, Guy?'

'Oh, fuck, yeah,' Guy says. 'Never fucking better.'

He's not, though; I think his legs must be giving out because I can see him wobbling. I need to help him but I'm supposed to open the gate and I need to move the car as well and the tractor engine sounds like it's throbbing or even being gunned, but probably the most important thing is helping Guy and I just don't know what to do first or in what order, and so I hesitate. I can feel myself hesitate; in fact I can feel myself starting to panic. I glance back at the car but it looks like Haze has gone to sleep.

'Actually, I'm sort of struggling here,' Guy admits. Even his voice sounds shaky.

'Shit,' Hol says, then moves in to Guy's left side. He puts his left arm round her shoulders, letting her take a lot of his weight. I think his legs have almost given way and he's mostly supporting himself on Hol and the crutch on his right arm. 'How's that?' Hol asks. To me she says, 'Get the gate first, Kit. Then move the car.'

'Brilliant,' Guy says. 'But now I'm going to wet me trousers.'

'Here,' Hol says, leaning in with her free hand and taking his penis in her fingers, directing the just-resumed stream of pee away from his legs. His cock looks very small and pale, in the cold late-evening light, like a soft little worm in her hand.

Guy clears his throat. 'Didn't know you cared, Hol.'

'Nothing I haven't handled before. And fuck off.' She looks at me, eyes flashing. 'Kit; the gate!'

I fumble the gate open, push it creaking back and latch it to a metal post, then jump into the Volvo, reverse it half a metre and then drive on up the lane a couple of car lengths.

'Oh,' Haze says from the back seat, stretching his arms and then wiping his face. 'Blimey. Yeah. Must have nodded off there. Is there some sort of problem?'

The tractor honks its horn then trundles, slowly, carefully, engine roaring, into the field past Guy and Hol. The giant trailer is very clanky.

Hol smiles wanly at the driver. I think he shouts something at her and she nods once and does a thumbs-up. The tractor and trailer bustle up the field towards the skyline.

'All under control,' I tell Haze.

'Oh, good,' he says, folding his arms and closing his eyes again as his head tips back against the headrest.

Hol is shaking Guy's penis as I reverse back down the lane, and just zipping his trousers up as I get out to help him back into the car.

'What about the gate?' I ask Hol.

'We've to leave it open,' she says.

As I'm putting Guy's crutch into the back of the car – Haze is doing his just-waking-up thing again and peering woozily at Guy – I see Hol stoop and dig her hands into some rain-wet grass on the other side of the gateway, then wipe them against each other.

Paul's Audi drives up and Paul leans out of the front passenger's window. 'Lost already?' he asks Hol.

'Shut up and follow this car,' she tells him, slapping the roof twice and swinging back in, slamming the door.

Yarlsthwaite Tower sits on the brink of the tallest cliff of Utley Edge, a ridge running north-east to south-west along the Pennines. Local lore has it that if you pronounce 'Utley' to chime with 'ugly', you're not local. If you pronounce it 'Ootley', you're an outsider pretending to be a local, and if you pronounce it somewhere in-between so it sounds more like 'Oatly' (though not *exactly* like that) then you can, tentatively, provisionally, on sufferance, be accepted as, probably, being one of God's own people; i.e., a local.

The tower is triangular, built of millstone grit – one of the local rocks – and is four tall storeys in height, with gothic battlements. It was built in the 1840s as a folly, to improve the view from Cherncrake Hall, hereditary seat of the Spilesteynes, to this day one of the area's biggest landowners. Even from the base of the folly you can see the square towers of the house peeping over its sheltering screen of trees. Guy and I took the tour round the place six years ago; he still grumbles over the cost of the tickets – no discount for local people – though the main thing I remember is the intricately tessellated floor of the orangery; the lord of the manor who had it built was into mathematics.

It occurred to me some years ago that if my mother is two-hundredth or whatever in line to the throne, and I am the illegitimate son of Guy and a local gentry woman, she might

116

have been from Cherncrake Hall. I've done a bit of research via Wikipedia, Google and so on, but from what I can see there was no female Spilesteyne the right age at the time I was born to fit Dad's (probably completely made-up) description.

'It's a fucking quagmire,' Paul says at the gate from the car park leading onto the path for the tower.

'I'm up for it,' Guy says, gripping the wheels of his wheel-chair hard and staring at the muddy, puddled surface of the path to the tower, fifty metres away.

'Yeah, good for you,' Paul says. 'You don't have to carry you.' He's wearing the same white parka-style jacket he wore to lunch.

'We can do it,' I tell everybody.

I'm wearing an old green wax jacket of Guy's and a pair of ancient black wellington boots that I had to patch with a bicycle repair kit last year. The jacket is so worn it has pale green crease marks all over the dark green. It's supposed to be waterproof but it isn't any more. I found a pair of green and white ski gloves in the jacket's pockets; they fit fine. They say Killy on them, a brand I've never heard of.

'Really sorry,' Haze is saying, 'but my back will be out for months if I . ... It's a real pain. I mean, like, literally, too, you know? A real pain.'

'Yes, you are,' Hol mutters, not quite loud enough for Haze to hear, I think. 'Rob? Take the other front corner?'

'On it,' Rob tells her.

'Together?' Hol says, squatting by Guy's knee and gripping the chair's metalwork near the small front wheel on the right. Rob is at the other front corner, Paul and I at the rear. We agree we're ready. A watery sunset is spreading pinks and reds across the western sky; the wind is dry, almost mild. Ours are the only two vehicles in the car park.

117

'Tell you what; I'll bring the brolly,' Haze says. 'Just in case.'

Haze is wearing an old Bewford University hoodie and has borrowed another of Guy's worn-looking huntin'-shootin'-'n'-fishin' jackets. I slipped an even older cycle cape over Guy before we left the house. It's the easiest way to keep him dry; the more layers he has on, the more painful it is for him to move his arms to get jackets and coats on and off.

'One, two, three – hup!' Hol says, and – only a little alarmingly, as Hol and Rob raise the front of the wheelchair higher than Paul and I can raise the rear at first – Guy is elevated to hip height.

'Sure we're all sober enough for this?' Guy says, holding even tighter to the chair's wheels as Paul and I adjust our grip and get him level.

Hol laughs. 'We're exactly drunk enough, I reckon,' she tells him as we start forward. 'Whoops!' she says, staggering. Guy is thrown to one side.

'Christ!' he says.

'Oh, fucking marvellous,' Paul mutters, looking down at where the wheel of the chair has left a dark mark on his white jacket. 'Oh well; had this at least a week.'

'Puddle deeper than anticipated,' Hol says. 'No problem.'

We set off again.

'How you doing there, Kit?' Paul asks.

'I'm doing fine, thanks,' I tell him.

'Yeah,' he sighs, 'you always are, aren't you?'

Alison and Pris are walking on the heather to the side of the path while Haze brings up the rear.

'Nice wellies, Hol,' Pris says. 'Those Barbours?'

Hol shrugs as best she can. 'Something like that.'

Alison glances down. One eyebrow rises. 'They're Le Chameau,' she tells Pris. 'Bit posh for you, Hol. Doc Martens not run to wellies?'

'They're from an ex,' Hol tells her. 'I got custody of the footwear. Were his; I need three pairs of socks and an insole not to walk out of them.'

'You should have stuck with that one,' Alison tells her. 'Boy who can afford to kiss off a pair of Le Chameau's probably loaded. Neoprene inside?'

'Neo-what?'

'They blue, inside?'

'Um . . . Sort of . . . fawn, I suppose.'

'*Leather* lining?' Alison says. Her waterproof jacket makes a hissy, sliding noise as she crosses her arms. She shakes her head. 'Oh my. You really did make a mistake there. Or . . . Oh, sorry. Did he dump you?'

'Mutual consent,' Hol tells her, her breath a little laboured. 'He found me too "abrasive" and I got fed up with his simple-minded obsession with female footwear.'

'Ah well,' Alison says. 'Maybe next time.'

'That is my sole ambition, patently,' Hol says.

At the tower, with the skies clearing to the west and the wind freshening and the rain-washed air making everything look nearer than it really is, even in the slanting light of late afternoon, we discover that the door that used to guard the stairway has been removed.

'It was metal,' Guy tells us. 'Nicked a couple of years ago by entrepreneurs who'd perfected the business model of swiping copper wires from railway signalling equipment and manhole covers from city streets and thought they'd branch out. Council put up a sign saying *Don't dare climb these stairs and it's at your own risk if you do,* but looks like that's been nicked too.'

'Requires investigating,' Paul says, stepping into the dark doorway and looking up the winding stair. 'Anyone else with me?'

'After you,' Rob says.

'Yeah, I'm up for it,' Pris agrees.

Alison sighs. 'Oh, I suppose so.' She hugs herself and frowns.

'You sure?' Haze says. 'There might be spiders and bats and all sorts.'

'You're right,' Paul says, taking off his white jacket. He holds it out to Guy. 'Warmed up anyway. You mind, Guy?'

'Ta. I'll use it as a blanket, keep me legs warm.' Guy takes Paul's jacket and arranges it over his knees.

'You be okay down here?' Paul asks Guy, with secondary glances at me and Hol.

'As rain,' Guy tells him.

'Brilliant.' Paul disappears up the stairs. 'Anybody got a torch?' he calls back.

'Oh, great,' Alison says as Rob motions her and Pris to go before him.

'Just wanting to look at my arse, Rob?' Pris says over her shoulder as she follows Alison into the dark doorway.

'Yeah,' he says. 'That's right.'

'No farting!' Haze says, following Rob.

As well as the sound of shoes on stone, there are ominous pretend-ghost whooo-hooo noises from the stairwell, some laughter and a couple of muffled curses.

Actually I do have a torch; a little credit-card-sized thing Mrs Willoughby gave me as a birthday present a couple of years ago, but it's for emergencies only, and I wouldn't call

120

this an emergency. If somebody falls on the stairs and needs help, that would be an emergency; then I could use it.

Of course if I let them have the torch, that might help prevent them falling on the stairs in the first place, so maybe I should loan it to them after all. However, by the time I think all this through it's a bit late anyway, and I might even cause an incident if I suddenly dash up the stairs after them, yelling about having a torch and saying I'd forgotten, sorry, but here it is – who needs it most?

I get quite hot thinking about all this; it's just the kind of thing that trips me up and makes me panic. I start taking deep, measured breaths, the way Mrs Willoughby taught me.

'You two can go if you want,' Guy says, looking up at me and Hol. He reaches under the cycling cape and takes a battered-looking rolly from a jacket pocket. 'Won't run away, I promise.'

'I'm fine here,' I tell him.

'Frightened of heights,' Guy says, nodding. 'Forgot.'

I am not unduly frightened of heights, and wonder how I may have given Guy the wrong impression.

'Bastard,' Guy says. He's having problems lighting the rolly; he's cupping his hand to shield the little plastic lighter and the cigarette from the wind but his hands shake a lot these days and because of the wind, or his shaking hand, the flame keeps blowing out. He peers at the lighter, tries to adjust it, shakes it a couple of times. 'Work, ye bastard,' he says, and tries again.

'Oh, give it here,' Hol says, taking both from him. She sticks the cigarette in her mouth, cups her hand and lights the rolly, handing it back as she exhales. The cloud of smoke is shredded and dissipated by the gusting wind. I don't think she inhaled properly. I have a swooning moment, thinking of the smoke leaking into her lungs and a single molecule of carcinogenic compound settling in an alveolus and triggering

121

cancer in one of her cells, starting a primary tumour that metastasises throughout her body, killing her, taking her away as well. But I really don't think she inhaled; not properly, just enough to get the rolly started. She lifts the cape and drops the lighter into one of Guy's jacket pockets.

Hol coughs. The cough is good, I tell myself; it means that she is clearing her trachea of the tars in the smoke, and, probably, that she isn't used to smoking and doesn't smoke in secret, even occasionally.

'Still a filthy habit,' she tells Guy.

'I'm full of them,' he tells her, drawing deeply on the rolly and sitting back to take in the view. I move to stand upwind, out of the smoke. Guy breathes out with what sounds like satisfaction. 'Ha. Used to be, at any rate,' he says. He looks up at Hol, grinning. 'That not true, Hol?'

'Yeah. One-man vice squad,' Hol says. 'That was you.'

Guy studies the glowing tip of the skinny roll-up. 'This is my last vice, Hol.' I think he sounds sad.

'Alcohol not count, then?' Hol says, smiling.

'Nah, not really. Don't enjoy it the way I used to, anyway. Don't enjoy much of anything any more. Last time I tried speed it nearly gave me a heart attack; same with coke. Ecstasy had me grinding my teeth to stumps and wanting to hug everybody.' Guy shudders at the memory. 'Got some Viagra from the doc to see if I could raise more than a smile but it just gave me a headache.'

I start humming to myself. I've got my phone with me, of course, and I'll have headphones in a pocket somewhere. Two concrete uprights against the west-facing wall of the tower show where there used to be a bench, but the wooden spars that spanned the gap and formed the seat have gone.

'Chased the dragon a few times, back in the day,' Guy

122

says. I think he sounds wistful. His voice has changed and it's almost like he's talking to himself now, as though Hol and I aren't here. 'Maybe I'll take up heroin if it all gets too fucking desperate and demeaning; get on the needle like a proper fucking junkie and go for an overdose.'

'Thought you had opiates to chug when the pain got bad,' Hol says to Guy, though glancing at me and sort of shrugging.

'Yeah,' Guy growls. 'That's all right, I suppose. Bit of a buzz off, that. Though it doesn't feel like a vice when it's medicinal. *Fucking* cancer,' Guy says, suddenly vehement. 'Even takes the fun out of opiates. *Fucking* shit!'

'Hey!'

We look up and see Paul waving from the top of the tower. He shouts something else but the wind is making such a noise it's hard to hear. We just wave back. The others appear at the parapet too and also wave, then they disappear.

'Wonder if they got into the rooms,' Hol says. 'Remember, even in the old days when the place was unlocked, you could never get into the three or four rooms that led off the stairs?'

'Wooden doors,' Guy says. 'Probably left those.' He looks at the tip of the rolly again. It's nearly finished. He stubs it into the white jacket across his knees.

'Guy!' Hol says, tearing the butt from his hand to throw it away. She pulls the jacket off him, spits on it and tries to brush the burned bit off, but it stays; a little black crater.

'Oops,' Guy says.

'What the fuck did you do that for?' Hol asks him. She glances up at the top of the tower but there's nobody there.

'Me hand slipped.'

'You lying fuck; you did that deliberately. What fucking age are you? You're acting like a spoiled brat!'

123

'Can I have that back, please?' Guy says. 'My legs are cold.'

Hol makes as though to throw the jacket back into his lap, then stops, thrusts it into my arms instead and quickly unzips her fleece. She wraps it round Guy's legs, tucking it in. 'There,' she says, as the wind tugs at her shirt and she does up the top couple of buttons by her neck. 'Make a mess of that and I'll make a fucking mess of you.'

'Thank you so much,' Guy says, like none of this has happened.

I think Hol is shivering. 'Would you like this?' I say, offering her Paul's jacket.

'No thanks,' she says, hugging herself and looking away to the view. Her shirt ripples in the wind.

'Our Holly has always favoured martyrdom over comfort,' Guy tells me.

'Twat,' Hol mutters.

'Right!'

'Come on!' With a noise of laughter and slapping soles, Paul and Rob appear, running down the stairs and bouncing out. 'Buckle up, you old bugger,' Paul tells Guy. 'The view's brilliant. We're getting you up to the top.' His face is flushed and he looks excited. Rob is laughing.

'I'm not going up those fucking stairs,' Guy says. 'Are you fucking mad? You'll tip me on me head and leave me prop- erly paralysed, you—'

'No, we won't,' Rob says. 'Just trust us.'

'I don't fucking trust you!' Guy protests, shouting now. 'I've never fucking trusted you!'

'Well, start,' Rob says, going to the rear of Guy's chair. Paul stations himself at the front, turning his back as he squats and grips the tubes holding the front wheels.

'Let me go, you cunt!' Guy starts kicking weakly at Paul's

back as he and Rob lift him and head for the tower's empty doorway. 'Hol! Kit! Make the buggers stop!'

'No,' Hol says, standing aside, still hugging herself.

There is the sound of applause from the top of the tower, where the others are leaning over, looking at us and clapping and cheering.

'Kit! The fuckers are going to kill me!'

'Guys,' I say, 'are you sure about this?'

'Positive,' Paul shouts back. 'We've worked it out.'

Hol looks at me. 'I'm assuming you have the local hospital on speed dial?'

I shrug. 'Just be 999, I reckon.'

'Let me go! I can see the fucking view from here! What do you think *that* is? Look!'

'Better up there,' Rob tells him. 'You need to feel the breeze. It's bracing.'

'I'll fucking brace you, you – mind me head!' Guy yells as they get to the doorway and nearly crack his forehead against the stonework.

'Can I help?' I ask, getting behind Rob as he and Paul rearrange themselves in the little vestibule at the bottom of the steps, Rob setting himself to go backwards up the stairs, holding the chair's handles, while Paul holds the front wheels up high. I have to shuffle round, then step back out again, to make room for this to happen.

'No room, Kit,' Paul says, breathing hard as Rob sets off up the narrow twist of steps. Paul follows. I step back inside again. And there is no room; Paul's shoulders are a couple of centimetres from filling the whole width of the stairwell. I think of offering my torch, at last, but I don't know how they'd hold it or what use it would be.

'I'll fucking sue!' Guy shouts, voice echoing up the

winding stair. He does look rather precariously balanced.

'Fine. I know a good lawyer,' Paul tells him.

'*You're* going to need a good fucking lawyer, you fucking maniac bastard!'

They go up one step each.

'Okay down there?' Rob asks.

'Fine,' Paul says. 'Keep going.'

They head on upwards.

'Bastards,' Guy mutters. His voice echoes.

'Leave them to it, Kit,' Hol says quietly from outside.

'I thought I could at least be a sort of human airbag,' I tell her. 'You know; if they fall.'

She smiles. 'Probably just break your neck too. You'll be more help waiting around to pick up the pieces if it does all go tits up.'

'You sure?' I say, as Paul's shoes disappear up the turn of the steps.

'When we get to the top and I ask you nicely,' I hear Guy say, 'will you toss me off?' Then he wheezes with laughter.

'No probs,' Paul says.

'I'm sure,' Hol tells me.

We stand outside, looking at the view.

The weather in the west provides a fine display of colours as the sun sinks between the ragged remains of the spreading clouds, and the hills and Dales crumpled against the horizon. The wind gusts, still smelling wet, rocking us as we stand there.

'I will take that jacket,' Hol says, and puts it on. I hold it open for her, something Hol taught me was okay to do. I used to think women would shout at me if I tried to do this but Hol says it's all right to offer and can even be done for men as well.

Hol glances towards the summit of the tower. 'You been to the top, Kit?' she asks.

'Yes, a few times,' I tell her. Four times, actually, but I'm wary of letting people – even Hol – know how much I count stuff. 'You?' I ask.

'Once or twice,' she says. She does up the jacket's zip. Paul's white jacket is far too big for her. She looks bundled up in it, half disappeared, like a child.

She glances back up again. Somebody – Haze, I think – waves from the battlements, and I wave back. Hol is looking out to the west.

'We came here once in a storm, twenty-odd years ago,' she says.

'That was brave.' As far as I'm aware the tower has always had a functioning lightning conductor, but still.

'Yeah, in the hearse.'

Dad used to drive a hearse. I suspect he was just trying to prove how wacky and eccentric he was, but he says it was dirt cheap and an outright bargain; a geriatric Daimler being replaced by a sleeker Ford. He was into surfing at the time and ex-hearses were relatively popular amongst surfers, allegedly, not so much because you can fit a board inside but because you can stretch out for a proper sleep in them and use them as sort of camper vans. You can fit a fair few people inside them, too, though the police take a dim view of passengers travelling lying down in the back without proper seats and seat belts.

Guy used to dress the part sometimes, too; he'd found an old top hat in the Bewford Oxfam shop and put black ribbons on the back, and he had a big black cane and a frock coat and all that stuff. He wore dark glasses and was often mistaken for a rock star. Or a twat, as he has himself admitted.

127

'You had to be fairly brave just to get into the hearse,' Hol tells me. 'I don't mean being superstitiously sensitive, I mean being mechanically aware; it was falling apart.'

I suppose back then the house wasn't. The quarry would have been shaking it every few days but the place must have been kept in reasonable repair. Maybe there's always been something in Guy's life that was falling apart. Until finally, as well as the house and the car and whatever else, the thing falling apart ended up being himself. Not that cancer makes you fall apart so much – that would be leprosy or something, I suppose – as add bits on. Cancer makes bits of you grow that are supposed to have stopped growing after a certain point, crowding out the bits you need to keep on living, if you're unlucky, if the treatments don't work.

I bet the old Daimler was falling apart, but I also bet I could have saved it. The older the car, the more you can do with it, self-maintaining and repairing. Of course, on the other hand, the older the car, the more need for maintenance and repair in the first place.

'Middle of the night,' Hol is saying. 'We were all drunk, all stoned or wired or whatever. One of those things that seemed like a good idea at the time.' She looks back at the door of the tower, then at the top. 'Near the end of term; we'd been celebrating. Came out here to watch the lightning after the rain had mostly stopped; there'd been a power cut back at the house so getting into the Daimler and going for a drive seemed like a wizard wheeze anyway. The rain was still coming down in bursts and gusts but you could see between the showers sometimes and watch lightning playing way over in the Lake District. So we stood out here and watched it, or sat in the car some of the time and watched it – we'd forgotten to bring enough warm clothes, or anything waterproof at all. The tower was closed, locked up, back then, so you could only shelter behind it, not get inside.'

Hol hugs herself in her big white cocoon of jacket. From this angle, I can't see the muddy mark on the sleeve or the burn hole on the back.

'Usual quota of ongoing emotional crises happening at the time,' Hol says. 'All part of the Willoughtree House merry-go-round. Your dad and I had been an item for a half a term in first year but then went our separate ways, amicably enough. Pris had succumbed to his charms too, a few times, but they were never really a couple. Ali had had a thing with Rob most of that term – this was second year – but then that had fallen apart a bit messily and she'd moved out for a week or two, slept on some girlfriend's floor. She'd been back that night to try and sort things out – with Guy, about whether she should stay the next term, not with Rob, who was enjoying being single again. She and I ended up sitting cross-legged like a pair of little pixies on the bench there.' She nods back at the two concrete uprights against the wall of the tower. 'We'd never really got on that well – she was closer to Pris, though I think Pris was sleeping in the back of the hearse at the time while the guys were off looking for interesting places to pee or something – but for some reason she decided I was her best friend that night. Said she was thinking about leaving the course, the uni, not just the house, because she was so upset at what had happened with Rob.'

'Oh dear,' I say, in a gap, while Hol is gazing out to the sunset.

'Thing is,' Hol says, sighing, 'I sort of had a quiet thing for Rob myself; had had almost from the start, but by the time Guy and I were apart he was with Ali, and after that he was enjoying screwing around too much . . . But he'd said just that evening that he was already getting tired of these mean-ingless first-year fucks – we had all the world-weary wisdom and ennui that comes from not being a first-year oneself, so—'

'Hey!' somebody shouts from the top of the tower. We both look up. Haze is waving at us. 'Where . . . ?' he shouts, then looks behind him, disappears briefly, comes back. 'All right!' he shouts down, voice almost inaudible in the stiffening wind. '. . . breath back! Or . . . thing!'

'Now what?' Hol says. We both go to the doorway. 'You guys okay up there?' she shouts up the stairs.

'Taking a rest!' Paul's voice comes floating faintly down. 'Heavier than he looks!'

'Fucking . . . !' Guy shouts too, but his voice is fainter still and we lose whatever follows.

'They must be on a landing,' I say. There are three small landings on the way up, where the doors to the rooms are. I guess the guys are resting on one of those. Hol shrugs. We go back outside, stand looking at the view again.

Hol just gazes into the distance.

'I didn't know all that,' I tell her after a moment or two when she hasn't said anything. I try to sound interested. I *am* interested, but I know that me being interested and actu-ally sounding interested are not always the same thing and I have to work at letting people know that sort of stuff. Anyway, this prompt works.

'Yeah, well, like I say; all a bit of a merry-go-round back then,' Hol says. 'Full of hope, hash and hormones.' She gives a small laugh. 'And wholefood. That was Haze's thing, mostly.' Hol shakes her head. 'That man discovered more types of lentil than we ever knew existed, or wanted to. Different ways of cooking them too, not all completely horrible. There was a while when Guy and Rob seemed to be competing over who could bed the highest number of women in a week; they were hardly out of their bedrooms and Haze was hardly out of the kitchen. I told Haze, he, Guy and Rob were all just the same, really; anything with a pulse.'

She looks up at me and smiles.

'Anyway,' she says, 'this night, I thought I'd spotted my chance to see what would happen with Rob and me. At the time he seemed like the happy medium between Guy and Paul. Guy was already starting to become his own tribute band; too full of himself and determined to be eccentric to be a decent . . . mate; all right for an interesting, exciting interlude but not proper boyfriend material.' Hol pauses, looks at me as if to see whether I'm going to take this adverse comment on my dad badly.

I just nod.

'Paul was always too sensible, too careful, too focused on shaping his life as a sort of support structure for his career,' Hol says. 'There was space in his life for a woman, but you always felt there was a pretty tight spec sheet involved and you'd have to answer an advert first, make the shortlist, have your CV polished to a high burnish and then hope to shine in the interview. Rob was smart, funny – in a quieter, drier way than Guy, but still with proper wit – and there was a sort of decency to his ambition at the time; talked about getting into activism, running a charity . . . Both of which he did, before he was headhunted and turned by the kleptocratic elite . . . But, that was later. That night, going on what he'd said to me earlier in the evening – which might just have been a sort of tentative approach in itself – I thought I might make my move when we got back to the house, or at least make it nice and obvious and natural that he could make a move for me. See?' She glances at me. 'I was starting

131

to mature, beginning to understand that some men like at least the illusion of control.' Hol looks up at me again and grins. She leans against me, puts her arm through mine.

This is a nice thing to do and gives me a good feeling. Of Dad's old housemates, Pris is the prettiest, but Hol is still an attractive woman and even though she's more like an aunt – and, just possibly, a lot closer than that – she's the kind of woman you can sort of have fantasies about and not feel she'd be horrified if she ever found out. Knowing Hol, she'd just sigh and shake her head. Of course I know nothing will ever happen, but I remember Hol herself telling me it was okay to fantasise, even quite wrong things, as long as the rudeness or other inappropriate behaviour remained virtual and stayed inside your own head. Better to fantasise about your lust or obsession honestly and explore it that way than refuse to acknowledge it at all and risk it bursting out into reality without warning.

'However,' Hol says, and sighs. 'Instead, I found myself telling Ali that Rob had told me he was getting fed up with bedding a succession of pliant first years.'

'Really?'

'I know. But there you are. I told her she was the second person to bare all to me that evening and Rob had said this, and that that probably meant he was starting to regret them splitting up and it was probably only your standard-issue male pride that was stopping him from telling her this and asking her to take him back, and she should just be honest and open with him without making herself vulnerable. Frankly I was sort of concocting my own little idealised narrative as I went along from relatively scant evidence, and enjoying spinning this tale for myself as well as for Ali, but it seemed to work; convinced at least one of us. So then the guys came back out of the darkness, and Ali got up and walked over to Rob and started talking to him, and next thing they were walking off round the back of the tower, arm in arm.' Hol lets go of my arm, hugs herself. 'Though there was one last lingering look back from Rob as they went.' Hol sighs. 'Or so I seem to recall. Light wasn't good enough to make it out exactly, but I've thought about that look a lot, over the years.'

'Wow,' I say. 'What? So . . . were they going to . . . Did they, like, you know . . . ?'

'What?' Hol says, frowning at me. 'You mean did they *fuck*? Round the back of the tower? Are you kidding? It was cold and windy and raining; we were already soaked through; last thing you'd have wanted to do was bare any more flesh to the elements. And any of us could have wandered round the back of the tower at any time, caught them. It's not even as though it would have been their first time and they were desperate. Would have had to have been a knee-trembler, too. Jesus, Kit; even we had *some* standards.'

'Ah. Sorry.'

'Nah, they were just talking, then hugging, kissing. But the point is: that was that. My chance, if there had ever even been one, had gone. I was being nice, and the girl's need seemed greater than mine.'

'Regretted it ever since?' I offer.

Hol shrugs. 'Well, I don't lose any sleep over it, but it might have been nice to have known.' She's silent for a few moments, then glances back at the tower.

I think I can, distantly, hear people going, '*Heave-ho!*'

'Ali and Rob were together from then on,' Hol says. 'If it had been me and him instead . . . Who knows what might have been different?' She shrugs.

My phone goes. It's Guy. 'Dad?' I say.

133

'Fucking terrible idea. Can you get up here, Kit? These lightweights are crapping out.'

'We are not crapping ou—' Somebody is protesting as Guy kills the link.

'I'm wanted,' I tell Hol.

'That must be nice.'

I walk up the narrow stone steps. They got as far as the second of the tower's three landings and had to admit they were never going to get Guy all the way to the top and back down safely. Paul is less fit than he thought, especially in the upper body, he tells us; he's more of a runner, a marathon man. Plus he had the harder lift, of course, from the bottom. He could probably make it, get Guy to the top, but it's better not to risk it with an already sick man. Also, it's a really heavy, old-fashioned wheelchair.

'Enough fucking excuses!' Guy yells, his voice echoing in the confined space. 'Get me back down for fuck's sake. Stupid fucking idea in the first fucking place!'

I take the front of the chair, holding the small front wheels up near my shoulders while Rob takes the top again. We make it down to the bottom of the tower without dropping Guy or cracking his head on the stonework. He grumbles and curses the whole way. The others are immediately behind us, complaining about the cold, though Rob and even Paul are both still sweating and I'm a little warm myself now.

Hol is standing at the bottom of the steps, just outside. 'That fun?' she asks Guy, grinning.

'And you can fuck off as well!' Guy shouts at her.

4

Guy falls asleep in the car. He's effectively still asleep when I help him upstairs. I leave him on top of the bed in his pants and vest with a cover pulled over him. He's missed some meds but sleep is probably better for him now. It's getting dark outside anyway, though I doubt he'll sleep through.

'Yeah,' Haze says, in the kitchen, where a large pot of tea is being prepared and biscuits sought. 'Reckon I'll hit the hay too, just for a disco nap.'

'That might not be such a bad idea,' Paul agrees. 'I brought some fig rolls,' he tells Pris, who is opening cupboards.

'Fig rolls,' Alison says, screwing her face up. 'I never got your thing about fig rolls.'

'Hey, Kit,' Pris says when she sees me. 'Any biscuits left?'

'Um, possibly not,' I tell them. There were none on special offer in any of the shops Hol and I visited this morning, or at least none I like.

'Yeah,' Paul says, 'I never really liked fig rolls that much either, to be honest. But I liked them more than anybody

135

else – everybody else kind of hated them – and so they got nicked and eaten only as a last resort, usually when people had the munchies. They lasted longer. Buying them just kind of became a habit after that.' Paul shrugs, frowns. 'I still don't really *like* them.'

'Jesus,' Hol says, walking in, wiping her hands. I can hear the cistern in the downstairs loo flushing. 'You saying you bought something you didn't like because we liked it even less so you didn't have to *share?*'

Paul frowns at her. 'That is pretty much what I just said.'

Hol shrugs. 'I missed the beginning.'

'You should have kept your biscuit of choice in your room,' Alison says. 'I did.'

Paul nods. 'I know. But that always felt like having an eating disorder.'

'Okay,' Alison says, nodding. 'Thanks a lot.'

'These digestives look viable,' Pris says, staring into a battered-looking biscuit barrel. She sticks her nose in, sniffs.

'They may be past their use-by,' I tell her. They are definitely past their use-by and I was saving them for the base of a cheesecake I was going to make, but never mind.

Pris sniffs them. 'They'll do.'

'Yeah,' Haze says, 'well, I'm taking myself off to bed. See you later.'

'Yeah, I'm going to pass on tea and biscuits, too,' Paul says.

'Nah, I'll take a couple of biscuits . . .' Haze says, grabbing two and only then making for the door.

'What?' Pris says. 'I'm making a fucking gallon of tea here, guys.'

'I might go on looking for the tape,' I tell people loudly, as Haze is in the doorway to the hall. 'That okay? I'll try to keep quiet, but . . .'

136

'Yeah,' Haze says. 'Yeah, no problem. Laters.'

'No probs,' Paul says. He takes out his phone as he follows Haze to the door. 'Chelsea score,' he says, clearly, to it, and leaves, peering at the screen. We can hear him tut and say 'Shit' as he heads to the foot of the stairs.

'Would be fucking Chelsea, wouldn't it?' Hol says.

'Not Man-U?' Rob says, yawning. 'Surprising.'

'Tea, Kit?' Pris asks.

'Yes, please. I'll take the big blue mug there; on the draining rack.'

I have several special mugs; the blue one is the biggest. I have my own special cereal plate and spoon, and dinner plate too. I know this is a bit childish but I don't see any harm in it and it's just comforting. I kind of keep Guy's cutlery and crockery separate too, nowadays, since the diagnosis. Before then I'd happily have shared stuff. I think it's some deep instinctive thing about being around somebody very ill; you want to set up and maintain certain boundaries. This is the reason I didn't finish Guy's eggy mug concoction this morning, even though I like it too (another memory of childhood).

I know Guy's cancer isn't contagious; you can't catch it off him, no matter how close you are physically or genetically, not even if you're his son. That's the thing about cancer; it's all yours – it's entirely, perfectly personalised. The cause might have come from outside – carcinogens in tobacco smoke or whatever – but that just triggered the runaway reaction in your own cells, and in that sense a fatal cancer is a kind of unwilled suicide, where, initially at least, one small part of the body has taken a decision that will lead to the death of the rest. Cancer feels like betrayal.

I take my big blue mug of tea and head up to the old servants' rooms. The last of the sunset light is leaching out of the sky. The lights up here tend to be bare bulbs hanging from the middle of the ceiling; old incandescent things that come on startlingly quickly, but which burn out more frequently too. Most don't work. I take the brightest – a hundred-watt bulb – from light fitting to light fitting, depending on what room I'm in, to see what I'm doing. This requires using an old T-shirt to stop it burning my fingers.

There is so much junk up here.

I find more old newspapers, stacked and yellowing, whole damp cardboard boxes full of ancient promotional stuff from the late nineties and early noughties when Guy worked at *North 99*, old suitcases stuffed with musty-smelling clothes and sorry-looking shoes, mostly men's, and entire tea chests crammed with empty plastic bags.

A lot of this crap could be usefully recycled, but Guy refuses to give me permission; for somebody with the reputation of a wastrel of legendary proportions, he can be remarkably small-minded and conservative about stuff like this. 'You never fucking know when something will come in useful.' So he's just a hoarder like any other, except he's foul-mouthed about it. I see this junk cluttering up the house and I itch to sort it and get it properly recycled, but I can't.

I like recycling. In some ways it's a bore, and I have a sort of inherited nostalgia for the old days, when – according to Guy – you just chucked everything into a big, shiny, cylindrical, metal dustbin and left it out for the bin-men (a simpler time), but recycling has its own rewards.

Nowadays we're expected to clean and sort almost everything; tins, bottles, plastics, paper and cardboard, kitchen and garden waste, wood, metal and residual landfill. Oh, and batteries, light bulbs, engine oil, mattresses, small and large

138

electrical items, tyres and so on. Technically it's a chore, but once you get into it it's sort of quietly satisfying.

First, you feel you're doing your bit for the planet. It might be a very small bit, it might be too late by some estimations and it might shrink into insignificance compared to the industrious carbon-loading going on elsewhere ('Are you still taking the sticky tape off that same fucking box? The Chinese'll have built another couple of coal-fired fucking power stations while you've been picking away at that last square millimetre' – guess who), but at least you feel you're playing your part, and while you might be with everybody else in the same big, ever-deepening hole, if nothing else you're trying to dig as slowly possible.

'This is your fucking religion, isn't it?' Guy said once, watching me use the special knife I keep for such tasks as I slit the label on a tin of beans, laid the label flat on a pile of others and rinsed the empty can. We were in the main outhouse, where I do all this stuff. He was leaning on his stick at the time, otherwise fairly ambulatory. Must have been about two years ago. Anyway, I thought about this.

'I don't think it's a religion,' I told him. 'But the process helps fulfil a certain need for order and ritual I seem to have.' Guy looked oddly furious at this. 'Order and . . . ordering,' I added.

'Just an excuse to go through my fucking bins,' he muttered, and stalked off.

And that's another reward: you feel more connected to your own life in a way, more aware of what you – and any others in the house – are consuming. It's a think-about-how-you-live thing. And a calibratory thing. I like calibratory things.

Lastly, you feel that even with this used, now seemingly useless, thrown-away stuff, you're bringing order to it, and so helping to make it useful again. And that's just a nice feeling.

Some of the music promo stuff bulging in these slightly damp cardboard boxes might be saleable on-line. I find some *North 99* 'Millennium Meltdown Survival Kit' goody bags, each complete with a candle, a T-shirt, a discount voucher for a station-branded, wind-up radio (apply by post to the *North 99* Post Office Box address in Bewford, enclosing a cheque or postal order, P&P inc.), a cigarette lighter and a decade-and-a-bit-out-of-date Eccles cake. Everything but the candle carries the old, garish station logo of *North 99*.

I wonder how much one of these will be worth on eBay. I have a bet with myself: a bit less than a quid. Still, we have two dozen of them, so that's maybe twenty, if I can sell them all. It would mostly be local people interested, too, so the postage shouldn't be off-putting either. None of the lighters I try works; their fuel's all leaked away or osmosed or something.

In the bedroom above Haze – I can hear him snoring – I find a cracked plastic stackable box full of old VHS cassettes, and I get hopeful, but they're just ordinary, not the special one that lets you play one of the smaller-format tapes inside it.

Something occurs to me and I go back to the room I looked in before, where all the old newspapers are; our collection of *Bew Valley and Ormisdale Chronicle and Posts*. I heave the great heavy bundles of damp, smelly papers out of their collapsing boxes and start sorting through them, looking for those from around the time of my birth and the year or so before.

When I find those I leaf through a few; they're hard to handle and easy to tear because they're so damp. I nearly give up, but eventually I find myself mentioned in the Births, Deaths and Marriages section. It's in an edition dated nearly five weeks after I'm born. 'To Mr Guy Hyndersley, a son, born 12 Arpil.' Arpil. I find it oddly depressing that even the – much delayed, shamefully terse, small-detail-of-not-mentioning-who-the-mother-is – announcement of my arrival into the world contains a misprint.

I look through a few other papers from the year before, to see if there's anything about us. All I find is a short obituary of Guy's dad.

Dad's parents split up not long after he was born. His dad went off to London with his new woman and his mum moved back here, to the family home, with her parents. She was an only child. She became a lecturer in Classics at Bewford and, later, the first woman ever to become a professor in the university. Her parents died within a year of each other while she pursued her career and brought up Dad with the help of various aunts and nannies.

Then, when Guy was twelve, she died of ovarian cancer. Her husband returned; they'd never divorced and she'd left the house to him anyway. He came back alone, though he had a few different girlfriends over the years once he settled here. I don't think Guy and his dad ever really got on.

When Guy was seventeen his dad met somebody else and effectively moved out, back to London again. He was an antiques dealer and apparently quite a gifted pianist, though not concert standard; he'd long before worked out there would be more money in antiques.

According to Guy, his father really only came back to the house to use it as a place to store stock he'd bought locally and would later move down to the showroom in London; he was back to see Guy every weekend at first, then every fortnight, then once a month, and so on. He died the year I was born, from a heart attack. 'He was a fat, boozy, sixty-a-day man whose main exercise was levering himself out of the car or away from the bar,' Guy told me, years ago. 'Well, that and industrial-scale coughing. His expiry did not exactly come as a total shock.'

'SHOCK DEATH OF BEWFORD MAN IN LONDON.' That and a single, not terribly illuminating paragraph is all that Guy's dad's death merited in the paper.

Anyway, all this might be why Guy ran a bit wild, before, during and even after his university years. But especially during, when he had so many accomplices.

There's a creaking, iron-framed, single bed in the room where the newspapers are. I leave the copies from the twelve months before my birth lying out on the old mattress, to dry as best they can. The mattress is stained, as though some-body's spilled a full pot of tea over it. I glance up at the ceiling; it's probably a leak up there that's caused this. The ceiling plaster looks damp. I haul the bed into the middle of the room, under a drier part of the ceiling, as quietly as I can, but the action still seems to resonate throughout the house. I pull the mattress off the bed – it's amazingly heavy – and dump it more or less where it was, except on the floorboards, not on the bedstead. The mattress may well have been providing a sort of floodplain for the leak above, trap-ping the moisture within it to stop it from descending into my room, directly underneath.

I start to lay out the newspapers I want to dry on the chain-link surface stretched between the side-bars of the bed frame.

'Found you,' Alison says from the doorway. 'Need a hand?'

'Oh, hi. Yes.' I've just finished laying the papers out to dry. 'Let's do the room above you. Or is Rob asleep?'

'Skyping with his dad,' Alison says, looking round the room, wrinkling her nose. 'Brazil or Argentina or something. Smells a bit in here, doesn't it?'

I try to keep a sort of mental Fart Log for such moments. Reviewing it, I can find no recent activity. 'Dampness,' I tell her. I nod upwards. 'The roof leaks.'

Alison sighs, looks like she's deflating. She shakes her head. 'Sad old place, these days,' she says quietly.

I don't know what to say, so I don't say anything.

After a moment I say, 'Let's try the other room.' I wrap the old T-shirt round my hand, reach up and take the bulb out. It goes very dark; the single window faces north and there are no curtains but there's little light left in the sky. There's no light in the corridor outside save for what comes up the narrow stairwell from the floor beneath. 'Just the one good bulb up here,' I explain to Alison.

'Marvellous.'

'I just think we need to do this logically.'

'Why is starting from the attic logical?'

'You need a programme for this sort of thing, Kit. A shape, a design, something everybody can follow. There has to be elegance. That's primary.'

'But the attic's just got lots of old empty boxes in it,' I explain.

'One of which might contain the tape.'

'Not really.'

'You can't be sure, Kit. The whole point is that it's somewhere we don't know, so we have to look everywhere. If we start from the top and eliminate that, then we've made progress. You need the feeling of making progress.'

'Uh-huh. Thing is, Guy got me to move everything heavy in the loft down here or into the outhouses years ago when

143

he started worrying about the house falling down; he thought it might be top-heavy.'

Alison frowns at me. 'Really?'

'That's what he told me. He was worried that the quarry edge coming closer might shake everything to bits and bring it all down on top of us.'

'That's not likely to happen, is it?'

'I don't think it ever was, but we did it anyway. All that's left up there is empty boxes that things like the TV came in, or computers, and, you know, other household appliances. All they have in them is the expanded polystyrene packing they came with.'

'So they're not totally empty?'

'They're as good as totally empty.'

'Maybe, but you can't be absolutely sure the packing material is all they contain.'

'I'm pretty sure.'

'Pretty sure doesn't cover it, mister,' Alison says, and makes an expression that I think indicates she means to be funny.

'I'd put it at about ninety-nine per cent sure,' I tell her.

This throws her, briefly. 'That's what I mean, though, Kit; you have to be one hundred per cent sure.'

'Yes, ultimately. But there's a lot of places in and around the house where the likelihood of finding the tape is a lot higher than one per cent, so we ought to prioritise those locations first, because we haven't got unlimited time; we really want to find this before lunch on Monday.'

'You still can't be sure it's not up there,' Alison says, her gaze flicking to the ceiling. 'And meanwhile we *are* wasting valuable time. So we should get to it.'

'Well, I was kind of . . . doing . . .' I say, waving at the boxes I've already checked. I can let her fill in the gaps.

144

We're still in the room above mine; I put the bulb back in when we got into this argument about how to conduct the search.

She nods once. 'So we need to move on. Come on.' She nods towards the stair head, where the trapdoor to the loft is. She makes to move, then stops when she sees that I'm not shifting. 'Look, Kit,' she says, hands on her hips. 'This is important to me. Very important. To me and to Rob. Most important to me, though. Do you understand that?' (I just raise my eyebrows.) 'There are things on that tape that would affect my career a *lot* more than Rob's, a *lot* more than Paul's. They're men; they're allowed to get away with more, they always are. I'm under more threat from that *fucking* tape than anybody else here; the men because they're men, and Pris and Hol because they have less to lose. I'm not running a couple of homes for pensioners stinking of urine, I'm not writing about films nobody watches in magazines nobody reads; I'm on course to have the kind of power that can buy and sell the sort of politician Paul *dreams* of being. So I *need* this done properly, do you understand? Now come *on*!'

This is a knotty one. I'm as good as certain the tape won't be up there, but there is some force to Alison's argument about absolute certainty, and a kind of elegance in having a clear top-down plan, only I'm starting to feel like she's insisting on this just to establish who's in control here (her, she would like), and my automatic reaction is to resist.

If she was a man I would definitely resist, because men tend to be more forceful and pushy and always trying to be top dog in situations like this, and that's sort of like bullying, which Guy always told me to fight back against, even if it hurt. But Alison's female, and I take her argument about things generally being easier for men, and them getting away with more, and so my instinct is to defer to her just so as to *not* be like a typical male, refusing to listen to women and sure that they (the man) has got it right. On the other hand, she has kind of been acting a bit like a man in this. Tricky.

Alison stops, half turns and smiles a big smile at me, tipping her head to one side, letting her neat blonde hair fall half across her face and sort of flicking it back a little as she says, in a subtly different, slightly lower, softer voice, 'Just do this for me, Kit; come on. Please?'

I have a suspicion this is what is called coquettishness. I believe I'm immune to it; in fact I'm so immune to it I did once think I might be gay, even though I'm pretty sure I'm not (better than ninety-nine per cent sure).

'Anyway, there's no light up in the attic,' I tell her. 'We'd need torches.'

'You must have torches,' she says, still smiling.

'I have a torch,' I tell her. 'It's small, though.'

Actually we have a ruggedised, plug-in, portable, five-hundred-watt, halogen work light on a long curly lead in the garage, which we could fetch and which would illuminate the whole loft, but frankly I'm trying to put her off so there's no need to mention it.

'Great.' She claps her hands, all business again. 'We've got some multi-squillion candle-power thing in the car. I'll get that.'

'Okay,' I say. 'You look up there, I'll look down here.'

'O— what?' This has thrown her too, as it was kind of meant to. 'No. We need to do this together, Kit,' she says.

'No we don't.'

'But yes we do. You're the local knowledge; we need your expertise up there.'

'But my local knowledge is telling me the tape isn't up there in the first place.'

'Ah,' she says, and smiles tightly and shakes her head, eyelids fluttering briefly closed. I think she means to look confident but in reality she looks like she's having to stall while she extemporises an answer to this. 'That's mistaking strategic knowledge for tactical knowledge,' she says (which is quite quick, I suppose). 'Leave the strategy to me, Kit; that's what I'm good at. That's my job. That's what they pay me for. Trust me.'

'Well anyway,' I say – breezily, I hope, because, although I've become a bit hot during our little exchange, I've also thoroughly enjoyed it – 'thanks for the offer of help, Ali.' (I don't think I've ever called her 'Ali' before.) 'I'm going to look in the room above yours. There's a stepladder behind the door of the last room on this side if you want to get up into the attic.'

Me and my working bulb head off to the room above her and Rob.

I think I hear her mutter 'Prick' in the darkness, but I'm not sure.

After a couple of minutes I hear her dragging the stepladder noisily along the hall into position under the loft trapdoor and banging it open, then clumping around above my head. It sounds like she's just letting the boxes fall to the floor up there, but they don't actually make much impact because, like I said, they're empty, or as good as.

Hol comes up after another couple of minutes and we get through the boxes in two of the old servants' rooms twice as fast, mostly in a companionable silence, save for the clumping.

*   *   *

'Dunder-headed, wart-raddled, slug-case of bilious turgidity.'

'Mollocking, mince-witted slack-jaw.'

'Gruel-brained, unlanced-boil-visaged, sense-prolapsed haemorrhoid-suckler.'

'Eew. Yuck.'

'Auto-stuprated, faecal-faced excrementiphage.'

'Binary-dumbfounded, synapse-deficient femtowit.'

'Why, you scrotum-faced, pillous-featured fartle-butt.'

'While you, sir, are a wit-wrecked, scurvy-tongued, mucus-palmed, cretinous pinprick.'

'Ooooh!'

'Well, you're a gangrenously, tripe-bollocked waste of flatulence.'

'Oh! Harsh.'

'You blunder-brained, coprophageous, cortex-curdled slap-basket.'

'Scrofulous, addle-pated geezertwat!'

'How dare you, you blither-wattled, sump-gargling breeze-blockhead.'

'Ham-brained, hair-fisted, cess-slathered pus-scuttle!'

'Scheech!'

'Space-wasting, worm-infested, bilge-veined, Hideometer-deforming scartle-dunce!'

'Did you say "Hideometer"?'

'That's what it says here.'

'What's a Hideometer?'

'Measures hideousness, obviously. Right, Kit?'

'That was the idea.'

'All right, but "*scartle*-dunce"? What's a scartle-dunce?'

'*I've* no idea. What's a "scartle", for that matter?'

'Kit?'

I shrug. My face is burning but I'm also smiling. 'I made

that one up,' I confess. 'I needed something for the rhythm of it and "scartle" just fitted. I was going to replace it with something better but in the end I didn't. I suppose I was kind of trying to see what I could get away with.'

'Quite a lot,' Paul says, 'by the look of it.'

He and Pris and Hol have been reading out some of my HeroSpace insults.

'These are brilliant, Kit!' Pris says. 'You're a fucking genius of insulting! And you actually win battles like this?'

'Well, not exactly battles, but there's a sort of game-engine-remuned subculture of insult trading, and providing you get the vote from your fellow gamers, there will be a victor and a vanquished, and so you can earn points, yeah. It's quite democratic, really.'

'You literally trade insults?' Paul says. He nods. 'That's quite cool.'

'Yeah, also,' Hol says, looking at Rob and Alison, sitting across from her, 'have you been tutoring the lad in your ludicrous management guru-speak?' Rob grins, Ali frowns. Hol looks at me. '"Game-engine-remuned", Kit?' Her eyes narrow. 'Actually, just "remuned"?'

'Leave him alone, Hol,' Haze says. 'Don't pick him up on every word.'

'No,' I say, 'it's fair; "remuned" is just a word that's used in the game to mean an activity or . . . a creation that's worth points. I don't think it's in the dictionaries. Well, not yet.'

We're in the sitting room after dinner. (I took a bunch of curries out of the freezer: a general thumbs-up, though a couple of dishes were judged 'a bit hot' and Haze gargled milk at one point. I think he was just trying to show off. I believe Dad was about to complain about them being too hot until other people did.) Now Hol, folded cross-legged on the couch, has her laptop balanced on her knees, plugged into HeroSpace. She has an account, an avatar – everything. I had no idea. She just likes to watch, she says. (That got an 'Ooooh!' from Haze, too.)

You can do that, in the game; providing you never try to accumulate points, you can just wander around most Territories, NearSpaces, Adjoinalities and Adjunctions without ever getting harmed. You're a bit like a ghost. Quite a lot of people do this, so they can follow a preferred player on their quests and campaigns – a travelling fan base – or just tour the scenery and the architecture; tourists, ogling, basically. Either way they get called Voys, but it's not too much of an insult. Not any more than, say, 'newbie' is – just a description. The game is so vast, so famous and so complex these days that a lot of people thinking of joining in as full-on, points-collecting Players like to spend some time as a Voy first, just to see if they think they're going to like it and fit in, and to start learning the rules and ropes by observation rather than bitter experience.

So Hol's a Voy, and she's followed me for over a year. I'm not sure how to feel about this: a little flattered, I guess, but also a little like my privacy has been invaded. She logged in to let the others hear some of my choicer insults from the last couple of seasons of the tavern-based, Pro Insult-Trading series. Now Paul and Pris are leaning over the couch behind her, one over each shoulder, watching her screen as she scrolls down the list of Previously Victorious Disparagements, which presents as gold-leaf-tooled gothic script on polished teak boards, a bit like the list of former mayors that hangs above the grand central staircase in Bewford city hall or the roll-call of vice-chancellors in one of the university's older colleges.

Paul points at the screen. 'Carbuncle-strewn, slump-buttocked denizen of the outer latriniverse!' he declaims.

'Limp-tooled, spunk-deficient, sputum-defiled, turd-stuffed crass basket!' Pris yells back. 'Ha ha ha.'

'Can we fucking go back to something resembling normal fucking English?' Guy says, pulling on a stunted rolly. 'This bollocks is doing me head in.'

'Nah, this is a laugh,' Haze tells him. He's rolling a joint. Ali has insisted on opening a window to let the smoke out; I had to fetch a blanket to cover Guy, who had immediately complained about the cold.

'Suppurating, brochette-brained chump-head,' Hol says. Possibly at Guy.

'Incompetence-redefining ignoramax!' Paul replies.

'"Ignoramax"?' Rob says. 'That another made-up one, Kit?'

'Yes,' I say. 'Also, earlier? I shouldn't really have got away with "breeze-blockhead", because that particular one was in a Dark Ages TymeShift Adjoinality, where breeze-blocks have yet to be invented.' I frown, thinking about this. 'I could still lose points, if somebody spots that.' They're all looking at me. 'I think it's because most Players are still American and they call breeze-blocks "cinder blocks", so they haven't noticed it.'

'Yeah, yeah,' Guy says. 'We get the point. You're so fucking clever, Kit.' He snorts. 'When you're finished blowing your own trumpet, don't forget to empty the spit-trap.'

'No,' Hol says, smiling at him. 'This is something different, Guy. It's called self-deprecation. It's more like sucking your own trumpet. You wouldn't understand.'

'Fuck off.'

'Yeah, you . . .' Pris has taken out her contact lenses for the evening and is wearing small rimless glasses (she's still

151

very pretty). She has to lean further over Hol's left shoulder to peer at the screen and read the words. 'You syphilivered, sense-redacted, bipedal tumour!' she says to Guy, and the last word is out before she realises.

Then her face falls and she sort of compresses her lips until they almost disappear, biting them. 'Oh,' she says, shrinking down, putting her chin on her forearms on the back of the couch.

'Yeah, that's maybe enough,' Hol says quietly, closing the laptop. She lifts her wineglass, drinks.

We're all looking at Guy, who's up-ending another John Smith's can to empty it. He smacks his lips and sticks the folded-up butt of the rolly into the can, then glances round at us.

'Yeah, I heard,' he says, wheezing. 'Sticks and fucking stones, ya bunch of wimps. You should hear the names I call me tumours. Makes that lot' – he nods at the closed laptop on Hol's knees. Handily for Guy, I am in line with him and the laptop so he's nodding at me too – 'sound like Jane Austen characters at their most excruciatingly fucking polite.'

'Yeah, well . . .' Haze says.

Pris keeps her head down and in a small voice as she looks at Guy says, 'Still; sorry, dude.'

'And I'll thank you not to "dude" me, either,' Guy says, though he doesn't sound upset. He looks at Haze. 'You rolling that fucking joint or growing it?'

'Nearly done,' Haze says, licking at a cigarette paper. 'Skilled job, this, isn't it? Can't hurry perfection.'

'There's your problem,' Guy says. 'Doesn't have to be perfect; just has to deliver.'

'Yeah, well,' Haze says, 'I take pride in my work, don't I?'

Pris snorts. Haze stiffens, hesitates, but then continues as though he hasn't heard.

'Oh, for fuck's sake,' Ali says. 'Do you two have to smoke at all?'

'It's my hobby,' Guy tells her. 'That and drinking.' He looks at me. 'More fucking wholesome than making up bollocks round-the-fucking-houses ways of insulting saddo losers in the cyberverse that you never really meet anyway and probably wouldn't want to even if you did have the chance.'

'Can't you at least smoke *proper* cigarettes?' Alison says. 'You know; the neat, undeformed ones you don't have to roll yourself?'

'Nah,' Guy says. 'Full of additives to keep them looking nice and stay lit, those are. You don't want to go pulling that shit into your lungs; might catch something.' He grins at Ali, who shudders, looks away.

'Cheaper, too,' Haze says. 'I get my baccy from a guy on the cross-Channel ferries. Cheap as chips.'

'Yeah, what language *is* that?' Paul says, coming to sit back where he was, beside Haze, and lifting up the packet of tobacco he's using. He inspects the small print, frowning.

Haze glances, shrugs. 'Dunno. Balkan, or Egyptian or something.'

'"Balkan"?' Hol says. 'That a new state I haven't heard of, Haze?'

''Spect so,' Haze says, sitting back as he lights up. He glances at me, grins. 'Kit makes things up, and so do I.' He pulls hard on the joint.

I tried smoking once but it didn't seem to agree with my throat. I was never going to take it up because of the whole good-chance-of-killing-you thing, but I thought I'd see what all the fuss was about. After I'd stopped coughing I felt a bit dizzy. Though that might just have been the coughing. Either way, it didn't seem like much. Definitely one of those moments when I've thought, *I am never going to understand people*.

'Hey, Humphrey?' Guy says to Haze.

'Just getting it drawing nicely,' Haze tells him. He hands the joint over. 'There you go, mate.'

'Ta.' Guy draws deeply, holds it in, then exhales a big cloud of smoke towards the ceiling, wheezing, then coughing. 'Heard a lot of crashing around upstairs earlier,' he says. 'Looking for the notorious tape, were we?'

'We've instigated a proper search,' Ali says. 'So far the attic is definitely clear.' She glances at me.

'Could have told you that,' Guy says. 'Nothing up there but mice, cardboard and expanded polystyrene.'

'There were no mice,' Ali says.

'Stands to reason,' Guy says, and coughs resonantly. 'Rats and sinking ships and that.'

'Kit and I are looking through the second-floor rooms,' Hol says. 'Still a few more to go.'

'I checked one of the outbuildings earlier,' Paul says. This comes as a surprise; I didn't know he had. The others look like they didn't know this either. Paul shrugs. 'Just started; there's a lot of junk in there. I could get into only one of them; there's a couple still locked. Plus there's the garage, of course. And the shed.'

'Our Kit is the keeper of the keys,' Guy says. 'Apply to him.'

'Just let me know,' I tell Paul, who nods. Most of the house keys are on a single big loop that lives in the old electricity meter cupboard near the back door.

'Can't see how it'd be in the garage, though,' Guy says.

154

'That's entirely Kit's preserve, isn't it, our kid?' Guy smiles round at the rest. 'Probably covered in oil if it is, eh?'

Actually I keep the garage and the car as clean, degreased and un-oily as is practicable with a sixty-year-old wooden garage and a thirty-year-old car to work with.

'But it's lost,' Ali says. 'It could be anywhere. That's the point.'

'Yes,' I say, 'but it's just misplaced. It hasn't been deliberately hidden.' I look at Dad. 'That's right, isn't it?'

'If it's hidden, it wasn't me hid it,' Guy says. 'I thought it was with the rest of the old VHS tapes in the boxes behind the corner unit with the new TV. Or thrown out by mistake.' Guy nods over towards the corner, where the TV is, above our ancient combo player that accepts DVDs and VHS, though I can't remember the last time we played a tape in it.

'There's a box of old VHS tapes behind there?' Ali says.

'Are you not listening?' Guy says to her.

'We haven't checked there,' she says, getting up.

'I have,' I tell her.

'But feel free to double-check,' Guy says as Ali goes over to the TV and leans over it, supporting herself with one hand on the wall.

'Yes, there's boxes,' she says.

I've checked, double-checked and triple-checked, so it's not there – it isn't even in the dusty space underneath the corner unit, only accessible from behind – but I still get a little twinge of fear as I worry about it being there after all, and the possibility, however remote, that I missed it three times.

'Help me move this thing, will you?' Ali says, glancing back at Rob and Paul, who both get up to help.

155

'Mind me fucking telly,' Guy says. 'Might be mostly shit on it but it's my choice of shit.'

They angle the TV out of the way, then Paul, who's tallest, reaches down and starts pulling out the old shoeboxes. They're square-tied with string, so they're easy to lift.

They check each one, but they're all just ordinary old VHS tapes; big, clunky, mechanical-looking things from another age, as out of place as vacuum tubes and steam pressure regulator valves in our era of slim, shiny DVDs and effectively invisible downloads and YouTube streams. A handful look unused, but most have handwritten labels with names of old films and terrestrial-channel TV programmes on them.

'If you find any porn, leave it out; I'll take it,' Guy says, leering.

'Thought you'd nothing to play it on,' Rob says.

'That is, sadly, true in more ways than one,' Guy admits, suddenly gloomy.

'Hello, *9½ Weeks*,' Paul says, holding up one tape. 'That was a bit filthy, wasn't it?' He looks at Guy. 'That count as porn?'

Guy shakes his head. 'Not these days.'

'You got to love Fellini,' Haze says, shaking his head.

'No, that was *8½*,' Hol tells him. 'Different film.'

Haze looks hurt. 'I knew that,' he says. 'Classic film!'

'Well,' Hol says, 'some memorable imagery, and the usual Fellini juxtaposition of a stultifying but respected Catholicism with a bracing new modernism, but overrated. It's about a film-maker struggling to make a film. Please.'

'So did you vote for *Vertigo* as the best-ever film in the poll last year?' Haze asks her.

'Did they ask *you*?' Ali says.

Hol looks at Ali. 'They asked me,' she says. 'I did not vote for *Vertigo*.'

'Overrated, I suppose,' Ali says, picking up another VHS cassette, dismissing it.

'Lush, intelligent use of colour,' Hol says, 'but the plot's idiotic. That matters, in film. It's not fucking opera.'

'What did you vote for, Hol?' Rob asks.

'*Citizen Kane*,' she says. 'I'm a traditionalist.'

'That's very . . . conventional of you,' Ali says.

'Yeah, conventional. That's me.'

'So,' Paul says, 'do we know where *any* of the S-VHS-C cassettes from the old days are?'

'Yes,' Guy says. 'We do. They're in my bedroom. So are the DVDs with the digitised versions of some of the tapes.'

'But not all of them?' Rob asks.

'Not all of which?' Guy asks. 'The tapes or the digi versions?'

'Well . . . either; both.'

'I think I've got all the mini-tapes – can't see any are missing apart from the one we're looking for – and there's only six of the tapes never made it onto DVD.'

'Why didn't they?' Ali asks.

'Two, it was quality control,' Guy tells her. 'Earliest ones, they're crap. I was leaving them to the last, if I transferred them at all. Other four, we just never got around to,' he says, glancing at me. 'After the VHS player packed up we had to send them off to get transferred professionally and that costs money. I'd just been diagnosed and had to leave me job at the time, so it didn't feel like the highest priority. Excuse fucking me.'

He cracks open another can of beer. I wish he'd drink less. Visits to the toilet – visits where he needs help afterwards;

157

if it's just a pee he can usually manage that by himself – are always messier, smellier . . . splashier, frankly, after he's drunk a lot of beer.

'Just asking,' Ali says, holding up one hand.

'And the ones – the mini-tapes – they've all been checked, all the way through?' Paul says. 'The one we're looking for hasn't been mislabelled or anything?'

'It's not fucking there,' Guy says, emphatically, though the effect is spoiled a little when he has to cough.

'So do we have the trick VHS cassette that plays the mini-tapes?' Rob asks.

'No, we fucking don't,' Guy says, wheezing. 'That's quite likely where the mini in question is. Inside it. Maybe.'

'What about a working VHS player?' Rob asks. 'That thing under the screen work?'

Guy is drinking from his can, so I say, 'It wouldn't work the last time we tried to use it.' I shrug. 'I wanted to take a look at it, see what was wrong, but—'

'—you're not a qualified fucking electrician,' Guy says. 'Not having you burn the house down before the quarry company's paid us the compensation.' He shakes his head. 'Not having that.'

'So if we find this tape, or a tape we think might be it, how are we supposed to test it?' Ali asks.

'I've still got a working player,' Haze says. 'Ancient old thing; top-loader, but it still works.'

'Well then,' Alison begins.

'But it's back home, though,' Haze says.

'Well,' Paul says, putting the last of the VHS cassettes back into the shoebox. 'We use the VHS player and the converter VHS cassette I brought with me. They're in the car.'

We all look at him. He smiles. 'Got them on eBay last week,' he says. 'Always be prepared.'

'Yeah, dib-fucking-dob,' Guy says.

'Keeping that quiet, weren't you?' Rob says.

'Not really,' Paul replies. 'Just waiting till somebody asked, or it became relevant.' He shrugs, nods at Ali. 'Ali asked, so I mentioned it.'

'Oh well, at least we know we can check any tapes we do find,' Pris says.

'Right,' Ali says. 'Well then. We could double-check the ones you have in your room.' She's looking at Guy. 'Just to be sure.'

'If that would be all right,' Rob says, also looking at Guy after what might have been a glance of exasperation at Ali.

'Be my fucking guest,' Guy says.

'Let's see if this one still works, first,' Paul says, nodding at the combo player under the TV.

'Kit,' Guy says. 'Fetch tapes, will you?'

'Okay.'

'Imagine if paintings were produced the way Hollywood films are – the *Mona Lisa* as we know it would be only the first draft; nobody would green-light something so dull and dowdy. In the second draft she'd be blonde; in the third smiling happily and showing some cleavage; by the fourth there'd be her and her equally attractive and feisty sisters, and the landscape behind would be a deserted beach. The fifth draft would get rid of the sisters, keep the seaside but make her a redhead and a bit more, like, ethnic looking? In the sixth, after the equivalent of a script doctor had been brought in, she'd have dark hair again but look meaner and be holding an automatic, and by the seventh or eighth the seaside would be replaced with a dark and mysterious jungle and she'd be a dusky maiden – no gun – wearing a low-cut wrap with a smouldering, alluring look and an exotic bloom in her long black tresses. Bingo – the *Mona Lisa* would look like something you were embarrassed your grandad bought in Woolworths in the early seventies.'

Hol is looking at me. They are all looking at me. This is sort of by way of a subtle revenge, I suppose, though it is also a sort of confession, almost a declaration.

'You *memorised* that, Kit?' Hol says.

I just nod.

'Do you have an eidetic memory?' Ali asks me.

'I don't think so,' I tell her. 'I forget a lot.'

'Vouch for that,' Guy says.

'I don't know whether to be impressed, flattered or disturbed, Kit,' Hol says, smiling and frowning at the same time. 'I wrote that years ago. I certainly couldn't quote it that precisely.'

'You're assuming it is precise,' Ali says. She digs into her bag, brings out her iPad. 'What was it in?' she asks.

'I can't even remember,' Hol says.

'*Saturday Guardian* magazine,' I tell them. 'I don't know the exact date.' I do know the approximate date – June 2008 – but I'm back-pedalling a bit now.

'Would be the fucking *Guardian*, wouldn't it?' Ali says, tapping at the screen.

'Yeah,' Hol says, scratching behind one ear. 'The national newspaper *not* owned by right-wing billionaires, based overseas for tax purposes. Funny how that's regarded as the eccentric choice. Never quite got that.'

'Yeah, well, you wouldn't,' Ali says.

'Fucking hell,' Guy says, glaring at me. 'Do you know everything our Hol's ever written off by heart?'

'Of course not.'

'Is that the article where you told people not to go and see any film where the posters feature somebody holding a gun?' Paul asks Hol, grinning.

'I said it'd be interesting if people did that,' Hol says.

'Fat chance, eh?' Haze says.

Hol nods. 'Well, quite.'

'Got it,' Ali says, staring at the iPad screen. She looks up at me. 'Quote it again?'

I shake my head. 'It's kind of gone.' This is a lie.

'*What?*' she says.

'It'll come back again in a day or two, probably,' I tell her.

I get glared at. She shakes her head, looks back at the tablet's screen. I see her eyes flicking back and forth, side to side. Haze starts humming.

'Humph,' Ali says, and flips the screen cover over the iPad, stuffing it back in her bag.

Our own VHS player still isn't working. We've used Paul's machine to watch some of the old films they made, back in the day. As ever, mostly I notice how young and slim and sort of innocent they all look. I'm not sure how they see themselves. They seem partly embarrassed, partly proud. They find these little mini-features much funnier than I do, but then there are, apparently, multiple references I don't get that they do. Some relate to films I've never seen that they have, and some to their lecturers and fellow students.

'I'd forgotten our Hitchcock was called *Sicko*,' Rob says, as we watch a black-and-white film about a Social Security investigations officer coming to the house to try to prove that the main character's mother wasn't a real person – just a dummy in a chair – and so there was a benefit fraud taking place. 'We anticipated Michael Moore by twenty years.'

'We should sue,' Ali says.

'No copyright on titles,' Paul mutters.

'We never paid enough attention to the hairstyles, did we?' Hol says, her gaze fastened to the TV screen. They are all sitting rapt, fascinated, watching themselves.

'Anyway,' Hol says, after we've watched the last of the films Guy never got round to transferring to DVD, 'that's all the labelled mini-tapes.'

'Let's watch the blanks, check those,' Ali says. There are half a dozen of the mini-tapes that have no label. In theory this means they have nothing recorded on them.

'Yeah, on fast-forward,' Haze suggests.

'No kidding,' Ali says, putting the first of the supposedly still blank mini-tapes into the VHS converter, 'there's an idea.'

We sit watching a sort of busy black-and-white haze for a while. Then we watch another one. Even on fast-forward, this takes a few minutes. It feels longer.

'Well, this is very experimental,' Paul says.

'Christ, it's like watching a Béla Tarr movie,' Rob says.

'Heathen,' mutters Hol.

Over the years, Hol has got me to watch lots of films I probably wouldn't have seen otherwise. She's brought some on DVD when she's visited, recommended (a few) new releases or (quite a lot of) old films in reconditioned prints playing at Bewford's New Campus Regional Film Theatre – though I only ever actually go there if she or Guy drags me along because I hate walking into a cinema by myself – plus she emails or texts to tell me there's something worth watching on TV.

She got me to watch black-and-white stuff like *Citizen*

Kane (good surprise ending, though I didn't really know what to make of it at first, so I guess she's right that it bears rewatching); *The Wages of Fear* (nerve-racking but a bit preachy – we might have watched the wrong version); *Seven Samurai* (quite violent, though a bit long, and very *muddy*); *The Misfits* (not getting it, though we watched it together and it made Holly cry); *Casablanca* (good, and very funny, though I think I both impressed and annoyed her when I pointed out that when Rick refers to 'German seventy-sevens' in the Paris flashback montage, there was no such calibre of gun, and, even if there had been, it was laughable that even an arms dealer would be able to identify it or them from just a few distant rumbles. Probably the writer was thinking, vaguely, of the anti-aircraft gun turned anti-tank gun, the eighty-eight. Anyway, when some of the foreigners are called after cars – Captain Renault, Signor Ferrari – it's probably a sign that not all that much in-depth research has been done); *The General* (not just black and white but *silent*! But funny. And short); and *L'Atalante* (not just black and white but in French too, and which I still don't get. Though quite short).

Then there were films that she was surprised I'd missed but thought I might like, like John Carpenter's *The Thing* (ultra scary); the original *Point Blank* (bit weird and dated, but good); *Taxi Driver* (which I didn't really like); *Delicatessen* (weird – must be an acquired taste); *Chinatown* (only okay; not seeing it, though another good ending; Hol reckons Polanski is a genius and you just have to ignore the alleged sex-with-a-minor thing); *Fargo* (great, though neither of us can work out what the bit in the restaurant with her old flame is doing in there. Hol hearts most of what the Coens have done – apparently I must watch something called *The*

Big Lebowski); *Goodfellas* (bit rambling, but good); and *The Godfather* (brilliant).

Some films she really loves felt too long to me, like *Apocalypse Now, Lawrence of Arabia, Kagemusha* and *2001: A Space Odyssey* (I fell asleep).

Others I just struggled with, like *Les Amants du Pont Neuf* and *The Conformist*. She reckons she should have kept those back for when I'm older, like she's keeping back *The Leopard* (which is not about a leopard) and *Tokyo Story* (which at least is set in Tokyo).

She is mostly okay with the first two *Terminator* movies and the first two *Alien* movies, which is a relief because I love them.

We disagree a bit about *Die Hard*, which I secretly think is one of the best films ever. The only rubbish bit is John McClane falling even a short way down the lift shaft and saving himself by catching hold of the lip of the air vent with his fingers; that's implausible. Hol dislikes it for the unnecessary dead-bad-guy-comes-alive-again bit at the end, especially as Al, the squad-car cop, then gets to reassert his own lost manhood and respect through a gun, by shooting somebody (even if it is a bad guy). And also for the dire sequels (though *Three* wasn't too bad), though it's hard to see how that's really the fault of the original film.

We disagree a lot about *Star Wars*, which I love and she hates. ('Rick Blaine gets a gun calibre wrong by eleven milli-metres and you pound on him; these guys are duelling with fucking "light sabres" and *that's* okay?' she said. 'And what about the fucking Nuremberg rally at the end?' I was forced to point out firmly that the film's only flaw is using 'parsec' as a unit of time.)

Oddly, we disagree about *Toy Story*, which she likes more

than I do. I think with her it's partly a technical thing. I feel the film's unfair to Sid, the set-up-to-be-horrible kid next door with the teeth braces and the vicious dog. His mash-up toys were *much* more interesting and imaginative than the boring Andy's ordinary ones. Unless you really do believe toys come alive and have feelings, in which case, okay, he's a monster.

We also completely disagree about all superhero movies (including *Batman* movies, even though technically, like Tony Stark in the *Iron Man* films, he's not a superhero). I think they're brilliant and she thinks they're brain-rotting rubbish. No matter how good they are. I mean, that's just mental.

She has no time for Bond movies either, which I suspect is actually unpatriotic.

Never mention the *Carry On* films, and how maybe they're a bit underrated and a good laugh really. Especially if you're just repeating something you've heard elsewhere and can't even begin to defend such a position. Which is 'cretinous', apparently.

However – to end on an upbeat, life-affirming note – we agree on the wonderfulness of *Jaws, The Searchers, Leon, The Outlaw Josey Wales, Catch-22, Get Carter, The Untouchables, Pulp Fiction* and anything by Miyazaki – in fact almost anything by Studio Ghibli.

'Nah, they were mostly shit, though.'

'No they weren't. They were interesting.'

'"Interesting"?' Guy says with a sneer as I plump his pillows up for him. 'That the best you can fucking do? What next? Fucking "compelling"?'

'Have you taken this one?' I hold up one of the pill packets from the bedside tray.

'What? No. Who cares?'

'Well, you should,' I tell him. 'I care,' I add.

'I've just watched those abysmally shit films we made when we were young and stupid instead of old and disillusioned; I've lost the will to live. What is that one, anyway? I don't even recognise it. Are you sneaking in new pills for me to take just for the sake of it?'

This touches a nerve, because I have occasionally thought about sneaking some Imodium into his meds regime, just to give me a break. Though sometimes he gets constipated anyway, without any help. Which is a relief, until the log-jam breaks.

I look at the label on the pill box. 'Claristipan.'

'What's that supposed to do?'

'I'm not sure. Might be a white blood cell thing. You should keep the leaflets that come with these. You're supposed to.'

'They've started disappearing. I can't find them any more.'

'That's because I'm keeping them. I have a loose-leaf folder. I rescue the leaflets from your litter bin and flatten them out and put them in clear plastic envelopes.'

'Well then, *you* tell me what . . . Clovistipan does.'

'Claristipan. I don't think I've got the leaflet for this one. I could look it up on WebMD.'

'Oh for fuck's sake. Don't bother. I haven't taken it. Give it here.'

Guy swallows one of the capsules. 'Fucking pills,' he says. 'I'd rattle when I fuck, if I could still fuck.' He coughs. 'If anyone still wanted to fuck me.'

'What about these ones?'

'What about what ones?'

'These; Genhexacol.'

'That was the first one I took!'

166

'Oh. Yeah.'

'Are you just mentioning my fucking meds to try and distract me? Are you embarrassed when I get morose? Do you not know how to cope when I start sounding depressed? Is that it?'

'No, no. What about these? Chloratiphene.'

'Fucking stop it! One of the few pleasures I have left is wallowing in my own fucking despair. You want to deny me even that!'

'It's not good to wallow.'

'I don't have anything else to fucking do. I don't know what else I'm good for. Wallowing is all I've got left.'

'You have your friends here. You've been . . . you've been brighter, more lively, with them around. Talking more, even moving better.'

'Stimulating company. Makes a pleasant change.'

'There you are, then,' I say, ignoring the part of this directed at me.

'Just fucking guilt brought them here, anyway. Or thinking there might be some money in it. Hoping they'll be mentioned in the will. They'll be fucking lucky.'

'That might apply to Haze. I think the rest . . . Actually I think they're all here because they want to be. Even Haze.'

'Still guilt,' Guy says, settling back into his pillows and looking like he's getting himself comfortable. 'I fucking guilted them into coming here. Come and see the dying man. Roll up, roll up for your last chance. Make your peace, settle your scores, square your conscience . . .'

'It doesn't do any good, thinking like that.'

'What, being fucking realistic? Have I missed something? Did we get the all-clear last week and I've got no cancer whatsoever any more and you're still doing all this because you just like the routine, or you've developed a fetish for wiping my arse and don't want it to stop?'

'I'm just saying. It's better to try to stay positive.'

'Oh, fuck off—'

'Dad, even the oncologists—'

'I take the fucking point that if you have a choice of being negative or positive about something like this, you might as well be positive; can't do any harm even if it borders on self-delusion and happy-clappy fuckwittery, but there's a funny fucking thing about having terminal cancer – I mean, apart from the hilarity of all the pain and the weakness and the fear and the general humiliation of the disease *and* the fucking treatments . . .' He breaks off to cough. 'It makes it hard to be fucking positive about any fucking thing, with the notable exception of feeling positive that you're going to fucking die. A prospect that seems like a blessed fucking relief, some days: *that's* a positive result, something devoutly to be wished for, when the pain's bad and you look back on a life that you wish you'd known was going to be this short so you could have shaped it different, and look forward to just more pain and increasing disability and helplessness, with the ever-enticing prospect of confusion and idiocy lying ahead, if and when the fucking cancer spreads into my brain. Oh yeah; lot to feel fucking positive about there!' He's been wheezing through the last half of this tirade. He collapses into another fit of coughing.

'Well,' I say, 'like I say . . .' God, this feels lame. It's like he infects me with his despair when he talks like this. 'You have to try to stay' – I'm looking for another word instead of 'positive', which I feel we've kind of devalued now – 'optimistic,' I end up with.

'Yeah,' he says, wheezing again. 'You know why you're supposed to be so fucking positive? Do you?'

168

'Well, I think people just think that—'

'Because people are piss-scared. That's why. Because nobody wants this to happen to them, and so they think, Well, it just *won't* happen to me. If they're God-botherers they think it's because their made-up God loves them and they won't get it because they don't deserve it. If they're not God-botherers they just think that it'd be different for them. If *they* got a whiff of anything ending in "oma" they'd escape its clutches with one mighty fucking bound through the sheer power of positive thinking. So they tell you to think positively, as though that's going to help with a metastasising cancer rampaging its way through your fucking body.'

Guy breaks off, coughs again. He's looking sweaty, his eyes are bright.

'You might as well walk into a burning building and try to put out the fire through the medium of modern dance. But it means when you do lose your brave fucking battle – because it always has to be a brave fucking battle, doesn't it? You're never allowed to have a cowardly battle or just a resigned one; that'd be letting the fucking side down, that would . . . Anyway, they can secretly think, Well, fucker didn't think positively enough, obviously. If that had been me, *I'd* have thought so positively I'd have been fine; I'd be fit as a fucking fiddle by now and out publicising my number one best-seller *How I Beat the Big* C and appearing on chat shows and talking with Spielberg's people about the fucking film version.' Guy coughs again. 'So you don't even get to die in peace; you don't even get to die without the implication that it's somehow your own fucking fault because you weren't fucking *positive* enough.'

It's your fault you smoked! I want to scream at him. I can feel tears trying to well up behind my eyes.

169

Guy looks up at me, face flushed and glistening in the bedside light. I should probably take a facecloth to him. He smiles. Or maybe sneers. It's something in between.

'Oh, it is my fault,' he says quietly. 'Of course. Silly me. I smeuked tabs, diven I?' He puts on this fake Geordie accent sometimes. 'Smeukin tabs' – smoking cigarettes, and its variations – is a favourite phrase.

I feel my own face flush, as though mimicking his. I hate that he can read me this easily, that my own thoughts and feelings are so transparent to him. Maybe they're this transparent to everybody! That would be even worse. I look away, blinking a lot, and pick up another pill packet, and would ask him if he's taken these yet, but he's kind of closed that option off too.

'Do you fucking understand I don't fucking want to die?' he says. His voice is quiet, and shaking. This is sort of a relief; I thought he'd be shouting at me by this point and spitting inadvertently and screaming that people got effing lung cancer before smoking was invented, or didn't I effing know . . .

Okay, so he's not shouting, but I almost wish he was, because I kind of know how to cope with that, with the shouting and the spitting, however inadequately, but I don't know how to cope with this: this low, impassioned-sounding voice. I don't know how to cope with it at all.

'Who fucking does want to die?' he says, staring up at me. 'Until something in your life gets so bad you feel it's the only thing that'll stop the fucking awfulness?' He looks away, into the darkness at the far end of the room. 'I'm scared to fucking death, Kit. Not *of* anything; not of hell or any bollocks like that; just at the thought of not fucking being any more. It shouldn't *be* frightening – it's just returning to the state you were in before you were born, before you were even

170

conceived – but it is, whether you like it or not, like your brain can't accept it's not the most important thing in the whole fucking world, the whole fucking universe, and it's terrified that when it goes, everything does.' More coughing. 'I *hate* the thought of the world and all the people in it just going merrily on without me after I'm gone. How fucking dare they? I should have had another forty, fifty years! I'm getting short-changed here and it's not even as though any other bugger is going to benefit from the time I'm losing. Just lose-fucking-lose, all round.'

He looks up at me. 'Fuck me,' he says quietly. 'You're actually crying. Reduced me own flesh and blood to tears.'

I take a big sniff. 'I'm sorry,' I tell him. 'Least I know you are my dad.'

'Oh, don't start,' he says, sounding suddenly tired. Which is also better than shouting, and I suppose I have to admit I was trying to shoe-horn in something about my mother there, and finding out who she is. I feel suddenly ashamed that I even thought of exploiting his obviously fragile emotional state just to find out something I want to know. Though, at the same time, doing all you can to find out who exactly your mum is doesn't seem all that unreasonable.

'I'll tell you now,' he says. 'If I'd known it was all going to end this early, I don't know that I'd have accepted responsibility for you, lad. Took the best years of my life, looking after you.'

Hearing him say this gives me a bad feeling in my belly. 'Sorry to have been such a burden,' I tell him, trying to stop crying. Failing.

'Too late for that now, isn't it? And you were just a babe in arms anyway. Not your fault. It was that bitch of a mother of yours.'

171

'Don't talk about her like that. Please.'

'I'll—' he starts angrily, then glances up at me and, after a moment, sighs, letting out as big and as deep a breath as he's capable of these days. His chest rattles and he nearly coughs. 'Ah well,' he says. 'Yeah. Not your fault, and I . . . appreciate what you've done for me, what you've been doing, recently. Suppose it's unfair you get the brunt of everything. But you're all I've got, aren't you? Eh?' He smiles uncertainly and reaches out to pat me on the arm, though he doesn't look me in the eyes. 'You're a good kid. None of this is your fault any more than it's mine.'

Less, I want to say, but don't.

'Yeah, well,' he says, and goes, I think, to try to put one hand behind his head, but then stops, grimacing with the pain, and lets his arm flop down by his side again. 'Maybe I've been wrong,' he says, and sighs. (And, just for a moment, I think he means that maybe he's been wrong to keep the identity of my mother secret from me all this time, and he's finally going to make amends now, and tell me. But no; we're back to him.) 'I most certainly do not believe in hell, purgatory or heaven or any of that dreamed-up, sado-fantasist bollockry. However,' he says, holding up one skinny finger, 'I am prepared to be pleasantly surprised, following my death, because I don't think I've been *that* bad a person, and if you can't expect a bit of magnanimity and compassion from God, who the fuck can you expect it from? If God is supposed to be less forgiving than your average council care worker, fuck 'im; what use is the twat?' He tries a smile, grinning up at me.

I think, in his own awkward way, he's trying to lighten the mood. The sheen of sweat seems to have gone now. He'll just accuse me of fussing if I try to wipe his face.

I think I must have a blind spot where religion is concerned. I just don't get it. Either it's telling you stuff that's just provably not true – like the Earth being six thousand years old, for example, when there are tree-ring records that go further back than that (I mean, tree rings!) – or it's telling you stuff that it swears is true but that it has no proof of, like life after death. That's such a big claim you'd think there'd be some pretty robust proof out there, but basically there's nothing, apart from claims in old books about miracles happening; old books often written ages after the events they describe.

Frankly I'm fairly sceptical about what I read in newspapers printed yesterday, when everybody's memories are still fresh, so this ancient stuff was never likely to appeal. And miracles seem in short supply, too, these days. Unless it's the sort that people talk about when a school collapses and all the children are crushed to death except one, who's pulled from the debris and people call that a miracle, though then it's hard not to feel, well, if that's a miracle, couldn't God have tried a little harder and let two of them live? Or, better still, the whole class, or the whole school?

The kind of people who seem to believe they know how their God thinks just sort of smile – regretfully, but still smile – when you say something like this, as though you're some kind of simpleton, but I don't think it's anything to smile about.

I am uncomfortably close to Guy's point of view in this. The last time he threw anything at the television was when one of the thirty-three Chilean miners, who were trapped down the bottom of that mine for two months in 2010, said that their rescue had been a miracle. 'No it wasn't a fucking miracle!' Guy screamed. 'A miracle would have been the

173

arch-fucking-angel Gabriel suddenly materialising amongst you and enfolding you all in his mighty wings to transport you instantly to the surface and your waiting loved ones in a display of dazzling radiance! *You* were rescued by tens of millions of dollars, mining experts from around the fucking world, the mobilised resources of the whole of the fucking state of Chile, months of hard, grinding work, calculation and expertise and *heavy engineering*, you superstitious Catholic FUCKWIT!' Then he threw a book at the telly. A paperback, thankfully.

I don't like Guy thinking he's influenced me too much, so I didn't tell him that I mostly agreed with all of this.

Anyway, from what I've been able to work out, if you're going to claim that you know something, then it should be provable, otherwise how do you know you know it? Just being surrounded by lots of people who agree with you doesn't prove anything. (Well, it might prove quite a lot of things, actually, but not what you might like to think it does, and quite likely not stuff you're going to be comfortable with, either.)

And faith is just mad; it's like you have to leap to the end of an argument or discussion about something and act as though you've been convinced, even though you haven't been, and then, apparently – well, allegedly – it all makes sense. But what wouldn't, if you've already committed to believing in it? You might stick with any sort of nonsense out of sheer embarrassment at admitting you'd been taken for such a fool. If you're going to apply this faith thing to anything, then anybody can just believe whatever they please, and then who's to say who's right or wrong?

I reckon claims to knowing stuff need to be open to discussion and argument, and the person doing the claiming has to be open to the possibility of having to change their mind because they realise they didn't have all the facts before, or because a new explanation just works better, otherwise how can you trust them?

From what I can gather, though, this idea doesn't seem to fit too well with religion.

Lastly, I think it's a very good sign if the various areas of the stuff you know about sort of all fit together. Like biochemistry and engineering fit together, even though they're completely different fields, because they're linked by clearly provable physical laws and mechanisms that make sense and that demonstrably work. I've met some very intelligent people whose thinking is all joined up until you get to religion, and then it's like that's an area that's been fenced off as out-of-bounds, not subject to the rules about proof and likelihood – even plausibility – that they'd apply as a matter of course in every other area.

Which might not be so bad if it was some fairly trivial area, like which is the best football team or something, but it isn't; it's what they regard as the most important part of their morality – even their personality – and it's worrying that this is the one bit they want to leave free from rational inquiry. I'd have thought that bit ought to get the most thoughtful attention, not the least.

Guy sighs. 'But I think I know there's nothing, son; just oblivion.' He closes his eyes. 'Oblivion; nothing else.' He's almost whispering now. 'Though,' he murmurs, 'that said; if there is an afterlife, depend on it I shall come back and haunt you like a fucker.' Then his eyelids flicker, and with that he's asleep.

Not in this house, you won't, I think, as I turn out the bedside light.

5

'Oh, Kit,' Paul says as I go back into the sitting room. 'Thought you'd gone to bed.' Paul is kneeling at the table between the two couches. The mirror has been taken off the wall above the mantelpiece and laid on the table; Paul is chopping up lines of white powder from a small pile near the centre.

'Should have gone to somebody's room,' Haze says. 'Told you.'

'Too bloody cold,' Ali says. 'Knew we should have brought our own heater.'

'Blow the fuses,' Paul says, brow furrowed as he taps at the mirror.

'That's all right,' I'm saying, as Hol sits back in her couch, rolling her eyes, and Pris says,

'Hope you don't mind, Kit,' and Rob is saying,

'He's a grown-up . . .'

'You won't tell Guy, will you?' Ali says to me. 'He'll be upset.'

'Yeah,' Hol says. 'Though upset as in jealous, not disapproving. That'd be the rankest hypocrisy.'

'No, it's okay,' I tell them. 'Doesn't bother me.'

'This is definitely the time to do this,' Paul says, chopping away with a black credit card. 'When we have all day tomorrow to recover.'

'Never used to need time to recover,' Rob says.

Paul pushes a line carefully to one side, making it parallel with half a dozen others. 'Also, we've all been getting a bit drunk there; this'll sharpen us back up again.'

'Yeah, align our excuses,' Hol says quietly, watching Paul.

'I think,' Haze says, 'the least we can do is include Kit in. Don't you think?'

'What, rather than exclude him out?' Hol says.

'Yeah,' Haze says, looking at me. 'Only if he wants. Not trying to force anybody or anything. Just polite. You use somebody's space, you offer them a share. Etiquette. Guy being indisposed, asleep, whatever; falls to our Kit, doesn't it? That's right, isn't it, Paul?'

'Sure is,' Paul says. He glances up at me. 'Cut you in here, chief?'

'Play your own game, Kit,' Hol says quietly.

'Yeah, sure,' I say, squatting on my pouffe. 'I assume that's coke?'

'Yup,' Paul says.

'Oh, I've done that before,' I tell them. They all look surprised. Hol most of all.

'My last birthday,' I tell them. 'Guy got us some. We both did it. Said in the old days he'd have been expected to take me to a brothel but this would have to do.'

'Wow,' Pris says.

'That's our Guyster!' Haze says, shaking his head and grinning.

'I think in the old days the brothel visit would probably

have happened earlier than your eighteenth,' Hol says, looking at me oddly.

'Modern parenting,' Rob says.

'Still a lot of lines there,' Ali observes, as Paul chops another couple.

'Guy took some of this just a couple of months ago?' Hol is saying, frowning. 'How did that go down?'

'Not great,' I tell her. 'I think he nearly had a heart attack. I was going to phone for an ambulance but he wouldn't let me. He said afterwards he thought he might have found a good way to off himself when the time came; a couple of Belushi-size lines and his heart would just thrash itself to a pulp.'

'You're not actually intending to take any, are you?' Ali is saying to Rob.

'Why the hell not?'

'Because we agreed—'

'No, honey,' Rob says. 'We talked about this but we didn't agree anything.' His voice sounds like he is talking at a business meeting, to an underling who is a bit slow. 'You have to learn the distinction between us stopping talking about something after you've had the last word in the latest part of an ongoing discussion, and us actually coming to an agreement.'

'Woh-oh,' Haze says.

'My mistake,' Ali says, looking at Rob.

'Jeez, guys,' Paul says, running a licked finger along the edge of the credit card and then rubbing his gums. 'None of this is compulsory. Just a toot or two. Lighten up.' He looks up at Ali, Rob. 'Yeah?'

'It's just, there are issues,' Ali says.

'Oh, God preserve us,' Hol mutters.

'Ali thinks I might be enjoying myself too much,' Rob tells us, smiling.

'I'm worried for both of us,' Ali says, hugging herself. 'We don't sit back, either of us. That's just not who we are. We tend to just go for things. We don't wait for things to happen to us, we go out and happen to things. Which is fine in some areas – it's what got us where we are, it's what Grayzr values in us – but not so good in other areas.'

'Like fun, apparently,' Rob says.

Paul is rolling up a fifty-pound note, looking thoughtful.

'Like potential addiction,' Ali says.

'Really?' Pris says. 'You're worried about that? Genuinely?'

'Are we going to do the coke or not?' Haze is saying.

'I think it's something we need to be aware of,' Ali says.

'Ali has talked about AA,' Rob tells us, shaking his head and breathing out hard.

'NA,' Ali corrects him. 'Narcotics Anonymous.'

'Same diff—' Rob starts to say.

'You fucking serious?' Hol says. 'Treating a psychological weakness like a so-called disease and submitting to a "Higher Power"?' She does the finger-quotation-marks thing. 'Fuck that. That's evangelism disguised as self-help.'

'It is a disease,' Ali tells Hol. 'You wouldn't understand. People don't when they haven't experienced—'

'Oh, wouldn't I?' Hol says. 'I had an ex went down this greasy path. He liked a drink. He liked drinking so much he preferred it to doing more than the absolute minimum at work or in his relationships. I was stupid enough, in lust enough, to think I could change him, but I couldn't. Eventually he decided he was an alcoholic; took refuge in this idea it's a disease—'

'It *is* a disease,' Ali says again.

179

'Nope,' Hol says. 'Bilharzia is a disease. Multiple sclerosis is a disease. Malaria is a disease. Weird sort of fucking disease you stop in its tracks by a simple act of will. All you have to do is reach for the glass' – she does just that, lifting her glass halfway to her lips, then replacing it on the table by the edge of the coke-decorated mirror – 'but then put it back down again. Same applies to smoking, or overeating. Just stop. Make the decision. Keep on making the same decision. Not saying it's easy, not disagreeing it's better to do it as part of a group if you are going to do it, but in the end it is just a decision; a neurological event inside your brain. Just decide.' She snaps her fingers. 'So-called "disease" over.' She lifts the glass again. 'Try that with bilharzia. Cheers.'

'It might be a different sort of disease,' Ali says. 'It's still a disease.'

'No it's *not*,' Hol says. 'It's a condition. It's a decision you keep on making to behave in a certain way rather than in another way. You can call it a psychological weakness or a lack of willpower if you like, but you can't call it a disease without making the word basically meaningless. You're insulting everybody who has a real disease by calling it one.'

'I'm guessing you and this ex didn't last very long if this was your attitude to giving him support,' Ali says.

'You guess correctly,' Hol informs her. 'He swapped one crutch for another: half-hearted alcoholism for half-witted, happy-clappy Christianity. Took up strumming his way to salvation in one of those big old north London churches where they think replacing the pews with beanbags is doing the work of the Lord.'

'So it did *work*,' Ali says.

Hol shakes her head. 'Nah, not for long. Last I heard from him was when he rang me up to tell me he'd decided he

180

actually was a sex addict and did I want to hook up later in a vodka bar?'

'Tell you what; I'll have yours,' Haze is saying, nodding at Rob as he sidles into position alongside Paul.

'Will you, fuck,' Rob says, grinning. He accepts the rolled fifty from Paul and bends over the mirror.

Ali looks at Hol and says, 'Thanks,' with a sneer as Rob snorts first one line, then another.

Rob sits back, offers the little paper tube to Ali. 'Sorry; should have been ladies first, I guess. You partaking?'

She snatches the note from him. 'Suppose I'd better stay in touch,' she says, pivoting towards the mirror. 'Hold my hair back.'

'*No?*' Paul says to Hol. 'Seriously? After all that?'

'Just making my point about disease and addiction,' Hol says. 'Wasn't committing to hoovering the marching powder.'

'I'll have yours, if you like,' Haze says.

'What?' Ali says, sniffing hard. 'You decided you might have a problem, Hol?'

'No,' Hol says. 'I just don't want to give money to the sort of people who produce – well, distribute – this stuff. I wouldn't wear fucking blood diamonds either.'

'It's a fucking *moral* thing?' Rob says, laughing loudly.

'Yeah,' Hol says, 'it's a fucking moral thing.' She sighs. 'I *like* cocaine. I'm good on cocaine. We get along very well, me and cocaine, and, one day, maybe, I hope, I'll get to start doing it again; if they legalise it and tax it and it's not distributed by murderous scumbags with dollar signs in their eyes. They make the fucking vulture fund operators look like hospice nurses.'

'I wasn't going to ask for a contribution, Hol,' Paul says,

tapping the note on the mirror, dislodging a little coke. He nods. 'This is just fun amongst friends. With my compliments.'

'You know what I meant,' Hol says.

'Also,' Paul says, handing the note to the waiting Haze, who swoops in immediately, 'I think you're doing a disservice to my dealer. Anybody less like a coked-up, ultra-capitalist, murdering nut-job is hard to imagine. If he was any more laid back he'd fall over. Backwards, obviously.'

'What?' Hol says. 'Does he travel out there himself and source it direct from a fair-trade cooperative of artisan bio-certified coca-leaf farmers?'

Paul frowns. 'Actually I think this stuff comes via FARC or somebody like that. They're the anti-government side, anyway, whatever their name. The guerrillas. This stuff funds the comrades.' He's looking up at Hol, who is gazing back down at him. 'Seriously,' he says.

'Uh-huh,' Hol says.

'That's good stuff,' Rob says, sitting far back in the couch and breathing in deeply. He looks at Ali. 'That is good stuff, isn't it?'

Ali nods, sniffing hard. 'Yes. Yes it is. It's good stuff. Very good stuff.'

Pris, who snorted after Ali in a very delicate, tidy, ladylike manner, is sitting with her head on the back of her couch, looking almost straight up at the ceiling. 'Mm-hmm,' she says. 'Missed this, have to say.'

'Fell for that line, did you?' Hol asks Paul, grinning.

Paul shrugs, offers the note to me, eyebrows raised. 'Just telling you what I was told, Hol. Didn't even ask for it. My man volunteered the information, unprompted. Didn't seem at all sure I'd approve, seemed to think I might refuse the deal, demand charlie produced by the right-wing cartels in league with the cops, army and torture cells or something.'

I take the cocaine, a line up each nostril. It tastes of almost nothing. I think the stuff Guy and I had was cut with crushed-up painkillers or something. This is much better.

I manage to snort without coughing or sneezing or banging my knees off the table and upsetting the mirror or anything. I nod to Paul, return the note, put my head back and sniff hard to keep the drug in there, then return to my pouffe.

'Sure I can't tempt you?' Paul says, offering the note to Hol. There are four lines left. 'All bought and paid for,' he tells her. He smiles round at the others. 'Suspect it'll all be going this evening, no matter what.'

'Yeah,' Rob says. 'Not releasing any unused stuff back into the wild.'

Haze giggles at this. He's rolling a joint.

'Also, I just wouldn't lie to you, Hol,' Paul says quietly.

Hol takes in a deep breath and then sighs heavily. 'Ah, what the fuck,' she says, and quickly unfolds her legs and sits forward, accepting the note.

'That's our girl,' Ali says. Hol ignores her, though I gain, anyway, the impression that what was meant to sound sarcastic ended up coming out almost affectionate. Or maybe the other way round.

Paul takes the last two lines and mops up the last little remnants, some with the note and some with a moistened finger, applying it to his gums again. Haze joins in from his side of the mirror.

Paul sits back. 'Hoo-*wee*!' he says, to the background of a lot of sniffing.

*   *   *

'The trick is to contra-rotate,' I tell Pris.

'What,' she says, 'you have to pirouette while you're stir-ring?'

'No! Not you; the teaspoon, and so the tea! I usually count eight rotations clockwise, then a brief pause, then seven the other way—'

'Not eight?'

'No, cos you're counting down, see? There's less undissolved sugar to stir into the tea by now. Then, after the seven anti-clockwise . . .'

'I *took* the train! Twice. I got the same racist fucking taxi driver both times,' Hol is telling Rob.

'You sure it was the same guy?'

'Positive! Asked where I'd come from and when I said London he fucking went on about how London had no real Londoners left in it any more, just people from "all over", and there were schools where the main language wasn't even English any more, it was Bengali or Pakistani, and how he blamed everything on the Somalis; there were streets in Newcastle where there was nothing but all these Somalis who couldn't speak a word of English but they were living the life of bleedin Riley on all these benefits and we should send them back where they came from and all our problems would be solved.'

'That is a bit old school.'

'I thought he was trying to have a really bad-taste laugh, I thought he was trying to be a local Borat or something. I was looking for the concealed cameras. I asked him, seriously: the country's bumping along the bottom after we baled out the fucking greedy, corrupt, incompetent bankers, while the poor are hammered and the rich have their taxes cut and he

184

blames the people who can't even vote, who have the *least* power of anybody?'

'And?'

'Yeah, he said that was about right. Get rid of the lot of them.'

'Good God.'

'I told him I felt exactly the same way as he did.'

'That'll have confused him,' Paul says. 'Just confused me.'

'About people like him; I'd kick out all the racists and the EDL shitheads. Ha!'

'What's EDL?'

'Jesus, Rob . . .'

'Then you can do surface stirring,' I tell Pris.

'What?'

'That's when you've put too much milk in your tea and there's hardly room even to put the teaspoon in, let alone stir the tea with it once it is in there.'

'Oh.'

'You've put the milk in but you've put in too much so the tea looks wrong.'

'Looks wrong?'

'Yeah, it looks like a brain or something.'

'A brain?'

'Or any folded organ compressed within an outer membrane, I suppose, but you know when you see a brain – a human brain, because they're the most folded, I think; not a mouse brain or something because they're almost smooth, but a human brain, with all those foldings on the surface?'

'Oh, right. Yeah.'

'Well, the tea looks like that, with these sort of pale areas – really volumes, but you know what I mean—'

'Uh-huh, uh-huh.'

'These sort of pale folds of milk slowly turning over under the surface tension of the tea within these borders of darker tea, and it just looks wrong, it looks evil!'

'Evil?'

'Yeah! Just evil! Disturbing!'

'I've not paid enough attention to my cuppa, clearly,' Pris says, looking concerned.

'This has to be after you've stirred the sugar in, obviously.'

'Obviously. Though I don't take sugar.'

'Never mind. But the thing is this technique won't have any significant effect on the main body of the tea, or the tea/ sugar layered mixture if you haven't done the main stirring.'

'Contra-rotating, naturally.'

'Of course.'

'So what is surface stirring?'

'You just blow gently across the surface of the tea; it's that simple.'

'Really?'

'Yes. Though you need to blow across to one side, if you know what I mean, not across the middle, to get a bit of circulation going. That's important.'

'Important?'

'Yes. It stirs the tea and milk together so it looks normal and you can drink a little of it, and then once you've done that of course there's room to get a spoon in now because of the reduced volume in the cup, if you need to, though you shouldn't need to, and that's surface stirring.'

'Wow.'

'No, but I just feel we didn't really give ourselves a proper chance. We bailed on each other too soon.'

'Haze, you were together for eleven years. How much longer did you need?' Ali says. Haze is talking to her and Paul. I'm listening in while Pris nips to the loo.

'Yeah, but it was a short eleven years.'

'What does that mean? How can you have a short eleven years?'

'I just mean it felt shorter—'

'You can have a short lunch-break, or a short weekend—'

'Instead of a long weekend, like this,' Paul says.

'That's just a weekend, isn't—'

'You can have a short *life*,' Paul says. 'Like some kid with leukaemia or something, but—'

'I'm just saying—'

'You can have a short holiday or a short summer, I guess,' Ali says. 'With any one of those you can find yourself looking back after they're over and thinking, *That went quickly, that went like it was really short, I really feel like I almost missed that entirely it went so fast*. But a short decade; in fact, a short decade-and-a-bit—'

'One point one decades,' Paul says.

'Yeah.'

'All I was trying to say—'

'I don't see how you can have a short one of those. That's just too long. That's not feasible. Won't fly. You're not even the same person after eleven years; you'll have changed, as a person.'

'Yup.'

'Well, it felt short to me.'

'Maybe so, but, like, really?'

'*This* is feeling long.'

'What is?'

'This. Me trying to tell you how I feel Pris and I never

187

gave it enough time to make it work. I feel like we were just on the cusp, you know? But she just . . . bolted. First with this Statoil guy—'

'Statoil? I thought he was called Bergquist—'

'Hernquist—'

'He *works* for Statoil—'

'Oh.'

'Then with this Rick guy.'

'Yeah, well . . .'

'Another thing I like to do is to do different things with my left hand and my right hand at the same time, while I'm making the tea,' I tell Pris when she returns.

'Really?'

'Like, I'll be stirring the tea—'

'Contra-rotating.'

'Naturally. And at the same time I'll use my left hand to open the fridge – because you can reach the fridge from the bit by the draining board where I do the tea – and take the milk out and close the fridge door with my foot and there's a way you can hold the milk carton so that you can grip it in one hand and unscrew the top at the same time, though obviously it can't be brand new because taking off the foil seal under the twist-off cap on a brand-new carton can't be done one-handed, so it has to be already started. But, see, the point is—'

'Kit?'

'What?'

'I'm getting bored with all this stuff about making tea.'

'Yeah, I know! It is a bit boring, isn't it? I think I'm boring myself. Thanks.' I take a big slurp of tea. I made tea for everybody; a great big pot.

188

'You're like Rick and his fishing.'

'I've never fished. Is it fun?'

'Not for the fish, I'm guessing.'

This makes me laugh.

'Also,' Pris says, 'not for the person having to listen to interminable tales of working out which fly is best in light rain under bright overcast as opposed to intermittent soft showers with a darker overcast and a changeable breeze, in autumn.'

'Should we get Guy up?' Rob says. 'Let him have a choice, have a chance to join in?'

'Why?' Haze says. 'Do you think we're making too much noise?'

'Are you crazy?' Paul says. 'The poor fucker's had an exciting day by his standards. Right, Kit?'

'Are we being noisy?' Pris asks.

'It has been strenuous,' I tell Paul and Rob. 'Just being up and awake through most of the day, and having so many people to talk to, I mean, you guys in particular, with so much to catch up on, and he has been looking forward for months to you being here, well, weeks at least, and then meeting new people, well, a new person – Rick – and then the whole thing with the tower; that'll have exhausted him, even though he was the one in the chair, for sure.'

I think I've just startled myself. Right there, I said 'for sure', and I never say 'for sure'; it's just not in my vocabulary, or at least not in my normal phrase-choice drop-down/pop-up menu or however you want to express it. Bizarre.

'We're not being that noisy,' Haze is saying. 'We're not, are we? Are we? We might be. But are we?'

'I don't know,' Pris says.

'Let the poor bastard sleep. Besides,' Paul says, gesturing to the mirror on the table, 'this stuff might be too much for him. Could kill him.'

'His heart really did react badly the time we tried it – I tried it, we did it – for my birthday,' I tell them.

'Guess it's how he'd like to go, though,' Rob says, staring at the small remaining pile of white powder. There's probably enough left for one last blast each. I wonder if that's it, or if Paul's got some more stashed away somewhere else he's not telling us about.

'Oh, that would look great,' Paul is saying to Rob. 'We turn up, get him ripped, his heart gives out and the cops show up.'

'We should turn the music down,' Ali says, looking at the dock where Haze's iPod is playing stuff like Happy Mondays and No Doubt and Oasis and Madonna and the Stone Roses.

'Why should the cops show up?' Rob asks.

'The cops?' Haze yelps, head jerking as he looks from the door to the window and back.

'Because we'd have a fucking dead guy on our hands?' Paul says to Rob, then turns to Haze. 'No cops, Haze,' he says calmly, 'no cops; just talking about if Guy pegged out on us while we're here. Purely hypothetical.'

'Yeah, but we wouldn't call the cops, we'd call an ambulance,' Rob says.

'I'll turn it down.' Ali gets up and turns the music down.

'When you have a corpse under retirement age involving sudden death, the medics will tend to want to call out the cops,' Paul says (Pris is nodding). 'Which might prove awkward for us if we're all pinging hysterically about A&E, babbling, with white powder lining our nostrils, and pupils like tunnels.'

190

'Aww,' Haze says. 'Ali!'

'Sh!' Pris tells him.

'So, no?' Rob says. 'We're not getting Guy up?'

'Very bad idea,' Paul tells him.

Rob sighs and runs a hand over his smooth scalp.

I shake my head emphatically to Rob's question, then nod equally vigorously to Paul's statement.

Rob looks over at the iPod, frowning. 'Music's gone quiet . . .'

'Kit! We need some thread!' Rob says.

'I'll get some!' I tell him.

Pris has been telling me about something totally fascinating called a Tea Tool so I've missed the context of the thread being required but it seems to involve Haze, and Ali covering her mouth with her hand and making an odd squealing noise.

'And olive oil,' Haze tells me.

'I'll get that too,' I tell him. 'Wait a minute; we only have groundnut oil or rapeseed oil or—'

'That'll do.'

I fetch these, then I have to go and wash my face so I go and wash my face in the sink in the downstairs loo and then I think I ought to go and have a quick look outside for some reason so I go and do that – everything's fine; hint of rain but some stars too, temperature still mild, though according to the forecast this is all just a respite and there's more heavy rain coming later in the night/early next morning – and when I come back Haze is sitting with a party popper in his hand and his tongue out the side of his mouth as he carefully pulls the little string away from the end of the popper – too gently to set off the party popper – and then starts tying a length of thread onto the string.

191

'I didn't know we had party poppers,' I say.

'Haze brought them,' Hol tells me.

'You really going to do this?' Ali says.

'Why not?' Haze is saying, tying off the extension to the party popper cord. He inspects his handiwork. 'Hmm,' he says. 'My loose ends are a bit long. Anybody got a pair of scissors?'

They all look at me, but Ali is reaching into her bag and bringing out a dinky little pair of scissors. Haze uses them to cut the ends off the knot; he does this again on another party popper he's already prepared that I hadn't spotted until now, then lines up the two pieces of thread and cuts them both to the same length. Then he gets some oil from the groundnut oil bottle I brought through and smooths it over both stretches of thread.

'The oil's an innovation,' Rob says. 'This your concession to Health and Safety, Haze?'

'Yeah. Thought I ought to do my bit.'

'Oh, Haze,' Pris says, shaking her head. 'This still your party piece?'

'Don't pretend you're not impressed,' Haze tells her, coating the threads with more oil.

'Definitely not pretending,' Hol says. Pris snorts.

Then Haze is snorting. Not more cocaine; the thread. He lies back on the couch with his head over one end and his nostrils pointing almost up at the ceiling, and he's feeding the lengths of thread into his nose; one up each nostril, then, once they've disappeared for about half their length, with much huffing and snorting—

'I can't watch this,' Ali says, looking away. 'This is so gross.'

'Nah,' Rob says, sitting forward to see better, drinking some more wine. 'A chap should have a hobby.'

—Haze leans forward and, holding the two party poppers near his chin, both in one hand, sort of coughs and makes throat-clearing noises until both lengths of black thread appear out of his mouth.

'Oh, yuk,' says Ali, who's glanced. She looks away again.

'You absolutely sure these are the same bits of thread you just snorted up?' Hol says. 'There could be a lot of shit up there.'

'Watch and be amazed,' Haze says. He lies back the way he was before, with his neck in a convex curve and the bottom of his nose pointing at the ceiling; he pulls the threads slowly out of his mouth until the bottleneck ends of the two party poppers disappear into his nostrils, then winds the ends of the threads round his index fingers. The threads seem to be slipping easily through the gaps between his molars, lubricated by the oil.

'Nutter,' Paul is saying, though I think he sounds affectionate.

'I can't believe you're still doing this,' Ali says.

'Fire in the hole,' Haze says. His voice sounds like he has a cold. He pulls sharply on the two threads.

Both party poppers explode, releasing little ribbons of coloured paper almost straight up into the air. The bangs are only slightly muffled.

'Yay!' yells Ali, clapping.

'Woo-hoo!' says Paul.

I look back at the door to the hall, worried about all this noise waking Guy up, but it's okay; I remembered to close it and he sleeps really soundly with all his medication.

Haze levers himself upright through the thin cloud of smoke and falling streams of multicoloured paper – it's like the spaghetti of confetti, I realise suddenly – and slowly pulls both party poppers out of and away from his nose, string and thread trailing damply after the spent bodies of the poppers. He's coughing and his face has gone very red. 'Ta-*dah*!' he says, then coughs some more.

'Doesn't that *hurt*?' Hol asks him.

'A bit,' Haze confirms, nodding, voice hoarse.

'Probably not advised if you're a wine taster,' says Paul.

Hol is shaking her head slowly as she contemplates Haze. 'Or, just . . . rational.'

'Best to do it after some coke,' Haze tells us, then coughs again. He points at his nose, which has started leaking clear snot like thick tears. 'Anaesthetises.'

'On which note,' Paul says, sitting forward and taking up his credit card. 'Thinking you should go first here, Haze.'

'Cheers.' More coughing and spluttering. 'Anybody got a hanky?' The smoke smells acrid.

Hol frowns, nods. 'Snot's turning red, dude.'

'Nah. 'T's okay. Meant to do that.'

Rob is looking intently at Hol, some time after we've all stopped sniffing. Mostly. The coke is all gone.

'I have no idea what you're talking about,' he tells her.

'Try listening, harder.'

'Oooh . . .' says Haze.

'Try explaining, better,' Ali says. She has been listening to Hol and Rob, leaning closer, looking like she wants to say something, for a while.

'Hey,' Rob says to her.

'Well,' she says.

'I'm calling it miraculist thinking,' Hol says. 'This is sort of my own term but if you can think of a better one, feel free.'

194

'Miraculist thinking,' Rob repeats.

'It's partly linked to millenarianism, but only partly,' Hol says.

'That's to do with hats, isn't it?' Haze suggests.

'Miraculist thinking,' Hol says, 'is that which assumes that only one of our ideas or behaviours – society's ideas or behaviours, humanity's ideas or behaviours – really needs to change, or be changed, to somehow suddenly – miraculously – make everything okay.'

'Such as?' Rob asks.

Hol shrugs. 'At its crudest it's the *Why can't we all just pull together?* argument.'

'That's hardly an argument,' Ali says.

'That's more of a plea,' Rob agrees.

'Why *can't* we all start being nice to each other?' Pris suggests.

'So, we all start following the same religion or something?' Paul suggests.

Hol nods. 'All religions are essentially miraculist, though they postpone until after death the instigation of the eventually-okay state that they promise, neatly skipping the requirement to back up such extraordinary claims with even ordinary proof. Marxism—'

'Oh, shit,' Ali says, sitting back, 'here we go.'

'Marxism,' Hol continues, looking at Ali, 'for all its clear-headedness and determination to be scientific, has been used as a miraculist crutch, and libertarianism is the new Marxism. To the extent they're miraculist, or are used in a miraculist manner, they're wrong.'

'Yeah, but what the hell has this got to do with romantic love?' Rob asks.

'Yeah,' Ali says.

'All I'm saying,' Hol says, 'is that the same belief – that if only everybody would believe in this or behave like that, everything would somehow come right: that there'd be no more of all the bad stuff, or at least an absolute minimum of it – is closely related to the idea of romantic love and that . . . that conviction that if only this person will love me, will agree to us being together – for ever – then my life will be perfect, and all will be well. You know; happy till the end of time, till the mountains crumble into the sea, till the rivers turn to dust, etcetera, blah.'

'So now you're shitting on love?' Ali says, folding her arms.

'Well,' Hol says, 'how often does that actually happen?'

'Well, hey,' Ali says, suddenly taking Rob's hand, 'I guess some of us are just lucky.'

Rob lets his hand be held, but is still looking at Hol.

Hol sighs. 'Yeah, but even after you're together with your perfect person – and I'm very happy for the two of you, obviously,' she says, with a smile directed at both of them, 'you still have to accept you continue to live in the real world, and there will always be problems in it, and even perfect couples – who, obviously, do completely exist – have arguments and disagreements and, at the very least, *risk* growing apart over time.'

Ali narrows her eyes but doesn't say anything.

'And this relates to *Independence Day* how?' Rob asks.

Hol rolls her eyes. 'Via Jeff Goldblum defeating the entire invasion of Earth with a bit of viral code on his clunky old laptop, delivered by a purloined, bad-guy space-fighter and the piloting skills of Will Smith. *Star Wars* and *The Lord of the Rings* indulge the same fantasy, only a little less outrageously. We all know it's total hokum, but deep down it's how we'd really love all our wars ended and our problems solved, with something as trivial but as crucial and absolute as a few lines of code or a shot down an exhaust port or the dissolving of a ring in magma, and I'm saying that it's very similar to this belief that if we can only find the right person, our mythical other half, all our personal issues will be sorted. They're both examples of miraculist thinking and they're both bollocks. As is the belief that some new piece of kit is going to change everything, suddenly and for the better. As is the belief that some new political theory will magically transform us into nicer or just more productive people.'

'You sound very disillusioned,' Ali says, nodding.

'So? Who would choose to be illusioned?' Hol asks.

'Well . . .' Pris says.

'Okay,' Ali says. 'I meant bitter.'

'What I'm saying,' Hol says again, just starting to sound tired, or at least as though she's struggling to be patient, 'is that there's never the equivalent of one little switch in the shared human psyche that can be thrown; there is no single line of code that – if only it were rewritten or corrected – would make everything okay for us. Instead there's just the usual slow but eventually steady progress of human morality and behaviour, built up over millennia; instead there's just the spreading of literacy, education and an understanding of how things really work, through research and the dissemination of the results of that research through honest media.'

Haze makes a noise like, 'Phht!'

'Everything,' Hol says, '– print, radio, television, computers, digitalisation, the internet – makes a difference, but nothing makes *all* the difference. We build better lives and a better world slowly, painstakingly, and there are no short cuts, just lots of improvements: most small, a few greater, none . . . decisive.'

'Remember when we spent three days running round half

of London trying to find a Wii?' Rob says to Ali. She frowns at him. 'Before Christmas, whenever it was,' Rob says.

'I remember we *got* one,' Ali tells him.

'Yeah, but in *Croydon*,' Rob says.

'Croydon,' Ali agrees, and shivers.

'Well,' Rob says, 'that was a bit like that, remember?'

'No,' Ali says instantly. 'I don't think it was like that at all, actually.'

'No? That feeling of needing that Wii,' Rob says. '*So* badly. And I've felt the same thing with the iPad and the Kinect when we couldn't get hold of them immediately either. Whatever the latest shiny new toy is. That feeling like an ache, like love, like an addiction.'

'Whoa,' Haze says, shaking his head. 'Back to drugs again. Tsk tsk tsk.' He's building a large joint on the mirror. He still has a twist of paper hanky stuffed up each nostril, though he's stopped coughing.

'It feels,' Rob is saying, 'like there's something wrong with the universe, or at least our lives, if we don't get it, soon, now. This thing, whatever it is.' He nods at Hol, looks at Ali, who is glaring back. 'And you get it and it's brilliant – it's so *new* – but then comes the comedown, sooner or later; the realisation that everything hasn't changed and you stop using it so much, and you realise it wasn't that great a gadget after all, or at least there's another, better one coming along soon, if you can only get your hands on one.'

'Well,' Ali says sharply, 'I fucking loved that Wii.'

'You loved the boxing game, hitting seven kinds of shit out of my Mii,' Rob says.

'And I love my iPad too,' Ali continues, 'and it's made a *huge* fucking difference to my life and I have no idea *what* the hell you're talking about.'

Pris yawns. 'I just want to say that I suffer from all the above.'

'Tired?' Paul asks her.

'Head full of snoozicles,' she says, stretching, 'though no idea if I'll be able to sleep.' She pulls her jumper back up from where it's slipped down her shoulder again. I think I caught a glimpse of some side boob there.

'Right,' Haze says. His voice still sounds very nasal. 'I've built this really strong joint, right? Aware of this wired-till-noon effect, so this is the antidote. If we all smoke this,' he says, holding the joint up in front of us, 'it'll precisely counteract the effects of the charlie—'

'Precisely?' Paul says.

'Precisely,' Haze says, nodding once. 'It's been carefully calibrated. It'll totally knock us out and reset our body clocks back to something like normal. Trust me.'

'No,' says Ali.

'Count me in,' Paul says. 'Though we do have all day tomorrow. Like I said. Cunning plan.'

'There's tobacco in that,' Ali says.

'Not all that much,' Haze says. 'It's mostly dope.'

'That's all right then,' Pris says, stretching again, and laughing. Her hair catches the light, a nimbus round her face.

'No,' Ali repeats.

'Nor me,' Pris says.

'Tobacco hurts my throat,' I tell Haze, when he looks at me. His shoulders slump.

Then he sits up again. 'Or,' he says, 'through the wonders of numerical deconstruction, I could turn this into a bong.'

'That's miraculist,' Rob observes.

'You'd need a bong,' Paul points out.

'I have a bong,' Haze says. 'In the car.' He waves the joint at us. 'What I want to know is, is it worth my time taking apart this beautifully and robustly rolled jay, this thing of beauty, and going out to the car and finding my bong and then taking the dopal contents and making—'

'The *dopal* contents?' Paul asks, grinning.

'Yes,' Haze says, nodding, 'the dopal contents, rather than the tobaccoidal contents of this here joint; taking them and making them into the contents of a bong bowl?' He looks round at each of us in turn. 'Are you with me? Are we together, compadres? Do we have a Fellowship of the Bong?'

'So, to be clear,' Paul says, 'no tobacco.'

'Correct,' Haze tells him. 'Zero tobacco. I will carefully separate one from the other.'

'Fair enough.' Hol nods. 'You talked me into it.'

'Yes, all right,' Ali says.

'Then that sounds like a feasible way forward,' Paul agrees.

'Yup,' Rob says. 'Nominal.'

'Suppose so,' Pris says, raising both arms above her head. 'Regret it in the' – she glances at her watch – 'later,' she says. 'But then that's sort of the tradition, I suppose.'

'I'll get some ice,' I tell them. I've seen Guy use a bong.

In the Rushlaan mountains there lies a Quest, the Quest of Metalarque, in the Liquile gorge. Somewhere beyond the gorge, beyond its ancient, teetering, half-fallen bridges, wind-abraded scramble ropes, worn climbing chains and crumbling, rusting brackets, beyond its howling, never-ending force of wind, beneath those impenetrable skies, beyond the mazes of flooded tunnels and half-awash, vertiginously pierced cliff galleries, and on the far side of the bestiary of ferocious guard-Revenantaries – so quick, when they kill you, that you barely have time to see them properly, leaving you with only a frozen glimpse of blurred mouth-parts scissoring shut – there lies a treasure, encased, according to the rumours, in a jagged fortalice of black diamond, and guarded by something so big and fast and powerful it preys upon the Revenantaries.

The goal, the treasure, at Quest's End, is unspecified, but the signs – spread geographically far and historically deep across the whole of HeroSpace – indicate that it must be of the first order. A Pax, a weapon of Absolution, an Imperator-level promotion, a Propagating ChronoSeam, or perhaps even something so potent, so unprecedented, that nothing like it has ever been seen before in HeroSpace. Perhaps the fabled Game-ender (a chilling, ludicrous, almost unthinkable thought), or – perhaps, and there are plenty of rumours to support this outcome too – just nothing: a Quest with an empty treasure chest at its end, or one holding only a slip of parchment with some sarcastic or dismissive message on it, to prove the vanity and idiocy of all Quests; a Quest to draw the most gifted, skilled and competitive away from all other, productive Quests, to leave space for less talented others.

Of course, the knowledge that the laborious, time-, strength- and morale-sapping heroics required to advance in the Quest of Metalarque may ultimately lead to nothing at all – may lead, in fact, to you looking like a dupe, like a fool, subject for evermore to knowing smirks and muttered jibes in taverns throughout the realm, perhaps even with a new, unwanted, unSecret Name – or that it may lead to the end of the whole game, the collapse of the whole world (however unlikely this may seem, especially given the revenues generated by the game for its creators and owners), is itself one of the most effective disincentives to pursuing what would be a dauntingly difficult, fiendishly challenging and just plain off-putting Quest even if you were absolutely assured of great treasure and vastly increased powers following its completion.

Hol nods, when I explain all this. 'That's a doozy, all right.' She pushes a hand through her shadow-black hair.

We're sitting in front of my main screen, set between the canted mirrors of the old dressing table; Hol's laptop sits on the raised side of the table. I've let her use my seat while I perch on my laundry basket. It creaked a bit when I lowered myself onto it but I don't think it's actually going to collapse. That would be humiliating.

We may be the last ones up. The coke might finally be wearing off and the narcotic effects of the final bong have sent all of us to our rooms, possibly even to sleep. I told Hol I'd probably stay up for a little longer, just to keep in touch with HeroSpace. I haven't played it in nearly twenty-four hours and I feel funny if I don't spend even just half an hour in-game each day. I won't be able to accomplish much – I'm too tired and feeling too slow – but there is, anyway, just a comfort in being back in there, just to hang out, all heroic efforts and accomplishments aside.

Currently, in such moments of relaxation, I've been manifesting in a feasting hall in Slaughtresgaard, mostly playing dumb-chance dice games and virtually drinking the local ale – which does interesting and uncontrollable things to one's vision – though also trying to track down a rumoured MovePass that might just help with the Metalarque Revenantaries. The MovePass is supposedly held by a bad-tempered dwarf who chills here, but he's partial to games of chance and might be persuaded to part with it for the right wager.

Hol said she'd like to see this – Slaughtresgaard is out-Law, and historically a bit tough and mean with Voys, who generally get used for target practice, so she'd never been – and so here we are; me on my computer, Hol on her laptop.

I do something a little underhand, letting Hol enter the hall significantly before me, so that it's not obvious we're together. The place is busy, with maybe a hundred avatars present, most of them probably real at this time of night rather than staffers and spear-carriers generated by the game itself – it's the wee small hours in dear old Blighty but it's prime evening playing time for West Coast American gamers.

Hol heads blithely for the bar while I pace a couple of steps behind her. Hol is a neat, trim figure in furs and fairly minimal cured-leather armour, lightly armed with a hand-blade hanging from each hip. She isn't tall, lithe, pneumatic or even Amazonially statuesque (like the barmaids here are). Instead she presents – sensibly for somebody at her level – as someone who wants to blend in, not attract attention. Her handblade scabbards are buttoned, which is akin to displaying a Peace badge, hereabouts.

My longsword sheath doesn't even have a button, and I keep it greased. This is about my eleventh or twelfth longsword; I've sold the rest for good money back in the real world. Serious, high-provenance, multi-kill swords look great and shout threat, but the truth is they don't make that big a difference; a good swordsman with a generic, off-the-shelf sword from a low-rep blacksmith will skewer a newbie toting the best steel money can buy, every time. It's like tennis rackets; if you're an average club player you can have the finest, highest-tech, carbon-fibre racket on the market, but it'll make no difference if you come up against somebody like Roger Federer; he could probably thrash you using a coal shovel.

Anyway, Hol patently presents no threat, but in a place like Slaughtresgaard that doesn't mean you won't get threatened. Arguably it almost guarantees it. And of course her attribute, skill and experience status are on show for all to see – you have no choice, as a Voy.

And attract attention is exactly what she does, almost immediately, while she's still a step away from the bar and marvelling at the giant snakes curled sleeping inside the glass bar top. (The snakes are there in case things get too rowdy; the staff just open the customer side of the cages and let the snakes out. The reptiles are kept hungry, so the place tends to clear pretty quickly; stops people smashing bottles off the counter tops too, on the rare occasions when the weaponry peace-bonding rule is actually being enforced.)

– 𝕽𝖔𝖚 𝖍𝖊𝖗𝖊 𝖙𝖔 𝖒𝖊𝖊𝖙 𝖘𝖔𝖒𝖊𝖇𝖔𝖉𝖞? Hol is asked, by a tall, thin, black-clad guy who looks suspiciously like Neo in the *Matrix* movies, even down to the shiny black shoes. (There are a lot of these guys about. Still.) He's presenting vaguely as a necromancer, but de-chromed, in the parlance; exact status hard to determine. Could be anything from a lowly wizard's even-more-lowly assistant to a TrueMage, though obviously we're meant to assume closer to the latter. I think I know how the rest of this exchange is supposed to go: Hol says . . . well, almost anything, and then he says something like, **𝕭𝖊𝖙𝖙𝖊𝖗 𝖍𝖔𝖕𝖊 𝖞𝖔𝖚 𝖒𝖊𝖊𝖙 𝖙𝖍𝖊𝖒 𝖘𝖔𝖔𝖓, 𝖑𝖎𝖙𝖙𝖑𝖊 𝖑𝖆𝖉𝖞** (or something equally rubbish), while he works up the gumption to knife her. Also, it's hard to treat somebody seriously when they insist on expressing themselves in **𝕲𝖔𝖙𝖍𝖎𝖈𝖐**. I mean, really.

'Whoa,' Hol says, over a stifled yawn, 'am I being hit on here, or threatened?'

'Threatened,' I tell her. In the game, I remain a couple of steps back. 'Ask him who he is, why he wants to know.'

– *Who wants to know?* Hol types (in a rare font I don't recognise).

But that's already too aggressive. Before Neo the Necromancer can reply – possibly by just knifing her without further ado – I flit forward and I'm suddenly at Hol's avatar's side, my left bicep touching her right shoulder, my gauntleted right hand resting easily on my belt buckle, mailed fingertips almost but not quite touching the pommel of my sword. (I'm still using a matched pair of Pro-level joysticks; people have claimed the Wii and the Kinect work better, but I disagree; for now at least a good set of joysticks gives superior accuracy.)

– She's with me, I tell Neo. (I use a *very* understated font. And I keep the size as small as you're allowed; the time it takes for somebody to have to peer more closely at their screen, or readjust the settings at their end, might be the difference between getting the first blow in or not.) I signify a smile, but I also give him a narrow angle on my full status.

He smiles back, after a moment. – 𝕬pologies, sir, he says. 𝕻lease: he offers me a contact, which I deign to accept because there's no need to be rude, even if I'm highly unlikely ever to need somebody like this. – If I can ever be of any help . . .

(I just nod.)

To Hol's avatar he says,

– 𝕷ucky, and then disappears. Not disappears as in disappears into the crowd; disappears as in disappears in a puff of smoke. Necros are prone to doing this.

Hol looks at me, in reality. 'Did we just avoid a Mos Eisley Cantina arm-getting-lopped-off scene there?'

'Sort of,' I tell her. This is pretty much exactly what I was hoping for (though at the low-violence end of the spectrum), and I feel elated and proud, because I protected her, and yet also a bit low and conniving for having set it all up in the first place. Had we swaggered into the hall side by side, only some nutter with a death wish would even have dared speak to her.

'Think I'm out of my depth here,' she tells me. 'I'm cutting out. You're the big beast here. I'll just watch you, from outside.'

'Your choice,' I tell her. Hol logs out.

I cut to the chase, quitting the feasting hall and dropping straight into the last place I got to in the Metalarque Quest. 'This is how big a beast I am against these guys,' I tell her ruefully. My avatar is standing in the gloom of a tunnel deep in a maze-mine hidden behind a waterfall. I kick open a door of pitted wood and rusting iron.

Usually in HeroSpace when you kick down a door the best technique is to charge straight in, before the splintered wreckage has a chance to bounce. I tried that here the last few times, though, and discovered you just get chomped by something on the other side you can't even see (lanterns, even shielded ones, have long since blown out, all lamp filaments melt at the threshold and even luminosity coatings stop working). This time I step to one side and wait to see what might emerge.

Something piano-black and shiny that might owe a little to the alien in *Alien* – but with two extra, very long, toothy heads where the arms would be on anything remotely humanoid – comes tearing out of the darkness and immediately engages. I'm experimenting with a metal-mesh throw-net, and chuck that over the bastard. Amazingly, this seems to work, slowing it down long enough to give me a chance to skewer it with my longsword. Only I'm too slow, reaction times degraded, and I miss the opening as its heads and grapple-limbs thrash, and it gets me, biting off my sword arm at the elbow.

I hit pause, sigh, log out, sit back.

'That is one mean motherfucker,' Hol breathes. 'Those things *common*?'

'Unique to the gorge, far as I know, far as anyone's telling,' I tell her. 'Which is kind of extra-daunting. Still; progress,' I say. 'Now I know the net works. Nobody'd mentioned that.'

'Trade secret?' Hol asks.

'Yeah, I guess.' The Metalarque Quest is, by the nature of the rumoured rewards as well as just the way the consecutive challenges are set up, strictly a solo affair. Only further rumours or outright – and unwise, or untrue – boasting gives you any idea how far others have got in the adventure, and what techniques they employed to get there.

'Do you keep a note of stuff like that?' Hol asks.

I nod. 'I keep a log,' I tell her, 'though mostly it's just a duplicate of what's in my head.' I pull open the drawer in the dressing table where I keep my notebook, then close it again, feeling foolish.

'What, written down?' Hol says, sounding amused, I think. Definitely smiling. 'That's very old school, isn't it?'

It's true; I keep a written log. I am almost superstitiously suspicious of storing anything so sensitive and valuable on the machine. Getting hacked is fairly unlikely – a lot of people Hol's age seem to assume that as soon as you become proficient at games like HeroSpace, you somehow automatically become a brilliant computer hacker too (a bizarre leap I've never under-stood) – but you can't be too careful, I reckon. The communi-ties of hackers and dedicated Players certainly overlap a bit, and while it's difficult to see how you could apportion enough time to do both to the required standard of excellence in either, it would take only one guy able and prepared to cheat like that to ruin or just steal what I've spent years building up.

'Well, you know,' I say, feeling awkward.

'May I see it?'

'Um . . .'

Hol touches me on the forearm. 'I suspect I'm still at the stage where none of it will mean much to me, hon, if you're worried that I'm going to cheat with it. But if you—'

'No, no; it's okay.'

I open the drawer, hand her the book. It's A3 size; two hundred pages, lined feint. It's mostly full. Hol leafs through it, eyes widening. 'Blimey,' she says. 'This is . . . comprehensive.' She smiles at me. 'Wow. Detailed. Thorough.'

'That's Volume Two,' I tell her, grinning despite myself.

'Jesus.' She riffles through the last half, the pages making a gentle noise like a stuttered sigh in the gently lit room. She hands the book back to me, putting her other hand to her mouth as she stifles a yawn.

'Most of it's just a log of what I've done,' I tell her. 'But there's, um . . . some analysis.' I have maps, on graph paper, too, which might seem like overkill, given that there's an automatic mapping function in the game anyway, but sometimes I like to double-check; you never know. Anyway, I don't show her those. They really are geeky.

'Hon,' Hol says, 'you could teach this game.'

'Oh, I don't know,' I say, and feel myself blush. I put the book back in its drawer.

'I haunt the HeroSpace forums, too, sometimes,' Hol tells me. 'Subtract the jealousy and sour grapes and there's a lot of respect for you in there. You're an expert in the field. World-renowned, Kit. Come on, now; no false modesty. You know this, you need to acknowledge it.'

'Yeah, well,' I say, blushing harder now. I'm glad the light is subdued in here. 'Those forums are full of a lot of . . . stuff,' I finish lamely, words failing me. Actually, it occurs to me, it's more the other way round; me failing words. I touch some possibly imaginary dust off one of the joysticks.

I'm aware, from the corner of my eye, that Hol is looking at me.

'I hope you haven't given up completely on the idea of going to university,' she says.

Hol has been gently pressuring me to think about tertiary education for the last four years at least, since I started getting good exam results (*some* good exam results – my record's patchy).

'Ah, you never know,' I tell her.

'Are you still thinking about it?'

'I think about it occasionally,' I confess.

'You could do it,' she says. 'I bet you could. I know you could. I know you think it's daunting, but . . . If you stayed around here, somewhere familiar . . . And Bewford would take you. Definitely. And you'd get support. You just have to not be shy about asking for it.'

'I don't know about that,' I say, and clear my throat. Actually there is a fair bit of dust in some of the folds of black rubber or whatever it is joining each of the joysticks' handgrips to the main body.

'I don't know about that, sor,' Hol says in a quiet, deep voice.

'Thank you, Ra—' I start to say, then correct myself. 'No; that was Ted, wasn't it?'

'Uh-huh,' Hol says.

'Ah.'

'Well, keep thinking about it,' Hol tells me. 'You got the grades, kid. Might be a waste not to.'

'It'd be a lot of work,' I say. 'And we haven't really got the money.'

'You should have, though, shouldn't you? From the house?'

'Maybe. Guy still talks about debts that have to be settled first.'

'Debts how big?'

'He won't say.'

'It's wrong he keeps you in the dark like that, Kit. He needs to tell you. He's got an obligation. You're his son, for God's sake. You have enough to worry about, with him dying, without that sort of uncertainty too. God, he's such a schmuck sometimes.'

I can hear the wind getting up, whispering round the edges of the house.

'Yeah, well. That's another thing, isn't it? Our form's not great in this family, finishing uni courses.'

I glance at her. I know she's supposed to be plain, but she looks so beautiful in the soft light of the screen saver. My screen saver consists of a proliferating three-dimensional maze of pipes; they start from nothing at some random part of the screen, then gradually fill it before vanishing, to start all over again. This iteration happens to have gone with a yellow colour scheme, lighting Hol's face with a golden glow a bit like you used to get from old-fashioned incandescent bulbs. I have to look away.

'Yeah, but that's Guy,' Hol tells me softly. 'You're you. Guy's just your dad. You don't need to be like him.'

'Might help if I knew who my mum was,' I say, and feel my mouth go suddenly dry.

'Maybe,' she says. 'But maybe not. Come on, Kit, you know how inheritance works; we're never just a fifty-fifty mix of whatever our parents are like. Some people are the spitting image of one of their grandmothers, or are "just like" some great-uncle; most of us don't differentiate out into some . . . parts list of attributes all traceable back to our immediate ancestors. It just doesn't work like that. You're your own man.' She sighs, rubs my upper arm with one hand. 'I know you want to know who your mum is, but . . . If and when you do find out, it probably won't solve any problems, apart from the . . . the just not knowing. You need to realise that, hon.'

I smile as I glance at her and try to sound jokey as I say, 'It's not you, then?'

Whatever Hol's next word was going to be catches in her throat. 'Excuse me?' she says, through a sort of brief, plosive laugh.

'Yeah, didn't think so!' I say, probably a bit too heartily.

'Oh, hon,' Hol says, hand squeezing my arm. 'You didn't really . . . ?'

'Well,' I say – and now I'm *really* blushing; I'm probably out-luminescing the screen saver – 'it did occur to me as, you know, just a theoretical possibility.'

I can't tell Hol that Guy told me she, Pris or Ali might be my mother, because I promised him I wouldn't, but I reckon it's plausible I might have thought of this myself. Having a reputation for obsessive-compulsive behaviour, Asperger's and/or taking things too far can come in useful.

'Could even have been any one of you, just in theory, like. You all went different ways after graduating. Didn't all meet up again for a couple of years.' I clear my throat again. 'I looked all this up, Googled, Facebooked, so on.'

Outside, it has started raining again. There's a damp rattling sound as a sudden gust throws drops against the main window of my room.

I glance at Hol. It looks like she has a sort of catch on the skin between her eyes, over the top of the nose, like it's material that's been snagged and pulled together. 'You were in Voluntary Service Overseas in Kenya,' I say. 'Pris was doing a post-grad year at Starmer Christian Ecumenical University, Missouri, and Ali was . . .' My voice trails off. My throat is quite dry.

'On the pampas, twirling her bolas and herding cattle on some distant relation's ranch,' Hol says.

I cough. 'Something like that. Supposed to be making a nature film but nobody's ever seen it.'

'Yeah,' Hol says, after a moment, with a big, heavy sigh. 'It was a good eighteen months . . . certainly at least a year, year and a bit, before we met up again, here. By which time you were indeed around. Guy's bouncing baby millstone, as he described you.'

'So. Just, like I say, in theory . . .'

'One of us could have nipped back here and dropped you on Guy's doorstep.'

'Put like that . . .'

'This was Guy, wasn't it?' Hol says, resting one elbow on the dressing table and settling her chin into her palm.

'What?'

'Guy suggested this. Guy said it might have been one of us.'

'Why would he say something like that?' I say. My voice has gone high, without me meaning it to. This is unbelievably annoying and embarrassing. I stare at the screen. The whole thing is full of yellow pipes. Oh shit, it's going to—

The screen goes black. Well; that deep, dark grey that we call black on a screen and think is black, until we compare it to real blackness. A tiny squared-off worm of crimson starts squiggling round near the centre of the screen, quickly starting to build up a red-themed pipe maze like a demented Technicolor Etch-a-Sketch. My face is burning. I'm glad humans can't see infrared.

'What a shit that man can be,' Hol says, through a sigh.

'If he had said anything, um, like that, and I'm not saying he did,' I say, already feeling miserable, 'then he would have made me promise not to tell anybody. Um. I'd imagine. And so, well . . .'

Hol pats my arm. 'Yeah, yeah, I get it. You haven't broken any promises, Kit.'

I have to clear my throat again. Maybe I'm coming down with a cold.

She sits back, folds her arms. 'It's none of us, Kit. I suppose, in theory, it would be possible, but it just isn't. It certainly wasn't me – it just wasn't – and I know Pris and Ali too well. They couldn't have kept that a secret; they were never that good at acting.'

'Well,' I say.

'Guy,' Hol says, 'was the star of our films.' She shrugs. 'Amazingly, quite a gifted actor. Though, inevitably, he really wanted to direct. Thought he was by far the best director of all of us.' She shakes her head. 'Actually he was entirely the worst. Just mannered, pretentious . . . no touch, all gimmicky camera-work . . . Hopeless with actors.' She taps me on the shoulder. 'Definitely not me, and I'd bet anything it wasn't Ali or Pris. Guy's fucking with you, Kit. He should be ashamed. Arsehole.' She looks away.

'*Please* don't say anything to him!' I ask her.

'Okay,' she says. 'Promise. But still. What a shit.'

'Oh well,' I say, cheerily, 'maybe my mum is a countess or something after all.' Again, I already feel I'm overdoing the breeziness, but I don't know how to modulate this properly. Using the twin joysticks to turn, step back, parry a blow and counterstrike all at the same time is easy in comparison.

'Told me it was a Traveller girl from Ireland,' Hol says.

'That's one of the others,' I confirm.

Hol is silent for a moment, and I listen to the noise of the rain, settling in now, growing heavier, then she says, almost as though just to herself, 'I suppose we could all have DNA tests done. Still can't believe it'd be either of them, though.'

'Well, anyway,' I say, sitting forward and feeling keen to change the subject. 'I might still go to uni. You never know. We'll wait and see. Probably best to take a sort of gap year anyway. I won't let Dad's bad example put me off.' I glance at Hol. Her face looks flushed now, lit by the increasing amount of red on the screen. 'And I'll *definitely* try not to get anybody pregnant.'

It's supposed to be funny, but Hol isn't laughing. In fact she isn't even smiling.

'Guy very nearly graduated, Kit,' she tells me. 'Came within a whisker. We all tried to help him. Even Ali, who was showing signs of advanced over-competitiveness, even then. We all did. And we almost succeeded. *He* almost succeeded.'

'Ah. Not the impression he gives.'

'I bet. Well; I know.' She shakes her head. 'Right at the end, after all those extra terms, those repeated years, those extensions upon extensions, those missed deadlines and those hilariously late essays, after all the times he was too stoned or too drunk or chasing after women, he was pretty much one viva away from a Desmond; really only had to turn up.'

'One what away from a what?'

Hol smiles. 'A viva; viva voce; an extended, formal, oral exam. I don't know about now, but at the time even the most tooth-squeakingly modern bits of Bewford like the Film and Media Studies department felt they were somehow not treating the educational process with appropriate respect unless they used archaic Latin terms . . . Anyway, Guy was, despite his best . . . his worst efforts, very close to getting a Two-Two. Hardly a golden apple, or any sort of glittering prize, but at least it would have been a result of sorts; something to show for all that time and effort. Mostly the effort of others, but still.'

'What happened? Did he forget to turn up?'

'No,' Hol says. 'He just had other priorities, as it turned out.' She nods. She's frowning, and I think she's pretending to indicate that this might even have seemed reasonable. 'It took me a *lot* of convincing of his tutor just to get the bastard his appointment,' she says, nodding, eyes wide, 'but in the end . . .' Her frown returns, deepens. 'Actually, I can't remember: he either buggered off to Orkney to watch a particularly fine display of the aurora borealis or he jumped into the hearse with his board to take advantage of some totally tubular Atlantic swells coming ashore at Newquay. He told me both stories within a couple of weeks at the time and I never did find out which was the truth. If either. And absolutely the funniest part, he thought, was that when he got to wherever it was, he got drunk instead; missed the Northern Lights or the monster surf entirely.' She looks at me, shrugs. 'He wasn't here or hereabouts; that was all I knew.' She shakes her head. 'Your dad's a feckless waster, Kit. If they'd done courses in Applied Indolence or just How to be a Complete Twat he'd have strolled a First and Honours without even having to study. It's no coincidence that the best thing that ever happened to him – that'd be you – was a mistake. He doesn't deserve you. I mean, you don't deserve

215

him, either, but you deserve better; he doesn't deserve you at all.'

'I, well, that's,' I say, and then have to look away.

'Sorry. I've embarrassed you,' Hol says.

'Well . . . But, thank you,' I say, moistening a finger and wiping the folds of the joystick clean of yet more dust.

'Okay,' she says. She yawns again. 'I really need to get to bed now. It's . . .' She looks at her watch. 'Officially stupid-o'clock.' She runs a hand through my hair, scratching the top of my head. When I turn to her she's grinning. 'Play your own game, Kit. Don't do or not do anything just because of what Guy did or didn't do.'

She stands, putting her hand to the small of her back and arching her spine, making her breasts suddenly prominent, outlined through the tautened material of her shirt. 'Feel free to learn all the lessons life spent so long trying to teach him that he never bothered with, but don't let him . . . shackle you. Okay?' she says, relaxing again, letting her arms hang by her side.

I nod. 'The opposite of lesson is moron,' I tell her.

This makes her laugh. 'Something like that.'

She leans down to kiss me on the forehead. I let her, then raise my head, look at her. I stand up, taller than her, put my arms round her, hug her gently. I can feel her arms round my back, her breasts pressing into the place between the top of my belly and the bottom of my chest.

'Goodnight, Holly,' I say, then push back slightly and look down at her. She's got that same puckered-brow thing happening, and opens her mouth. So I kiss her.

She sort of lets me, and I try slipping my tongue slowly into her mouth, but then there's a pressure on my shoulders as her hands push back at me and a vibration as she tries to say something or at least make a noise, then she's pulling her head away and to one side.

'Whoa, whoa, whoa,' she's saying, and I'm holding her tighter now, pressing myself against her. I have a fairly serious erection and I bring myself forward, pushing into her so she can feel it. She pushes harder with her hands, though, and I have to let her go or it'll start to feel like we're wrestling or something. I'm still holding her, and she's still resting her hands against my shoulders, but we're otherwise disengaged. 'Kit, honey,' she says, very softly, 'what do you think you're doing?'

I look at her, frowning. I wasn't aware that what I was just doing was really open to more than one interpretation. 'Sorry,' I say. Mumble, more like.

'Oh, sweetheart,' she says, reaching up and touching my cheek with one hand. I want to catch that hand, kiss her wrist, have her respond, catching her breath, biting her lip. But I don't. She shakes her head, smiles, even laughs a little. 'I shouldn't even be slightly tempted.'

'So you are, then?' I say, pulling her forward a little again.

'Yeah, well, you're pretty cute when you get to know you, but, Jeez, Kit . . .'

'I haven't . . .' I start to say. I need to clear my throat again, so I do. 'I'm sorry if I'm being, well, whatever. It's just I haven't done this. This is all new for me. I'm still, you know, a virgin, technically.'

'Oh, honey,' Hol says, with that same frown/smile combination. She touches my cheek again; tenderly, I think, but probably, I'm guessing, not the right sort of tenderly. 'Trust me, your time will come, but maybe not with somebody old enough to be your mum, huh?'

'Yeah; and I'll definitely believe you're not my mother if . . .' I pull her a little closer still.

'*What?*' She laughs, then slaps me on the front of my shoulder with the back of her hand. She's still shaking her head, grinning broadly. 'Yeah, you really are your father's son, aren't you?' She snorts. 'Try anything, work all the angles.'

'I just think you're very, really . . . sexy.' Damn! I thought my brain was leading up to something better than that! I've sort of rubbed my groin against her a bit as I said that too, and she looks down.

'Whoa,' she says again. She even reaches out, touches, briefly holds my erection through my combat pants, giving it a squeeze. 'Fucking hell, Kit; you didn't get *that* from your old man.'

'Well, it's all yours if—'

'Now, just . . . just stop that,' she says, pushing away again and folding her arms, looking up at me. I'm still holding her, but it's starting to feel awkward now.

'It's really sweet you think I'm "sexy", but so did your dad, twenty years ago. That—'

'That was twenty years ago.' My, that almost sounds adult.

'Yeah, but if I – if we . . .' She shakes her head. Emphatically, I'm sorry to see. 'That would be a new . . . be a new some-thing for me. Low, high, I don't know, but it's not somewhere we're going, Kit. Sorry. Kit, I—'

I look down, between us. My cock feels, if anything, encour-aged by this slow, kind, ongoing rejection. The swirling camo design looks like it's emphasising the size of my erection.

'Yes,' Hol says. 'That's very, that's . . . that's quite, but . . . you should . . . Can you put that away? It's distracting.'

I reach into my pocket, get a hold and pull my cock up so that it stops sticking straight out and nestles against my belly instead, at least partially restrained by the elastic of my underpants.

'Thank you,' Hol says. 'Kit, I love you like . . . an auntie, I guess. I think Pris feels the same. Maybe even Ali. Though I guess she hides it well. But . . . Oh, honey,' she says, sighing, coming forward and hugging me now, though with her head turned to the side, across my chest, as though she's trying to listen to my heart. 'Ah, wouldn't it be great if sex was just sex? Eh? But it isn't. Well, sometimes it is, when you just bump into somebody, just for an evening, a night, and you both know that's all there'll ever be, or – maybe – the start of something, but . . .' She looks up into my face for a moment. 'But that's not where we are, hon. That's not where we're starting from.' She puts her head back against my chest. I wonder if she can hear my heart, hammering, urgent. 'We've known each other too long.'

'Established in our roles,' I say. It comes out more morosely than I'd meant.

'I like being your friend, Kit. I want to keep on being your friend. For the next twenty years, the next forty. However long.'

'It's because you changed my nappy, isn't it?'

She laughs, tightens her arms round my back, squeezing. 'Yeah, that'll be it.' She looks up at me. 'You had the tiniest, cutest, little plump pink bum, then, and a tiny, *tiny* little willy.' She holds up a little finger, waggles it. She pushes away, slaps me softly, open-handed, on the side of the shoulder. 'And *haven't* you grown?' Another pat on the shoulder. 'Well done. But now,' she says, with another yawn, which she stifles with a fist, 'I really need to get to sleep.' She steps back, bends at the waist, sticking her rear out behind her, one leg coming forward like a ballet dancer as she bows, arms out. 'Goodnight.'

'I'm really sorry,' I say.

219

She shakes her head as she straightens. 'Well, just don't be. I'm sort of flattered, and you behaved like a gent.' She wobbles her head a little. 'Pretty much.' She grins. 'So don't be sorry. Sorry is how we'd both have felt in the morning, or even before, if we had.'

'Can we keep this between the two of us, as well?' I mutter, looking down.

'Yeah, of course. What the hey. Enough secrets in this house. One more makes no difference. You sleep well, hon.' She heads for the door, then out, closing it quietly.

I look back at the dressing table. The screen saver reaches saturation point again, disappears. For an instant, before a little green squiggle starts in one corner, I can see the reflection of my face.

Somewhat to my own surprise, I'm smiling.

6

I go for my walk round the garden. It's nearly noon but I haven't seen any signs that anybody is up yet. I've looked in on Guy – still fast asleep, breathing normally – opened the dishwasher and unlocked the front door. All the cars are where they were last night.

It's dry for now, though the garden is damp and the skies to the west, where the weather is coming from, as usual, look dark and heavy with more rain.

Earlier, I took our old combi VHS player up to my room from the lounge to take a look at it. An internal fuse had blown; I fixed it in ten minutes and by far the longest part of that time was taken up with removing and then refitting the case. I put the player under the telly, checked it worked and disconnected Paul's machine.

I feel a bit hung-over, though not badly. I drank a lot less than everybody else last night, but then I'm not used to drinking very much in the first place. I probably had the same amount of cocaine as the rest, and about half as much of the bong. Dad says it helps to be young, too; you can grossly mistreat your body long into the night and still wake up bright-eyed and bushy-tailed the next morning in a way that just isn't possible once age has started to take its toll. So he claims; he might just be making excuses.

The familiar route round the garden is soothing, my feet falling easily into the little hollows I've worn over the years. I've put a gilet on over my T-shirt and farmer's shirt, because it's chilly. I had a shower this morning, again. That's two in two days, which is way more than I'd normally have even in summer, when I might actually get sweaty. Sometimes in winter I don't bother for up to a week, and even then it's my increasingly bedraggled hair that finally forces the issue. But after Hol said I was a bit whiffy when she first arrived and I got that initial hug, I've started showering like a girl. Ah well.

I waited a good ten minutes last night, just in case Hol changed her mind and crept back into my room and slid naked into my bed, but she didn't. Still, just thinking about this meant it was only about another thirty seconds before I was ready to roll over and go to sleep.

One of the outhouse doors is hanging more open than it needs to – it never shuts completely – probably because one of the others has been looking in there for the tape. I lift it and push it to, wedging the door against its frame so it won't bang in a strong wind.

I think we're okay, Hol and I. I probably shouldn't have tried what I did, but – oh, for goodness' sake – I've still to start properly, and even amongst the less than A-list male teens back at school (some of them, frankly – even making allowances and trying to be kind – distinctly unprepossessing) there was a majority who claimed they'd had sex, and a majority of that majority who said they were pretty much sexually active on a regular, ongoing basis.

I don't think I have any illusions about my own fitness, either physically or as a repository of this slippery quality of 'coolness' (I don't have any), but, again, even allowing – allowing hard – for that, this just seems unfair. If these slack-jawed proto-cretins are getting it, why aren't I?

I comfort myself with two thoughts: they might be – indeed, they probably were – lying and, even if they weren't, then I probably wouldn't really want to have sex with the kind of girl who'd agree to bump uglies with boys so lump-like and dim anyway. Though, at the same time, being honest with myself, I strongly suspect that if one of those girls had thrown herself at me, I would have taken full advantage. But then (I immediately think), that would only have been because it was my first time. Once I'd got over that first, daunting hurdle, I'd be as picky and restrained as I think somebody with my obvious gifts of the mind ought to be.

Anyway, all theoretical for now. Hol rejected me, but it was done with some sympathy and I feel we're still friends. I take her point about not risking a relationship that might last decades yet, but on the other hand I'm disappointed she wasn't prepared to be a bit more adventurous and just go, *Oh, what the hell* . . . I suspect the devil-may-care promiscuity of her and Guy's generation might have been much exaggerated.

Various flowers are starting to push up through the earth, both from old, weed-bedraggled flower beds and just from random places where seeds must have fallen. The snowdrops have been and gone.

The trees are producing buds, too; little green packages full of the promise of spring. I feel an odd, even stupid sympathy for the trees and the bushes and flowers that will, in all likelihood, just be starting to come into flower when the house is demolished and the garden drops into the quarry, destroying everything. I suppose I could save some of the flowers, maybe even a few bushes; dig them up and transplant them elsewhere, though of course I don't know where I'd put them because I don't know where I'll be.

It probably won't all happen at once anyway. The house and the various outbuildings are due to be demolished in any event, as soon as they take over the land, but after that the quarry people will clear strips of foliage and topsoil along the advancing edge of the quarry only as they need to. I've seen this process at work on the quarry's other boundaries: clear and strip a ledge about ten metres wide, exposing the bedrock and giving the plant and machinery a solid new surface to use as a sort of rough roadway, then a few days or weeks later drill the holes, set the charges, detonate the explosives and bring the latest section of rock crashing down. It might take months or even years before the quarry finally eats away the whole back garden and gets to where the house once stood. It'll all depend on the demand for stone, I guess.

I get to the rear wall, and the place where you can climb up to look over. I feel slightly self-conscious, knowing that there are people in the house who might be able to see me, but I reach up, grasp a stone near the top of the wall, put my foot on the protruding bit of iron and pull myself upwards. I stand on a couple of footholds, relatively high up, so I can sort of balance on my belly on the worn round coping stones, giving me a good view to the base of the wall.

Which is a bit closer to the quarry's edge than it was the last time I did this, maybe a couple of weeks ago.

It looks like there's been a minor landslide. The strip of ground between the base of the wall and the lip of the quarry, which was about two and a half to three metres wide the last time I looked, is down to about a metre, for about half

224

the length of the garden wall. This bitten-away-looking chunk is centred more or less on where I am. Just below me, there's only a path-sized strip of grass; maybe half a metre. The rest of the ground has slipped away, forming a shallow, crumpled slope of dark-brown clods of earth, some of them stringy with the pale roots of plants and some of them lying toppled at all angles, fringed with patches of scrubby, straw-coloured turf.

One arm-thick tree root angles across the slip, its rough brown spiral slowly thinning before it forms a sort of elbow a metre away from the lip and heads back again to disappear into the ground, as though avoiding the edge. There are a few big boulders in the mix too. The soil doesn't look like it's been washed away much, or smoothed by the rain, so it probably happened in the last week; maybe just in the last few days. I think back to try to remember any unusual noises from this end of the garden, but I can't recall any.

It doesn't look like the rock beneath has fallen; it's all just the topsoil and earth, maybe two metres deep, which has slumped away towards and – partially – over the lip of the quarry. Probably all the recent rain added just enough extra weight and lubrication to send it over the edge. I doubt we're in any danger or anything – the rock here is solid, which is why you have to drill and blast it to get it to fall and break up – but I do feel suddenly exposed and vulnerable, perched on the wall like this. It's not impossible the wall's been destabilised by this latest ground movement and having an extra hundred kilos draped over the top of it could, conceivably, be just enough to trigger another landslip, taking the wall with it. And, right now, me too, of course. I look to either side. The wall still appears straight and level, not bowed or slumping.

I take a final, measured look round, just to prove to myself

I'm not *that* intimidated and fearful, then get carefully back down and retreat from the wall, standing there and looking for a while at the ground at its foot, in case there's any sign on this side that it's been undermined or started to shift.

Then I continue my walk round the garden, though with a frown on my face.

Because there are some changes on this side of the wall that are recent, too. Nothing as obviously dramatic as the landslip on the quarry side, of course, and nothing to indicate that the wall is in immediate danger of collapsing, but changes, all the same, from the last time I walked this way, which was a full three days ago (a long time by my standards of regularity).

The marks made by the rubber foot on the bottom of a standard NHS-issue forearm crutch are generally fairly shallow, unless there's been a lot of rain previously and the ground is soft. Even then, you could easily miss the signs, and if there was just one, you probably wouldn't spot it at all.

When there are a few, though, measured out at roughly one-pace intervals on the sodden, winter-thin grass by the side of the little path here, and a little freckle of further indentations, just in front of the centre of the wall, as though somebody stopped there for a short while, shifting their weight from foot to foot and foot to crutch, perhaps, while they did something, presumably with their hands, then – if you're sort of observant by nature, which I guess I am – it's all kind of obvious.

I go back into the house and stand in the back porch for a moment, then step into the kitchen itself and stand quietly for a moment longer. I can't hear anything; it seems there's still nobody else up.

I go out to the garage, where the Volvo sits wrapped in its smell of oil. Hanging on the back wall there's a big looped clump of climbing rope from about ten years ago when Guy thought he might take up rock climbing (he frightened himself, first time he tried, so never did). The rope's here in case, for some highly non-foreseeable reason, the car ever needs a tow-rope fifty metres long. I think that way Guy feels its purchase wasn't a complete waste of money.

I take the rope, sling it over my shoulder, then remove the pair of binoculars from the car's glovebox and put those round my neck. I leave the garage and go round the back of the little copse of oaks between the garage and the garden's west-facing wall. There's a way over the wall here too, provided by an old oil drum standing upright. Guy was going to turn it into a barbecue, but never got round to it.

On the other side, at the edge of a broad, darkly ploughed field, I walk up to the corner where the quarry edge begins, keeping close to the wall so I'm not stepping on the ridged brown earth and so that I can't be seen from the house.

At the corner of the field where a double wire fence joins up with our wall and the quarry drops away, the landslip further along looks slightly less dramatic.

Once I'm over the two fences I loop some of the rope round one of the strainer posts and walk out to the edge of the quarry, keeping the rope tight. I get to the very edge, just centimetres from the drop; closer than I've ever been, made confident by the rope twisted round my arm and gripped threefold in my hand. I look into the quarry, straight down the face and along.

The vertical walls, greyly slick with the recent rain, stretch away, circling back round to the kilometre-distant gap where the buildings and machinery sit.

Relatively little of the landslip seems to have gone over the edge and fallen to the roadway, thirty metres down.

Beyond that broad shelf there's another cliff and then, maybe fifteen metres down, the base of the quarry, largely filled with two giant pools separated by a sort of causeway of rubble, one truck wide and rutted.

When I look carefully, more of the landslide becomes obvious. I use the binoculars, one-handed, scanning all I can of the earth and rocks that have fallen, both where the debris has been caught by little ledges on the way down, and where it's hit or been washed down onto the rock platform at the base of the cliff. I can hear a buzzard mewling somewhere above my head and feel a faint breeze flowing upwards out of the quarry, cold and damp. It moves my hair about, blowing it over my forehead. I remember the feeling of Hol running her fingers through my hair last night, and shiver without warning.

One or two of the ledges down there have been around long enough for a few small plants to have taken root, though they look pretty lean and scraggy. Their dark greens, browns and beiges are about the only interruption to the slate-grey bedrock. A crude shape of brown twigs on one ledge halfway down might be an old birds' nest. I inspect the rest of the ledges carefully, and the base of the cliff that runs beneath our garden wall.

I leave the edge, unloop the rope and throw it over my shoulder again, then start to sidle along the wall with my back to the stonework, looking down towards the exposed jumble of boulders, clods and turf marking the new edge.

I'm breathing fairly quickly, and my heart is hammering away like it was last night when I thought I might finally be going to get laid, because although the slope of crumpled ground looks stable in its new slumped configuration, what the hell do I know? It might be poised to slip again as soon

228

as the first idiot comes lumbering along, disturbing things (this would be me).

I crab my way along the wall until I get to the bit just below where I was balancing on top earlier, where the strip of remaining grass is only just wide enough to take my boots.

The thick tree root protruding from the slip feels reassuringly solid. I tie the rope to it near where it's thickest and first emerges from beneath the wall. I tie the other end round my chest, keeping this part loose to pass the rest of the rope bundle through and slinging it over my shoulder again, then I tighten up the knot in front of me, settling the rope under my armpits. I'm good with knots; it's my mountaineering technique that is doubtless rubbish. Still, the rope seems to pay out okay and if I do fall it should tighten up and stop me. I think I'll keep a really good grip on the rope anyway, just to be sure.

Tromping backwards through the mud and earth, roots and stones to the edge is pretty unpleasant; my boots sink in up to the ankle. I'm leaving a really obvious trail, too. Just before I get to the lip, the ground gives way beneath my feet and I go down with an 'Oof!' I can do nothing about, landing partly on my knees on a thin covering of muck right on the edge, and partly on my elbows in thicker earth, as I pull tight on the rope. My feet must be hanging over the edge. I can hear stones and lumps of soil clattering and thudding down the cliff just beneath my shins.

'Uh-huh,' I say to myself, and haul hard on the rope as I pull myself back up. I risk a glance down. It looks more sheer from this angle. Not encouraging.

I stand right on the lip, pay out a little more rope until I'm leaning out over the drop, then – with a dust-dry mouth and a heart spasming so hard and fast it's making my vision pulse like a faulty strip light – I start down the cliff.

We did this kind of thing once on an adventure day with the school, though I seem to recall there was more than just one rope involved: lots of ropes, they had, and a variety of shiny and very colourful carabiners of anodised aluminium, plus buckles and harnesses and safety helmets and other highly reassuring bits of patently over-engineered climbing paraphernalia.

'If I die a virgin, Hol,' I whisper to myself (it's always a sign I'm nervous when I talk to myself), 'I hope you have the good grace to weep at my funeral.'

Mostly I'm terrified of the tree root turning out to be not actually attached to anything else after all, and getting pulled out of the earth by my own weight, sending me plummeting to the rock below. But losing my footing and thudding into the cliff face, my insides constricted by a mis-tied knot over-tightening round my chest, is something to consider as well. I'm starting to re-evaluate my sticking-to-one-hundred-kilos weight-management policy.

'A little late, admittedly,' I mutter to myself, walking slowly down the cliff backwards, trying to pay out rope at just the right rate to keep me at an angle that makes this frankly bizarre mode of travel possible.

My phone goes. 'Aww . . .' I hear myself say, exasperated. It's Guy's ringtone. He'll just persist if I don't answer. The rope's wrapped round my right hand so I have to use the wrong hand to dig awkwardly around in my gilet pocket for the phone. I nearly drop it, but manage to catch it against my chest, then bring it up to my left ear.

'Hello?'

'Where the fuck are you?'

'I went for a walk,' I tell him. Technically, this is true.

'Well, get your arse back here. I need getting up.'

'I'll be maybe ten, fifteen minutes. Can you manage till then?'

'No, I bloody can't, but I'll just bloody have to, won't I? I can smell some bugger making toast, too, and it's fucking tormenting. I'll struggle out of bed myself, or shout for somebody. Just you enjoy your morning constitutional, young sir.'

'Aww, Dad,' I begin, but he rings off.

I put the phone into a more convenient pocket.

I lose my footing once, trying to swing out to one side to investigate a particular ledge. I pendulum in and thump against the cliff wall, twisting slightly to the left as I go, so that when I hit I have to absorb the blow on my right shoulder. The binoculars clatter.

'Shit,' I say. At least the rope hasn't strangled my chest. I push back out, get my legs to the right angle on the second attempt and resume the position, then collect myself – let my hammering heart slow down a bit, for a start – and then pay out a little more rope and swing to the side, bounce-walking along the cliff face. The rope, stretched tight over the lip of cliff above, dislodges a little earth and a pebble or two as I go, spraying and rattling down to one side.

The interesting stuff on the ledge I was trying to reach proves to be a few weathered, sun-bleached bones; they're those of a sheep, maybe a lamb. I let myself further down the cliff.

I get centred under where the landslip happened, watching the edge above for any boulders deciding to fall on top of me. My arms and legs are aching and the rope is digging painfully into my back and the sides of my upper ribs. I think I need to ascend soon.

I look down again, then bring the binoculars up with my

left hand. This is enough to destabilise me once more; one foot, then the other, skids downwards off the rock as I lose grip. I thump into the rock a second time, the binoculars whacking into my chest.

'Fuck!' I say. I don't like to swear, so I must be upset.

I pause for a moment, sort of kneeling against the cliff face. My shoulders and ribs are really hurting now. I take one last look with the binoculars, at a ledge near the bottom of the cliff. The extra distance means I have to adjust the focus, while keeping hold of the rope means I have to do this one-handed, which is not easy.

More white straight lines, sticking out of the fallen earth of the landslip, on the last ledge before the stone roadway beneath. Maybe bleached bones, maybe not. The twisted, grey-brown branches of a stunted bush get in the way.

'Hmm,' I say to myself. I rest the binoculars against my chest and push away from the rock, then start walking upwards, pulling on the rope to keep the angle right. This is harder and more strenuous than it sounds. It was definitely easier on the school adventure-day outing to the climbing wall. I suspect the harness they used – it went under the groin as well as round the shoulders, like you were a para-chutist or something – meant we were properly balanced somehow, whereas my cobbled-together arrangement makes the whole business more awkward, difficult and, for that matter, painful. I'm trailing great long dangling loops of untidy rope now, too, because, clearly, my gathering-it-over-my-shoulder regime has proved lax. This can't be great; what if it gets snagged on something further down?

It takes a lot of muttered cursing before I get to the lip of the cliff. Even there I lose my footing as I try to step up the very last bit and impact with the stone and clodded ground again, getting a mouthful of earth in the process. I spit and splutter as I hang there, nearly gagging. My back and upper chest feel like they're on fire. My hands are right on the cliff edge, sunk in soft soil and small stones. I kick out, heave and haul, and my legs flail like a cartoon character trying to run through thin air, but, at last, I get all of me over the edge and kneeling in the muck a couple of metres in front of the wall where the rope is tied.

'Oh. Hello, Kit.'

I nearly fall back into the quarry. I stare at the top of the wall, where Haze is looking down at me, just his head and one hand holding a roll-up visible. 'You all right there, mate?' He takes a drag, exhales a cloud of grey-blue smoke.

'Ah!' I say, breathing hard, still shaken. I stagger to my feet, plough forward through the soft ground, trying to untie the knot over my chest. 'Yeah! Fine!' I tell him, stumbling back to the relative safety of the base of the wall.

'Looks like there's been an avalanche or something, doesn't it?' Haze says from above as I lean back, exhausted, against the stonework, shaking, breathing hard and picking ineffectually at the now very tight, hard knot over my chest.

'Uh-huh,' I say.

'You do a lot of climbing, then?'

'No,' I say, half shouting. 'Not really.'

'They let you go climbing in the quarry, do they?'

'Well, you know,' I say, still trying to get my breath back. 'It being a Sunday. Nobody about. Not much activity, these days anyway.'

'Ah. Right. Anyway, it's all exercise, isn't it?'

'Yup.'

'Yeah . . .' I can hear him pulling on the cigarette, then it goes arcing over my head, falling into the quarry. 'I've got the kettle on,' he tells me. 'Going to jump back down now. Oh; you need a hand getting back over or anything?'

'No. No, I'm fine.'

'Splendido. I'll get a brew going. Milk and two sugars, isn't it?'

'Yeah.' The knot is just starting to loosen. 'Milk and two. Please.'

No point keeping a low profile now; I climb over the wall where I'm standing – it's not easy, I'm trembling so much, muscles aching – and tramp back to the garage to dump the rope and binoculars, then leave my boots at the back door and brush off what mud I can from my clothes before entering the porch.

'What the fuck have you been doing?' Guy asks, sat at the head of the kitchen table in the old army greatcoat he uses as a dressing gown. Ali is sitting across the angle from him, looking submerged in her fluffy white robe. She just stares at me. There are big circles under her eyes.

'I fell,' I tell Guy, and head for the hall.

'Tea's on the table!' Haze calls from the sink as I leave. He's wearing a different T-shirt. Carter, it says, in dramatic black and white.

'Back in a min,' I tell him as I go for yet another shower.

But there's a queue, because everybody seems to be getting up at the same time. Paul's standing outside the bathroom with a towel over his arm.

'Hey, Kit,' he says, voice croaky. His hair's dishevelled.

I shower in Guy's en suite instead. He doesn't like me doing this, but too bad. I even leave some grit in one corner of the shower tray, rather than rinse it carefully away as I normally would, just to make it clear I've been here.

'Yeah, that'll show him, Kit,' I tell myself.

But then, as I'm towelling down outside the shower, I start to feel foolish and petty, so I reach into the shower and hose away the little V of grey dirt after all, until it's all spotless again.

'Much better,' I mutter.

'You fuckers! You might have fucking woken me up! Kit! Why didn't you get me back up?'

'You were sound asleep,' I tell him.

'You could have woken me!'

'You'd already taken your sleeping pills; you'd have been too groggy to move.'

'Well, let's think what plant-based chemical substance is world-renowned for making people feel wide fucking awake, almost instantly, shall we? Oh, wait a fucking minute. I know!'

'Dad, the last time you took coke you nearly had a heart attack,' I remind him.

'My heart, Kit. My fucking heart, not yours. My heart, my life, my choice.'

He's wearing his ancient, faded red *North 99* baseball cap today instead of the woolly hat that looks like a tea cosy. Maybe because there's a hint of sun in the sky. He puts one hand up to the brim and for a moment it looks like he's actually going to tear the cap off and throw it onto the table in disgust, but he doesn't.

'Stop biting the kid's ear,' Hol tells him. 'We just didn't want to risk you dying on us. At least Kit was thinking of your best interests; the rest of us were just scared about explaining ourselves to the cops when they turned up in A&E while the medics were drawing the bloods that would prove you'd OD'd on the devil's dandruff.' She smiles at Guy. 'You need to elevate your guns a bit, love. Pick on those of us not quite at point-blank range.'

'*That* was a movie,' Haze says, nodding.

'Talking about heart attacks,' Ali says quietly to Rob. I think maybe she taps his leg with hers, under the table.

'What?' Pris says to Haze.

Rob drinks from his coffee mug, looks up from his iPad at Ali. 'Now what?'

'*Point Blank.*'

'How many cups have you had?' Ali says.

'That with John Cusack?' Paul asks, sounding sleepy.

Rob redirects his gaze from Ali to Paul. 'That was *Grosse Pointe Blank*,' he tells him, going back to his iPad. 'This was late sixties; John Boorman, Lee Marvin.'

'I make it three,' Ali says to Rob, who doesn't look up. 'You just don't usually drink this much. You know what it can do to your heart.'

'Never saw it,' Pris says.

Rob frowns at something on the iPad.

'Thank fuck,' Guy is saying to Hol, 'I have friends prepared to go to such lengths to protect me in my final months and make sure I don't over-enjoy myself, or peg out before my properly constituted . . . allotment of pain, misery and humiliation.'

Ali releases a long sigh.

'You're welcome,' Hol mutters, munching her toast and reading her magazine.

'So. You two were up late,' Ali says quietly. Nobody seems sure who she's talking about at first, though she's looking at Hol as she says this. Then she looks at me. Uh-oh.

'Hmm?' Hol is saying.

'Just, I saw you sidling quietly out of Kit's room, late on; very late on, last night. When I was going for a pee.'

Hol snorts, going back to her magazine. 'Yeah. We're secret

lovers.' She nods sideways at Guy. 'I'm collecting the set.' She pauses, looks up at Guy. 'Your dad; he's not still alive, is he?'

'No, but we could dig him the fuck up,' Guy says. 'Would that be acceptable?'

'I was watching Kit play his game,' Hol tells Ali, with a small smile on her lips. 'Being a big bulgy hero and taking up arms against a sea of scary monsters. It was surprisingly interesting.' She nods, frowns. 'Almost worryingly interesting.' She gazes at a point just above Ali's head, fingers drumming on the table. 'I may be even more of a geek than I was already worried about.' She shrugs, goes back to her magazine.

'Okay,' Ali says, though she somehow sounds like she's only pretending to accept this. She turns her face to me. 'Kit, are you blushing?'

'I don't think so,' I tell her, suddenly angry at her. 'Am I?' I ask Paul, who is sitting looking sorry for himself and cradling a large mug of tea. The round of toast on the plate in front of him is untouched.

'Hmm?' Paul says. I don't think he's been listening.

Hol is looking at me, elbow on table, chin on hand. 'Dunno. Are you blushing, Kit? Have you reason to? Should I be flattered? Vaguely disturbed?'

'Well, *now* I'm blushing,' I tell them, grinning.

'Hmm,' Ali says, but just drinks her tea.

'You got a girlfriend yet, Kit?' Haze asks.

'No,' I tell him.

'Who'd fucking have him?' Guy says, glaring at me.

'Guy!' Pris says. She looks at me. 'He's just jealous, Kit,' she tells me. 'You're cuter than he is; way cuter.'

'Yeah, maybe now, just,' Guy mutters.

237

'Thank you very much, ma'am,' I say quietly, head down.

'The trick,' Haze says, 'is just to get out there and not be afraid to get the occasional knock-back.'

Hol looks at Haze. '"Occasional"?' she says.

'I agree with m'learned friend,' Paul says quietly, pushing his plate of toast to one side and gently lowering his head to lay it on the table. 'Put yourself about a bit, Kit,' he tells me.

'Do you not want that toast, then?' Haze is saying.

'. . . *We* sure as hell did,' Rob mutters.

For a moment there's silence in the kitchen, and nobody meets anybody else's gaze.

For a few moments, actually.

I think it's a sex tape.

'Right,' Ali says, 'if we're going to do this properly we need a programme.'

'Jeez, here we go,' Rob says, rubbing a hand over his shiny scalp.

Ali looks at him. 'We only have so much time, and so many able-bodied searchers.'

'Oh, ta,' Guy mutters.

'Don't sweat it, Guy,' Paul says quietly, his head still lying on the table. 'She may have been referring to me.' He sighs loudly. 'Don't feel very able-bodied right now.'

'Yeah,' Hol says. 'We may not all be at our best here.'

'I'll draw up a doc,' Ali says, reaching for her iPad. 'Assign us roles and areas of study.'

'You're missing work, aren't you?' Rob says.

Paul groans.

'Let me do that,' I say, reaching to grab the A4 pad from its drawer. I pull the pencil out of the ring-binder bit at the top, flip over to a clean sheet and quickly draw eight lines down the page.

'Kit,' Ali says, raising the iPad one-handed. 'I've got it covered.'

'This is quicker,' I tell her, starting to scribble letter groups along the top of the page: Dad, Me, Hol . . . 'Race you!' I tell her, glancing up. Pri, Ali, Haz, Rob, Pol. Down the side of the page I start listing the various bits of the house, beginning with 'At' for Attic.

Ali places the iPad on the table. 'Well,' she says, 'if it keeps you happy.' She nods at the pad in front of me. 'You've got all of us, yes?' She leaves a space for me to confirm that I do, but I just keep on writing. 'Then,' she says, 'you need all the places we can look, then some free space for other categories, like somebody who can liaise between all the rest, or . . . make the tea or something.'

'Got it,' I tell her.

'Or we could do it like ants,' Haze suggests.

We all look at him. '*What?*' Guy says. I suppose somebody had to.

'Yeah,' Haze says. 'Only, I saw this documentary, see? The ants don't have, like, a plan between them, not like a proper, thought-out, like . . . plan, but the way they just sort of all mill about, right, it looks . . . it looks, like, totally random? And it sort of is, at first, but then they end up communicating with . . . like, chemicals, and these trails let them explore everywhere but then, like, concentrate on the bits where they need to, yeah? See?'

'Not really,' Pris says.

Ali looks back at me as I get to near the bottom of the page, writing OH (for Outhouse/s) 1, 2, 3 and Gar. There's about an eighth of the page left for Any Other Business.

'And maybe,' Ali says, 'another column for promising areas too big for one person to cover in the time that would benefit from further research and additional resources being brought to bear.'

'Got you,' I say, drawing another line down near the right margin.

'But that's what I was saying . . .' Haze says in a small voice.

'Might I make a suggestion?' Guy says. 'Given that this is my fucking house and home?'

'What?' Ali says.

I look at Dad, pencil poised.

He looks at me. 'Let's have a big fucking bonfire. Clear all the shit.'

Hol glances at the door of the bedroom. 'You did okay, by the way,' she tells me quietly. I raise my eyebrows. 'Over breakfast,' she says. 'Good deflecting. Saying, "*Now* I'm blushing." That worked.'

I might be starting to blush again now. 'I'm getting better at this stuff,' I agree. 'That box ready?'

'Ready to go. Take it away, young Kit.'

My principal role is liaison and logistics; this is what I've been tasked with. Mostly this means carrying boxes. I take the box down the stairs to where Guy sits in his wheelchair by the open back door in the kitchen porch. I plonk the relatively shallow cardboard box – it originally contained bananas – down on an upturned plastic crate I brought from my room to sit in front of Guy. He leans over, peers into the box. 'Books,' he says. 'Charity shop.'

'Righto,' I say, lifting the box.

'This you?' he says, nodding at some of the mud and soil I left behind earlier, lying just outside the door.

'Told you; I fell.' I head for the garage to add this box to the couple already in the car.

'Yeah,' Haze says, pulling out a crumbling cardboard container from beneath a pile of old curtains. We're in what Guy and I have always called the old outhouse, because it's even more dilapidated than the others, but which for the purposes of our organised search we're calling Outhouse Two. 'I was sort of given . . . well, I was thinking, you know, that maybe Guy was getting us here to, you know, pass on some of his worldly goods or whatever. You know, rather than wait. Rather than involve the lawyers more than they need to be, know what I mean? Maybe tell us what he was handing on, to, like, you know, acknowledge what we'd all meant to each other. Or something. I don't know.'

'Yeah, well,' I say.

I peel back the flaps on top of the box. Inside, there is a lot of wood and fabric stuff, like bread bins, chopping boards and light shades.

'Do you think Guy's got any surprises lined up, or anything?' Haze asks me.

I think about this. 'No,' I tell him.

'Look at these! We can't throw these out!'

'It's not really throwing out,' I tell Pris. 'We're just going to recycle some.'

Pris is in Guy's room, with full permission to get rid of any clothes she deems fit for disposal. She has a laundry basket for things to be recycled and a big cardboard box for things to be burned. She's holding up some old stuff; things I think must be from the time of Guy's parents. A white silk scarf, fronded, a slinky dress of silver, frayed, an old pair of

241

yellow cords, so thick they look ploughed, an electric-blue dressing gown with vivid, colourful Chinese decorations, delicately pitted by tiny burn holes down the front.

'Do *you* want to take anything?' I ask Pris. 'For you?'

'Hmm, I don't know. I'd mostly only be taking them for other people. Friends.'

'Shall I get another box?'

'Do you think these would fit Rick?' she asks, holding up the pair of yellow cords.

They look big and baggy and old-fashioned. 'Yes,' I tell her, sticking strictly to remit.

'Hmm.' She holds them out in front of her, puts her head to one side. This is an action humans share with dogs. I've never worked out why either species employs it.

Technically I'm still waiting for an answer to my question about getting another box; however, I'm starting to think Pris missed it somehow. Eventually I say, 'Do you think Rick is a thick yellow cord kind of person?'

Pris first purses her lips, then sort of shifts her whole compressed mouth to one side. She frowns. 'Maybe not,' she concedes. 'I've never seen him in anything like this. But that doesn't mean he shouldn't try something different, does it?' She looks at me.

'Does he have much that would go with them?' I ask her.

She shakes her head. 'Not really. Need to be part of a whole new outfit.'

'Hmm.'

She puts them down on the bed. 'Do you *like* my new man, Kit?'

'Rick?'

'Well, duh.'

'He seems perfectly nice.'

242

'You don't think he's . . . ?'

I look at her.

My initial assumption – naturally, I think – is that Pris isn't sure what she wants to ask me, but then I remember one of those handy-tips-when-having-an-adult-conversation I got from either Hol or Mrs Willoughby (maybe both): sometimes when people leave a question like that hanging it's not because they've suddenly been distracted or have simply forgotten what it was they set out to ask; they're doing it deliberately (or instinctively) because they want to see what you think. They want to know what *you* believe they were about to ask; either that or they're giving you permission to raise something that was on your mind anyway.

This applies especially with a question couched as Pris's question was, as 'You don't think . . . ?' The implication is that the person is worried that you think badly of somebody or something they care about. If she'd said, '*But* don't you think . . . ?' then the meaning would most likely be reversed. People use this latter form when they think you might be thinking too well of somebody or something they believe needs criticising.

The trouble is, I don't really have any strong or deep feelings for Rick either way, so I can't really help here.

'Don't think he's what?' I ask, resorting to the kind of conversational Route One tactic I'd have used in the old days regardless. It still has its place.

'I don't know,' Pris says, lifting an old black cape with a maroon lining and dusting something off it. 'I thought maybe, you being, you know . . .' She sighs. 'A sort of independent observer, you might be able to judge whether he . . . what the others think of him, or what he . . . how he appears

243

compared to the rest of us, you know?' She looks up at me briefly, goes back to brushing at the dark cape.

I have a think. 'He's younger than you lot.'

'Do you think they resent that?'

'No.'

She looks at me. I get the impression this may have been the wrong answer somehow, even though it seemed the obvious right answer to me. 'Really?' she says.

'Well, I don't think so.'

'He's not that much younger,' she says, almost to herself. She smiles at me. 'I suppose I worry they could look down on him. Because, I don't know. Because he didn't go to uni. I mean, he could have, but his career, you know, just took him along a different path.'

'I'm not going to uni,' I tell her.

'No?'

'Probably not.'

'Some people can be a bit, you know, snobbish. Towards people who haven't.'

I shrug. 'Their problem.'

She sort of stares at me. Her eyes go wide for a bit. 'Yes, it is, isn't it?'

'He seemed okay,' I tell Pris. Which is truthful, though of course we all have our own definitions of what 'okay' means, and we each might have several different definitions, depending on context. Which allows a lot of room for ambiguity and even misunderstanding. I sort of disapprove of such terminological inexactitude and laxity, frankly, but Hol assures me sometimes this sort of leeway is exactly what people are looking for, especially in a situation where they hope to be reassured.

You get to say something vague that means one thing to

you – maybe something not really that complimentary – and the other person is allowed to interpret it as being entirely positive and supportive. As long as they don't actually misquote you or cite your opinion, as interpreted, as the whole reason for a subsequent, disastrous course of action, this is regarded as a good outcome for both parties.

'Rick, I mean,' I add, realising I've left a bit of a gap here. 'He seemed okay.' I try hard to think of what Hol would want me to ask here. 'Is he . . . nice? Is he a decent guy? To you?'

Pris is nodding, still looking at the surface of the cape and picking at it. 'Yes. Yeah, he's sweet. Can be really funny, once you get to know him. Lots of mates. And he gets on really well with Mhyra. You know; my little girl.'

'Yeah, of course. She's . . .'

'Hmm?'

'She is . . . your only child, is that right?'

'Uh-huh,' Pris says, frowning at me.

'Well, there you go,' I say.

'It's just,' Pris says, going back to picking at the cape, 'we're such a . . . bunch of Heathers, you know?' She smiles at me.

'Heathers?' I say, not getting whatever it is I'm supposed to be getting.

'Film?' Pris says. '*Heathers*. Winona Ryder, Christian Slater?'

'Not seen it.'

'Well, long time since I did, I suppose, but I just remember it being about this clique of really bitchy girls, all called Heather. And sometimes I wonder if we're a bit like that.'

As recently as only a year or so ago, I'd have said something obtuse here like, 'But you're not all girls.' However, now I'm a bit less stubborn about such things and I've accepted Hol's point that you have to partner people in conversations; it's

245

generally supposed to be a cooperative, not an adversarial, process. You're helping each other to feel your way to some sort of shared meaning, not jousting from either side of a fence.

Unless it's Ali, and sometimes Rob, and other people like that, who often do appear to be trying to score points off you. Then the rules are a bit different.

'Swings and roundabouts,' I tell Pris. 'It's good being part of a gang or a group, but there are negatives too. Bound to be.'

This is close to something Mrs Willoughby's said, though I also know a little about this kind of thing from first-hand, because I've usually – well, always, so far – been on the outside of any given gang, group or clique. Which I don't mind, because I think you see more as an outsider. ('Yeah, you see more but you feel less,' was Hol's reply when I told her about this.)

'I've got lots of other friends,' Pris tells me. 'People from work, from dance classes, pals from my local. Too many, I think, sometimes . . . But it's like you always need to come back to the people you sort of half grew up, half matured, with, from uni days, from then, to . . .'

'Calibrate,' I suggest, after a decent interval, as Pris stares unseeing at the cape in her hands.

'Calibrate?'

'You calibrate against a known reference point or standard.' I shrug.

She nods, looks away. 'Yeah, we're always measuring ourselves against others, aren't we?'

It's not quite what I meant, but if that's the point she needed to reach, I can't really contradict her. She's brushing the cape smoothly now, with the nap, as though trying to soothe it. Her phone goes.

'Hey,' she says. 'Glo; everything okay?' There's a pause, then her face relaxes and she sees me smile. 'Have you now?' she says. 'My. Who could that be?' Another short pause, then, 'That wouldn't be a certain snooky-wook, name of Mhyra, would it? Oh! Is that *you*? Is that my little shnuggy-wuggums, sounding all grown up already?'

'I'll get that box,' I tell her.

'Can't seem to pick up the WiFi here,' Ali says, when I visit her in Outhouse One. It's cold and damp in this old stone shed of a place and she wears a padded shirt and a thickly quilted gilet of shiny electric blue.

'WiFi?' I say, not wanting to give anything away.

'Yeah,' Ali says, bringing an ancient, sagging cardboard box down from a shelf. She places it on an old gateleg table she's opened up. 'Saw you had broadband and a hub, in your room,' she tells me, opening up the box.

'Oh. You were . . .' I listen to my voice trail away. I locked my room this morning when I knew we were going to be conducting this search, after assuring people I knew it inside out and that it was one place where the tape most certainly wasn't. It was Ali I was thinking of, specifically, when I locked it.

'Oh, I popped in the other night, looking for a spare socket to recharge something, you know,' Ali says. 'But I was admiring your games set-up and I saw you had broadband connected and just wondered how come there was no WiFi signal anywhere.' She smiles at me. The cardboard box in front of her is full of tapes, but they're the wrong sort; ancient reel-to-reel audiotapes in plastic cases, probably from when Guy was in local radio. Ali starts flicking through them anyway.

'Yeah, there is no WiFi,' I tell her.

'Really?' Ali says. 'How does that work? Or not work?'

'Mostly by me not turning it on.'

'That's a little selfish, isn't it?' Ali says immediately, as though she already knew this, had gamed our exchange and prepared her reply.

'Yes, it is a little,' I tell her. 'I need it for playing HeroSpace. Paid for it myself.'

'Well, that's very enterprising of you, but don't you think you could afford to share a little? Hol's indoctrination of socialist values not taken fully after all, hmm?' she asks.

I just stare at her.

'Wouldn't cramp your style as a games wizard too much to turn it on, would it? Bet we'd all be grateful.'

'You're all going home tomorrow.'

'Mm. I suppose. What about Guy? Wouldn't he like to have WiFi?'

'Probably not. He's not that bothered. Have you seen his phone? Hasn't even got a camera. Its only game is Break Out. It's a joke. And he's never really got on with computers.'

'Does he know?'

I could pretend I don't know what she means, but I suspect there's no point. 'No, he doesn't.'

'Oh,' Ali says, as though I've just disappointed her. I'm giving her quite a good hard stare but it's unappreciated; she's still flicking through the tape cases, her finger knocking them delicately from one angle of lean to another. 'I see,' she adds.

'But I'm sure he'd love to have something else to dig me up about,' I tell her. This is a bit bold, but I'm pleased with it; it sounded quite adult. I think Hol would approve.

Ali gets to the end of the audiotapes and closes the box again. She leans her elbows on it, smiles at me. '*Do* you know where the tape is, Kit?' she asks.

'I wouldn't have let all this happen if I did,' I tell her, gesturing around. I am not blushing. I think this is a true statement. It is also an instruction. Just think steely, I tell myself. 'I don't need you guys to do all this. I could clear the place myself. I'd rather, in a way.'

'What was that you were clearing from the room with all the papers, into your room?'

Good grief, the woman sees everything. Yesterday evening I shifted the year's worth of copies of the *Bew Valley and Ormisdale Chronicle and Post* out of the upstairs room where I'd left them drying and into my bedroom, so they wouldn't get thrown out. 'Old newspapers,' I tell her.

'Lot of old newspapers.'

'Fifty-two,' I say. 'One year. From the one with the announcement of my birth, back.'

'Oh,' Ali says.

'I thought there might be some sort of clue in the papers that would help me work out who my mum might be.'

'I thought she was a Jewish princess from NYC,' Ali says. 'From this fabulously wealthy family of ultra-strict financiers; some naive exchange student Guy seduced while her body-guard's back was turned, bringing shame on the whole family. So they couldn't possibly keep the baby. Something like that?' She's shaking her head, frowning. 'No?'

'It depends who you talk to, and that seems to depend on what Guy's told that particular person.' I pause, look thoughtful. 'Though that is a new one. Jewish princess. That would make me Jewish, too.'

'It would?'

'It's a matrilineal . . . faith . . . inheritance thing.'

'Oh. Did you turn up on the doorstep . . . ?' Ali says, looking pointedly at my groin.

'No,' I tell her. 'Though I don't think you really need that bit of evidence to be reasonably sure this is another of Dad's fantasies.'

'Probably.'

'I mean, don't tell him I told you this, but he did once suggest my mum might be one of you. Hol, Pris . . . you.' (I've decided I don't care that I promised Guy I wouldn't say anything about this; the more I've thought about it, the more I've come round to the conclusion he was just trying to manipulate me.)

Ali grins. 'Did he now?' she says.

'He sort of retracted immediately, but I think that was part of the act, too. He just liked bringing it up, putting it out there, to mess with my head.'

'Does sound like Guy.'

'So; not you, then?'

'No, not me,' Ali says. 'Can't really see it being Hol or Pris either. Hol, if anyone, but even she might have been more, you know, attentive, don't you think? She'd have been to see you more, if you were hers.' She purses her lips. 'Though she does visit quite a bit, doesn't she? Always has.' Ali looks – I think – thoughtful. On her, this is a slightly worrying expression. 'And she did knock back that move to something better and brighter in Manhattan. Hmm.'

'Yeah. I still don't think it's her, though.'

'No,' Ali says, nodding, though with her eyes slightly pursed too now, as though her head might think one thing but her eyes take a different view.

'Anyway,' I say, holding both arms out, 'that's why I was

250

saving the old newspapers; keeping them from getting re-cycled or thrown on the bonfire.'

'How's the fire coming along?'

'It's growing. Should be a . . . good big blaze, when we light it.'

Ali catches something in the way I say this. (I think I might have sort of widened my eyes and moved my ears back a little as I said it.) 'What,' she says, 'do you think we're getting overenthusiastic?'

'I just worry we might chuck out stuff we shouldn't. Burning's kind of final.'

Ali nods slowly. 'I suppose that might be the next time we all meet up, mightn't it?' she says.

'When?'

'At the crematorium. Once Guy's gone. It's only meant to be a few months now, isn't it?'

'That's . . .' I find I have to clear my throat to cover the time it takes to cope with this sudden change of direction. 'That's what we're all expecting.'

'I'm sorry. Should I not have said anything? You look upset.'

I don't think I do; I don't feel it, anyway. Maybe she expected me to be.

'My bad,' she says. 'I'm not the world's best at pussy-footing round this sort of thing. Too head-down confrontational, that's me. So Rob tells me, anyway. Can't help calling things like I see them. Cutting through all the euphemisms and excuses. It's a failing. I suppose.'

'He had talked about being buried in the garden,' I tell her, 'but then with the quarry going to eat into it over the next few years . . . Well, can't do that. So, yes, the crema-torium. Probably.'

'Do you think you'll miss him?'

251

I've thought about this. 'Yes,' I tell her. 'Probably more than I expect to, as of now. Apparently that's the way it tends to work.' I'm aware this might sound kind of cold and emotionless, but I think it's all you can say about something that you won't really know the full truth of until it happens. Anyway, as an answer, this seems to satisfy her. More so than it might most people, perhaps.

'Hmm.' Ali nods. 'Anyway,' she says, patting the box of tapes. 'Can't really burn these. Too toxic, I guess.'

'A lot of this old crap is,' I tell her.

Rob has the task of looking in all the miscellaneous store cupboards dotted round the house. He's one and a half down, so far, with lots to go.

'Anybody near finished yet?' he asks me, standing on the upper landing outside a walk-in. 'There's a lot of these to get through and they're even more stuffed than they look.' Wood, cardboard and plastic boxes of various types and sizes are scattered all over the floor around him.

'Not really,' I tell him. 'Haze should be . . . he's got the least to do, I think.'

'Huh. Right; those can go. There's stuff there from even before our time. You're running all this past Guy, yeah?'

'Yes. Think that's more than one trip; I'll be back.'

I take two boxes of ancient bills, business and official letters and bank statements down to Guy, let him look at them and have a good old grumble about security and how we should have bought a shredder and you can't let this sort of stuff just go for recycling, just in case, and so am directed to dump everything onto the steadily growing structure of the bonfire.

'I hadn't realised Guy was such a hoarder,' Rob says when I return. 'Always thought he was the use-it-and-throw-it-away

252

kind of guy; use-it-and-lose-it, just careless, with everything.'

'I think it was his grandparents started it,' I tell him. 'His mum was fairly meticulous and liked to keep everything neatly sorted, and Guy sort of inherited the habit. He'd throw things away but then he'd feel bad and sort through them later, file them away, in case they ever came in handy or they were asked for by . . . officialdom. Even his dad used to keep lots of ancient stuff. Receipts, mostly, I think. He sort of collected those.'

'Yeah, met his dad a couple of times,' Rob says. 'Cold, disapproving kind of guy. Stank of fags. You didn't miss much.'

'So I hear. Dad doesn't seem to have thought very highly of him either.'

'Well, at least they were still talking to each other.' Rob grins. 'My old man won't talk to me at all. Hasn't for twenty years.'

I just widen my eyes. I think it's that kind of statement.

'Wow,' I say, when Rob just keeps on grinning and the silence goes on so long I feel I kind of have to make some sort of noise. I think I knew Rob didn't get on with his parents, or his dad, at least, but this is an unexpected detail.

'All I did was tell him I'd voted Tory in my first general election, in ninety-two,' Rob tells me. 'Dad was a Labour man, right? Union man, too; shop steward, down-the-line socialist. Staunch. Staunch as they come.'

'Ah,' I say, because it seems required. Rob's family is from Newcastle or nearby, though you'd never tell from his accent.

'Told him over tea at my nan's in Gateshead, thinking I was doing the right thing, the brave thing, the manly thing, the reasonable thing, thinking I'd get a reasoned argument, instigate some sort of measured discourse.' Rob shakes his head. 'He just stopped eating, looked at his plate and thought for a moment, put down his knife and fork and went upstairs. Wouldn't come down until I'd left, gone back to uni. We see each other at family funerals – four, so far – but even then he won't say so much as hello. Lost count of the number of aunts and uncles who've tried to act as peacemakers. Won't hear of it.'

I nod slowly.

'Thing is,' Rob says, 'I always admired him for his ideals, for sticking up for what he believed in. Told him that. Always did tell him that. But times change. Patterns, ways of life, economic circumstances, ways of doing business and making things: they all change, and if you don't move with the times, the times just roll over you and bury you. That's all I was doing, voting for the team in the blue corner; moving with the times the way he'd moved with his. But he couldn't see that. He'd have been the type who'd burn at the stake before they'd renounce their particular brand of faith, even for one right next door.' Rob shrugs. 'I told him, via my mum, I'd voted for Blair in the ninety-seven election, but that didn't seem to make any difference.' Rob laughs. 'One strike and you're out, with my dad. Must be great to have convictions, eh, Kit?'

'That does seem . . . a bit, ah, harsh.'

'That's life. Families, at any rate. Anyway. Effluent under the bridge, I guess. But enough about me and my mad family. Back to business.' He kicks one of the boxes. 'There are statements and letters in here from banks and building societies I've never even heard of.'

'I think we can safely assume those are all closed then.'

'Hope your inheritance amounts to something more than all this crap and a heap of bills, young Kit.'

'Me too.'

254

'You going to be okay? Financially? When he goes?'

'I'd like to think so.'

Rob frowns at me. 'You don't have to be diplomatic with me, Kit. I don't have any illusions about your dad, or owe him anything. Other way round; Guy was nearly as bad as Haze at the casual tenner loan and then the seemingly innocent forgetting. That was one set of records never kept, never made in the first place. What is the situation; don't you know?'

'No, I don't know,' I tell him. 'Dad won't tell me.'

'More boxes, Kit!' Hol calls out from a bedroom doorway at the other end of the landing. 'Hey, Rob. Progress?'

'Slow,' Rob says loudly. Hol shrugs and goes back into the room. Rob looks at me. 'He won't tell you?'

'I'm not sure he knows himself. He says there are debts to be covered from the sale of the house. Some days he says things like, "Don't you worry, kid, you'll be rolling in it after you've got shot of me," other days, mostly when he's really low, he says I'll be lucky to see a penny and how did it come to this and he's sorry he's been such a rubbish dad.' I shrug. 'Take your pick.'

'You should ask Paul if there's anything legal . . . any legal procedure you can follow to find out the true situation.'

'Probably a bit late to start that now. I was expecting all that stuff to be settled, you know, afterwards.'

Rob sighs, squats by an opened box, takes out the half-dozen plastic folders it contains, briefly riffs through each and replaces them. 'Yeah,' he's saying as he does all this. 'See your point. Probably take years and you'd be overtaken by events. Well, one event.' He glances up at me, returns his attention to the folders. 'Just more money for the lawyers anyway. And the accountants, of course. Can't forget the accountants. Mustn't leave them out.' He stands, kicks the flaps back over the box. 'Clear. Ready to go.'

I take the boxes down for Dad's inspection. My back is starting to hurt.

'Help me move this, will you, love?' Hol asks when I go back for the boxes she's left on the landing. In the room, we shift the bed away from the wall, exposing more long cardboard boxes and some old rolled-up carpets wrapped in giant clear plastic bags.

'How's it going?' Hol asks.

'Good,' I tell her. 'We're getting through lots of stuff. Haze and Paul are a bit slow.'

'Paul's damaged,' Hol says, climbing over the bed to lie on it and open up one of the boxes. Her bum looks good in her tight jeans. 'Haze . . . well, Haze is damaged too, but with Paul it's mostly temporary.' She pulls back the flaps of the box.

'Also, I've checked with Pris and Ali about the whole them-being-my-mother thing? I don't think they are either.'

'*Carpet* tiles?' Hol is saying, batting away some disturbed dust. She glances back at me. 'Nobody did, hon. Including Guy.'

'I know, but I thought I'd better ask, just to be sure.'

'Well, hope that's put your mind at rest.'

'I suppose,' I say, pulling out one of the wrapped carpets. 'Hol?'

'Kit,' she says, pulling up wads of grey carpet tiles but then letting them fall back again. 'There's nothing else in here,' she mutters. 'These can go.'

'You know that money?'

'What money, hon?' She closes the box flaps again.

256

'That you've been looking after for me.'

'Oh. Yeah.'

'About how much are we talking about? Just roughly?'

'Oh,' Hol says, still lying on the bed, opening another box between it and the wall. 'Not sure, offhand.'

'Ah. I thought maybe you'd, like, brought a cheque. This weekend. Like we . . . you know . . .'

'Well,' Hol says, not looking back at me. 'I sort of have. Well, I *have*,' she says. She lifts out another carpet tile. This one is olive.

'Oh.'

'Couple of grand,' she says quietly. She rummages in the box of carpet tiles.

'Ah.'

I'm saying 'Ah' – and saying it the way that I said it – because I thought I'd built up significantly more than that; closer to five or six times that.

Hol throws the box flaps closed, twists on the bed. Her face might look a little flushed. She sits up on the bed, then jumps off it and goes to the door and closes it quietly, then stands in the window recess, folds her arms and leans against the windowsill, with a bright, milky sky behind her. 'I don't have all the money, Kit,' she tells me, her gaze fixed on me. 'Not all of it. Not right now.' She pauses, swallows, and I think I'm supposed to say something but I don't know what to say.

Suddenly my insides don't feel so good. It's like going over a sudden dip in the road when your dad's driving and you're just drifting off to sleep and suddenly the world just drops away beneath you. I sit on the bed.

'You will get it,' Hol is saying. 'It'll all be there, with interest, but I don't have it right now. I'm sorry. I'm really

257

sorry. But, look, you don't need it right now, not *right* now, do you? I mean, I've got a cheque with me, for you, for two thousand. That'll definitely clear. That won't be a problem, but the rest . . . it's another eleven or so, all told, I guess . . . you can wait just a bit for that, can't you? Can you?' She's shaking her head. It's hard to see because, framed by the window, she's against the light, made a silhouette of, but she might be crying a little. 'Or have I just . . . ? Is this . . . ? Christ, I feel like I'm just . . . I'm really fucking you over here, Kit, I'm so, *so* fucking sorry, but—' She breaks off, stands up, turns away, puts her hands to her face.

'Well,' I say, after clearing my throat. 'Two thousand's . . . two thousand,' I say, lamely. 'We're not destitute, and . . . there might, there should be money left after the house is sold and everything. Probably.'

'I mean, it's not like you . . . you do okay, you two, don't you?' Hol says, not looking at me. She's looking out the window instead.

I'm back to not knowing what to say again for a bit, because I think I already covered this in what I just said.

'What happened?' I ask her, after a while.

She shakes her head really quickly. 'Life happened, Kit. Tax codes happened, rent rises happened, friends letting me down happened, boyfriends with bad habits happened, hot new magazines and websites folding before they ever got round to paying their contributors fucking *happened*.'

Hol sounds angry, and I think maybe she sounds angry with me, which leaves me feeling a bit confused because I can't see what I've done wrong. I sort of want to stand up and go over to her and put my arms round her and cuddle her and reassure her – not even anything sexual . . . though definitely that too, if I'm being honest – because she sounds

258

hurt, and it would be good to try to take that away from her, try to make that better, because she's Hol, after all.

And yet this isn't fair, because I'm the one who's been let down here. I realise Hol's had problems and people have let her down, and I feel sorry for her for that, but it wasn't me who let her down and now she's letting me down.

We did an experiment in Physics class once with a van de Graaff generator where the whole class joined hands and one person got to touch the shiny globe at the top of the machine and the shock passed instantly to every one of us, making us all flinch, yelp, jump or scream, and I remember thinking, *Oh, thanks; so we all get to share the pain.* And this feels like that: like pain passed on, for no reason. At least, for no fair reason.

Hol turns round, sniffing and wiping a finger under each eye. She doesn't look flushed any more. 'You'll get your money, Kit,' she says, and her voice sounds slightly flat somehow. 'I won't let you down. I mean, I won't . . . this won't . . . this isn't *it*, this isn't permanent. I just . . . things, timings . . . kind of . . .' She shakes her head again, settles back against the window. 'This isn't me,' she says quietly, as though talking to herself, and shaking her head. 'This isn't what I'm like, I don't do this, I don't pull this kind of . . . I can't believe I'm having to say this.' She looks up at me. 'You will get your money, Kit,' she tells me.

I sit, nodding. 'Well, okay,' I say. 'Good.'

'Oh, Kit, Jesus. Is that all you can say?' It sounds almost like she wants to laugh, though her voice sounds wavery, like she might be about to cry, too.

'I suppose,' I tell her, shrugging, 'I don't know what else to say.'

She laughs a little at this, then gives a quick, sharp sigh.

'You'd be within your rights to shout and scream at me, Kit.' She clears her throat. 'If it'll help, feel free. Won't change anything, of course, but just let it rip if you need to.'

'I don't really see the point.'

'Going for silent, wounded disapproval instead, are we?' she says. 'How terribly British.' She sounds bitter, I think, again as though this is somehow my fault.

'I'm a bit . . . numbed, I suppose,' I say.

'Yeah, well,' she says, voice clipped. 'I guess numbed is a good way to be these days. Feeling less, being pre-disappointed, armoured by low expectations of people. And . . . oneself. Definitely the way to go. Smart move. Well done. Proud of you.' She folds her arms again. Her voice changes once more, goes deeper, slower, as she hangs her head. 'Oh, Kit, I'm so sorry.'

Oh bugger it, I'm going to hug her. I get up and go over and put my arms round her. She's stiff and it's awkward at first but then she brings her head up and lays it on my chest and puts her arms first on my hips, as though she might be going to push me away, but then round me – well, as far as she can reach, anyway – as well. We do a proper hug. Her hair smells clean, of coconut.

Hol stiffens again. 'Kit,' she says, 'have you got a fucking erection?'

'Oops,' I say, letting go and backing off.

'Jesus,' she sighs, folding her arms again and looking away.

'You check the rugs,' I tell her, kicking one of the rolled-up carpets. 'They might be sellable. I'll come back for the carpet tiles.'

I take the boxes in the hall down to Guy.

7

'I might have found something,' I tell Paul. He's sitting in the shed, on an old bar stool he and Guy nicked from a pub, twenty-plus years ago. He's been taking out whole drawers of junk from the various chests of drawers crammed into the shed; some under the workbench, most piled around the walls. In places they are three chests tall. They all look ancient.

Mostly, Paul's been using a blunt wood chisel to lever the tops off a variety of nine-tenths-empty paint tins, which seem to form at least a quarter of the ecology of clutter, debris and scrap the shed contains. Then I take the drawers out to the big pile of stuff in the middle of the lawn and dump them.

So far, the stacked drawers are making up a large part of the overall shape of the slowly building bonfire. All that old paint should burn well, though I guess there will be a lot of blackened tins left afterwards.

Even the weather is cooperating; the skies are almost clear, the wind is gentle and the air mild and the next rain isn't forecast until tomorrow afternoon, when everybody will have gone, though there is a chance we might get some this evening; I'll check the latest forecast soon.

'We're probably going to contravene some Clean Air Act, when we burn all this ancient shit,' Paul is saying, and then looks at me. '*What?*'

'I might have found something,' I tell him again.

'The tape?'

'Maybe. I'm not sure. It's not very accessible. It'll need to be checked out.'

Paul looks round the dim interior of the shed. 'Not in here, I take it?'

'No.'

'Whose . . .' He smiles. 'Whose jurisdiction is it under, then?'

'It's not where any of us are looking,' I tell him.

He stares at me. 'Kind of renders this whole operation somewhat moot, doesn't it?' He sighs, puts the chisel down. Its wooden handle is splayed at the top where it's been repeatedly hit with a hammer over the years. Paul sighs. 'I say moot, I mean pointless.'

'It might not be the tape we're looking for,' I say. 'That might still turn up, somewhere in the house. Out here; wherever.'

Paul does not look good. You can see he's hung-over, and tired. He frowns. 'So why can't you just—'

His iPhone, lying on the workbench, rings. His eyes close and he grimaces, then he opens them, leans, looks at the screen. 'Oh, fuck,' he breathes. 'Excuse me,' he says to me. He picks up the phone. 'Ben, hi. What?'

He listens for a while, making a variety of funny faces as he looks out of the window. Eventually he says, 'Yeah, well, they'll just have to . . . Well, no, they just will. That's—' He looks at me as the other person talks to him some more. I can hear their voices, though not what they're actually saying.

Paul puts on an expression like a stupid person and slowly crosses his eyes. I smile. Then, after a sigh or two, he says, 'Ben . . . Ben . . . Ben. Ben? Ben. Ben. Yes, right. See, the thing is; that's . . . that's just not covered. It's not there, in what we have, in our instructions. This is a new direction, new proposal, new ball game, so it just isn't something we can speak to. This is a client decision, and they're not contactable until Tuesday p.m. earliest; more likely Wednesday, on past form. Even then, they're never going to come back with a clear yes or no immediately. They'll go away and think about it. Probably for a mystifyingly long time. So . . . So . . . No, yeah, I hear you, yeah, loud and clear and unam-fucking-biguous, partner, but, well . . . Yeah, understand. Understand, yeah, yep, understand. Totally understand. Totally understand. Don't sympathise, barely care, but completely understand . . .' Paul gazes up at the ceiling of the outhouse for a moment, as though looking for a sign. Or cobwebs. We have plenty of those.

Then, with a sigh, he says, '. . . Yeah, well, this is, clearly, an unspeakable human tragedy for them, but wait for another day or two is exactly what we're going to have to ask the poor little souls to do, bless them . . . Well, God knows it's a big ask, I realise, but they'll just have to try to draw the strength from somewhere. Maybe there's some therapy with heated coprolites of just the right healing frequency they could . . .'

The person on the other end is talking again. Paul takes the phone away from his ear and puts it to the outside of his right thigh, pressed against the fabric of his jeans. He looks at me and shakes his head. 'Dear fucking God,' he says, then sighs again and brings the phone back up to his ear.

He listens for a bit, then he holds the phone in front of

him – I can hear the voice of the other person almost well enough to make out the words – and presses the screen. The voice stops. Paul holds the iPhone's top right button down for a few seconds until the power-off screen presents itself, then he slides his finger along the top of the touchscreen, which goes black. 'There,' he says with a small smile, putting the phone back on the bench, face down. 'And if I could take the fucking battery out, I would.'

He turns to me. 'So,' he says. 'This thing that might or might not be the tape, that you can see but can't . . . access.' He shakes his head, looks confused. 'Is it in the window of a shop or something?'

I put some of the paint-tin lids into the latest cleared drawer, stacking them neatly against one side. 'It's a little complicated,' I tell him.

Paul's eyes close briefly. 'Oh, goody. Please, do tell, then. I . . . I feel the need for some additional complexity in my life, goodness knows.'

I push the tin lids from one side of the drawer to the other. Then I push them back the other way. After a moment, Paul says, 'Kit?'

'It's a sex tape, isn't it?' I say, looking at him.

Paul sighs mightily. His head goes down, his chin almost on his chest. 'Yes, Kit; it's a sex tape. A porn tape. *Debbie Does Bewford*, I do believe we called it.'

'Aha.'

'Yes, as you say; aha.'

'So, embarrassing.'

Paul nods. 'Embarrassing would be one word for it, at the . . . at the very mild end of the spectrum of adjectives one might care to employ. Yes.'

'So, which of you guys would be most . . . embarrassed?'

Paul smiles. 'Oh, I think we'd all find it quite thoroughly embarrassing if it came to light and was ever seen by . . . well, anybody, but clearly it might be potentially harmful for my political career, in particular. Hence my close interest in the matter. There; are you happy?'

'So, is it, like, one couple, of you, I mean, or a threesome or—'

'It's pretty much all of us getting it on with everybody else. We kind of got carried away. It's utter filth from beginning to end, Kit, with erect cocks and close-ups of penetrations all over the place, not to mention come-shots and some anal and a little guy-on . . . male-on-male action and . . . and quite a lot of lesbian stuff too, and even simulated sex with a dog at one point.'

'Wow,' I say.

'Yeah; *simulated* sex with a dog. But simulated quite convincingly, if I say . . . I mean, no animals harmed, etc. Though . . . even so, obviously.'

'Was this the dog Dad used to have?'

'Yup. Old Brassica himself.'

'*Brassica?*'

'Yeah. Brassica. Why?'

'I thought he was called Mixtape. Because he was a mongrel.'

Paul shakes his head. 'No. Guy told us he was called Brassica because he was a collie.' Paul looks thoughtful. 'He looked mostly collie.'

This is not exactly LOL territory. Actually I'm not even sure this is worth a little cursory half-breath-down-the-nose micro-laugh, so I don't bother. 'Maybe Mixtape was like his first name and Brassica was his surname,' I suggest. Paul looks at me. 'Or something,' I add.

265

'Yeah, or something,' Paul says. 'Or this is just Guy being Guy again. Or they were different dogs entirely.'

'Okay,' I say, nodding. 'Yeah.'

Paul gazes into the middle distance. 'I blame the E,' he says quietly. 'We did far too much Ecstasy back then. Amongst other stuff, but . . . a lot of E.' He shakes his head.

'Mm-hmm.'

'And the camerawork is . . . terrible, it has to be said. Well below our usual standards. Really shaky, focus poor. Or on a tripod with nobody manning it; we're part out of frame half the time. But still, ample footage to get us all as fully disgraced and as fired as our respective employers might deem fit.'

'It's all starting to make sense,' I tell him.

That's me almost out of filler phrases, apart from '*Really?*' Hopefully we'll get back to the conversational main sequence shortly.

'So, where is it?' he asks. 'Or where might it be?'

(Aha!)

'It might be in the quarry,' I tell him. 'On a ledge about four or five metres up from the base of the cliff, the work-face just over the back garden wall.'

He looks at me. 'So you've seen it?'

'I've seen something that might be it. I tried to get down to it earlier but the rope wasn't long enough and I got too tired. Climbing up from the bottom shouldn't be too difficult. There's a ladder in the garage that might reach without any real climbing at all.'

'Can we get into the quarry?'

'Definitely. Might even get the car in; depends on whether the gate's been locked at the far side.'

Paul looks out of the shed window for a moment, nodding

as though to himself. 'Well, I don't think I'm fit to drive, frankly, but you could.'

'There's a charity shop in town that lets you leave stuff for them outside the back door, in these sort of skip things, plus the recycling centre is open seven days a week; I thought I'd wait until I have to make a trip, then just come back via the quarry.'

'Volvo filling up, is it?'

'Fairly quickly. Another half-hour or so and I'll have to head into town. Or its springs'll collapse.'

'You okay to do all this yourself? Or do you need help?'

'Fine myself. Just letting you know.' I pause. 'Of course, we could just tell the others.'

'Yeah,' Paul says, taking up the old wood chisel. 'We could, but let's not.'

'You not wanting to keep this stuff?' Guy asks.

It's a box of old drawings – things I did when I was a kid.

I pick up a sheet of A4 with some incomprehensible crayon scrawls on it, mostly purple. 'Not really.'

Guy leans down to the box and picks up a truly ancient sepia-coloured school book. It has his name on it, but that's been crossed out and my name substituted. He flicks through it.

'This was one of mine,' he says. 'No idea why I kept it the first time either. Remember this?' He holds up the book, fanned open. There are lots of imaginatively drawn numbers of various sizes.

'No.' It looks like it might be my childhood doodling style, but it means nothing.

Guy laughs. 'Think that was the first time I knew you were going to be a proper handful.'

267

'*Really?*'

'You asked why there were no capital numbers.'

'Capital numbers?'

'You said there were capital letters so there ought to be capital numbers too, like at the start of big numbers, or important ones.'

'Oh,' I say, squinting at one of the scrawls. 'That's why this three is so big and the point one four is so small.'

'Took me a day to realise there *were* capital numbers,' Guy says as I drop the book back in the box. 'Only they're roman. Big v's and little v's and suchlike.'

'So, no capital zeros,' I say.

Guy nods, sighs. 'Yeah, that's what you said back then, too.'

'I'm going out in the car now,' I tell Paul. He's finished with the paint tins and is stacking old offcuts of wood into a rusted wheelbarrow. The floor of the wheelbarrow is fifty per cent hole, but he's put a bit of plywood over it to stop everything falling through.

'Want a hand?' he asks. 'I could hold the ladder or something.'

'Okay.'

We're in luck; there's a truck-sized side gate to the quarry itself that allows access without entering the compound where the buildings and machinery are, and this gate's closed but not locked.

We've been to the recycling centre and the skips at the back of the charity shop off Bishopsgate. Paul wanted to go to the quarry first but understood when I said the car was too laden; we'd ground it on the rough quarry roads unless we got all the weight out the back first.

I close the gate behind us and drive up the shallow ramp of crushed rock to the right, taking the north-west side round the great scoop of removed rock. The quarry's two great stagnant pools, divided by a single thin causeway of crushed rock, lie still and dark green at the lowest level, five metres below us. A modest ten-metre cliff circles the next tier up, its base level with where we are now. The main, most recently worked face is above us, taller still and set back even further.

Paul leans forward in his seat. 'Fuck me. You don't realise how big it is from up top, do you?'

'They've removed about twenty million tons of rock from here,' I tell him. I think that was the latest figure I heard quoted. Whatever; Paul looks suitably impressed.

We're in second gear and going quite slowly, but the car's meeting lots of grey and khaki-coloured puddles, deeper dips and hollows, and the sort of random, jagged stones and small boulders on the track that a truck wouldn't notice but which a car struggles to cope with; we're getting bounced around a lot.

Paul's holding the dashboard and looking a little pale. 'You okay?' I ask him.

He stares out through the windscreen, swallows, nods. 'I've been better,' he admits.

I slow down, go into first gear. The bumping and jostling becomes less violent. When we get to the top of the ramp that leads to the shelf around the base of the main cliff, the road levels out and the surface becomes more even; we can do nearly twenty without getting thrown around too much. Big boulders the size of hatchbacks line the cliff edge like outsize traffic bollards. Ahead, at the far end of the quarry, the bit where the little landslide took place is just about visible

269

if you know what you're looking for. The wall of the house is a small straight line across the skyline, its tilted roofs like dark tents against the clouds, sheltering behind the trees, though the house disappears as we get closer to the far south wall.

Paul looks relieved as we get out of the car. Little piles of earth and turf and dirty-looking stones lie at the foot of the cliff, beneath the site of the landslide. We both have a look round but there's nothing man-made lying around down here. I'm not even sure from this angle whether I can tell which shelf I decided might hold the thing that might or might not be the tape. I un-bungee the ladder from the roof-rack and slide it out to maximum extension. We lever it up against the cliff, roughly in the middle of the landslip. We make sure both feet are firm and slightly embedded in the track, then Paul holds the ladder while I climb it.

It all looks quite different from when I was dangling on the end of a rope earlier. I get to the top, take a good look around. The ledge I saw before is, I think, about three metres away to my left, but a metre higher than the top reach of the ladder.

I climb back down. 'It's over this way,' I tell Paul.

We reposition the ladder, step back and wait while some earth and small stones shower down, rattling and bouncing, and then I go up again.

'Should have brought a hard hat,' Paul says.

The ledge is a bit more than a metre above. I climb again until I'm standing on the topmost rung of the ladder. The cliff is pretty rough and there are numerous holds so it's not difficult.

'Fuck's sake, Kit, be careful,' Paul yells.

'Yeah!' I shout. 'Don't worry!' Which sounds a bit point-less, but I suppose you have to say something.

270

My head's still not quite at ledge level. I look down, find footholds, and use the earth-spattered lip of the ledge as a handhold to steady myself as I push up.

'Jesus, Kit!' Paul shouts.

'Just keep the ladder where it is,' I tell him, trying to sound reassuring.

I feel for another couple of footholds. I find only one but that should be enough. There's a straggly-looking but sturdy-feeling bush growing on the ledge. I use this to steady myself, push up again and slide chest-first onto the ledge, which is about half a metre wide and sloped with dirt.

I hold onto the bush with one hand, find a handhold on the cliff behind with the other, and sort of pull and wriggle myself round until I'm sitting.

The straight-edged white objects I saw from further up this morning are still plausibly some bleached bones from a fallen lamb or a large bird; or something man-made, maybe plastic. Whatever they are, they're about another metre away along the ledge to the left, past and partly underneath another misshapen, dead-looking bush.

I'm sort of half sat on the narrow ledge now, legs hanging over the edge, bum balanced on the angle of soft earth. This would be a lot easier if there hadn't been a landslip, turning the ledge from a flat shelf to a slippy, unstable slope. If I'm to get over there I'll have to bump my way along on my backside for a metre, over more slidey earth and past this other bush. I think I can probably do it, but there's nothing much to grab at if I start to slip, apart from this lifeless-looking shrub. Or I could turn around again – a bit dangerous in itself – push up to stand on the ledge and then sidle along. Then have to get back down to this sort of level to pick the tape up. Or kick it over the edge.

271

I bend at the waist, look down and shout, 'Can you re-position the ladder again? Metre that way?' I nod.

'Okay. Hold on.'

Paul struggles to lever the ladder away from the cliff. I'm starting to worry he'll pull it back and lose control and it'll land on the car, or go whanging over the cliff behind and down into the deepest level of the quarry.

'Just sort of turn it,' I tell him.

'What?'

This takes some explaining. We get the ladder to where I want it eventually, just under the relevant bit. I bump along in that direction, digging little heel-of-the-hand holds as I go. My hands are getting absolutely filthy. Getting past the dried-up bush is slightly exciting, too.

'What can you see?' Paul shouts.

'Well,' I shout back down, 'one corner of a white plastic TDK-branded VHS tape case, partially covered with earth.'

'Well, yeah!' Paul shouts.

With my left leg dangling only half a metre above the end of the ladder and one hand holding onto a two-fingers-wide handhold, I swing over and plunge my hand into the earth, just shy of where it needs to be. I bump closer, having to trust to the bush now. I think it feels trustworthy. I've already opened one big gilet pocket, for the tape.

Finally, I pull the tape case out of the loose earth around it.

'Well, it's not empty!' I shout to Paul. I bump back a little along the dirt-smothered ledge, get my hand back to the good hold on the rock, then risk letting go – trusting the compacted earth beneath my bum to hold me on the ledge – and using both hands I slide the cassette most of the way out.

It's a Sony inside, not TDK. It isn't an ordinary VHS tape; it feels unbalanced somehow and half of it has a sort of

272

smoke-brown window over it, with a smaller tape visible inside.

I shove the cassette back into the case and stick the case into the big outer pocket of my gilet.

'Got it!'

'Brilliant!'

'Okay,' I shout. 'Hold it steady. Coming down.'

I edge back a little the way I came, about a bum-width. My camo trousers are going to be filthy as well.

'What are you doing?' Paul shouts.

'Just getting in position. Keep the ladder where it is.'

I get as firm a grip as I can with one hand, then turn round, using the other hand to grab a hold on the cliff behind. My legs should be directly above the ladder; I can't look to check, but now I can control myself better.

'Is the ladder beneath my feet?' I shout.

'Yes!' Paul hollers back.

I lower myself slowly, swinging my feet from side to side a little to feel for the ladder. Clonk. Got it.

'You're there!' Paul yells.

I get both feet on the ladder and start stepping down, a rung at a time, until I can grasp the sides of the ladder again.

I pull the tape case from my pocket, then the cassette from inside the case. 'That what you're looking for?' I ask Paul.

He nods, takes it. 'Could well be.' He slides a switch on one surface, tries it a few more times. 'Hmm. Jammed. Surgery may be required.'

I start bringing the ladder down, walking the bottom further out from the cliff so it clatters down the rock face. 'Suppose that makes me a professional climber, now,' I tell him.

'Yeah,' Paul says. 'Don't worry, Kit. You'll get your money.'

'What are you going to do now? Do we tell people?'

'Let me take a quick look, assuming I can get it working, and then, yes, we'll tell people.'

'Okay.'

I get the ladder flat on the ground, unclip it and collapse it. We put it back on the roof-rack. I take some time to brush off all the dirt that I can from my clothes but then put an old bin bag between my bum and the Volvo's seat anyway. The Volvo's driver's seat is kind of stained and filthy already, frankly, but there's no need to get it totally minging. I use a rag to clean my hands as best I can.

Paul looks a little healthier and happier as we head out of the quarry. He sits with the tape on his lap. Before we get to the quarry buildings and the gate he's taken out his wallet and extracted five fifty-pound notes, folding them and depositing them into my gilet's left breast pocket.

'Bonus for the hair-raisingly risky climbing,' he explains.

I smile. 'Ta.'

'So,' he says, after we're clear of the quarry approach track and back on the public road. 'How do we think the tape got there?'

I have a think about this. 'That's a very good question,' I tell him. I am extremely pleased with this answer.

'Any thoughts?' Paul asks.

'About how it got there?'

'Yeah, Kit,' Paul says, 'that's kind of what I thought we were currently talking about.'

'Well, a few,' I say, reminding myself not to get too cocky. 'It's just . . . I don't want to accuse anybody.'

'Strictly between us, then,' he says. 'I'll give you my word it won't go any further.'

'Your word?' I ask him. I'm not even entirely sure he's being serious, though he looks like he is. I don't think

274

anybody's ever offered me their word on something before. It sounds so old-fashioned.

'Yes, my word, Kit. Believe it or not, that actually counts for something, for some of us. Try not to gasp.'

'Okay. But it's not just that; I'm not even sure whether the landslip happened first or afterwards.'

'Do we . . . think somebody buried the tape? On the far side of the wall? Is that . . . ?'

'Not very likely. I think it must have been thrown over the wall.'

'And . . . who would do that?' Paul asks.

'Not me,' I tell him.

'You must have theories,' he says.

'Hmm . . .'

'So . . . on balance. Take a guess; was the tape thrown over before the landslip, or after?'

'I think . . . after, from the way it was lying,' I tell him. 'Though more stuff had sort of dropped on top of it too, I think, so it's hard to be certain. Don't think it had been there all that long. It's not faded with sunshine or anything. Well, apart from the spine, compared to the front and back, but that'll have happened in the house, I suppose, when it was on a shelf.'

I guide the Volvo through the narrow lanes, coming to the T-junction where we turn left and head up the road that leads to the house. The tree branches are arched above like too many thin, tented fingers.

'Wonder why someone would want to throw it away,' Paul says, as we pull out of the junction.

'I can't imagine,' I tell him. I'm guessing he knows this is an outright lie and I'm just trying to be discreet, or protect somebody.

*   *   *

'Where the fuck have you been?'

'Took longer than expected,' I tell Guy.

Paul has gone back to his outhouse. I have a big backlog of boxes and assorted bits and pieces to run past Guy and either take out to the car – I've left it parked closer, to make this easier – or dump on the steadily growing bonfire. Which is bigger than it was when we left; obviously some people have been adding to it themselves without waiting for me to do the donkey work.

I go back to emptying the house, shuttling the rubbish onto the bonfire and the recycling into the Volvo.

There's a break for tea and bacon sarnies. 'Think I'll take a little snooze, after,' Paul tells people. 'Just an hour or so.'

'Have you finished with the outhouse?' Ali asks. She's busy carefully stripping the little glistening lengths of fat from the bacon rashers, depositing them at the side of her plate.

I'd have cut them off with scissors before grilling if she'd said, or done her rashers longer to turn the fat into something more like crackling or even just let her have trimmed medallions if she'd wanted, but she never said. She uses her nails to remove the last bits of fat, then rebuilds her sandwich. It'll be cold now. If enough people do this I'd happily grill up the remains till they're crispy and have them myself, all lovely and crunchy in a folded bit of bread.

Paul isn't really going to have a snooze; he's going to use the time in his room to try to get the mini-VHS tape working and play it in the VHS player he brought with him.

'Yup,' Paul tells Ali, yawning. 'All done. Just a last few boxes for Kit to take away.'

This isn't entirely true; there are still a few drawers to be looked through but I'm pretty sure I know what's in all of them and I've agreed to check them and then do whatever needs doing; won't take long.

'Is there any more brown sauce?' Haze asks.

'Think that's it done,' I tell him.

'Good bacon sarnies,' Hol says, not looking at me.

'I'll be glad to get shot of you gannets,' Guy says. 'Thought Kit ate a lot. Christ.' Guy insisted on a full-size sandwich like everybody else, though I know he won't finish it. He's taken only two bites.

'On our way home tomorrow, bright and early,' Rob tells him.

'This has been fun,' Pris says, smiling, looking round at all of us. 'Don't you think?'

'Yeah,' Guy says, bringing his sarnie up towards his mouth and focusing on it. 'Just like the old days, except with me dying.' He puts the sandwich back down on his plate again.

Ali takes a long-drawn-in breath and fixes her gaze at the table; Rob purses his lips and restirs his tea. Hol is looking blankly off to one side. Haze appears fascinated by Guy's sandwich.

'Oh, Guy,' Pris says, her face pinched. 'Honey, is there really nothing—'

'No. Nothing,' Guy says. 'Tried everything.'

'Have you tried alternative or holistic—'

'No. Not fucking going to, either. You can keep that bollocks. Whatever I've got, the fucker can keep growing despite industrial fucking doses of gamma radiation and laugh in the fucking face of chemicals they originally used in mustard gas. I therefore find the prospect of it being turned around by tiny amounts of infinitely diluted water or the power of closing one's eyes in a nice dark room and thinking about pink ponies somewhat unlikely, to say the least.'

'Well,' Pris says, frowning. 'It's just—'

'No, love,' Guy says. 'Whatever you're going to say, it's not.'

Pris frowns and looks round at the rest, finds no support, and with a little shake of her head says, 'Well, it's you . . . It's your body, Guy. I guess none of us can live your life for you.'

'You can die my death for me, petal,' Guy offers, sounding almost jovial now.

Pris appears, I think, hurt at first but then looks up at him and gives a small explosive laugh when she sees him smiling, winking at her.

'Anyway, remissions happen,' Ali says. 'You can never give up hope. You mustn't. You can't.'

'I *live* in bloody hope, Alison,' Guy tells her. 'Permanent bloody resident. Every morning I wake up thinking, *Hey-hey; maybe it's gone and I'm fine!* Never has been so far, but I don't let that discourage me.'

'I think you're finding your own way to be positive about it all,' Pris says.

'Mr fucking Positivity, that's me.' Guy raises his teacup. 'To fucking Positivity!'

We all toast fucking Positivity. Even me, and I don't normally swear.

Paul gazes up at the top of the still unlit bonfire in the centre of our lawn, then down at Guy. 'This isn't a . . . pyre, is it? You're not going to throw yourself on top of it, are you?' he asks.

'Will you fuck off?' Guy says. 'I have to listen to this bollocks every fifth of November.'

Paul reappeared from his room after about forty minutes,

and went to work with Rob, going through the various cupboards. When I raised my eyebrows at him – Rob was too near for us to talk properly – Paul just blanked me.

The fire is finished, or as finished as it's ever going to be before it's lit. It's about four metres high and the same across, largely composed of bits of ancient soft furniture too old to have fire-resistance labels attached, various worn, moth-eaten carpets, lots of old drawers and their associated chests, assorted bits of vintage plastic and many boxes and bin liners full of papers and old clothes Guy doesn't want to go for recycling.

There's still more stuff that might get added to the bonfire, and the temptation is to leave lighting it until dark, in an hour or two, but the latest forecast is for heavy rain around the same time and the sky to the west is already thickening with dark clouds, so we need to get it going now.

I've packed the heart of the fire with the most combustible stuff, like sawdust, small dry bits of wood, oily rags and the old paint, and left a hole in the side of the fire to give access to the centre. Guy leans awkwardly on one stick and holds a last oily rag from the garage. I use a lighter on the knotted rag and it catches, flames pale in the last watery light filtering through the outskirt tatters of the clouds massing to the west. Little coils of black smoke lick up round the sides as Guy gives it time to catch properly, then he sort of half throws, half pendulums the fiery rag into the heart of the bonfire.

Five minutes later it's already a decent blaze; we stand watching it, transfixed both by the ever-changing flames themselves and the slowly seeping, waving smoke, and by the progress of the burning as it spreads through the fabric of the bonfire, catching quickly on the oily rags and paint-soaked sawdust, producing quick bursts of fire and thick, dark smoke, and crawling more slowly along pieces of wood and crumpled cardboard before starting to lick and lap at the bulging sides of the bin bags, which are beginning to melt and slowly split, exposing and oozing out their contents like bursting sausages in a frying pan. Things are starting to crackle.

Within ten minutes we have to start retreating from the heat, stepping back across the grass. Flames are shooting from the top and beginning to spread laterally everywhere. It feels like the fire has awoken and begun reaching out, as if before it was something small and lazy that was just happening to the pile of stuff that is the bonfire; a function or property of the massed debris, like its height or its mass. Now it's like it's become its own thing, like it's something alive and separate inside the pyre, something with its own independent life and needs and a determination to feed and grow.

There's an urgency to the rise and flick of the flames now as they feed on their own heat and more and more air is sucked into the blaze, to be heated and used and transformed, the resulting gases thrown upwards through the writhing basket of fire. Before, the smoke was rising the way steam rises from a plate of hot food, gently curling through the air, all relaxed and lazy; now it looks propelled, excited, turbo-charged, throwing itself at the sky like something furious, impatient, angry.

It must be the melancholic in me that can already look forward, past the time when the fire is at its peak, fully ablaze – when even where we're standing now would be impossibly, damagingly, skin-crispingly close – to when it's starting to die back again, and then to when it's half collapsed and then fully fallen in, to – hours and hours from now, even if the rain somehow holds off – when it's just black cinders, grey ash and a few half-hidden, low-glowing embers producing a little heated air and not even any smoke any more.

It's like a river, I think suddenly. It starts small and hesitant, becomes bigger, quicker, more assured as it grows, bursts with power and fury in its prime, then returns to slow, meandering quietness towards the end, eventually giving itself to nothing, recycled into its constituent parts.

It's hardly uncommon: something going from near-helpless small beginnings, through childhood and youth to vigorous adulthood, then decrepitude, and an end. So a process, like many others, but short enough and vivid enough for those of us with the time and interest to observe it and draw our own comparisons, if we're that way inclined.

I'm not stupid. I *am* weird and I don't think the way other people do, I realise that, plus, like a computer, I struggle with some stuff that normal people find easy to the point of not even thinking about, but I'm not stupid. I know that part of the reason I'm finding it so affecting standing here looking at the fire – especially with these people, especially with my dad at my side, leaning on his stick, his skeletal fingers clutched like talons round the knurled top – is because this is like looking at an image of our own lives, our own abandoned histories, our own past, baggage and legacies; all that hoarded meaning going up in smoke and flame, reduced to no more than bulk fuel for a mindless chemical reaction.

It's been nearly quarter of an hour now, I reckon, and I don't think anybody's said a thing. If they have, it's been very quietly, and just one person to another, right beside them. I've never heard this lot so quiet when they're all together.

Then there's a sound over the roar of the flames. Guy sounds like he's choking at first, and I start to turn to him. He isn't choking. He puts his head back then jerks it forward and spits into the fire.

Against the riot of flames, it's hard to tell whether the

gobbet of spit gets there, falls short, or is even vaporised by the heat before it can land. Anyway, it vanishes.

'Well,' he says. 'Before we all get totally fucking mesmerised and turn into . . . fucking . . . Zoroastrians, d'you not think it's time for another cup of fucking tea?'

'Well, we have a result,' Paul tells me, after tea and biscuits, on the first-floor landing, while the rain is just starting and we're clearing the last walk-in cupboard.

'And?' I ask, when he doesn't add anything immediately.

'Tell you in the big reveal,' he smiles. 'Shall we just stick to the truth? About the sequence of events?'

I have a think. 'Maybe not mention the money?'

'Agreed. Let's say you just asked me for help after we'd done the recycling, that was the first I knew.'

'Okay.'

There's the noise of the loo flushing, and when Rob reappears, I'm already heading downstairs with another box. My back is quite sore now.

'Yeah, but it's true, isn't it?' Haze says, nodding slowly, eyes partially closed, staring into the middle distance, or at least whatever portion of it is available within the confines of the sitting room. 'When you stare into the void, it, like, stares back at you.'

'Does it, fuck,' Guy snorts.

Haze looks at him, blinking rapidly.

We're just finishing a curry we had delivered. Paul paid for it. Everybody thought Haze was going to cook tonight but it turns out he accidentally brought a bag full of football gear instead of his collection of specially mixed hand-ground spices and secret sauce bases. He was full of apologies.

We ordered too much, which is great; there's another four full meals here – more if I boil some rice to go with it. In my head, I'm already reorganising the contents of the freezer to make room for everything. And this is even allowing for further grazing on the most snackable stuff. I may tidy up fairly soon to get the surviving main-meal portions safely out of the way and remove them from being tempting. This is sneaky, but frankly we've all gorged ourselves and it'll probably be better for their waistlines.

More beer and wine has been opened, though everybody agrees they can't get too drunk as they're all heading home tomorrow. I'm drinking some medium-sweet white from a wine box Pris brought.

'Whoa, dude. I'm just saying what I felt,' Haze says, through a small cloud of exhaled smoke. Ali, sitting nearby, waves it away with quick, sharp flaps of her hand.

'No you're fucking not,' Guy tells him. 'You're just repeating a load of ego . . . drenched, self-regard-saturated, pseudo-mystical bollocks.'

Hol mutters something about 'calling my homie Freddy N on one of his greater insights', though she says it so quietly I think maybe only I hear it as Rob sighs and says,

'Just give up now, Haze.'

'Is that from *Touching the Void*, that climbing—' Ali says, as Guy jabs one bony finger at Haze.

'How does the fucking void stare back at you?'

'I was just saying, I was looking into the quarry this morning—' Haze begins.

'How the *fuck* does the fucking void stare back at you?' Guy demands, louder. He's already complained about having a headache this evening and he's taken more painkillers than he really should. Sometimes when he's in a lot of pain he gets more angry and combative and, well, vicious. 'Where are its eyes, where is its fucking nervous system, where is the brain that is receiving the results of this so-fucking-directed staring? Staring implies looking, looking implies – requires, fucking demands – something to stare with, something to interpret and consider and fucking philosophise about the results of this "staring". How does any fucking absence of rock or other material cobble together the intellectual wherewithal to do anything as organised as fucking *stare*?'

'I think,' Paul says, 'it's generally regarded as being just a metaphor for the connection you feel when you gaze upon something . . . profound.'

'Really?' Guy sneers. 'I think it's an excuse for the intellectually challenged and . . . pretentious to make themselves feel important. Wow, man,' Guy says, suddenly switching to a deeper, stoned-sounding, slightly posher voice and slowing down a fraction, 'like, I'm so fucking the centre of the world I can't stare into this crack in the ground without it showing me the respect of, like, staring back at me, like, you know? Cos I'm, like, as vacuous as it is, yah?' He shakes his head, switches back to his normal voice as he says, 'Jesus,' and drinks from his can of Newcastle Brown.

For a moment I can hear the rain spattering against the windows. It was heavier earlier. I checked on the fire ten minutes ago and it's almost out, a lot of stuff only half burned.

'Whatever you say, dude, but I felt something,' Haze says, shrugging. He hands the joint to Guy, who takes it and says,

'Whatever you felt, it wasn't being fucking stared at.'

'Have it your way,' Haze says, sitting back and exhaling some more smoke.

I think Guy's being a little unfair on Haze. I know what

284

it's like to stare at something and feel fascinated. Even trivial things can do this. I remember getting that feeling for the first time with a kitchen tap, and water. I was just a kid and standing on an upturned bucket or something so I could reach the big main sink and I was experimenting with the cold tap, turning it on and off and trying to regulate it as accurately as possible.

The phenomenon that really entranced me was when I got the flow just right, almost but not quite closed off. You had to start with the tap running, not from it being off – it works only one way, on our taps at least. You reduce the flow to just before it cuts into individual droplets, and, if you get it right, it suddenly turns into a single thin column of water, looking somehow so still that it might as well be made out of glass; you can't see any sign of it flowing at all. The very first time I did this I was young enough to imagine that it literally had turned into glass, and had to stick my finger into the stream to see.

I loved the fact that you couldn't see the water flow; you had to look into the sink, where it was hitting the white ceramic surface, to see that the water was actually still falling from the tap and heading down the plughole.

Of course, since doing Physics, now I know that what I was observing was an example of laminar flow, and that when you open the tap up a little further the stream's behaviour modulates into standard non-laminar flow – with turbulence, which is the norm – but at the time I remember being mesmerised by the effect, and thinking that I was somehow connecting with something deep and mysterious.

(I also loved letting thin, clear honey or syrup dribble off a spoon and onto a slice of bread – from high-enough up – so that the hair-thin stream of it at the bottom wriggled and darted about the place as it hit, like a mad thing. Though that didn't feel quite so profound and Zen as the static stream-of-water thing, maybe because it was about frantic, erratic movement rather than stillness.)

'Anyway,' Haze says, sounding almost upset. 'The sodding void *did* stare back at me; only it was Kit. He was in it, in the quarry, or at least, like, just climbing out; he stared back at me. Didn't you, Kit?'

Now they're all looking at me.

I try to keep calm and not blush. 'Yes I did,' I agree, nodding and trying to look serious and unflapped.

'In the fucking *quarry*?' Guy says.

'There's been a landslip, just over the back wall,' I tell him, then look round at the rest. This is something I've been thinking about, preparing for. 'I wanted to check it was just the topsoil that had fallen away with all the rain, not the start of the rock crumbling, so I got a rope from the garage and took a look.' They're all still staring at me. I nod in what I trust is a reassuring manner. 'We're fine. Just topsoil and . . . stones and a few roots and stuff. No problem.' They're still staring at me. In the silence, I almost add, 'You're welcome,' but that might be a bit too cheeky.

'Is this where you were when you should have been helping me get up this morning?' Guy asks.

'Yes.'

'*How* do you know it's safe?' Ali asks. 'You're not a geologist.'

'Bit dangerous, no, Kit?' Rob says, smiling.

'You daft bugger; you could have fucking killed yourself!' Guy says. 'Who'd look after me then?'

'You didn't think to *say* anything?' Hol is saying. She's been mostly quiet this evening. She drinks from her glass of red.

'Well, before, I didn't want to worry anybody,' I tell them. I shrug. 'After I'd done it, I felt kind of foolish for worrying myself, so I didn't say anything then either.'

'And you,' Hol says, looking at Haze. 'You didn't say anything.'

'I just thought, like, this was something Kit did every day or something.'

'*What?*' Hol says.

'For exercise,' Haze says, looking down, as though he's only now realising this sounds a bit odd.

'. . . Anyway,' Paul says. 'On to other business. We have the tape.'

He smiles widely.

I can hear the rain; a flurry hits the window, dies away again.

'No fucking kidding?' Guy says, as Pris says,

'When were you going to tell us?'

'Yeah, no kidding,' Paul says to Guy, then looks to Pris. 'This is me telling you now, honey,' he says.

'When did you find it?' Rob asks.

'Where was it?' Ali demands.

'Let me hand you back to my capable colleague, Mr Kitchener Hyndersley,' Paul says, waving one hand in my direction. 'Kit; if you'd be so kind.'

'Oh,' I say, suddenly on the spot. 'Okay.'

So I tell them about looking down from the cliff and seeing stuff on ledges below me. Then about asking Paul for his help and us going to the charity shop and recycling centre, and then driving into the quarry and using the ladder to climb up to the ledge.

'You've had it since this *morning?*' Ali yelps, glaring at Paul, then me.

'Yeah,' Paul says, 'but we weren't sure we had the right one until I'd got it working. It was jammed. I wanted to be sure it was the right tape before I said anything. That took a while. Didn't want to stop people searching in case the real one was still out there.'

'So . . .' Rob is saying, glancing from me to Paul and back again. 'It is definitely the tape?'

'Almost certainly,' Paul says.

'Only *almost*?' Hol says. 'What the fuck else could you mistake it for?'

'Has . . . Kit seen . . . the tape?' Pris asks.

'Nope,' Paul says. Meanwhile I'm shaking my head, to confirm. 'Want to see it?' Paul asks, looking round at us all.

'With Kit here?' Rob says, frowning.

'Yeah.' Paul is smiling. 'That's not actually going to be a problem. Trust me.' Paul looks at Guy. 'Guy?' he says.

'What?' Guy looks angry.

'You okay with this?'

Dad stares at him. 'Fuck it, yeah. Let's at least watch the start, eh?'

Paul stands. 'I'll get the gizmo.'

Once Paul has left the room, Guy looks at me. 'Keeping this very quiet, weren't we?' he says.

'I'm getting another drink,' Haze announces. 'Anybody else?'

I shrug. 'Like Paul says, didn't want to say anything until we knew.'

Another couple of top-ups and cans are requested. Haze leaves the room.

Rob is switching on the old combo player under the telly. 'Yeah,' he says. 'When did this start working?'

'When I fixed it,' I tell him. They all look at me.

'So,' Guy says, 'do you know what was—' He breaks off to cough. 'Do you know what's on the tape?'

'Something embarrassing,' I tell him.

'One way of putting it,' Ali says.

Hol is looking at me. It's a funny look, like she almost doesn't know who I am. I don't think I remember her ever looking at me like that before. It gives me a strange feeling in my insides; not a nice one.

'How the fuck . . . ?' Rob says, pointing the TV remote and clicking repeatedly.

'Let me,' Ali says, reaching, but he turns away so she can't take the control from him.

'No, I can—'

'Will you just let me do it? You're never any good . . .'

'It's just—'

'Will you give it here?'

More pointing and clicking. 'Maybe the batteries . . .'

They keep on arguing.

Guy looks at them with what might just be an affectionate sneer. Definitely a sneer, anyway. 'Well, ladies and gents,' he says, in an old-style, radio-DJ voice, 'we seem to be experiencing a few technical difficulties at the moment, but we hope that isn't spoiling your enjoyment of the smooth sounds here on RTFM . . .'

'Fuck *off*!' Rob says, as Ali tries to grab the remote from him.

'Give it to the kid,' Guy says.

'You're just being stubborn!' Ali tells Rob, trying to take the remote again. Rob, still on his knees in front of the TV, has to raise the device over his head to stop her getting it.

Guy leans forward with a grimace, takes the remote from Rob's hand and throws it to me.

His aim's a bit off but I reach and catch it, then click a couple of buttons. The TV screen flashes, then fills with the fuzzy monochrome visual static I sort of vaguely remember from watching VHS tapes long ago. 'There you go,' I say.

'Wait a minute,' Haze says from the doorway, laden. 'Was it a Newkie Brown or a Guinness, Guyster?'

'Has it got alcohol? Is there a "Y" in the day?' Guy asks, accepting a brown can of the former. He sticks the remains of the joint in the old can, drops it to the floor.

Ali looks at Rob, then me. 'That's what I was going to do,' she tells him.

'*That's what I was going to do,*' he mimics back at her in a pretend-lady voice.

She sort of almost smiles and slaps him on the arm.

'Sit your fat arse on the couch,' he tells her. This is unfair, as Ali does not have a fat arse.

'Sit yours on my face,' she tells him, still nearly smiling, then goes back to sit.

'You should be so lucky.'

'Yeah, I should,' she says, lifting her wineglass.

'That's the wine box empty,' Haze tells Pris, filling her glass from the silver pillow he's extracted from it. He puts the remainder into mine, showing me how to get the very last drops out by careful squeezing and getting the tap-angle just right. Useful.

'Ate viola,' Paul says, returning, brandishing the trick VHS cassette.

The tape starts with more visual static and the sound of crackling. Then it switches to a view of Bewford, probably taken, I reckon from the angle, from the field that rises between the house and the city. You can tell it's old because

290

there's what looks like a microwave tower on Almsworth Hill, and it appears they're just building the multi-storey car park near Marshgate. The picture quality isn't great.

'The Irreconcilable Creative Differences Film Partnership Presents,' says some cheesy-looking digital lettering across the middle of the screen. Ali sighs.

'Are you sure Kit should be . . . ?' Pris is saying.

Paul holds up one hand. 'You'll miss the soundtrack,' he says, as some organ music starts.

'Christ,' Hol says. '"Je t'aime" . . . etc. I'd forgotten.'

'Seriously, Paul,' Pris says, sounding panicky. 'We can't let . . .'

Her voice trails away as the music stops abruptly and the screen flickers, goes dark, flickers again, shows what might be a half-second of the same panning footage of Bewford, with some cursive writing in pink starting to slide across the screen – you can see the edge of the pane of glass it must be written on – before going grey-black again. I think the word in pink said 'Debbie', but only because Paul already told me the film was called *Debbie Does Bewford*; really it's gone too quick.

Then there's more scratchy static and then, suddenly, we're looking at an interior, and the retreating back of a man . . . who is my dad, we realise, as he sits down on a seat facing the camera. He smiles. Actually the smile is more of a gurn. He's sitting where he's sitting now, in the same seat, in this same room. He looks only a year or two younger. He still has the comb-over remains of a full head of blond hair.

'Right then,' he says. He sits back in his seat and folds his arms. I wouldn't have thought you could fold your arms pugnaciously, but Guy manages it. 'The standard fucking disclaimer. If you're watching this I must be dead. You lucky

291

fuckers. Patently all your meagre supplies of talent were sublimated into staying alive.'

Paul asked for the remote when he inserted the tape. Now he points it at the VHS machine, clicks, and the image judders, stalls. It doesn't freeze tidily like a paused DVD or something off a hard disk; it sort of slides to a stop halfway across the screen, the picture all mushed up and smeared like it's a still-wet painting that somebody's wiped with a damp cloth. Seems to have gone monochrome, too.

Paul looks at Guy, who is gazing at the screen with an odd expression that might be sadness, resignation or even mild amusement. 'I listened to the first bit of what follows, Guy,' Paul says quietly. 'Do you want the rest of us to hear it?'

Guy looks into his can, then nods. 'Yeah, why not?' he says. 'Why should you have all the fucking fun?'

'Okay.' Paul restarts the tape.

'Right,' Guy says, from the screen. 'Obviously I don't actually want to die, but I am trying to find what positives I can in the shitty circumstances, and one of those is that I shall be glad to see the back of this poxy little country and this fucked-up world and this bunch of fucking morons constituting my fellow stakeholders in the species *Homo* so-called *sapiens*.'

(Rob sighs heavily and looks at Ali, though she doesn't look at him.)

'I shall,' Guy says, from the screen, 'consider myself well rid of this island's pathetic, grovelling population of celebrity-obsessed, superficiality-fixated wankers. I shall not miss the institutionalised servility that is the worship of the royals – that bunch of useless, vapid, anti-intellectual pillocks – or the cringing respect accorded to the shitting out of value-bereft Ruritanian "honours" by the government of the fucking

292

day, or the hounding of the poor and disabled and the cosseting of the rich and privileged, or the imperially deluded belief that what we really need is a brace of aircraft-free aircraft carriers and upgraded nuclear weapons we're never going to fucking use and which would condemn us for ever in the eyes of the world if we ever fucking did. Not that we can, anyway, because we can't fire the fucking things unless the Americans let us.

'I shall not have to witness the drowning or the starvation through mass-migration of the destitute of Bangladesh or anywhere else low-lying and impoverished, or listen to another fuckwit climate-change denier claiming that it's all just part of some natural cycle, or down to sunspots, or watch as our kleptocrat-captured governments find new excuses not to close down tax havens, or tax the rich such that the fuckers actually have to pay more than they themselves or their lickspittle bean-counters deem appropriate.'

(Rob is shaking his head. Hol is half smiling, half sneering at the screen, eyes bright. Haze says, 'Yeah, tell it like it is, dude!' as he builds another joint.)

'And I shall not miss being part of a species lamentably ready to resort to torture, rape and mass-murder just because some other poor fucker or fuckers is or are slightly different from those intent upon doing such harm, be it because they happen to worship a very slightly different set of supersti-tious idiocies, possess skin occupying a non-identical position on a Pantone racial colour wheel, or had the fucking temerity to pop out of a womb on the other side of a river, ocean, mountain range, other major geographical feature, or, indeed, just a straight line drawn across the desert by some bored and ignorant bureaucrat umpteen thousand miles away and a century ago.

293

'None of these things shall I miss. Frankly it's a relief to be getting shot of the necessity of watching such bollocks play out. I would still rather have the choice, mark you, but, as this would appear to be being denied me, I am making the best of a bad job and looking on the bright side: I shall be free, at last, of that nagging, persistent sensation that I am, for the most part, surrounded by fucking idiots.'

Paul points and clicks. The picture judders to a stop again.

'I fast-forwarded from about here, Guy,' Paul tells him. 'Didn't catch much else you said.' He looks round at the rest. 'Okay to do the same now?'

'There anything at the end?' Rob asks. 'Of what was originally on there?'

'Nah,' Guy says. 'I said my piece then left it running to the end of the tape. Though what I had to say still filled most of it.'

'Almost all,' Paul agrees.

'I assume the next line was something about present company excepted?' Rob says, swigging his wine. He nods at the screen with its frozen image of a slightly younger Guy poised like he's about to open his mouth and start talking again. 'That – this whole tape – was meant for us, for us here, yeah?'

'Yeah,' Guy says, glancing round everybody else in the room. 'Basically for you lot.'

'So when you say "surrounded by fucking idiots" you mean other people, not us.'

Guy looks at Rob for a moment. 'Partly,' he says eventually. 'Though the next couple of minutes might not make particularly . . . ego-boosting . . .' He looks angry, waves one hand. 'The next couple of minutes might not be particularly edifying for any of you.' He grins. 'I spend the time detailing the personal inadequacies of each of you and listing the many ways you've failed to live up to your early promise and your own ambitions, however preposterous and pathetic. So, I wouldn't advise watching any further. Not now we've reached the watershed.'

'Well, I want to hear what you said,' Ali says.

Rob looks at her. 'About you, or me?'

She only glances at him. 'Both,' she says. 'All of us.'

Guy shakes his head. 'I wouldn't.'

'Yeah,' Paul says. 'I wouldn't.'

We all look at him. He shrugs. 'I said I stopped *about* here,' he explains, nodding at the screen. He looks at Guy for a moment, and Guy looks back at him. Paul nods, 'Thank you for your comments, old friend. All grist to the mill, even the negative feedback.'

'Fucking welcome, mate.' Guy grins. 'My pleasure.'

'Were you actually as . . . forthright about the others?' Paul asks, glancing around.

Guy grimaces. 'Only to the extent that I could be,' he says. 'With your higher public profile and potential for doing harm through high . . . or even medium or low office, I felt you required singling out for special attention.' He holds one hand up to Paul. 'No need to thank me, lad. Just doing my bit as a public-spirited citizen.'

Ali opens her mouth, but Guy is already saying, 'Anyway, my tape, my house, my rules. Fast-forward from here,' he tells Paul. 'If you'd be so kind, my good fellow.'

'I think we each have a right—' Ali is saying.

Paul clicks the remote and the image jerks into motion, plays enough tape at something close to normal play speed for one garbled, squeaky word from Guy, then goes into fast-forward. Not a very *fast* fast-forward, but enough to make Guy look comedic as he sits there, hands jerking about as he scratches one ear, the other ear, his nose, the back of his head, and does so repeatedly. He crosses and uncrosses his legs almost too fast to see, waves his arms like he's having a fit.

Something in me winces at the idea of the tape physically having to race past the read/record heads, wearing itself away for our convenience. I've felt the same way listening to a diamond stylus scratching and twitching its way through the groove moulded into a vinyl record. Compared to digital it just all feels so crude, so ancient, so *damaging*.

'You're a lawyer, Paul,' Guy says, watching his own twitchy image on the screen.

'Yes, I am,' Paul confirms, not looking at Guy.

'Then would I be right in thinking that this tape is still my property?'

'I think you would have a case,' Paul says. 'I seem to recall you bought the relevant batch of tapes, and while the original film might, arguably, though without the benefit of a formal, written contract, of course, have been our joint intellectual property – especially given the rubric about the Partnership at the beginning – this would look like it's all yours.'

'Then would you be good enough to furnish me with the aforesaid heretofore fucking mentioned tape when we're finished staring at this haunting from my slightly younger and marginally less-decrepit and despairing self, if you'd be so kind?'

'Why certainly,' Paul says.

The rain must have gone off, or the wind's switched direction.

Then suddenly the Guy on the TV screen is up and

bounding out of his seat and across the room, right up to the camera so it goes dark, then the darkness wipes away and we're looking at almost the same scene but not quite – the angle's changed, slightly to the right, slightly up – and we're watching Guy tearing across the room to the hall door and then the screen goes almost black until you realise all he's done is put out the room light and it must be night outside because apart from a little sliver of light from the hall showing round the edge of the not fully closed door, that's all there is.

In less than a minute, the screen changes to a sort of different, more complete darkness, then there's a quite audible clunk from the tape player under the telly, and the TV defaults to its standard black standby screen with the letters AV2 glowing at the top left corner. It sounds like the tape has started rewinding itself automatically.

'And that's all, folks,' Paul says.

'So that's it?' Hol says, glowering at Guy. 'You recorded some sort of living *will* over it?'

'As I say, more a series of rants, really,' Guy says. 'Best you don't hear the rest of it until I'm safely gone and that thing about suddenly thinking hypocritically well of the recently deceased has kicked in. Cheers.' He drinks from his can of Brown.

'What about the bit where you portion out your worldly goods to your best pals?' Haze asks, sort of laughing.

'Oh, *yeah*,' Guy says, nodding, eyes wide. 'Except that's in the disappointingly but predictably inferior Hollywood remake,' he says. 'And in a different universe.'

'So you still have the video camera?' Hol says.

'Yeah,' Guy tells her. 'But it only works off the mains adaptor, and I can't connect it up to the screen; lost the lead.'

'You sure there's nothing else on there apart from that bit at the beginning?' Ali asks Paul.

'Checked it twice, staring intently all the way,' Paul tells her. 'Then ran it normal speed with the sound down. Nothing. That's four times now. It's one smooth continuous take, apart from the bit where Guy stops talking and – I assume – checks it's all worked, then switches it back on to record the empty room over the rest.'

'Spot on, old bean,' Guy says.

'I've heard there can sometimes be traces of earlier stuff on these old tapes,' Ali says. 'Even after they're recorded over.'

'Oh, don't fucking worry,' Guy says, as the tape clunks to a stop inside the machine. 'That was my fourth or fifth take, recorded on top of different versions of roughly the same rant going back several years. I just updated it a little each time. Took me a while to perfect my . . .' Guy looks at me. 'What's the word I'm looking for? Jesus. Not peroration. Angrier. Like . . . invective!' he says, looking relieved. 'Took me a while to perfect my invective.' He shakes his head, mutters, 'Fuck.'

'I think you're tired,' Pris tells him.

'Tired of hearing excuses for my brain letting me down,' Guy mutters. Paul goes to kneel in front of the VHS player.

'Better yet, our Paul,' Guy says to him, 'just record over it. All of it. Record BBC fucking One over the entirety of the fucker; anything, but bury what's on there.'

'You sure?' Paul asks him.

'Much as it goes against my nature to spare any of you fuckers the pain, yes. What's on there is just embarrassing; I devote far more time to tearing you all apart than any of you remotely deserve. Scrub it. BBC1; might catch *Antiques Roadshow* or something, some pablum almost worth watching.'

298

'I protest,' Ali says. 'We have a right—'

'No you don't,' Guy tells her. To Paul he says, 'Press the red dot button now, if you would.'

Paul says nothing. He uses the controls on the player itself. The appropriate red light starts winking, indicating it's recording. Paul sits again.

'So how come the tape was in the quarry?' Ali says. She's looking at Guy. 'Did you try to throw it away?'

'I have no idea how it got there,' Guy says, not looking at her.

'Well,' Ali says, frowning, 'somebody—'

'So, are we happy, now?' Guy asks.

'You're sure there are no copies?' Paul asks him.

'None I fucking made.'

'And you had it, all the time, yeah?' Rob says.

'Suppose,' Guy says.

'"Suppose"?' Ali says. 'What does that—'

'It means it was here,' Guy tells her. 'In my possession, through-fucking-out. Even when I didn't know exactly where the fuck it was, it was always in the house.'

'Except when it was in the quarry,' Haze points out.

'I think we should get to the bottom of why it was in the quarry at all,' Ali says, crossing her arms.

'You've seen your fucking tape, there's nothing on it to get your knickers in a twist about any longer,' Guy tells her. 'It's getting recorded over, again, and there's no copies of it. Is that not fucking enough?'

'No,' Ali says, frowning. 'I think—'

'Just leave it, Ali,' Rob sighs.

'I don't see that we can leave—'

'Let's take a vote, shall we?' Hol suggests. 'All those who think we should pursue this topic, please raise your hand.'

299

Ali raises her hand. She's the only one. She looks around, her gaze settling on Rob. 'Thanks for the support,' she tells him.

Rob shrugs, grins. 'Any time.'

'Right. Fuck it,' Paul says, clapping his hands once and rubbing them. 'Obviously we're still sticking with the not-drinking-too-much thing, but I think this calls for a celebration. I just happen to have a case of some of Madame Bollinger's finest . . . well, some of her finest non-vintage, in the car.' He looks round at them all, appearing poised to get to his feet. 'Shall I?'

'Fucking yeah,' Guy says, licking his lips. 'Bring on the fucking bubbly.'

Pris claps her hands. 'Woo-hoo!'

''Twould be churlish to refuse,' Rob agrees.

'Hmm,' Ali says, uncrossing her arms. 'Well, this still isn't over. But I suppose . . .'

'Here we go,' Hol breathes. Again, I'm not sure anybody else can hear her.

'Way to go,' Haze says. 'Twelve bottles of Bolly! You beauty!'

'Well, six,' Paul says, standing. 'Champagne bottles tend to come by the half-dozen. Cos they're heavier, I suppose.'

'Yeah,' Haze says, slapping his forehead. 'Of course!'

'I'll get some glasses,' I say, following Paul to the door.

'You got flutes?' Paul calls as he heads down the hall to the front door. 'I've brought some, if not. Enough for all.'

'Better bring them,' I tell him. 'We may be down to jam jars.'

'Oh, I made good use of it, on consecutive occasions on consecutive nights over consecutive weeks,' Guy says. 'Thank you very much.' He raises his glass.

'Jesus,' Hol says. She glances at me, but I pretend not to see. Nobody's used the terms 'sex tape' or 'porn', but otherwise they've become a bit less coy about the whole subject.

'Oh, you mean – oh,' Pris says, then pretends to gag.

'What?' Guy says, as though innocently. 'What else are these things for?'

'Thanks for sharing,' Ali says.

Guy leers. 'It was my pleasure, darlin.'

The tape inside the VHS player did a final clonk a minute ago and rewound automatically again. Paul's just checked the start; looks like we've recorded half an hour of *Holby City*.

Guy holds out one hand to Paul, who is kneeling in front of the TV, extracting the tape from the machine, then the mini-tape from the carrier cassette. 'May I have my tape, please?' Paul hands him the chunky little mini-cassette. He stuffs it into an inside pocket of his jacket. 'Thank you.'

'Welcome,' Paul murmurs.

Guy sighs, wheezing a little. 'Thank fuck that's done.' He looks round at all of us. 'Actually, the really fucking embarrassing thing on there was that I spent a minute or two telling you, despite all the foregoing, how much I loved you all and how it had been a privilege to know you and I hoped you'd think well of me and miss me.' He drinks his champagne.

'Aaw,' Pris says, smiling broadly, and puts a hand on Guy's arm.

Hol is looking at Guy. 'Seriously?'

Paul is frowning. 'Yeah,' he says. '*Seriously?*'

Ali just snorts. Rob looks on, breathing a little heavily. Haze is lighting the next joint, humming.

Guy shrugs as best he can, drinks some more, grinning. 'Never fucking know now, will you?'

*   *   *

301

'You're holding it wrong,' Paul tells me.

I look at him. 'It's a glass,' I tell him. Actually maybe it's not a glass, not technically, as it feels a bit heavy and I think these thick, tall flute things Paul brought in from the car might be crystal, whatever the difference is. Maybe even lead crystal, though that sounds vaguely poisonous. Either way, it's not like I'm holding it by the rim, or upside down or something.

'Yes, but it's got champagne in it,' Paul says. 'Same with white wine.' He holds his glass up in front of my face to show me how he's holding his glass. 'With both, you're supposed to drink them while they're still cold, or at least cool. So you hold them by the stem, and that way less of the heat from your hand transfers to the glass and the wine. With red wine it's okay to hold the bowl, because red has more of a bouquet and that benefits from being gently warmed.'

We're all standing in the kitchen, where we've been clearing stuff away in a sudden fit of communal enterprise. Then people started feeling hungry again and so we warmed over some of the starters in the microwave, though they go a bit soggy when you do that.

'Or you just get it down your neck so quick you don't need to worry about all this pretentious bollocks,' Guy says. He's the only one not standing as we snack, sitting at the head of the kitchen table with a couple of untouched samosas on a plate in front of him.

Paul glances at him, sighs. 'Yes. Or you can guzzle White Lightning down the local park, piss against the trees and shit in the bushes, as your father points out.'

'How you doing?' I ask Hol, sort of sauntering up to her as she stands looking across the kitchen sink, through the window towards where the fire was. Her champagne glass

302

lies on the draining surface, at an angle. I'm holding my glass by the stem. The champagne is a bit dry and if Paul hadn't looked appalled when I suggested mixing it fifty-fifty with a nice sweet white wine, I might have done just that. He wouldn't even compromise on medium-sweet. On the other hand, it's giving me a very nice warm glow.

'I'm fine,' Hol says, not looking at me. I glance at the sink in front of her and think about showing her the laminar flow trick with the tap, but decide that might appear a bit childish. I gaze out the window too, searching for any sign of the fire, but it's pitch out there. There's no rain hitting the window though I can hear a medley of steady drippings.

Then I realise Hol is looking at me, but via the window. She's looking at my reflection.

She does a sort of half-glance behind her, drops her voice and says, 'I am sorry, Kit. I'll make it up to you. It'll all be there. I just need some time. I just hope you're not as disappointed with me as I am with myself.'

'It's okay,' I tell her, via this V of photons apexed on the window glass. Though it's not really okay. Not properly, completely okay. It might never be absolutely okay ever again. But it's sort of okay, because I still mostly trust her and I think she means what she says. I'll feel better once the initial cheque for the two thousand has cleared, I suppose. Then it'll be a bit better, a bit closer to properly okay. In the meantime there's no point me haranguing her or blanking her. She's still my friend. 'We're okay,' I tell her.

I put my arm round her shoulders, squeeze in a chummy sort of way, then let go.

I think she relaxes a bit. 'You're sweet,' she says quietly. 'I never thought I'd let anyone down like this. Least of all you.'

'Seriously. It's okay,' I tell her. 'I trust you.'

'More than I deserve,' she mutters. She breaks eye contact, finishes her glass, turns round and leans her bum against the sink front. 'Any more bubbly?'

I take her glass. By the stem. 'Allow me, ma'am.'

'I meant every fucking word,' Guy is telling Pris and Hol. 'I think you're all fucking berserk; *we're* all fucking berserk, except I'm not going to be around much longer to take responsibility for the fucking mess we're in, so I'm fucking absolving myself. I used to think we were a bit lame, our generation, a bit wimpish and conformist compared to students from ten years before us, but we were the fucking Angry Brigade compared to the little twats running around the campus these days. They occupied the Old Quad for a week with a dozen tents and sat completing their latest essay on their tablets to make sure they'd be in on time and then seemed genuinely fucking surprised the bankers didn't all hand their bonuses back and reform the entire international banking system just on the strength of that. They should be manning the fucking barricades, stashing petrol bombs and standing shoulder to fucking shoulder with the workers, such as are left; there should have been a general fucking strike when the banks weren't all straight-out nationalised.'

We're in the sitting room. More drink has been taken. We're on the fourth or fifth bottle of champagne, and most people have some sort of chaser too.

'Oh, for fuck's sake, Guy!' Rob yells suddenly. We all look at him. Even Ali. 'You just don't get it, do you?'

'Get fucking what?' Guy says.

'That the world's fucking changed, Guy. Again? You know? Like it always does?'

304

'Babe,' Ali says, reaching to touch Rob's arm, but he pulls it away, keeps his gaze fixed on Guy, who is glaring back at him.

'And like it always will? And just because you don't like it, that doesn't matter a fuck. Jesus Christ, Guy, none of us are glad you haven't got long to go, but it's like that's just an acknowledgement of how cut off from everything you and people like you are – have been – for years, decades.'

'Babe,' Ali says again.

'Yeah, the world isn't fucking perfect, Guy,' Rob says, 'but it never fucking was and it never fucking will be, not with us in charge. The fact you don't like the way things have been going since before . . . before even you were able to vote, is just too bad. Dying . . . being on the brink of death doesn't give you any right to just sit there—'

'Babe,' Ali says a third time, reaching out to Rob again. He shrugs her off, spilling some of his champagne onto the carpet. At least it's not going to leave much of a stain.

'Leave me alone, will you?' Rob says to Ali. 'We've been creeping around, pussy-footing around this all weekend – in fact, no; all of the last two fucking *decades*. Guy, Guy, Guy, seriously,' Rob says, wiping his mouth and sitting forward, putting his glass down and holding his hands out like claws towards Guy, who is looking, I think, vaguely amused. 'We don't want you to die, but you're going to go . . . still bitter, still fuming against stuff there's no, no reason to fume against.'

'What?' Guy breaks in. 'I cannot rail against the injustices of humanity in my own fucking house because I might curdle my karma or something? What fresh bollockry is this?'

'The world has *changed*!' Rob shouts. Ali looks like she's going to reach out to him again, but then makes her mouth go tight, folding her lips inwards so that they sort of disappear inside her mouth. She sits back, arms folded, gaze fixed on the table. 'It'll change again and the people who grew up while it's . . . while it's like the way it is now will be upset at *that* and wish it would return to the way things were when *they* were young, but it won't ever go back, not to their time, now, or to yours, twenty years back or more, not to anybody's time.'

'So I should stop whining about it?' Guy says, with an expression somewhere between a grin and a sneer.

'Yeah,' Paul says, with a sort of half-hearted laugh. 'Stop bellyaching about it.'

'But I like whining,' Guy tells him. 'I enjoy bellyaching about shit happening and it's one of the very few pleasures I have left, harping on about how stupid people are and how fucked-up the world is.' Guy looks from Rob round at the rest of us, then back to Rob. 'Fucking entirely take your point, Robert. But do not attempt to deprive me of one of my last . . . last . . . retained enjoyments. Shit!' He looks at me. 'What was I . . . ?'

'Last remaining?' I say.

Guy snaps his fingers. 'Fucking "remaining"; trust me to go for the marginally more obscure term.' He shakes his head.

'So we should just roll over and let ourselves be double-fucked by the bankers and the governments that govern in their interests but our name?' Hol asks Rob.

'Oh, fuck,' Rob says, laughing. 'Here we go. It's the last Marxist in the shop. What, Hol?'

'Don't have the discipline to be a proper Marxist,' Hol tells him. 'But it's not really about politics, just fairness; justice. Being decent to your fellow human beings.'

'Well, there are lots of ways of trying to be fair,' Rob tells her. 'And the one we've settled on is obviously capitalism and the market; we've sort of tried everything else and they didn't work, and even if those other possibilities were strangled at birth by big bad capitalism, it's no good trying to resurrect them. We have to work with what we've got.'

'What, to each according to his greed?' Hol says.

'We're *all* greedy,' Rob says loudly. 'Some of us are greedy for different things, not always money, but we're all greedy. You're greedy. I'm greedy, we all are. The system we have to work with just acknowledges that, that's all.' He sways slightly, even though he's still sitting down, as he picks up his glass and drinks. 'You should try working with it sometime, Hol. Try going with the flow. You'll get further.'

'Not in any direction I fucking want to go,' Hol says.

'Well, tough,' Rob tells her. 'Cos you're being borne along in that direction all the time anyway whether you like it or not.'

'Yeah, we should all swim faster towards the next precipice, the next great fall,' Hol says. She drinks too. 'Woo-hoo.'

'Have we all quite finished?' Pris says. 'You guys . . .' She shakes her head, ventures a smile.

'Yeah, come on, guys,' Haze says, rolling another modest joint (supplies are low).

But Rob is looking at Pris with his lip curled and saying, 'Oh, stop being the fucking school matron, won't you? You think you're holding us together or something? Balm for our jaggedness or what the fuck? Who appointed you—'

'Right,' Ali says, sitting forward. 'Babe, Rob, come on—'

Rob ignores her, still glaring at Pris, who wears a frown. 'You're so fucking jolly-hockey-sticks for a council-house girl made good,' Rob tells her. 'With your latest dumb-ass bloke in tow and this pathetic desperation that we all think he's "okay" and not too much *not* like "one of us".'

'Christ, Rob,' Ali says, like she's going to cry now, and sits wringing her hands.

'Like that fucking matters,' Rob says. 'Like we represent anything worthwhile, like we're anything else apart from a bunch of people who came together for a few years because we were in the same uni and the same department and then went our separate ways to our own pathetic individual disappointments, and became the sort of people we'd have run a mile from when we were the age we were when we first lived here. Well, your guy *isn't* okay, Pris; none of us think so. But none of us is going to risk hurting your fragile fucking feelings by saying so, not even Mr I-Speak-the-Truth Guy here.' Rob wipes his mouth again. Pris seems to shrink in on herself. 'Pris,' Rob says, leaning towards her, 'your new guy is . . .' Rob looks at Hol. 'What's the—' He snaps his fingers, looks back to Pris. 'Lumpen; yeah, that's what he is, he's lumpen.'

'Okay, you need to stop now,' Ali says quickly, clutching at Rob's elbow.

He shrugs her off. 'Oh, don't give me the fucking wounded puppy eyes,' Rob tells Pris, his face contorting. 'This is the fucking point: if you love him or just like him or he's a good fuck or something or good with your kid, fine; why the fuck not? Sincerely hope you're happy. Sincerely. But don't look to us for some sort of fucking endorsement. You don't need it. We're a bunch of fuck-ups; not one of us is doing what we really ever wanted to do. Not one.'

'Speak for yourself,' Hol says.

'Why the hell should we have to stick with what we wanted to do when we were basically just kids anyway?' Paul says.

'What?' Rob is saying to Hol. 'You *wanted* to be a

penniless film critic? So shit at managing her own finances you have to ask your friends for loans? Really? Seriously?'

'Fuck you,' Hol says, staring at him, voice flat.

'What?' Ali says. Haze looks startled.

Rob grins at Hol, waves one hand at her regally. 'Ah, repay me any time, but get off my fucking case about what a corporate sell-out I am, or whatever this week's line is. Helping to keep *you* afloat, honey.'

'Repay *you?*' Ali is saying. Her face looks pale. 'It's all in joint . . . do you have a fucking separate *bank* account? Where—' But Rob is still looking at Hol. He is smiling. She is not. 'God fucking dammit,' Ali says. 'Look at me when I'm—'

She wraps her fingers round his elbow again and Rob tries to shrug her off once more but she keeps her grip, and then Rob sort of half turns to her and jabs his elbow – his whole arm – back so hard he hits her in the bottom of her ribs and you can hear the thud and the wheeze of breath being knocked out of her and her involuntary gasp and yelp of pain.

'Christ!' Paul says, getting up, going towards Rob or maybe Ali. Haze is just sitting looking stunned, Pris's mouth is hanging open. Even Guy looks surprised.

'You fucking—!' Hol is bouncing out of the couch and coming at Rob, planting one foot on the table between them and looking like she's going to leap across it.

Ali is sliding off the couch to her knees, wrapped around herself, doubling up on the floor, kneeling, head down, blonde hair hanging.

Rob leaps to his feet, in front of Hol. 'Yeah, Hol?'

Hol is half on and half off the table. She swings her balled right fist at him but he just pulls his head back and she misses, unbalancing herself. She staggers back and to the side, one foot scattering glasses on the table. She starts to fall; the wrong way for me to save her. I'm getting up from the pouffe as fast as I can. Haze is holding the book he's rolling the joint on up and out of the way.

Hol flies to one side, falling between the table and the end of the couch, but sort of catching her left knee on the corner of the table and the back of her head on the arm of the couch; Guy has stuck a foot out under her, to try to help cushion her head before it hits the floor.

'Fucking *enough*, Rob!' Paul yells, getting to Rob from one side and trying to put his arms round him. Rob is watching Hol as she falls in a ragged, disorganised heap; the sound of her hitting the floor is loud, and I feel the floor bounce. Rob wriggles in Paul's embrace, not wanting to be held.

Ali is still on her knees, also between the table and the couch, on the other side. Pris has got to her, kneeling with one hand on Ali's back.

Rob relaxes and lets himself be held by Paul. He turns to him and says, 'This is nice; finally coming out, are we?'

'Oh just leave it, Rob, for the love of fuck,' Paul says, sounding weary.

'Give us a kiss.'

'Fuck off.'

I've gone round the back of the couch to help Hol. Guy is leaning forward, grunting with the effort, one hand on Hol's shoulder. Hol is stirring, one hand gripping the edge of the table, trying to get up. I get to her and start trying to help.

'So, how are we now?' Rob says jovially, looking round at us all as best he can while still trapped in Paul's arms. 'Better, worse, or just the same?'

*   *   *

310

We're in the kitchen again. Hol is sitting at the table, an improvised ice pack held at the back of her head, a pack of sacrificial frozen peas on her injured knee. I am washing up and drying, and Guy, walking with just his stick, is putting away, one-handed. He hobbles across the kitchen every so often, carrying one plate or glass at a time. Paul is sitting beside Hol, his head on the table again, like he was this morning.

Rob seemed happy enough to go to his and Ali's room, though there was some crashing and banging up there afterwards and it did sound like he was wrecking the place. 'We should set him loose on the rest of the house,' Guy said. 'Save the quarry people some money tearing it down.'

Ali thinks she might have a cracked rib. She rang a taxi to take her to A&E. Pris went with her.

Haze went to sleep slumped on a seat in the sitting room. He had to be woken to be sent to his bed.

Guy is whistling. He stops long enough to say, 'Well, we should do this more often, don't you think?'

'Yeah,' Hol says. 'Every weekend.'

'I'm free next one,' Paul says, then; 'Oh, no; no I'm not.' He doesn't take his head off the table as he's saying any of this. 'But yeah. Actually . . . I may just move back in. Commute.'

'You really that hard-up, pet?' Guy says to Hol, as he passes, carrying a saucer.

'Hard-up enough to have to ask Rob for a loan,' Hol says dully. 'Draw your own.'

'You should have asked me,' Paul says.

'That's very . . . gallant of you,' Hol tells him. 'Trying to protect what little is left of my reputation in front of these two. But let's stick with the truth, eh?'

311

'Ah,' Paul says from the table. 'Okay.'

Hol catches me looking at her. 'Paul already loaned me money.'

'I see,' I say. I go back to drying.

And so this last evening seems set to dribble away into nothing, while we go to our respective beds.

Ali rang from A&E to say she and Pris wouldn't be back; Pris had gone to Rick's hotel in Ormiston and Ali had booked herself into the George, in Bewford city centre. She was still waiting to be seen by a doctor. Hol is limping almost as bad as Dad. Paul has a sore head and has taken some ibuprofen and some co-codamol. I settle down a surprisingly cheery Guy, make sure he takes all his meds, and then collapse into bed, too tired to play any HeroSpace or even have a wank.

I wake up to hear Guy coming hobbling along the corridor, approaching my door. I look at my phone. Half an hour since I went to sleep. The door opens, sending a widening bar of light across the floor and the far wall. Dad comes in but it's not him after all; the figure is slighter and straighter. I realise it's Hol as she closes the door, shutting off the outside light. A few standby lights and charging LEDs on things like the computer and socket transformers and so on provide just enough illumination.

'Couldn't sleep,' she tells me. She comes up to the bed, limping a little. She's wearing a thin, dark dressing gown. She stands so close I can smell her; coconut – from her hair, I remember – plus some other perfume, just faint, but deep and musky.

It too is something I've smelled on her before, but there is a last, elusive, hinted tang coming off her as well, something

312

sharp and fresh and somehow animal at the same time, something I sort of know but don't know, something bewilderingly, undeniably, unavoidably exciting, as though the higher regions of my brain and self have nothing to do with the experience or the effect it's having on me.

If I reach out now, I think, *I could touch her.*

'Um,' I hear myself say. My mouth has suddenly gone very dry. 'Why, ah . . . Why are you . . . here?' I ask her.

I think I see her shake her head. 'I don't know myself,' she tells me. I hear her blow out a breath. 'I feel like I . . . Like I can't do the right thing, like there's no right thing to be done, just a choice of which wrong one to do, trying to work out which is the least . . . damaging, least . . . humiliating or mean or selfish or . . . I don't know—'

'Sh,' I tell her.

'Yeah,' she says, putting a hand into her dishevelled hair and rubbing the back of her head, 'I'm sort of wittering, I suppose. I should—'

'No, I mean, *sh*,' I tell her, pushing myself up to a sitting position and turning my head towards the window. 'I can hear something.'

She turns too. 'What?'

'Something . . .' I say.

'Yes, but—'

There's a noise. I recognise it. 'That's the car,' I tell her.

'Whose car?' she says. 'Ali coming back after all? Rob going for a long midnight drive of the soul?'

Actually it's nearly four in the morning, but I don't say this. 'No,' I tell her, pushing the duvet back. 'That's our car. That's the Volvo.'

I swing out of bed and pull on my underpants – facing away from Hol so she can't see my erection.

'*Guy?*' she says into the darkness. 'He can still *drive?*'

'If he takes enough painkillers,' I tell her. (So many you wouldn't be allowed to operate heavy machinery, or drive, though I don't say this.)

I can hear the engine sound getting louder as the Volvo leaves the garage. 'Let me listen a moment,' I whisper. We both hold our breaths. The car moves off down the drive without pausing. 'He's not gone back to close the garage doors.' I shrug down my T-shirt, pull up my camo trousers, reach for my gilet. 'I'd better check his room,' I tell her.

Hol swivels, gasping with pain as she puts weight on her injured knee. 'Give me one minute,' she says, hobbling for the door. 'I dress fast.' She leaves the door open; I follow her ten seconds later, still buckling my belt.

Guy isn't in his room. The bed is still warm. Snores come from Rob's room. Hol comes back out of her room, a fleece held between her teeth, hopping on her good, bare foot as she pulls a boot on over the other, nearly falling, and grimacing with pain and muttering muffled curses.

'Check—' I start to say, as she stops at Paul's door and opens it. There's a grunt from inside.

'Present,' Hol says. She looks at me, then has to sit on the top step of the stairs to put on the other boot. 'Take it we're hot pursuiting?'

'Think we should,' I say.

'My car,' she says. 'You'll have to drive.' She nods. 'This is my clutch leg; doubt it'll work right.'

I can see tail lights in the distance as we head down the drive, then lose sight of them as we come down to the public road.

Hol's seen them too. 'Think that's him?' she says. She's staring over to where the lights were, south, heading

314

south-west, though we're too far down in the half-sunken, tree- and hedge-lined lane for her to have any chance of seeing them from here. It's so dark you can't tell that, though.

'Only lights I could see,' I tell her.

'Me too,' she says, arming her way into her fleece.

'Where's the wipers?' I ask Hol. It isn't raining now but drops from earlier are still dotting the screen.

She reaches, flicks a stalk. 'Here.'

The little Polo feels dainty, tinny and delicate after the tank-like Volvo. I crunch the gearbox a couple of times but Hol doesn't complain.

'If he'd turned the other way, into town,' I say, 'we'd probably not have seen him.'

'So it might not be him we're following.'

'Maybe not.' The Polo's engine makes lots of noise but doesn't make it move very fast. It hangs on okay in the corners, though.

'I take it Guy isn't in the habit of doing this? Going off in the middle of the night?' Hol asks.

'Never,' I tell her. I had to resist the strong urge to take a moment to close the garage doors when we ran out of the house a couple of minutes ago. At least Guy had closed the front door of the house.

'Think he might be going off to end it all?'

'Worried he might be,' I confess, glancing over at her.

Hol has her mobile out, puts it to her ear. 'Trying calling him. You never know.'

'I think he might be going back to Yarlsthwaite,' I say, suddenly realising. 'To the tower. Or the cliffs.'

'Maybe he just wants to get there under his own power,' Hol says. 'Climb it himself, to prove . . . that he can, without people trying to help.'

I shake my head. 'I don't think so.'

The car park at Yarlsthwaite is empty. There's no sign of the Volvo at Ullisedge community park either: another clifftop location notoriously popular with suicides. And doggers, I've heard, though there are no obvious signs. The night is mild and the gentle breeze smells damp and fresh.

'Where now?' Hol asks.

'Leplam lake,' I tell her.

We head under the motorway at the Ormiston interchange, make for the lake. No sign there either. There used to be places where you could just drive straight from the bit beside the proper car park into deep water, but the council have closed that section off with a berm and boulders and there are chained bollards protecting the rest.

'I always thought, if I wanted to end it all,' Hol says, 'I might just drive really fast down the motorway and then into . . . I don't know. Some bit of concrete. A bridge support, maybe. Though they seem to have protected all that stuff with crash barriers. Or take an ordinary road, and hit a tree, or swerve into the path of a truck. Only that seems a bit selfish; hard on the trucker. Not that I've a lot of time for – what?'

'We can go back that way anyway,' I tell her.

'What way?' she asks as I spin the car round and head for the car park exit and the road.

'Just this place I know,' I say.

Cresting the moor road, approaching the bridge that arches high above the motorway – the bridge that I usually reach from the other side, by walking for nearly an hour over the fields and the moor, where I've stood and stared at the traffic and watched for random jams – we can see that there's a car – an estate – sitting in the middle.

316

Its headlights are pointing towards us. Getting closer, as we start to descend, we can see that it is the Volvo, and the driver's door is hanging open. Closer still, from the place where the bit of relatively modern approach road gives out onto the bridge proper, we can see there doesn't seem to be anybody around, and nobody in the car either, unless they're lying down or hiding.

'Oh, fuck,' Hol says softly.

I can feel my mouth going dry. The traffic beneath us is flowing normally, though, in both directions. It's not even five yet, but there's a respectable amount of trucks and cars labouring or thundering or just humming along beneath us, and all of it without the benefit of lots of flashing blue lights.

We drive onto the bridge, stop in front of the Volvo, get out.

The car's engine is silent. The headlights look a normal kind of brightness so it can't have been here that long; the battery needs replacing and doesn't hold much of a charge.

Guy's head pops out from behind the rear of the car, looking down its grimy flank at us. 'Fuck me, can a man get no peace to contemplate his imminent demise? What's up? Has Rob attacked somebody else, or Ali come back with the rozzers?'

'*Christ*, you had us worried,' Hol says, walking up to where Guy is sitting on the little kerb, a metre or so behind the rear of the car. His stick lies at his side.

'Did I now?' he asks. 'How thoughtless of me.'

'Hi, Dad.' We both sit on the kerb with him. Then I get up again, turn the Volvo's lights to sidelights only and close the door. I sit back down.

'Just . . . heard you going, taking the car, not closing the garage door,' I tell him.

'Yeah, well, didn't want to risk leaving time for somebody

317

to come out and try to stop me,' Guy says. He pulls out what looks like one of Haze's joints, lights it and inhales deeply. There are the remains of two joints in the gutter between his feet. 'You know, with some spurious . . . concern that I might be off to do what people commonly refer to as "something stupid", i.e. top meself.'

'That what you were going to do?' Hol asks.

'Might still.' Guy shrugs, glances behind us towards the railings and traffic moving beneath. 'You two could help push me over. Fuck Dignitas.' The traffic makes a coming-and-going noise like surf on fast-forward.

'Was that really what—' I begin.

'Oh, yes,' Guy says, pulling hard on the joint. He puts his head back and it's like that bit in *The Wrong Trousers* when a light goes off in Gromit's kennel and you suddenly see he's been crying. Guy's upper cheeks and the sides of his nose are wet with tears. 'Took some extra opiate, just so I could move better, not trying to overdose . . . But yeah, that was indubitably the fullness of my attention, oh yes. Intention, I mean. And there; that's why.'

'What?' Hol asks.

'Think it's going into my brain, Hol,' he says, his voice hollow. 'Can't think of the right words, increasingly.'

'Everybody gets that,' Hol says.

Guy shakes his head. 'I never.'

Hol puts her arm round him. Guy hesitates, then puts his head on her shoulder. I do the same from the other side. To my surprise, after a moment or two, he rests his head on my shoulder.

'Well,' Hol says, 'it's your life, Guy, but I don't think either of us is sorry we disturbed you.'

He says nothing for a while, then sighs deeply, wheezing

a little. 'Oh,' he says at last, 'I just want to be shot of all of you, and let you be shot of me. I just wanted to say, *Fuck you all*. Not so much to you, not to the . . . everybody here this weekend, but to everybody else; to the world as revealed in wank-rag tabloids and any quick channel-hop. That was the mistake I made earlier: put the telly on, caught some repeated drivel; game shows, show-pony sport, special-agent spy wank. *That's* what I want to say *Fuck You* to; to the world and his wife and his fuckwit children, to all the idiots bought off with puerile telly and corrupted sports and brainless movie product and fame for the fucking sake of it, and the slow but steady rehabilitation of torture at all levels, whether it's watching some witless D-list celeb scranning witchetty grubs and showering in dung beetles or hearing that our brave fucking boys have ripped the balls off another teenage rag-head in some-or-other dusty Benightistan. All that shit. All that fucking shit.'

Hol is silent for a while. Eventually she says, 'Yeah, well, we haven't exactly covered ourselves in glory, our generation. But there's always another one coming along. They might do better. Even when it'd be less painful to just make our peace with despair and get on with it, there is always hope. Whether we like it or not.'

'Not for me there isn't, Hol,' Guy says, and just sounds weary.

Hol sighs. 'Which is always going to colour your judgement of everything else, isn't it? Even if it feels like all that's happened is you've escaped your last illusions and you're finally seeing things clearly.'

Guy laughs silently against me. Or maybe he's weeping. But I think it's a laugh, in the end. 'Yeah, Hol,' he says, reaching down and flicking one of the dead joints along the side of the kerb. 'We are all of us in the gutter.' He pulls on the lit joint. Because his head is still on my shoulder, some of the smoke goes into my eyes, making them water. 'But some of us,' he wheezes, 'are staring down the drain.'

I feel Hol hug him gently.

'Anyway,' he says, coughing. 'I still couldn't jump, in the end.' He pulls on the joint again. 'More of a coward than I thought.' He laughs. I feel him shiver. 'Thought I could at least control something, take fucking charge of something, impose my own fucking schedule on what was happening to me, rather than just being . . . prey to it.' He raises his head from my shoulder, looks at the Volvo. 'Specially as, like I say . . . all these little . . . attacks of aphasia, lately.' He looks at both of us in turn, grimacing as he turns his neck this way and that. 'My bum's cold,' he announces.

He starts trying to get up and we both help him; he opens the estate's tailgate and sits in there, looking hunched and shivery. I pull the blanket from the car and wrap it round him, then I sit back on the kerb again. Hol stands, instead, arms crossed, on the road, looking down at Guy.

'But then I chickened out,' he tells us. 'I mean, I'd worked out how I could have levered myself over the railings using my stick and everything . . . but then I started thinking that maybe it doesn't look high enough to kill me outright, and that would be a bit shit, and then what about the poor fucker I throw myself in front of, even if I wait till there's a gap in the traffic? Then I thought I could wait for a Range Rover or a big Merc or a Beemer or an Audi – something flash, with a personal twat plate – try to fucking *aim* for that, on the plausible grounds that whoever was driving it would be a rich fucker and like as not deserved a bit of compensatory trauma in their pampered fucking life.' He shakes his head.

320

'Then I thought, *But what if they've got kids in the car?* Even if they are spoiled, over-indulged brats, do I have the right to . . . ? So I gave in to fucking . . . *compassion* in the end. Me! Things have come to a pretty pass, I tell you.' He hangs his head, shakes it. He pulls in a deep, wheezing breath, and looks up again, blinking.

'And then I realised I was just looking for excuses for myself, and I wasn't going to do it anyway. So I gave up and sat meself down here to have a smoke and think about it.' He smiles at both of us and says, 'And so, my friends, I have smoked, and I have indeed thought about it. And . . .'

He doesn't say any more. He just looks away, towards the downward brow of the hill where the floor of the cutting and the motorway fall away and where all the white lights blink into existence and all the red lights suddenly disappear.

There's a silence then, filled from beneath with the rise and fall of the noise of the traffic, and I smell the diesel fumes, laid out across the cold, early-morning breeze, and I wait for Guy to say more, or for Hol to say something else, but neither of them does say anything, so eventually I ask, 'Do you want to go back home now, Dad?'

8

'Doesn't look much bigger, really, does it?' Hol asks. It's summer and the sun is coming and going behind lots of little puffy white clouds, painting the ground and half the curved wall of the quarry with sliding patterns of shade. We're standing on the loop of the driveway, just in front of where the house used to be. We're looking through a chain-link fence into the quarry. Big yellow trucks, made toys of by the distance, trundle about the place.

'I did think it would look . . . bigger,' I agree. 'Fast work, though. Didn't think the house would be gone this quickly.'

Guy died two months ago, in the Bewford hospice. He was only there for the last week; I managed him at home until then.

The day Dad died, I stayed in the spare room at Mrs Willoughby's, which was kind of her. I was alone in the house the second night, and felt almost nothing at first, but then woke up in the middle of the night with an already sopping pillow, crying. I sobbed quietly for some time, curled up round a pain in my belly I worried for a while might be the start of my own illness, my own cancer, somehow inherited despite everything, but it was gone by the morning and has never reappeared.

The Power of Attorney action was dropped by the council a week later, coincidentally on the same day I got the notice informing me the house had to be vacated in ten days, after the final appeal against the quarry company's land purchase was turned down.

Not everybody was there for the funeral. Ali was in Indonesia and couldn't make it; Rob felt embarrassed by his behaviour on that last weekend we were all together, and declined. I got to speak to him on the phone, at his office in London, after a few days of persistence, but he still couldn't be persuaded.

The evening of the funeral – the wake was back here, and fairly subdued – I ended up sitting on a couch between Hol and Pris, crying a little and being hugged from both sides and falling asleep between them. They saw me to my room together. I fell asleep on top of the bed with all my clothes and one shoe still on. I had a dream that I woke up to find somebody standing over me in the darkness, holding a tape-measure, but it wasn't anybody I recognised, and my imagination may have added the detail of the tape-measure afterwards.

The estate isn't settled yet but the lawyer says there ought to be some money coming to me after Guy's many debts are settled; maybe twenty-five to thirty thousand, which is not exactly life-changing – my life has changed quite enough already, frankly – but also not to be sniffed at.

Hol's cheque for two thousand did clear. She was borrowing from Paul and Rob to pay me back.

The only part of my inheritance I've received so far is a name and address:

Mrs Elisabeth McKelvie
28B Tonbridge Avenue
Maroombah
NSW 1124
Australia

The lawyer had instructions to pass this on to me as soon as Guy died. I'm still trying to decide what to do with this. Maybe nothing. Maybe I'll just write a letter; that would seem the most obvious thing. Or maybe I'll fly off to the other side of the world without telling anybody and turn up on her doorstep and ring the bell. That would be fitting. Though, knowing Guy, this could turn out to be a joke, and she'll stand there blinking uncomprehendingly at me and we'll have no connection of any sort whatsoever.

Since the funeral, Rob and Ali have split up. Rob is now based in Mountain View, California. Ali is in Dubai.

Pris seems happy with Rick; we hardly hear from her. They're still on the south coast.

Paul has been offered a promotion within his company that will mean relocating to New York City. The news leaked and there is already talk of him being deselected as Labour party candidate for the Bewford City constituency at the next election.

Haze – amazingly – appears to be on the run in France after certain financial irregularities came to light at the women's football team he managed, following his abrupt dismissal. Hol says it's hard to know whether this is hopelessly tawdry or actually quite impressive.

Hol and I live together, for now, in her little flat in Maida Vale. I have the boxroom, which has just enough space for a sort of upper-bunk single bed with a desk underneath

– this is where I play HeroSpace – and a clothes rail. There is no room in the tiny kitchen for a washing machine; we go to a launderette. Hol is paying me back the remainder of what she owes by still covering all the rent. I chip in for half the other outgoings. This suits both of us. Hol is fairly house-proud herself, but I keep the place extremely neat and tidy.

No more has ever been said about the night that Hol came into my room, or what might have happened, and Hol is a little more formal and correct with me than she used to be, I think.

I'm not sure I really like London very much; it's so noisy and frenetic and people seem to struggle to find the time to be polite to each other. But, still, it's exciting, and we've been to see lots of places I'd only ever heard of or seen on TV or film, which is fun. I suppose London will do for now.

I can't decide if I want to move back up here at some point, or not. I miss it, but Hol says sometimes missing somebody or something is just a natural part of your life, and doesn't mean you absolutely have to go back to that person or place.

Tricky one.

Also, Hol takes me along to as many films and previews as she's allowed to, which is nice of her. I've started a film review website of my own to try to look as professional as I can, though not all the distributors and preview theatres are falling for this. The website is doing okay, actually. I can't dissect a film the way Hol can, or put it in the context of others going back to way-back-when, but apparently I have some fresh and original insights. So there.

'Well, Kit,' Hol says, giving the chain-link fence a rattle just for the hell of it, then dusting her hands off, 'in the end we're just standing here looking into a big fucking hole in the ground.'

'Yes,' I say, and take one last look round at the expanded emptiness of the quarry. 'We are.'

'Never mind.' She looks at her mobile. 'Come on,' she says, stuffing it back in her pocket. 'Time for tea with Mrs Willoughby.'

We get back into Hol's little faded red Polo and drive off.